W9-BVO-659

"This profound and beautiful debut is a sharp exploration of racial divides and community in America."
—*NEWSWEEK*

"*The Kindest Lie* is an easy, accessible novel filled with hard, important truths."
—*NEW YORK TIMES BOOK REVIEW*

"Powerful insights emerge on the plurality of Black American experience and the divisions between rural and urban life, and the wealthy and the working class. Johnson's clear-eyed saga hits hard."
—*PUBLISHERS WEEKLY* (STARRED REVIEW)

"This modern-day depiction of a woman in crisis and what she discovers about what she left behind is well-written, timely, and oh-so-memorable."
—*GOOD MORNING AMERICA*

"Hope and change upend quickly in Johnson's timely, heartwarming debut."
—*O, THE OPRAH MAGAZINE*

"A heart-wrenching story of family, racism, poverty, and love."
—*GOOD HOUSEKEEPING*

"[A] BEAUTIFULLY CRAFTED DEBUT." —JODI PICOULT

Praise for
The Kindest Lie

"A profound look at racial and economic injustices in America."
—Refinery29

"This heart-wrenching story teaches us how long love really endures."
—*Woman's Day*

"Johnson's powerful debut novel examines the racial injustices and class inequalities in our country."

—E! Online

"Generational secrets, class divides, motherhood, and American life on the edge of political and economic change are all examined in Johnson's engaging debut. . . . Through well-developed characters, Johnson provides a realistic portrayal of middle America in the tumultuous era of economic collapse."

—*Booklist*

"Similar to *The Vanishing Half* by Brit Bennett, *The Kindest Lie* is an engrossing story about race, class, and coming to grips with your past. . . . *The Kindest Lie* will not only pull at your heartstrings, but it will also make you want to call your family, fight racial injustice, and hold on tighter to those you love. With every page you turn, you'll see just how powerful unconditional love really is."

—PopSugar

"*The Kindest Lie* is the story of one family that reveals the larger story of America itself. Taut and surprising, Nancy Johnson's debut novel tackles complex issues—ambition, romance, class—with the lightest of touches."

—Rumaan Alam, *New York Times* bestselling author
of *Leave the World Behind*

"Race, class, family, and secrets are all on a collision course in Johnson's extraordinarily moving, timely read. Like a heat-seeking missile, her novel hones in on who we think we belong to and why, following the merging lives of Ruth, a Black female engineer who seeks out the child she gave away, and Midnight, a young white boy struggling to find his place in the very poverty Ruth managed to escape. A gloriously written, stunning heart-scorcher about who we are and what we could be."

—Caroline Leavitt, *New York Times* bestselling author of *Pictures of You* and *Cruel Beautiful World*

"In this winning portrait of circumstance, sacrifice, and forgiveness, the lines that separate past from present and right from wrong are erased and redrawn—oftentimes with earth-shattering consequences. Rife with rich language, shocking revelations, and easy-to-fall-into characters, *The Kindest Lie* is the kind of novel you'll feel in your bones."

—Zakiya Dalila Harris, *New York Times* bestselling author of *The Other Black Girl*

"In *The Kindest Lie* Nancy Johnson takes us into both a bygone time—the dawning of the Obama era—and the tender heart of her protagonist, Ruth. This is a novel that seeks to discover the beauty of our journeys despite the lies we tell each other and ourselves."

—Rion Amilcar Scott, award-winning author of *The World Doesn't Require You* and *Insurrections*

"One of the most buzzed-about books of the season."

—*New York Post*

"Johnson makes powerful points about our connections and communities."

—*Real Simple*

"It takes tremendous talent to seamlessly combine social commentary with a powder keg of a plot, and Nancy Johnson accomplishes just that in her gripping debut novel, *The Kindest Lie*, addressing issues of race, class, privilege, and upward mobility. . . . A fictional callback to Isabel Wilkerson's *Caste*, *The Kindest Lie* also brings to mind Brit Bennett's *The Vanishing Half*, in which another young Black woman returns to her hometown to try to reconcile her past, present, and future. Don't miss this powerful debut."

—*BookPage* (starred review)

"In *The Kindest Lie*, Nancy Johnson gives us two unforgettable characters. Ruth and Midnight represent different Americas: one trending up, one spiraling down. Johnson—through graceful sentences, tenderness, dramatic expertise, and overflowing empathy—is able to twist these Americas into a singular portrait of a country in transition. This enviable debut enlightens while breaking your heart. A truly beautiful achievement."

—Gabriel Bump, author of *Everywhere You Don't Belong*

"A heart-wrenching portrayal of an unlikely bond and a profound nod to the fallacy of post-racial America—*The Kindest Lie* is nuanced, spellbinding, and necessary."

—Margaret Wilkerson Sexton, award-winning author of *The Revisioners*

"Johnson has built a cast of beautifully complex characters. . . . This story speaks to race, class, and what it means to be a family."

—She Reads

"Essential, powerful, wrenching: Johnson's debut tells a history of family secrets and lies shaped by the racism that permeates modern America. A riveting story and a searing lesson on why Black Lives Matter is today's crucial social justice movement."

—Sara Paretsky, *New York Times* bestselling author

"*The Kindest Lie* is a soul-stirring, vividly told saga that demands to be read! Johnson presents a story with dazzling prose and textured, complicated characters that haunt you long after you've closed the book. It's hard to believe *The Kindest Lie* is Johnson's debut, as it's told with such an assured voice and graceful conviction. I thoroughly enjoyed and *highly* recommend it!"

—Catherine Adel West, author of *Saving Ruby King*

"*The Kindest Lie* is not only a superb *debut* novel, it is also, without qualification, a superb novel *period*. Nancy Johnson endows her characters with a generous grace that slowly embraces the reader as the plot unfolds, accomplishing what the very best novelists do—tell the stories of strangers so well we are ultimately compelled to discover the strangers within us all."

—James Anderson, award-winning author of *The Never-Open Desert Diner* and *Lullaby Road*

"Nancy Johnson's eloquently written, introspective, and emotionally resonant debut novel, *The Kindest Lie*, is a timely commentary on social justice, race relations, and what it means to be Black in today's America. . . . With subtle details as rich as they are emotionally resonant, author Johnson takes readers into Ruth's intimate struggle to find peace and come to terms with being an imperfect mother. *The Kindest Lie* is a visceral depiction of being Black in America, the quest for understanding and acceptance, the struggles of motherhood, and the strength of family amid the backdrop of a racially divided country."

—Washington Independent Review of Books

"Johnson's debut novel will appeal to a wide range of readers, who will be drawn into the despairing lives of her characters. Ruth's predicament comes to a most satisfying conclusion."

—*Library Journal*

"Timely, layered, and perfect for your Zoom book club."

—HelloGiggles

"[A] graceful, well-crafted exploration of class, race, and culture; of motherhood; and of family ties. Johnson's memorable characters are forced into uncomfortable situations that feel vital to understand in a divided America."

—*Christian Science Monitor*

The
Kindest Lie

For Lindsey

The
Kindest Lie

a novel

Enjoy reading!
Nancy J

NANCY JOHNSON

wm

WILLIAM MORROW
An Imprint of HarperCollins*Publishers*

P.S.™ is a trademark of HarperCollins Publishers.

HarperCollins books may be purchased for educational, business, or sales promotional use. For information, please email the Special Markets Department at SPsales@harpercollins.com.

A hardcover edition of this book was published in 2021 by William Morrow, an imprint of HarperCollins Publishers.

FIRST WILLIAM MORROW PAPERBACK EDITION PUBLISHED 2022.

Designed by Nancy Singer
Illustration of house on title page spread by Joel Holland
Illustration of woman on title page spread © Atlas Studio/Shutterstock, Inc.

Library of Congress Cataloging-in-Publication Data has been applied for.

ISBN 978-0-06-300564-8

22 23 24 25 26 LSC 10 9 8 7 6 5 4 3 2 1

For my parents.
My heart. My home. Always.

The
Kindest Lie

One

RUTH

No one talked about what happened in the summer of 1997 in the house where Ruth Tuttle had grown up. In fact, there were days she remained certain she had never given birth at all. Somehow, she convinced herself that her life began when she drove away from that little shotgun house in Indiana without her baby. She had been only seventeen.

A lie could be kind to you if you wanted it to be, if you let it. With every year that passed, it became easier to put more distance between her old life and her new one. If the titles of *doctor* and *lawyer* had signaled success back in the day, then *engineer* had to be the 2.0 symbol that you'd made it. And she had. With Yale University conferring her degree and lending its good name to her, there was no question. And if the proof weren't in her pedigree, it manifested in her marriage to a PepsiCo marketing executive.

The upcoming presidential election stirred an unusual optimism in her husband, Xavier, and he fancied himself having everything new. First, he convinced her they should buy the new town house in the Bronzeville neighborhood on Chicago's South Side. Then a new Lexus LX 570 that could easily seat eight. He wasn't just angling for more leg room, either. Sooner rather than later, he wanted a baby. *It's time.* When Xavier repeated those words, Ruth stretched her lips into a smile, neglecting to mention she was already a mother, if in name only.

On Election Night, a light snow fell outside their town house, reminding her of confetti after a sports championship. But they couldn't get ahead of themselves. No one knew how this night would go. Pacing in their bedroom, Ruth tugged at the twists of her hair, and they detangled easily for once, loosening between her fingers, as she breathed in avocado and coconut and promise.

"You look good, babe." Xavier splashed cologne on his neck and popped the collar of his mustard-yellow blazer. He was one of those brothers who had the confidence to pull off risky, bold colors. She wouldn't call him conventionally handsome, but no woman in her right mind would kick him out of bed, either. Removing a stray thread from his lapel, she pulled him closer and kissed his full lips. "You clean up pretty nicely, too, mister."

He smiled and they fist-bumped, something they'd been doing long before Barack and Michelle made it cool to some and subversive to others. He brushed by her quickly to answer the doorbell. "This is it. Game time."

In the full-length mirror, Ruth took in her tall, bony build, with her twiglike legs. After searching many boutiques, she had finally found this jewel-toned emerald-green fit-and-flare dress that gave her the illusion of curves. Her wide, luminous brown eyes caught people's attention first, as they loomed so large on her angular face. It had taken years for her to love her own dark skin, almost the color of their shiny new walnut hardwood floors. Before she left the bedroom, she dipped her index finger in gel and smoothed a few fine baby hairs at her temple.

Ruth could hear the booming voice of Harvey from the post office as she made her way to the living room. They'd become friends when he delivered mail at their old apartment building.

"Am I in Obama headquarters?" he said, debuting a little two-step, finished off with a spin.

Ruth hugged his neck and picked up a tray of their signature cocktail for the evening, handing him a chocolate martini. "You think we'll make history tonight, Harvey?"

"I'm no betting man, now, but if we came out and voted like we were supposed to, I think it can happen." The old Black man had yellowed eyes and a face creased with lines resembling the rings of a tree. He'd banked on retiring early, but when his wife got laid off from her job a few months ago, he'd had to delay his plans. Still, tonight, a flicker of light gleamed in Harvey's eyes.

It felt like they were hurtling toward inevitability, and as guests arrived, the mood in their living room became electric. But were they setting themselves up for a fall? After all, their hope rested with a man whose name reeked of improbability with its questionable linguistic roots. *Barack Hussein Obama.*

She thought of Mama and Papa, her grandparents who had raised her. Even before Ruth's mother walked away from their family, the woman hadn't done much mothering, so her grandparents had taken care of her and her brother, Eli, since day one. She and Eli had entered the world with legacy status as living history with biblical names, the descendants of Hezekiah Tuttle, named for the king of Judah. Ruth smiled when she thought of an autoworker and a hotel maid setting up their grandchildren to be royalty from birth, and all she and Eli had to do was live up to their names.

Her grandmother had suggested that she be named Ruth. Papa had nodded in agreement, and so that's what her mother chose. One syllable, old school and biblical. A name that Ruth's grandmother said would at least get her to the interview. You couldn't tell Mama that an ethnically ambiguous name could only take you so far and couldn't inoculate anybody from a bigot or a bullet. Still, all that old-school planning had served Ruth well in chemical engineering, where being a woman was almost as much an anomaly as her Blackness. Like Obama, she, too, had been called *articulate.*

Guests jammed every square inch of the living room and kitchen, checking various television stations periodically for updated vote counts and projections. Penelope and Tess, an attorney couple who practiced intellectual property and antitrust law, respectively, brought rib tips from Lem's on the South Side, which, through bulletproof glass, served the best barbecue in town.

"Are your grandmother and brother doing a watch party tonight?" Tess asked. She and Ruth had met through a local Yale alumni group.

"I don't know. I doubt it. I'm not sure what happens in Ganton these days," Ruth said ambivalently, going from sipping her martini to draining the glass. When people heard the name Ganton, they thought of Fernwood, the auto plant that made parts for GM cars. The factory where Papa and Eli had worked for years. The town wasn't known for much else.

"You better claim your people and stop trying to be bougie." Xavier had a bad habit of dipping into every conversation. He grinned and bumped her shoulder with his.

He had jokes, but he had no way of knowing that Ganton's very soil was a trapdoor, a gateway to nothingness that few people climbed out of. The welcome sign that greeted visitors bore no warning.

"I know this is not the child of Mrs. Shaw of Jack and Jill of America, Incorporated, talking." Ruth made sure to enunciate each syllable in exaggerated fashion. Her imitation of Xavier's mother irked him, and when she needed that ammunition in an argument, she used it.

"What's this got to do with my mama or Jack and Jill?"

Penelope jumped in then. "I think what she's trying to say is that if y'all had been alive in slavery times, your people would've been in the house."

By now, they had an audience and it turned into everybody's debate. Harvey said, "See, that's what Obama wants to do. Even it out so those of us in the field can join you in the house, Xavier."

Her husband's mouth twisted at the corners, trying to stifle a laugh. "I'm telling you that we fell on hard times, too. Well, sometimes." Xavier added that qualifier knowing how pathetic he sounded, trying to weave a poor man's narrative from the finest silks of prosperity.

Ruth raised an eyebrow. "Okay, tell me this. When it rained outside, did it also rain inside your house?"

"No, but we did have that can of bacon grease on the back of the stove."

Everybody hollered. Ruth shook her head, laughter snatching her breath. "Seriously? That's about being Black or maybe just country, but not poor."

"I'll admit my people may have had a little money, but I didn't." Xavier slid his arm around her shoulders and winked. "When I begged for a G.I. Joe as a kid, they made it real clear I didn't have a pot to piss in or a window to throw it out of. I lived in their house rent-free and my lease could be up with a quickness and without notice."

"They were teaching you a sense of responsibility. That's good parenting, babe, not poverty." The rest of the crowd laughed or added their own hard-luck tales to the buoyant mood.

This game of who had been worse off crowned no victors, and to be fair, Ruth hadn't been mayonnaise-sandwich-eating poor growing up, but they often missed that five-day grace period for their lease payments on the house.

"Hush, y'all, c'mon! They're about to make a projection," Xavier yelled.

Huddled in front of the television, Ruth and her friends watched the red and blue colors of the electoral map fill in, their collective breaths held. Xavier, gripping a miniature American flag, crouched close to the screen like he did right before the buzzer sounded at the end of a close Chicago Bulls game (during the lean years, mind you, not the Jordan glory days).

She felt Tess's fingers dig into her shoulders when television anchors finally pronounced Barack Hussein Obama the forty-fourth president of the United States.

Her whole life, Ruth hadn't dared to believe this could happen, and she almost forgot to breathe. A picture of the little house where she grew up in Ganton came to mind, its low ceilings and narrow hallways. Mama at the kitchen table counting money on the first of the month. Papa's body quivering underneath his plant uniform as he tried to walk straight in the early days of his illness. Maybe, just maybe, everything they'd all been through had been for this. To get here, to this moment. To this man with the funny name. To this day in history.

Xavier whooped and gave her a ball-drop, New Year's Eve–style kiss. The town house vibrated with their jubilation. Guests lifted their glasses and their voices in a toast to their own manifest destiny. Out of the corner of her eye, she saw Harvey, who was usually the loudest in any room, rocking quietly in a chair with his folded hands pressed against his lips.

Then they rolled up the living room rug to do stepper sets and slides, with Xavier break-dancing like he was thirteen instead of thirty-two.

Somehow, she needed to store every part of this moment, burn it into her being, so it would still be real when she lived it again as memory. She wanted to scoop up this feeling, bottle it, and tighten the cap so none could seep out, ever. But at the same time, her instincts told her to share it. So, she opened the windows to give the neighborhood a contact high.

Keeping it old school, the Gap Band's "Outstanding" blasted from the speakers and they took turns strutting down the *Soul Train* line. Xavier's breath warmed Ruth's neck, and from behind, he wrapped his arms around her waist, and they rocked gently to the beat. With his wife at home, Harvey managed to slide into a dance sandwich between Penelope and Tess, who always humored the old man. Their feet felt light and their chests, too, the weight of *wait your turn, not so fast,* and *never* having lifted, at least for one night.

Ruth and Xavier ate and danced until the sun poked through the blinds, bathing their town house in a groggy afterglow, spotlighting barbecue-stained plates and her high-heeled shoes slung in a corner of the room. In the early hours of the morning, Ruth lay on the love seat, the high still buzzing in her head, Xavier's face inches from hers. She stared at his profile and ran her forefinger down his long nose to his lips, past his chin to his pronounced Adam's apple. His skin tone reminded her of the rich Mississippi soil where Mama was born, with flecks of red and yellow just under the surface.

He was prone to faking sleep, and it wasn't until she blew a noise-maker gently in his ear that his lips moved.

"You think our kid could be president someday?" His voice had turned rusty from all the celebrating.

This was the first time Xavier had spoken of anything as tangible as an occupation for their not-yet-born, imaginary child. In the morning sun, the thought of babies unmoored her. "Aren't you getting ahead of yourself?" she said.

"I don't know. Maybe you're right. We have plenty of time to map out that kid's future." He lifted one eyebrow. "What I do know, though, is now that we got a Black president, I'm taking chitlins to the office today." After a few seconds of silence, he laughed, and she did, too, their heads falling back like dominoes from the force of it. Maybe she laughed a bit too hard in relief that he was no longer talking about children.

She poked his side. "You are ridiculous. You better leave your chitterlings at home," she said, emphasizing each syllable for effect. "At least until the man takes the oath of office. Don't mess around and get your Black butt fired now."

They stayed like that for hours, giggling softly and smiling at everything and nothing, wrapped in each other's arms, hungover with hope.

Two

RUTH

ays later, Ruth lay stretched out on the cold leather table of her gynecologist's office with a paper sheet on her lap, legs dangled over the edge. She didn't want to be here, but they'd made the appointment months ago. This day had been so far into the future that she'd almost forgotten about it.

"You know I came prepared. Just call me the iron man," Xavier said, unfurling a paper bag and pulling out a banana, a can of cashews, and a bottle of iron supplements.

She laughed. "Silly. You know I can't eat all that before Dr. Joshi comes in."

Knowing she was having her IUD removed that day, she had already eaten beans, spinach, and a baked potato for lunch. Several of the health blogs she followed revealed stories of women who bled heavily, some for as long as ten months, after the removal of their IUDs due to hormonal imbalances. A last-minute iron intake may have been futile, but she had to try.

Xavier couldn't be still and kept flipping the window shades, looking out onto the street, a goofy grin on his face. Flashes of sunlight made her shield her eyes. She half expected him to open the window and shout the news that they were one step closer to being able to get pregnant.

She forced herself to picture the life Xavier imagined for them—their new home filled with babies. A family needed to be rooted somewhere to flourish. It wasn't impossible to see them raising a child in Bronzeville, even with the errant gunshot ringing in the distance. Living near a few blasts from bullets conferred a certain street credibility, proving you hadn't completely sold out. Overgrown weeds in empty lots dotted her community, but the seeds of new Black-owned businesses sprouted, too. Somehow, Black people had reengineered gentrification there—rehabbing houses, stimulating the economy, and turning the place into their own mecca. The neighborhood reminded her of herself, a process of tearing down and building back up, making something out of nothing. The baby she'd have with Xavier one day could be her *something*.

"You're in good hands already, I see." Dr. Ranya Joshi, a slight Indian woman, entered the exam room. Her movements were small, too, and Ruth had been relieved when she first saw her gynecologist's tiny, delicate hands.

"Okay, Doc, how soon can we get pregnant? We're ready to make some babies." Xavier rubbed his hands together like he was starting a fire between them.

"Look, let's just get this over with. We can talk about fertility at my next appointment," Ruth said. All this talk of babies still left her as cold on the inside as this table felt on her bare back.

Dr. Joshi laughed and opened her arms as if she were presenting them with a gift. "Well, you should both know there's nothing to worry about. The IUD is like any other form of contraception. Once you stop using it, you can very well conceive on your first cycle."

Ruth lay back and her slender fingers pressed on her flat belly. She pictured it swollen and taut the way it had been once. Back then, her body had resembled a string bean smuggling a basketball under its shirt.

She shivered at the memory. Her nakedness on the table made her feel like a slab of meat, a specimen to be studied and talked about, and she crossed her arms over her flowered gown, drawing her knees up to her chest. She thought back to when she was seventeen, with Mama and Eli looking down on her half-naked body in the bed, their faces tight with worry, urging her to push.

Every sensation seemed magnified now. Xavier's hand squeezing hers. Then the speculum, hard and cold, entering her vagina. The tensing of her muscles. She had felt secure for years knowing the IUD was inside her. A shield protecting her from another pregnancy she wasn't ready for.

It was funny how on paper you could feel prepared for something, yet on the inside you felt anything but. Xavier had recently been promoted to vice president at PepsiCo, and she worked as a chemical engineer at a consumer-packaged-goods company. Their financial adviser had assured them their investment portfolio was *on track*. And now that they'd bought a town house, they could build equity and take advantage of tax deductions. Almost every box had been checked, and the only task left incomplete was to grow their family.

"Just breathe," Dr. Joshi said. "I'm looking for the strings." The cold instrument pulled and stretched her vaginal walls. "Okay, got them."

With her eyes closed, Ruth balled her fists as the IUD slid through the opening of her cervix. She sighed loudly, not realizing she'd been holding her breath. When her eyes fluttered open, she saw Xavier's smile hovering over her and then felt Dr. Joshi prying her fingers open to press ibuprofen into her hand.

"You did just fine." Xavier brushed her twists off her forehead so he could kiss her. A look passed between her husband and her doctor, one of satisfaction, as if they were in cahoots and some long-ago-conceived plan had finally come together.

ON THE TRAIN RIDE HOME, RUTH WRAPPED HER ARMS AROUND HER stomach. The el careened around a sharp turn, its roar and rumble vibrating inside her, aggravating her cramps.

Xavier said, "You know we'd kill the parenting game, right?" He nudged her with his thigh. "Our first son should be Xavier Jr. Carry on my name."

Ruth swallowed her unease and played along. "Mmm. And if it's a girl, how about Xena?"

Xavier frowned. "What kind of name is Xena?"

"Xena, the Warrior Princess? Hello? Any girl of mine will be a fighter. She needs a fierce name."

"Okay, if we're going the cinematic route, let's go real old school. When we have our second and third daughters, every one of them will just be Madame X. Kind of like George Foreman naming all his kids George."

Ruth punched his arm lightly. "First of all, what makes you think I'm birthing all these babies? And if I'm doing nine months of hard labor, the baby will have some variation of *my* name."

"As long as none of the boys is named Rufus, I'm cool," he said.

Up until now, their discussions about children resembled the way they talked about taking a trip to Antarctica. It made for good dinner table conversation, but they never called a travel agent or booked a flight. But this time, when Xavier slung his strong arm around her shoulders, she pictured those arms guiding their child's swing of a baseball bat or pushing a little one off on a two-wheel bike for the first time.

"We can do this, babe," he said. "It's time."

She closed her eyes and rested her head against the window, letting those fantasies marinate, when a commotion at the front of the train forced them both to sit up in their seats.

A Black boy sat cross-legged on the train floor beating a five-gallon yellow bucket. He lowered his head until his long locs swung in a furious rhythm, thick ropes slapping the sides of the bucket, loose and free and defiant.

When he turned his face, Ruth recognized him as one of the drummer boys who often tapped out beats for tips on the el platform. Never on the train, though, like this. Usually, the bucket boys were older, not boys with baby faces, but men in their early twenties. This boy couldn't have been more than fifteen.

Instinctively, Ruth glanced at the other passengers to gauge their reactions. A few white folks smiled appreciatively or simply stared, mildly curious at this oddity. Others jammed earbuds into their ears, pretending they didn't hear the drumming or see the boy.

A middle-aged Black woman pumped her fists in the air and swiveled her hips in her seat. "All right now. Do that thing. Yes, we can," she said, echoing the familiar Obama campaign slogan, the high from that night still sweetening the air.

The door to the train car in front of them swung open. A white police officer in uniform walked down the aisle. Xavier stiffened in the seat beside her.

Many of the bucket boys came from housing projects near Bronzeville, and they were in and out of jail, often simply for drumming in the wrong places in front of people who didn't embrace their entrepreneurial spirit.

Ruth felt the tension in Xavier tightly coiled, as if he might spring into action. She put her hand on his arm and he flinched. Burying her nails in his skin, she tried to silently telegraph to him not to move.

Her eyes stayed on the gun in the cop's holster.

She thought about her brother and how, when he was nineteen, a cop had stopped him for speeding and found a dime bag of weed in his car. Not a lot of weed. But enough to send Eli to jail for three weeks. A stupid kid move on his part, but not criminal enough to do time. Since that day, just the sight of a cop made her skin itch.

No one on the train moved. They stayed quiet, whatever they had to say pushed down inside them by fear or shock or something else.

The only sounds: the clatter of the train swerving along the tracks and the loud, insistent drumming.

The boy, so carried away by the music he was making, hadn't noticed the cop.

Or the toe of his black boot almost touching the rim of the bucket. Not until the cop stomped. Hard, loud.

The sticks went still and fell to the floor. The boy's eyes, brown and wide with fear, slowly traveled upward and stopped at the officer's gun in its holster.

"Hey, kid. Get up! What the hell do you think this is?" The officer's hands rested on his waist, inches from his baton and gun. Ruth heard Xavier mutter under his breath, *"Don't fight. Just do what he says,"* and she squeezed his arm.

Frozen, the boy sat there for a few seconds without moving. The officer stomped his boot again. "Are you deaf and dumb? I said get up, or I'll haul your ass to jail." This time the boy scrambled to his feet, tucking the bucket under his arm. He didn't make eye contact with anybody. When the train lurched to a stop, he scurried off, the cop right behind him.

Ruth didn't realize her hands had been shaking until Xavier covered them with his own.

Nothing bad had happened. No violence. No one hurt. It had been nothing.

Yet her muscles contracted, leaving her body rigid. She thought of her own son, just a few years younger than that bucket boy. What if that had been him with his legs wrapped around a bucket and a cop standing over him?

The country had just elected Obama president, giving their dreams wings. But that was then. Now, the clarity of a new day trimmed their feathers as it always had, making it damn near impossible to take flight.

BACK HOME, XAVIER TUGGED AT THE HEM OF HER SHIRT, AND SOON she lay on the sofa, staring at the halo of his neatly cropped Afro. His lips on hers held her in place, and she looked into his eyes, as soft and brown as chocolate orchids in bloom. She wondered if most people kissed with their eyes closed to block out all senses except for touch. But she needed to see his eyes, to determine how he might handle her truth if she ever found the courage to share it with him.

She had tried to tell him so many times—during their Netflix binges, on the way to Firestone to get an oil change, or in bed when they recapped their days before falling asleep at night. Those times when they lay side by side, the quiet of the dark would sometimes give her permission to speak, and she rehearsed what she might say. *Remember when we saw that cute kid at the mall? Well, I have one of those.* Or *You wouldn't judge me if you found out I had a kid out there somewhere but didn't know where, would you?* All of it sounded ridiculous and impossibly wrong when she played it out in her head.

A man took pride in his seed, a flag in the ground that said he'd been there. A Black man trying to find his way needed something to call his own, a part of him that would endure beyond anything the world threw at him. Ruth's son didn't grow from Xavier's seed.

"Not now. Not tonight," Ruth said, peeling his hand from her thigh.

"Okay, you've had a long day. Just let me hold you." They repositioned themselves until they were spooning, her back pressed against his chest with his arms folded around her.

Xavier had always been a patient man, proposing three times before she was finally convinced that happily ever after could be hers, too.

"You'd be the perfect mother," he'd whisper to her on the street as they watched grimy kids with potato chip crumbs at the corners of their mouths being cursed and dragged by baby-faced mothers.

Ruth couldn't tell her husband that she was no better than those young women and, actually, probably even worse, since she'd walked away from the life she'd created, leaving some other, nameless, faceless woman to mother her child.

Three

RUTH

Chicago glittered at night along the Magnificent Mile, people bouncing along in a fog of unadulterated bliss. They passed pristine holiday window displays that Ruth swore had to be video frames lifted from a Hallmark Channel movie. The only discordant note was the car horns punctuating the strains of Christmas music floating along Michigan Avenue.

Ruth inhaled to take it in fully, and a blast of cold air mixed with roasting coffee beans from a nearby café filled her nostrils. The muscle of this city flexed around her, and she stood so small next to the skyscrapers. In Ganton, the most massive structure in town was the Fernwood plant. But in Chicago, she got whiplash every time she walked in the Loop trying to absorb every sight.

Tess and Penelope strolled a few feet ahead in their matching white pantsuits with white faux fur wraps. Their locs slapped their faces when they twisted their heads excitedly to point out various shops and gift ideas. Every few blocks, Ruth glanced up at Xavier to see if he was just being coy about not knowing where they were headed. With a hint of mischief on his face, he smiled, pretending to be more clued in than he really was. He carried a folding table under his arm like it was a newspaper and bounced along with that happy warrior countenance as usual. She swung a picnic basket by her side, enjoying the tingling sensation of flirting with the unknown. They were joined by other friends and casual acquaintances heading to the secret, undisclosed location, and the mystery added to their giddiness.

Only the man at the front of the crowd, in the white top hat with the matching white cane, knew their destination. Victor was a casual acquaintance of Xavier's, whom he'd met on the treadmill at the East Bank Club. Having lived in Paris for a few years, Victor had been a frequent attendee of Dîner en Blanc, the invitation-only, pop-up event that hadn't made its way from France to the United States yet. When Victor relocated to Chicago, he'd brought his own unofficial, bootleg version with him.

As the group of about forty moved west of Michigan Avenue, people on the street stared at this merry band of Black folks waving their white cloth dinner napkins. Crowds parted like the sea to let them go by. Ruth tried to imagine how they must have looked to the white and Asian people they passed. *Don't make a spectacle of yourself,* Mama often said. *They already think we do nothing but sing and dance. Don't give them a reason to believe it's true.*

You could pay a price for thumbing your nose at respectability. Ruth knew this. If she'd eschewed respectability, she wouldn't have made it to Yale or the consumer-packaged-goods company. She wouldn't have this life where she could put on a white chiffon dress and white leather boots to prance down the street this time of year just to be irreverent.

Caught up in the magic of this night, though, Ruth didn't care what anyone thought. She alternated between observing this bougie tribe of hers as if she were an outsider and taking in the actual experience of it. Strutting down State Street, loud and proud, the wind carrying their laughter.

Parading through the Loop, Tess took Penelope's hand in hers. It was the first time Ruth had seen them publicly act like a couple. A startled expression crossed Penelope's face for an instant, and then she squeezed Tess's waist. A subtle yet unmistakable act of possession. Ownership. Not ownership of each other as partners but of themselves, their identities, their place in the world.

At one Yale alumni barbecue, Tess had pulled Ruth to the side. She said, "Don't ever take this for granted." Confused, Ruth asked what she meant.

"I mean your husband." Tess gestured to where Xavier stood getting a hamburger off the grill. "You can bring him here and to your work functions and nobody bats an eye. It's just routine. Nothing is routine for me."

The urge to question Tess further passed and they never spoke of it again, but seeing her friend and Penelope showing affection so openly made her realize that something had emboldened them after Election Night.

An odd sense of sadness overtook Ruth when she watched them and how free they'd become. She wanted to move into this new existence with them, but her feet remained stuck in the quicksand of her past. How could she enjoy that kind of ease when she carried something so heavy? Thoughts of her baby boy flooded her mind. She couldn't shake the feeling that she'd relegated her son to a life of misfortune in Ganton.

When they walked under the el tracks, Ruth spotted a Black man and woman huddled under a blanket, and she suspected they were close to her own age even though they appeared to be twice as old. The woman's cheeks drooped, and her face had collapsed from all the missing teeth. Her companion, a man in a dingy brown overcoat and red plaid pajama bottoms, pulled a wrinkled, dirt-stained Obama T-shirt from under the blanket and waved it at them. Seeing the ragged couple troubled her on a personal level. Lately, she'd been having the same nightmare about a little boy, waif thin and filthy, in an alley begging for food. In her dream, she reached out to him, but he couldn't see or hear her.

"Ten dollars! Yes, we can," the man called out in a tired voice, repeating the familiar campaign slogan.

Consumed by their own revelry, no one in her group seemed to even notice the man's postelection sales pitch.

The man's hollowed, bloodshot eyes found hers. When she slowed her stride, he zeroed in on her hesitation. "For you, miss, five dollars." She held up an empty hand as if to say she had no cash.

Xavier leaned over and whispered in her ear. "Just don't engage."

The man tried again. "Hey, lady. At least I'm not out here robbing people. I'm a businessman." The woman by his side rocked back and forth and Ruth inadvertently shivered, imagining how cold she must have been with only that threadbare blanket for cover.

Ruth refused to meet his eyes again, even as guilt flipped her insides. The only way she assuaged that guilt was to remind herself that she and Xavier made annual donations to charities that qualified as tax-exempt with the IRS. Legitimate organizations with listings in the proper registries.

Tugging at her white coat sleeve, Xavier pulled her along. "C'mon now. I admire that dude's hustle, but you know those shirts are hot."

Penelope linked her arm with Ruth's. "I'd represent you in court, but my fee would be about fifty times as much as that shirt costs. Probably not the wisest financial move."

"You don't even do criminal defense work," Ruth said, welcoming the light banter.

"I took a class in law school. Close enough."

Ruth allowed herself to be swallowed back into the group as Victor led them toward an empty, rehabbed warehouse. The building stood as a gray ghost, windows boarded up, lips sealed about its industrious past. The rattle of an el train sounded overhead, and Ruth couldn't imagine any kind of party in this drab place. But no more than a half hour later, the inside was transformed into a white wonderland.

White tables. White linens. White flowers. White wine. Even a white bird squawked in a cage.

"If that ain't some internalized racial self-hatred, I don't know what is," Harvey had said half-jokingly when he declined their invitation to attend. In spite of their coaxing, he'd smiled and said, "Thank you, but I'll pass."

If only Harvey could've seen how beautiful they were that night. A kaleidoscope of colors. Every shade of black popped against the white backdrop. They were sculptors and scientists. Bankers and builders. The world was their oyster. And they knew it. That had never been truer than now.

They dined on blue cheese canapés with walnuts, melon caprese salads, and Parmesan tortellini bites. Each table and food display more extravagant than the last. No matter how many bougie parties she attended, Ruth would never get used to some of this fancy cuisine. She nibbled and moved food around on the tiny white plate.

What would Eli think of this spread? She and her brother had grown up eating fried baloney, not bologna sandwiches on Wonder bread, and chasing it with red drink. You couldn't retrain taste buds on a whim. But she had slowly groomed her palate to appreciate decadent desserts. Her contribution for the night: her famous chocolate martinis and Dom Perignon champagne truffles from Teuscher Chocolates on Michigan Avenue. Dark chocolate flown in every week from a kitchen in Zurich, Switzerland.

A woman in a floor-length white mink applauded Barack Obama for marrying well, for choosing Michelle—an attorney with her own well-established career, an inherent sense of confidence, and beautiful dark skin.

Tess agreed. "You don't have to look twice to know she's a sister!"

Nodding, Xavier added, "I know that's right. She's a descendant of slaves. That matters."

In a French accent that hadn't diminished in the five years he'd been back in the States, Victor tapped his white cane to get everyone's attention. "You American Blacks are always consumed with the question of race."

Penelope shot back, "Since when is Detroit not in America? You were born in Detroit, right?"

Bolstered by her friend and bristling herself at Victor's conde-scension, Ruth raised an eyebrow and kept her voice low. "And who do you think you are? Are you not claiming Black these days?"

Having been raised by grandparents who had lived through the ugliness of the Jim Crow South and the oppression that continued when they migrated north, she couldn't let Victor minimize the last-ing impact of racism in America.

He lifted the rim of his top hat to reveal his hazel eyes. "I'm a cit-izen of the world, to put it plainly." Ignoring the eye rolls in the room, he continued. "What we have to get a handle on is class warfare. We must lift ourselves economically, and I know we can do it."

Xavier stood and smoothed the jacket of his white linen suit. "Ruth is right and so are you. It's both. We can't ignore race, but we also have to pool our money together and raise the capital to start something of our own. Look at the talent in this room. We got engineers, accoun-tants, lawyers, and me to market the shit out of this thing. We're sitting on a gold mine if we figure out how to leverage it right."

A familiar fire lit in Xavier's eyes, and soon a local alderwoman and Victor were both trying to convince Xavier to not only pursue his en-trepreneurial dreams but also consider a future in politics. Obama had gotten his start with grassroots community organizing and then state politics, and Victor, having served on the incoming president's campaign committee, told Xavier he could follow a similar model. She couldn't deny her husband's natural affinity for moving and mobilizing people.

Ruth remembered the night five years ago when she'd met Xavier, at a Bronzeville art gallery exhibition where he spoke to the audience about Blacks who settled in Bronzeville during the Great Migration. The first thing she noticed was how tall he was, towering over most of the crowd. He stood with his feet hip-width apart, the toes of his dress shoes pointed outward. His stance exuded confidence and power, but not in an arrogant way. As he detailed the history of the community, the audience leaned into him that night, hanging on to his sentences, like plants bending toward the sunlight.

From a corner of the room, Ruth watched him, equally impressed and skeptical. Her suspicion often roused around men with silver tongues after Ronald, her high school boyfriend, had seduced her with his manipulative wordplay.

That night they met, the gallery had been filled with beautiful women whose bodies contracted and expanded in the right places, while Ruth's arms and legs hung long, her entire body one straight line. Even she couldn't stop staring at the other women, their skin glistening like they'd just stepped out of the shower. Their hair—the conventionally *good* kind—welcomed a hard rain instead of shrinking from it.

Xavier politely acknowledged their thirsty gazes and then singled out Ruth, asking her opinion on gentrification, embracing her challenge to a statement or two he'd made that she found obtuse. Even though she felt out of her element, she surprised herself by holding her own, springing forth like a baby chick hatching and pushing her way out into a new world. Abandoning the social traditions that she'd grown up with, Ruth pursued him as much as he pursued her. Leaving her son behind had been about running away from Ganton and everything her hometown represented, but she'd never run toward anything until Xavier.

Ruth scooped rotisserie chicken salad and spread it on a cracker while listening to the others plan the trajectory of her husband's career. She stewed over the direction their lives could go in next. For the second time this year, she'd been passed over for a promotion and had politely and diplomatically applauded the rise of another engineer she'd mentored. Unsure of her own future with the company, she worried that Xavier would let others stoke his ambitions, forcing him to risk too much when they needed stability right now.

But no one wanted to be practical in the bubble of this special night. As hedonistic and heady as it was, to Ruth it still felt fragile and new. Like if you pulled the thread of a coat button, it would surely unravel until the button fell off. Yet no one else seemed to be consumed with caution. And so they partied the night away in white, embodying the title of the famous Lorraine Hansberry play *To Be Young, Gifted and Black*. With a brother on his way to the White House, they had state-sanctioned permission to dream.

Four

RUTH

On Thanksgiving, candles scented the house with cinnamon and cloves. They usually spent the holiday with Xavier's parents, but this year, the Shaws—unbelievably young and spry at sixty—had flown to Costa Rica for a week of hiking in a rain forest and kayaking through mangroves. The timing worked out well for Ruth, who much preferred to be home alone with her husband on their first Thanksgiving in their new home.

Ruth provided the Honey Baked ham, which she swore tasted just like home cooking. Xavier, who had handled most of the culinary duties since the day they married, made broccolini and candied yams.

"You put your foot in it this time." Ruth spooned her second helping of yams onto her plate. "Even better than your mom's, but don't you dare tell her I said so."

"Everything I know, I learned from her. Don't let the prissy fool you. She can throw down in the kitchen."

She gave him the side-eye. "Yes, I know that. When she doesn't have dinner catered, that is."

"She only did it that one time to impress you when y'all first met. Must've worked." He grinned. "You married me." Ruth held up a corn muffin and threatened to throw it at him.

For dessert, they ate sweet potato pie (never pumpkin) while sitting in the windowsill of the living room, their legs intertwined.

Ruth figured Mama and Eli had probably long finished their Thanksgiving meal. She often wondered if they still spent the holidays together now that Eli was married with a family of his own. Growing up, the four of them ate an early holiday supper, no later than two in the afternoon. A few hours afterward, the second and third cousins and play cousins would come over with aluminum foil and Styrofoam containers, prepared to take home whatever they couldn't eat at Mama's table. As if they hadn't taken a bite all day, she and her brother would help themselves to more mac 'n' cheese and potato salad, the two dishes Mama was famous for. When they had a family quorum, everyone held hands while Papa said grace and they took turns recounting what they were thankful for.

Putting her plate on the coffee table, Ruth, inspired by the memory, got up and went to the kitchen. She returned with a stack of orange, yellow, and brown notepaper left over from an abandoned scrapbooking effort.

"Let's start a gratitude box. Once a year, we'll write down what we're grateful for, share with each other, and then keep the notes in here." She held up a small wooden box with a golden latch. "We can read them the following year and remember how blessed we are." They took turns sharing their gratitude for everything from love and health to hummingbirds, rum, Stevie Wonder's *Songs in the Key of Life* album, short lines at Whole Foods, and all the ways they were fulfilling their dreams.

On his last piece of paper, Xavier quickly scribbled something and stared at it for a long moment before scratching his brow and folding the note.

Sensing his hesitation, Ruth pulled the paper from his hands and unfolded it. In his careful cursive, he'd written that he was grateful for *our 2.5 children on the way.*

Nausea rose inside Ruth and it must have shown on her face.

"Okay, okay," Xavier said. "I'll erase the point-five so you don't think I'm trying to be slick rounding up to three kids."

"You are so not funny." Absently, she creased the corner of the orange sheet where he'd put his wish in writing. Something about seeing the words on paper unnerved her, creating what she knew would inevitably grow into a chasm between them.

He reached for a Sharpie, took the note back from her, and crossed out the number *2* and replaced it with the number *1*. "Better? Even though I do think children without brothers or sisters can grow up with some issues. I know I did. But we can start with one and take it from there."

"Will you please stop?"

The stack of paper fell from Ruth's lap to the floor, but she didn't bend to pick it up. Xavier disentangled his legs from hers and rested his back against the opposite end of the windowsill. "Tell me what's really going on. If you don't want to have kids with me, just say so."

"Nothing is going on."

"Now, we've been married long enough for me to know that 'nothing' really means 'something.'"

"No, that's not it. Things are just complicated." She couldn't meet his eyes.

"Every time I mention kids you act like I just asked you to rob a 7-Eleven. You hardly want to make love anymore. There's nothing complicated about a man and his wife having a family. Is it my wide forehead? You don't want our kids to inherit it?" He laughed at his feeble attempt at a joke, but it came out hollow, devoid of any humor. His face tightened like he was in pain and his mouth twisted at the corners.

She bowed her head. Xavier continued without waiting for her to respond, his voice increasingly ragged.

"I know you think I was born into some kind of Black aristocracy. But we were still regular folks who sat down at dinner every night and talked about regular shit. My parents worked damn hard to send me to prep schools and overseas immersion trips. They wanted to give me every shot possible at making something of myself. When I married you, that's all I could think about—giving that same amazing life to our children. That's what being a real man is about, leading a family. Is that so wrong, for a man to want that?"

Ruth's throat squeezed, and her voice emerged tinny. "I love you, Xavier, I do, but have you considered that I may be dealing with my own thing, something that has nothing to do with you or your precious manhood? Have you thought about that?" She wrapped her arms tightly around herself, her hands buried in the sleeves of her sweater.

"All I know is I shouldn't have to build a case and have to persuade my own wife to have kids with me like we're in a *Law and Order* courtroom."

When they were dating, they had talked about having kids someday, but it lurked in the recesses of her brain as a future aspiration, something abstract. She had thought she might warm to the idea at some point down the road. If not, she could push it out of her own mind long enough that it might escape his and he'd forget, and they'd never have to discuss it again.

Xavier paced across the living room floor to the kitchen. "Penelope and Tess were even talking the other night about having a kid, whether or not they can legally marry. Here we are married, and look at us right now. Something's wrong as hell with this picture."

"Our friends have nothing to do with this. Can you please leave them out of our marriage?"

"Fine. You're right. But why don't you tell me what, or *who,* this is about then? I'm trying *real* hard to understand here. If a man's wife doesn't want his child and can't stand to have him touch her anymore, it's usually because there's *another man.*" He choked on those last two words and they came out hard and brittle. Even in his anger, he'd been careful to use the third person, not to accuse her directly, but it meant the same thing. Her husband suspected she was having an affair. How did they get here?

Xavier gathered their plates and utensils from the table, dropping them in the sink with a loud clatter. Gripping a scouring pad tightly, he scrubbed a serving bowl. She watched the pulsing veins in his hands and thought back to how gentle those hands had been the night they'd met.

After the art event was over, the street outside the gallery had sparkled from the rainfall, and Xavier had reached for her hand, claiming it was his duty to ensure she didn't slip and fall in a puddle and sully her sundress. Her hand had felt safe and protected in the cushion of his soft, larger one.

All that old-school attention had impressed her, which she hadn't liked to admit back then, but she knew game when she heard it, too. While not begrudging him any player points, she had remained engineering-school practical. She hadn't fully trusted a man since Ronald left her with a hole in her heart and a baby in her belly.

After they talked for three hours under the moonlight that night, Xavier began referring to her as *his girl,* and she'd promptly asked him to take a week to clear the field. He had the nerve to look brand-new. She slowed her speech to give him a chance to catch up.

"It means that you might want to tie up any loose ends with other ladies before pursuing me."

Xavier laughed, and she saw one crooked front tooth breaking formation, turned the wrong way as if in rebellion. That little imperfection endeared him to her even more.

"You don't need to worry. I don't have a girlfriend."

"But is there a woman out there who *thinks* she's your girlfriend?"

He opened his mouth to give a quick answer but closed it just as fast. "All fields will be clear by next weekend, in time for our first official date." Then he'd saluted, making her laugh, and she knew then, under that star-filled sky, that she had met her husband.

Standing behind Xavier in their kitchen now, helpless, she touched his arm gingerly, as if it were a flame that could burn her. "There is no one else. You know that. Will you just talk to me?"

He flinched. "I've been talking for months. I've been the only one talking while you've been running. Making excuses. *Lying.*"

She hadn't seen her husband this angry since their engagement, when he'd asked to meet Mama and Eli to get to know them and receive their blessing for the impending marriage. When Ruth had dodged his request as long as she could, she eventually flat-out refused, and Xavier assumed she was ashamed of him and likely had no intention to marry. Every time her bond with Xavier had stretched thin enough to break, it was because of her grand attempts to keep her worlds separate, to protect the lie of her past at all costs, even if that cost included her husband.

The truth could serve as a needed relief valve, lowering the pressure inside their marriage before it exploded. She had confessed to him about unpaid parking tickets and finally told him that his "famous" foot rubs were more ticklish than tantalizing.

But this was different. The birth of her baby seemed to have happened in another lifetime. To another person even. What did a wife owe her husband? How much retroactive truth-telling could be expected?

For what seemed like an eternity, Xavier scrubbed the same dish over and over in silence, just the way Mama used to when she couldn't figure out what else to do with her emotions.

She wanted to see his eyes. She needed to see them. She needed him to at least look at her. But she knew he wouldn't as long as she kept silent.

In a small voice, Ruth spoke, unsure at first whether she'd said the words aloud or only in her head. "You're right. I've been lying to you."

When his hands stilled in the dishwater, she knew he'd heard her. Without turning to face her, he said, "I'm listening."

Hail battered the windows of their town house and the wind roared. Ruth sank into the closest kitchen chair. Xavier dried his hands and sat down opposite her. There was no easy way to begin a story that was years past its due date. Eleven years, to be exact.

"I was seventeen. My senior year in high school. I messed up. Badly. His name was Ronald Atkins." She rubbed her hands together in her lap, her mouth going bone dry when she spoke her old boy-friend's name aloud.

Xavier had no way of knowing what she'd say next, but he re-coiled on instinct. Maybe it had been the way she'd avoided his eyes when she said her ex's name. Or maybe it was just the sting of hearing another man's name on his wife's tongue before a confession.

"I got pregnant."

A noise came from him that reminded her of that burst of air from a deflating balloon. She went on anyway. "I didn't want to have an abortion. You know I was raised in the church and Mama wouldn't have let me even if I'd wanted to."

Xavier laughed as if she'd just told the funniest joke he'd ever heard. The sound he made tapered off in a little titter and then he cleared his throat. "I can't be hearing you right."

"I'm sorry."

The expression on his face clouded and he shook his head slightly as if to clear the fog. "You have a kid." It was a statement, not a ques-tion, as though he needed to say the words himself to believe them.

"Yes."

"And you never said a word all these years? What the *hell*, Ruth?"

"I'm sorry, Xavier. I was scared to tell you and I'm scared now. So, let me finish before I lose my nerve." She rolled a napkin ring between her fingers. "I had a baby boy. Then I gave him up. I couldn't keep him. My freshman orientation was a few weeks after he was born. I left town and I tried to put all of it behind me. Have been trying to ever since."

He stood, shoulders curved, his head shaking, mouth open. "How could you keep something like this from me? After a year of dating and then four years of marriage, you never found a conve-nient time to tell me you had a *son*?" He paced in front of the stove, his voice getting louder.

The ham and all the leftover sides sat cold and congealing at the center of the table, and Ruth kept her eyes on the thin layer of grease forming on top of the corn. When she finally looked up at Xavier, she recognized the hurt in his eyes. Anger would have been preferable. He looked at her like he didn't know her. All she had to offer him now was more of the truth.

"I didn't grow up like you did," she said.

"No, don't give me that. You're not going to use the size of my family's bank account to excuse your lies all these years."

Ruth gestured to the granite countertops, steel cabinets, and floating shelves. "Every day I walk around this house like I belong here. But inside, I'm that poor pregnant Black girl from Ganton, Indiana. I didn't want your family to think less of me. I didn't want you to think less of me, either."

Xavier sat down again. "I wouldn't have judged you. Remember Shavonne, my cousin on my daddy's side? The one with the light eyes that you met at the family reunion last year?"

Ruth nodded.

"She got pregnant her sophomore year in high school and dropped out. She still talks about getting her GED. The same thing could have happened to me. I messed around with my share of girls in high school and didn't always strap up."

"But it's different for guys," she said. "People don't shame you for it. You still get to walk away and have a future."

Xavier paused at that, then said, "I just wish you'd trusted me more. Or trusted me at all."

He rose from the table again and moved to the sink to continue washing dishes, and so did she. They moved like an assembly line in the kitchen, washing and rinsing plates and scooping leftovers into Tupperware containers. When Ruth had first told Xavier that her grandmother didn't believe in dishwashers, she thought he would laugh and consider it old-fashioned like she had.

Mama always said dishwashers were *nothing but a waste of water, and besides, nothing beats good ol' elbow grease.* Xavier accepted that as reasonable and suggested he and Ruth wash and dry dishes together as a team. They usually talked while they worked. Not this time, though. The hinges of their new cabinets squeaked louder than usual, it seemed, when they put away each dish.

THROUGH A NARROW OPENING OF THEIR BEDROOM DOOR THAT night Ruth heard Xavier moving about the house. The announcer on ESPN analyzing plays in a football game. Then the pop from the opening of his bottle of Sam Adams. About two commercial breaks later, the sound of him using the guest bathroom.

Sitting in bed alone, she pulled the comforter around her shoulders and rocked lightly against the headboard. She thought about the first guy she'd built her world around, only to have him back away from her.

She remembered Friday nights in Ganton, no particular one because they were all the same. Fast-food islands every few miles teeming with pent-up adrenaline. Taco Bell and Walmart as destinations, not pit stops on the way to something more exciting. Malls jittering with girls telling jokes Ruth didn't get. When she dreamed of her future, she imagined being on an airplane looking down on Ganton from ten thousand feet, then twenty and thirty thousand feet, until the clouds obscured her hometown altogether. There had to be a world out there that didn't revolve around high school football.

As luck would have it, though, it was football that introduced Ruth to Ronald. His sweat-streaked face had glimmered in the moonlight, black and shiny like fresh asphalt after a hard rain. He wore shades even in the dark and a tribal tattoo snaked down his neck, inviting her to follow wherever it led. But it didn't matter whether he noticed her, because she'd always pitied girls like her best friend, Natasha, who had to rely on their looks instead of their brains to attract boys.

So when Ronald stopped her on the street after a game and asked her name, she was surprised by her body's unconscious response to the attention. Inevitably, she tried to think of something coy that Natasha might say. Instead, her brain went to mush and the only comeback she could think of was, of all things, biblical.

"Jezebel," she teased.

He laughed and came back hard. "All right now. Got to watch out for y'all church girls. I know everybody on their knees ain't praying."

She blushed at how brazen he was and looked down at her hands, the nails unpolished and bit to the quick. Hastily, she shoved her hands into her pockets.

He stepped closer. "Look, I know you're a good girl. I'm not trying to take advantage. I see you around school. I don't say anything to you, but I see you and I know you're about something."

I see you. When Ronald said that, it was like turning the key in the ignition of a new car, hearing the engine rev for the first time. She wished she had something to lean on to steady herself. Mama and Eli had been too consumed with their own problems to really see her. They moved through the same rooms, but they didn't get her the way Ronald did.

I see you. She couldn't get that out of her head because everyone saw him, not her. As a star athlete, a football legend, he didn't get patted down at parties or followed in stores like Eli did.

Still, this boy was dangerous. Not in the clutch-your-purse kind of way that some white people considered Black boys dangerous. Not because of anything criminal or even borderline criminal. The threat Ronald posed wasn't to her body. It was to that deep part of herself she was still trying to get to know. Back then, she existed as this little knot of unripe fruit.

For months, they met in the most clandestine spots—the thirty-yard line of the football field after the stadium lights went out, the aisles of the GoLo gas station, and sometimes his cousin's apartment. Why they met in secret she didn't know. And she never asked why he wouldn't kiss her, but she assumed this was the natural dance of men and women. Everything about their relationship felt like walking on the edge of a cliff, one she wanted to plunge over again and again.

"We fit together like a puzzle. R and R, baby," Ronald said. He made it sound like poetry, with the rhythm and soul of spoken word, and she said little because his eloquence said it all, overwhelming and consuming her in a deluge of new emotions. She imagined their alliterative names on wedding invitations someday, *Ruth and Ronald* embossed in the timeless elegance of calligraphy.

They blasted their boom boxes and finished each other's sentences and hip-hop lyrics. This was the nineties and music provided the anthem to their lives. If Ruth had to name one song that embodied their love story, though, it would've been the Fugees' "Killing Me Softly."

With Mama taking on extra hours cleaning at the hotel and Eli putting in long shifts at the plant, her family unit barely existed anymore. On most days, she found herself alone.

The first night she joined Ronald down in the basement of the house he shared with his mother, she took in the sparse furnishings. A ratty brown leather couch with one seat cushion that had turned black and slick where Ronald usually sat. In a corner of the dimly lit room, a floor lamp with a dull bulb. She watched him move with ease across the room to the hi-fi, where he nimbly tuned the FM channels until he settled on one with the DJ whispering in a low, raspy voice. Almost intoxicating. And then a slow jam played.

A wave of nerves overcame Ruth and something inside her like an alarm screamed that she shouldn't be there. She'd never done more than kiss a boy, but there she was alone with one in a dark basement. Still, she convinced herself she was being silly, too uptight as usual. This was Ronald from school, not a stranger. *Be cool,* she told herself.

He'd poured glasses of grapefruit juice for both of them. When he passed her the bottle of vodka to mix with it, she froze. It smelled like nail polish remover. Other than sneaking a sip of her grandfather's beer when she was eight, which had made her gag, Ruth had never tried alcohol. Ronald must have sensed her discomfort.

"Breathe in, then just sip on it. Nice and slow," he told her. He was sitting close to her on the couch. Too close, their knees bumping. A jolt of excitement intensified by fear ran through her.

She put the drink to her lips as he had instructed. It reminded her of one of those nasty-tasting medicines Mama had forced her to drink as a kid. The vodka burned the roof of her mouth and then her throat and stomach, too.

Still, something about the delicious danger of drinking, and doing it with Ronald, ignited her whole body.

The next time she found herself in Ronald's basement, she came prepared, knowing what could happen, but also not knowing, either. His mother had worked late that night as a nurse aide at the hospital, filling in for someone else. When Ronald called her to come over, it was already late, but she hurriedly changed into her pretty lace thong that Natasha had convinced her to buy on one of their trips to the mall. Not the granny panties Mama bought for her, five in a pack. She dabbed perfumed body oil on her belly button and the insides of her thighs. All those little details she had picked up from tales of Natasha's exploits that Ruth had stored in her mind. Finally, it was her turn.

The low ceiling and the close walls made Ronald's football player body seem unusually large and awkward. He excited her. He terrified her, too. Wordlessly, he fumbled with the hook of her bra and she turned her head, avoiding his eyes, suddenly shy, maybe even a little remorseful. Yet if she tried hard enough, she could be a girl who didn't care about bad reputations and grandmothers' expectations. She could just be.

It hurt until it didn't anymore. Sex was like salve on old wounds. When he entered her, he filled the aching, empty places left by a dead grandfather and parents she never knew. They didn't talk about protection because he was her protection.

The day the doctor confirmed Ruth's pregnancy, Mama didn't say a word. There was no surprise on her face. No shock. It was as if she had been awaiting official confirmation of what she already knew. People said there was something about the way a girl walked from the very beginning when she was carrying a baby—a spread to her hips, the parting of her legs—that you could just tell.

Mama took her anger out on a frying pan, scrubbing it so hard the nonstick coating peeled off like an onion skin. That night, Ruth saw her kneeling in the closet, her face wet with perspiration, trembling, a moan rising from her throat, petitioning Jesus to intervene.

Ruth couldn't even look her grandmother in her eyes in those early months of pregnancy. She had messed up big time, carrying her shame in front of her, that shame walking into rooms first, pressing against the kitchen table where they said grace as a family.

Keeping the baby a secret from Ronald had never been the plan, but he barely looked at her during that first trimester. When he got sidelined from football in a late-season game with an anterior cruciate ligament tear and his college scholarship dreams began slipping away, he withdrew into himself. That's the only way to put it. As soon as he stopped touching that ball, he stopped touching her, too.

Still, Ruth kept making plans for them and the baby on the way, hoping he'd eventually stop tripping. On an Excel spreadsheet she kept private, she mapped out her strategy, which included Ronald attending community college to start and then joining her at a four-year university where she'd study part-time and raise their baby, and he'd play football.

The college prep books had advised making two lists: one for "safety" schools and another for "I'll die happy if this ever happens" schools. Yale, with its reputation for fostering big ideas and curiosity, had been her reach-beyond-the-cornfields-of-Ganton, her reach-for-more. She had watched Angela Bassett in the movie *Waiting to Exhale* dozens of times, and the Yale graduate inspired her. There was something about the way she moved—her back stick straight, head high—and every time she spoke, brilliance dripped from her lips. A Yale-made woman.

After college graduation, Ronald would be drafted to the NFL and she would find an engineering job in whatever city he landed in, and by then, they would consider having a second child.

In those early months of her pregnancy, before she began to show, she told herself that if Ronald knew the truth, maybe his eyes wouldn't be so cold and distant. But every time she tried talking to him about anything, he either snapped at her or stayed quiet.

She tried to explain how the Pythagorean theorem related to football interceptions, but he wasn't interested. She offered to ice his knee, but he didn't want her to touch him. Could she make him a sandwich? No.

One night, they were sitting on the couch at Ronald's place watching an old *Martin* rerun and she suggested they go together to a party that Friday night, something to take his mind off his knee injury. And if she were honest, anything to get out of his mother's basement.

Without looking at her, Ronald pulled hard on the Velcro strap of his knee brace. "You can do what you want on Friday nights, just not with me," he said.

How could she tell him about the baby after that? What if he blamed her and thought she had trapped him somehow? People labeled certain girls in school who zeroed in on potential husbands like a laser, some going as far as to poke holes in condoms. Ruth wasn't one of those girls, yet she desperately wanted him to know they'd created a life together. Keeping the baby a secret almost destroyed her, but every time she opened her mouth, no sound emerged. She couldn't do it.

Her long talks were instead with the baby. *Do you think he still loves us?* Her tongue would itch, and she'd crave something sweet, like caramel apples or Tootsie Rolls. That would be a sign from their baby that everything would be okay.

Then she'd say, *If Ronald really loves us and wants us to be a family, kick once for yes, twice for no.* Sometimes, she wouldn't feel anything for a long stretch of time, and then if there were two kicks, she told herself the baby had misheard the question. She'd ask it again until she felt a single kick.

Now, the silence between Ruth and her husband coated the air, thick and pungent, the discontent almost choking them. When there was no more good TV to watch, only infomercials for blenders and thigh thinners, Xavier finally came to bed. He wasn't a man to pout or lick his wounds. But they'd never fought over anything this consequential before, either, and as well as she knew her husband, it was impossible to read his mind. And honestly, this hadn't even been a fight. A fight would have been easier. He moved around their bedroom, careful to avoid any physical contact with her.

Ruth turned out the lights and lay beneath the sheets with her eyes closed and hands clasped over her chest, pretending she hadn't moments earlier been pressed against the door trying to anticipate his mood. Her head burrowed in the thousand-thread-count pillowcase, made of Egyptian cotton designed to softly caress her cheek. But on this night, it just chafed, and she couldn't get comfortable with Xavier so close, yet so far away.

He sat on the edge of the bed for a few minutes before stretching out on top of the covers, then rolling onto his side. Curling into a ball, she tucked her legs beneath her, facing one wall while he faced the other. He had always been a generous bed partner, never hogging the covers or manspreading. In the infancy of their marriage, she had stayed awake through the night watching his chest rise and fall as a mother would do with her baby, admiring the bridge of his nose and the length of his eyelashes. She had been afraid to go to sleep. Afraid he might not be there in the morning.

For her, love had always been about holding on too tight. She could never get the grip just right. When sleep finally came, her body shook with fresh dreams of her son hungry and helpless in a Ganton alley. Her nightgown, damp with sweat, clung to her skin like Saran wrap.

Five

MIDNIGHT

Midnight lay facedown on the back seat of Daddy's Chevy Silverado pickup truck. The truck smelled worse than the dead frog from science class that had been soaking in formaldehyde for weeks. This was not Midnight's day to spend with Daddy—usually that was Mondays and Fridays—but he jumped into his father's truck whenever he spotted it around town.

He listened to the rumble of the wind and the purr of the engine, trying to ignore the anger in the voice of the man yelling at Daddy. Fights seemed to find Daddy and his friends. Their bodies ready to give a punch or get one. Midnight had seen so much in his time that Granny called him an old soul. Even without sitting up to look, he knew the voice of the other man belonged to Drew, the guy who let Daddy live in his place after the plant closed. Midnight would've moved in, too, but Granny said it didn't look right for a boy his age to live with two men. So he was stuck at her house.

From inside the truck, he could hear Drew saying, *"You owe me rent money, Butch. You better get it to me by the end of the week."*

Then Daddy: *"I told you I'd pay you. Get off my back."*

Midnight didn't sit up to look, but he could hear their grunts and the slapping of fists against jaws. With his eyes shut, he felt each bump and bang on the side of the truck, not sure if Daddy or Drew was winning, but sure he had time. A few minutes at least.

All the truck windows were white with snow. On all fours, he crawled to the center console, opened it, and pulled out the plastic clips that led to the secret compartment where Daddy kept the gun. Well, not a real gun, because Daddy hid those underground. *The feds won't get these,* he said. The gun he'd bought for Midnight looked real except it had an orange tip on the end and shot plastic pellets. Daddy was trying to teach him how to shoot. But the only time Daddy let him fire it was when he wore special clothes and something to protect his eyes.

"Don't be scared of it. Hold it like you mean it," Daddy said the first time he took him out for practice shooting.

That day, Midnight had extended his good arm—the left one—wrapped his fingers around the trigger, closed his eyes, and then lost his grip, the gun falling to the ground.

"Pick it up and do it again without being so reckless."

He let Daddy's words in his ear guide him. *Square your shoulders and lean forward. Don't pull the trigger, squeeze it like you're making a fist.* On Midnight's fifth try, Daddy dropped his head and was quiet at first, his eyes misting. Then he worked his mouth into a half smile, slapped Midnight on the back, and said, "Good job. That's my boy."

Midnight would always be a one-arm shot. The boy with the gimp arm. Forever damaged goods, and he feared no matter how brave he was, Daddy would only see his scars.

There was no one in all of Ganton as fearless as Daddy, who called himself a good guy with a gun. He'd whipped it out once at the laundromat to stop a man he swore he saw choking his girlfriend and slamming her head against the washing machine. Both the guy and the girl said they were just goofing around, but Daddy didn't believe them.

And there was that time somebody was breaking into cars late at night in one area of Pratt, and Daddy patrolled the street with his hand on the Sig in his waistband, the same nine-millimeter that cops and Navy SEALs carried.

Now Midnight practiced his shooting position, aiming the gun at the steering wheel, the floor mats, the power locks, then the passenger window. Tucking his elbow in close to his rib cage, he made himself smaller. Then he lined the muzzle of the gun up with the side of the front seat, using it as cover the way he would if he were a cop trying to sneak up on a bad guy. But then the stomp of boots in the snow outside the driver's-side door got louder and Midnight quickly tossed the gun back in its hiding spot and shut the console. Even though it was a pretend gun, Daddy didn't like him playing with it unsupervised. Midnight hunched down on the floor of the back seat.

The door to the truck opened and Daddy got in and revved the engine long and hard. The truck charged ahead, making Midnight bump his head on the back of Daddy's seat. He let out a yelp.

"Patrick, what the hell are you doing in my truck?"

That's how he knew Daddy was mad. Usually, he called him *kid* or nothing at all, rarely his real name. Daddy and Granny and the teachers at school were the only ones who called him Patrick. The name didn't feel right for him. After all, Patricks had a certain look, like Patrick Mulligan in his sixth-grade class. Red hair combed neatly, freckles all over his face, and navy-blue pullover sweaters. That's what a Patrick looked like.

Daddy didn't like the nickname *Midnight*, and he hated where it came from. In third grade, Midnight had started noticing Black boys who made the coolest shapes with their hair and somehow it stayed in place and never fell in their eyes. Boys who casually dropped the *g* on words sometimes, like when they told him to quit buggin' when he said something silly. They walked with that cool limp, the dip that had a rhythm to it like music always on beat. One time he followed them into class imitating their walk until their teacher, Mrs. Thornton, made him stand in the corner, calling what he'd done *inappropriate*. She never explained why he was being punished, but he'd learned early on that grown-ups didn't have to explain themselves to kids.

From then on, he became known as the little white boy who acted

Black. Whatever that meant. The Black kids at school started calling him *Midnight* and he wasn't sure if it was because they liked him or because they were making fun of him.

The seat reclined, and Daddy leaned back, still fuming under his breath, his long brown rattail hanging below his wool hat. He guided the steering wheel with one hand, small red scratches dotting his white knuckles, with a Camel dangling from his fingers.

"Did you know you can hold your breath for seventeen whole minutes without passing out?" Midnight leaned forward with his elbows on the armrest between the two front seats.

"Sit back."

"Oh, and if you cut a snake's head off, it can still bite you hours later."

The traffic light at Shepherd Street had just turned yellow and Daddy floored it, making the truck skid, forcing him to jerk the wheel to keep them going in a straight line.

"Damn ice," he said.

"Did you know there's ice on Mars in the polar ice caps and on some glaciers? They say that people may be able to live there someday."

When Daddy turned his head from side to side to watch traffic, the rattail he'd been growing for years slithered across the headrest. He raked his hands over it, something he probably didn't even realize he did. Whenever Granny asked when he planned to chop it off, he flipped it, a way of flipping her off, too.

"You do your homework?" Daddy said, not sounding too interested in the answer.

"School's out for Christmas the end of this week. We don't go back till it's the new year."

"Hmm."

Midnight opened his backpack and took out a pair of scissors, the ones with the green rubber grip handle and blunt tip, school-sanctioned official scissors. With a shaky hand, he opened the scissors and placed the rattail between the blades, and that's when Daddy slammed the brakes. The truck's wheels ground in the snow, throwing

Midnight forward into the back of his father's seat. The scissors fell to the floor.

"What the hell?" Daddy yelled, either at the red light he almost ran or at the tug he felt at the nape of his neck. Midnight wasn't sure whether he would've had the guts to go through with it or not, but because of Daddy's crazy driving he'd never know.

On the side of the road he saw Tank, a guy who used to work with Daddy at the plant, but who now spent all day collecting cans he could trade for cash. He was one of those people who always wore a stupid grin even when nothing was funny.

Tank motioned for Daddy to pull over to the shoulder of the road. The hazy lights of a police car came into focus through the rearview mirror.

"Get out, kid," Daddy said.

The cops weren't chasing anybody. They were leading a procession of long black cars with dark windows, the kind where those inside can see you, but you can't see them. Following was a line of regular cars and pickup trucks, all with their lights beaming in the heavy fog. Snow hit at a strange angle, hurling little spiky balls at them, and Midnight buried his head in his jacket to shield his face.

Daddy grabbed Midnight's good arm. "Get your hands out of your pockets and put your head up. Show some respect."

The cold and snow stung Midnight's eyes and he squinted against the force of it. Daddy saluted, and Tank did, too, as the funeral cars rode by with the American flag waving frantically on sticks in the windshields.

A few cars in the funeral procession honked their horns in greeting, breaking the silence of respect like some guys did when they laughed too hard at the pastor's joke, as if they were in the bar and not church.

"That was Elroy Richards, you know. When he retired from Fernwood, he always said he wanted to own a bait and tackle shop. He did it. He did the damn thing," Tank said, holding his dingy baseball cap over his chest.

"Hell, yeah, he did. One of the best guys on the line. Put in his thirty years. Never let anybody down. A good man. What happened?" Daddy dropped his head.

"Cancer. He was bad off and Marie said they couldn't afford chemo or any of that."

"That's rough. A damn shame."

They watched those slow-moving long black cars with their bright lights until they blended into the afternoon sky.

When they got back in the truck, Daddy got real quiet and ran his hands through his greasy hair. He was in a bad mood. He had been in a bad mood for a long time. For years.

"Thinking about Mom?" Midnight said.

"I'm not always thinking about your mother. Will you give it a rest already? Sit back and be quiet. Fasten your seat belt." Daddy gunned the engine, maybe to drown out anything else Midnight might have said.

MIDNIGHT STOPPED TALKING, BUT NOT EVEN DADDY COULD CON-trol his thoughts. What went on in his mind belonged to him, no guardrails, no judgment from the grown-ups, no rules to break, just a private space in a cluttered world that was his and his alone. A space to be with Mom.

She used to move around the kitchen in their old house, her hands soaking wet with Dawn dishwashing liquid, her hair growing wild as prairie grass. She always winked at him when she made his scrambled eggs and pancakes in the mornings, her eyes a deep blue or maybe green. He couldn't remember. He never saw her mad. Some-times she mussed his hair and called him her little mad scientist, just like Einstein. When she smiled, her whole face lit up and you wanted to get closer to the flame.

The night she and Daddy told him he was getting a little sister, they went out for hot fudge sundaes before dinner. A drop of choco-late stained Midnight's wide-ruled notebook paper where he made a list of all the things he'd teach her: the right way to throw a spitball, how to dig for worms, and the proper form for pitching a curveball. Midnight would always have a seven-year head start and she'd never catch up. He liked it that way. When she was old enough, he decided he'd take her to the junkyard to sift through metal for something special, like the time he and Daddy found a grille and lights from a damaged cop car. Daddy had let him keep both in his bedroom to show off to his friends when they slept over.

"Can I hold her when she gets here? I won't drop her. I swear I won't," he'd said to Mom.

"Yes, sweetheart. I promise," she'd answered, looking him in the eye.

Daddy just grinned like he always did back then, even when he had to work overtime at the plant to bring in extra money for the crib and all the other baby stuff. The night Mom's water broke, Daddy ran all the red lights to get them to the hospital. He sang the whole way to keep Mom calm.

The hospital smelled funny, like a mix of Lysol and cough syrup. People in white coats and what looked like pastel pajamas rushed around holding clipboards and checking their pagers.

They didn't allow kids inside the birthing room, so Granny waited with Midnight down the hall, close enough though to see Mom's room. They tried to decide who his little sister would look like— whether she'd have Daddy's long, narrow nose or Mom's pink lips and sandy hair.

Just when he and Granny were about to start playing Uno, the door to Mom's hospital room swung open and Daddy flew out of it like he'd been knocked back by a blast from an explosion. Even now, Midnight could still see Daddy's body hitting that wall behind him and sinking to the floor. Granny jumped from her seat quicker than Midnight had ever seen her move. He got up, too.

A tall doctor walked toward them, his head down, and it looked to Midnight that the man's eyeglasses might tumble from the tip of his nose. When the doctor finally spoke, he said Hannah didn't make it. It took a couple of seconds for Midnight to recognize his mother's actual name, and he didn't know right away what *didn't make it* meant until Granny fell against a chair and Daddy squeezed his head between his hands as if it would fall apart unless he held it together.

All the lights went out in Midnight's brain and he couldn't make sense of what anyone said after that. Later, Granny would remind him that the doctor had said Mom and his little sister had died of something with a weird name. *Preeclampsia.* It had something to do with high blood pressure, which made no sense. Granny was his mom's mom and she had that, and she still lived to get old. His sister hadn't even lived long enough to get a name of her own.

Midnight wondered what he had done wrong. Why had Mom lied about all the things he'd get to do with his little sister? Was she mad about that time he tried to stick her tampons up his nose? Or because he never cleaned his room when she told him to? Or helped her wash dishes?

Midnight watched from the doorway of her hospital room as Daddy and Granny tiptoed in as if Mom were asleep and might wake up if they made too much noise. From the doorway, he saw her in the bed, but with everybody gathered around, they were blocking her face. He almost screamed and ran away but didn't want Daddy to think he was a little punk, something he called him when he refused to touch a dead possum or a snake slithering on the side of the road. So, he stood there, close enough to prove his manhood, but far enough away that his clearest memories of his mother would not be of her lying there in that bed, dead.

No matter how hard he tried, he couldn't forgive her. To him death was just another way people broke their promises. A way for them to leave and have the last word.

Six

RUTH

Every time Ruth held her key card up to the wall reader on the twenty-third floor, she heard a soft click, then saw a green light that brought her more relief than she cared to admit. That small token granted her access through the electric-powered doors into the inner sanctum of Langham, the consumer-packaged-goods company where she'd worked since graduating college.

Nothing had been the same with Xavier since Thanksgiving, when she told him the truth about her baby, so when she walked into the reception area at Langham the Monday after, the air felt different, lighter somehow. Here, she could surround herself with the certainty of product testing and avoid the variability in her personal life. The laboratory had always been her refuge, and she immersed herself in building laundry detergent formulas. Yet lately, she felt the way she had as a kid in gym class teetering on the balance beam, where one misstep could land her in a heap on the floor.

Once a week, Ruth sent her lab coat out for dry cleaning, because she preferred it neatly pressed, the fabric crisp and white without blemish. After a few years on the job, some of her colleagues had settled into a more casual relationship with the company, their dress sporadically slouchy and their performance erratic. But when you came from where Ruth did, you knew what the bottom looked like, and you couldn't slip and fall back there again.

Shelley, the Black assistant who sat at the front desk to greet visitors, nodded to Ruth in sisterly approval. Obama's win had widened her smile more than usual and Ruth grinned back.

"You're working it today, girl," Shelley said, as she did most mornings when Ruth stepped off the elevator. But all Ruth was really working was the customary uniform of any laboratory scientist from the research and development team: long pants and long sleeves under a lab coat, closed-toe shoes, safety goggles, and purple gloves.

It was nearly impossible to be cute in this getup, but Ruth recognized what Shelley meant without either woman having to verbalize it. Their conspiratorial looks said Ruth had made it and so had Shelley, by proxy. Just her mere presence as a chemical engineer made a statement: a road map for the handful of Blacks in the company and an unwritten, unspoken exclamation point for anyone who doubted they could dominate in the sciences.

The lab's fluorescent ceiling lights illuminated the brown liver spots at the top of her boss Clayton's head, the open terrain that his sparse mud-brown hairs failed to cover. Side by side, they poured surfactant into beakers.

She cleared her throat and said, "I see Max's getting his name on lots of patents lately."

Had her tone sounded casual, as she'd intended? Or had her insecurity bled through her practiced nonchalance? Holding the beaker eye level and swirling the liquid inside, Clayton said, "Mmm. I'd say our entire group is innovating."

Defending her statement would seem just that, *defensive*, so she kept quiet. Max had joined their team as a scientist just two years ago, and after she trained him, he was quickly assigned to core brands and then new innovations. In Langham lingo, they were the *high-market-value, high-market-share* products.

No one in the workplace was indispensable, yet when senior leaders said they wanted a detergent with ten times more cleaning power than that of their main competitor, Ruth busted her ass to make those claims true. In the early days, Clayton often referred to her *enviable talent*.

Three years into her tenure with the company, Ruth began working on core brands, but recently, Clayton asked her to only make small tweaks to formulas. Nothing more challenging than that. Now was not the time, despite Xavier's eagerness, to get pregnant and have Clayton question her commitment to Langham. In spite of Clayton's early praise of her work, she feared her own position would always remain tenuous. A bull she would ride for as long as she could hold on without it bucking and knocking her to the ground.

She had met Clayton at a National Society of Black Engineers recruiting event on Yale's campus a few months before graduation. Her knees trembled beneath her somber gray interview suit when she faced him as he scouted new talent at the networking reception.

Her grandmother's voice rang in her head that night. *Stand up straight. Don't slouch. Look them straight in those blue or green eyes, because they're no better than you. Let them see how smart you are.*

It didn't take long for Ruth and Clayton to bond over being born and raised in the Midwest—the Indiana auto factory town for her and a dairy farm in Wisconsin for him. Even though she was Black, and he was white and older, they had similar roots. The same values. Corn-fed folks. Sturdy. Good, decent people at the core.

They laughed at their mutual preference for no-frills cuisine with names that were easy to pronounce. But it was their banter over biochemical interactions and thermodynamics that lit her up, and before they knew it an hour had passed. Their conversation was so all-consuming that Ruth forgot her fear and left behind the shamed teen mother from Ganton who had been intimidated by the Ivy League freshman year. By this time, she had become a butterfly shedding her cocoon, finding her legs and then her wings.

Now, Max stood on the other side of Clayton, his hands stuffed in the pockets of his corduroys.

"Which mission are you on?" Max asked their boss. Splotches of red dotted the skin of his neck just above the collar of his lab coat.

For weeks now, the two of them had been talking endlessly about *Star Wars Battlefront: Renegade Squadron*. Clayton said, "I'm on Korriban. We got Han Solo unfrozen from that carbonite. Now we're attacking Emperor Palpatine."

Max said, "Okay, you're on the ninth mission then. Just wait till he gets trapped and you have to help him get into the shield generator base. Pretty gnarly."

At night, Ruth found herself googling the adventures of Han Solo so that she could add something to these conversations. But it was as if Clayton and Max were speaking another language that she didn't have the patience to learn.

Trying to ignore their voices, Ruth turned on the propeller mixer and watched the cloudy haze of blue color mix with a cleaning agent. It always reminded her of a smoothie in a blender.

She felt someone's eyes on her and looked up to see Nigel, a scientist from Ghana, glance at her quickly before returning to his acid-level test. The sting from his furtive gaze burned her cheeks. She wished she hadn't confided in him her fears about Max cozying up to Clayton and leapfrogging over her in the company.

"You just have to work harder is all," Nigel had said dismissively, before launching into a diatribe about what he called the abysmal work ethic of American Blacks.

When he joined the team, Ruth had rejoiced at having another person of color in R&D. Without exaggeration, Nigel's skin could be described as blue black, that you-can't-see-your-hand-in-front-of-your-face level of darkness. Yet his snobbery reminded her of Victor. As Zora Neale Hurston once said, *All my skinfolk ain't kinfolk.*

CHRISTMAS ADS, CHRISTMAS MUSIC, AND CHRISTMAS DECORATIONS seemed to sprout everywhere like overgrown weeds she wanted to trample with only a week to go before the holiday. The brightness of window displays that had delighted her days before blinded her now, and she blanched at their lack of subtlety. All this festivity shoved Ruth into the arms of cheer she didn't really feel and actively resisted.

Back in the day, her grandparents had a scarcity mindset, always pinching pennies, even at the most indulgent time of the year. They gave one present each to Ruth and Eli, instilling in them the value of family, not frivolity. Not that she and her brother had appreciated the larger lesson back then.

Ruth had been three years old when their biological mother left them. Very few memories of the woman lodged in her brain, but on the last Christmas they spent together, Joanna wore a short red Santa dress with bells dangling from her butt. The bells jingled when she walked, and that sound made Ruth laugh. She would have followed her mother anywhere.

In every fleeting, possibly phantom memory of their mother, Ruth had to begrudgingly acknowledge the woman's beauty, her high cheekbones and those dimples Ruth had liked to press to see if they'd pop back out. That Christmas, Joanna surprised her with a mesh bag filled with marbles in every color imaginable. Ruth remembered being enamored with the marbles, rolling them on the kitchen floor, delighting in the noise they made, until Mama scooped them back into the bag and yelled at Joanna. Too young to understand the argument and desperate to play with those marbles, Ruth cried uncontrollably. It wasn't until years later that Mama would relive that day, saying Joanna should've known better than to give a three-year-old a toy she could choke on. *Careless,* Mama said. *Always careless.*

Eli would've been nine that Christmas, and she couldn't recall what their mother had given him, if anything. Whenever she tried to get her brother to tell her what he remembered about Joanna, he changed the subject. She suspected their mother's disappearance had been harder on him because he'd known her longer, loved her longer, had more memories to suppress.

Christmas became a more sensible affair when she went to live with her grandparents. There was that time in Walmart when Ruth threw a tantrum after not getting the Cabbage Patch Kid doll she'd begged for, the one that came with a birth certificate you could frame. Their chubby cheeks and pinched faces fascinated her. Papa had been ready to cave, usually pliable after her desperate pleas, but melodrama around Mama rarely yielded more than a swat to the backside. She said, *A girl your age doesn't need to be playing house. No babies for you no time soon.*

That night, Ruth had seen Mama kneeling in the closet, murmuring something to Jesus to ward off any nascent baby-making spirits. Oh, the irony of embodying her grandmother's unanswered prayers, becoming everything the old woman had feared most.

XAVIER WASN'T HOME FROM WORK YET, WHICH GAVE RUTH uninterrupted time to wrap his Christmas present—a pair of Magnanni leather shoes, handcrafted in Spain. He had fawned over them obsessively on one of their trips to Nordstrom, admiring how the toasted-almond leather shone in the glint of the store lighting. He had vowed to own them one day. In a spontaneous moment, or a desperate one depending on how you looked at it, she had stopped at the Michigan Avenue store on her way home from work to buy them. He would whoop in delight at the sight of these shoes, and she needed to see him smile and watch his face erupt in joy again.

The last few weeks, she and Xavier had moved through their home like roommates, careful not to invade each other's space, leaving notes that revealed just enough information about their whereabouts to stave off any missing-person reports to the police. The silences between them stretched like a rubber band about to snap. When they did speak, it was only to communicate the mundane: *Have you changed the furnace filter yet? I bought a Christmas gift for Harvey and put both our names on it.* Their marriage reminded her of the trunk of a tree in late winter or early spring, and already she could see the cracks, the gradual splitting of the bark. In time, new wood grew around a tree's wound, sealing it off from further decay. She held on to the hope that Christmas Day would be their new wood.

WITH THE WRAPPED MAGNANNI SHOES TUCKED UNDER THE Christmas tree, Ruth felt ambitious that night, her impulse buy inspiring her to change into a dusty-rose silk negligee and drape a string of pearls across her body. She felt a bit silly. Besides, Xavier had never required a lot of packaging pretense; he had told her many times how sexy she looked in a baggy, ratty old T-shirt. But when he'd said that, he had no idea she'd been lying to him since the day they met. And besides, he'd been begging her to make love. She would do more than oblige him. She would do what she'd always done—overperform and exceed expectations.

Staging herself seductively on the bed, she tried multiple poses: Lying on her side with one hand on her thigh. Kneeling on all fours. Finally, she settled on a playful pose resting on her stomach, a position that made her tiny breasts puff up like dough popping out of a biscuit can. Then, she waited.

The first thing Xavier did when he walked into their bedroom was toss his keys on the nightstand. Still in his starched white shirt and dark gray slacks, he sat on the ottoman across from the bed, opening his laptop. Obviously, he saw her on the bed, but gave no indication that he noticed her body wrapped in silk and pearls.

Holding her breath, she sucked in her stomach to camouflage the slight pooch that became magnified by the thin fabric of her negligee. She wondered what on the computer screen had him so preoccupied. He unbuttoned the cuffs of his shirtsleeves, still barely looking up at her. When he finally spoke, he sounded as officious and routine as a doctor in a patient exam room.

"Okay, I know you want to check in on your son. What information do you have? I assume you've got the adoption papers somewhere. Who are his adoptive parents? We need a plan. He could be in New York or China for all we know."

Cold air chilled her bare skin. "No, I don't know. I don't know anything."

She curled into a ball on the bed. Xavier could see her there in her sexy display, but he hadn't reacted at all. Nothing. And why so many questions all of a sudden when they hadn't spoken of the baby in weeks?

Quickly, she grabbed her terry cloth bathrobe and shoved her arms into it, too embarrassed to look up at him. His sudden, practical questions made her dizzy. Normally, she operated just as logically, applying the scientific method to every decision. As heavy a burden as her secret had been to carry alone all these years, Xavier's probing seemed to double the load on her shoulders.

"What's gotten into you all of a sudden?"

Laughing roughly, he said, "It's not all of a sudden. You've had four years to come up with answers. The more I think about it, the more it burns me up that you could say nothing all these years. And now, when I'm trying to help, you don't want to talk about the adoption papers."

"I never signed any papers. I don't even know his name." Just admitting that carved out a pit at the base of her stomach. The image from her dreams of a wide-eyed, lost boy wandering the dirty streets of some big city made her nauseated.

When she'd gone home to Ganton the summer after her graduation from Yale, she'd seen little boys in the grocery store and at the bank and the post office and she'd felt a mix of fear and anxiety, wondering if a child standing near her in line could be hers. To this day, the backs of boys' heads always caught her attention. She had become quite skilled at maneuvering until she saw their faces, the shapes of their eyes, the contours of their lips and noses. She even measured the heights of foreheads in her engineer's mind, estimating how her son's face had grown over time. And always, she looked for the birthmark on his left cheek. Parks and playgrounds toyed with her imagination the most, and she wondered if certain faces and smiles should feel familiar. But in reality, she doubted her son's adoptive parents would've taken him somewhere else outside Ganton.

Xavier looked incredulous. "You don't even know who he is or who's raising him? How is that even possible?"

"I told you I was just a child myself," she said, her voice thin and brittle.

"But you weren't seven. You were seventeen and old enough to ask questions and keep some records."

In all the years since she'd given birth, she'd convinced herself that naïveté explained her inaction. But Xavier's words cut to the bone and revealed something she hadn't considered—abject stupidity on her part. He hadn't asked a direct question, so she didn't give an answer. Her eyes roamed their bedroom and she looked everywhere she could except at him.

"Once you were grown, you still didn't ask any questions about the adoption? And what about your grandmother and brother?"

There had been an agreement with Mama and Eli that they would take care of everything and she would go on with her life, never looking back. But now, that pact felt ridiculous, and seeing everything through her husband's eyes, she felt embarrassed and couldn't believe she'd let things go this long.

In a small voice, she said, "I did the best I knew how at the time."

Forcing herself to hold his gaze, she looked into his deep-set light brown eyes. From the day they met at the art gallery, she'd always seen laughter and mischief in them. She searched them now for that warmth, but she could tell his stare would not thaw anytime soon.

Xavier sat with his legs wide apart, rapidly tapping both feet. She could sense his growing frustration. "I just can't believe you didn't tell me. I told you about my mom and how she used to step out on my dad when I was growing up. That's something I never told anybody." Pinning her with his eyes, he said, "Nobody. Except for you."

Xavier worked his mouth the way he did when he had food stuck between his teeth. She turned away, realizing he was trying not to cry.

Shortly after their engagement, he had confided in her that prim and proper Mrs. Shaw had been unfaithful to her husband, to Xavier's dad. From what Xavier had said, it wasn't just a one-time slip-up, either. Apparently, she'd been "addicted" to the thrill of being pursued by various men.

His confession had torn at her insides. She imagined his humiliation, the way he always wondered as a kid what he'd done wrong to make his own mother turn away from her family. At the time, she'd vacillated between feeling endearment that he'd shared something so painful and guilt that she couldn't or wouldn't reciprocate.

Somehow their family recovered, and Ruth suspected that had a lot to do with Mr. Shaw's deep capacity to forgive. Ruth hoped for similar forgiveness from Xavier.

She pulled the ties of her robe. "I don't know what to say. I'm not as strong as you are."

"Don't do that. Don't try to make me feel sorry for you."

"That's not what I'm doing," she said, hearing the pleading in her tone. "If I could turn back time, I'd tell you everything, but I can't."

Xavier stood above her, his arms folded across his chest. "Would you? Would you tell me about your kid? Because honestly, I don't believe you would. I *trusted* you, Ruth, but you couldn't trust me."

He looked at her as if she were a stranger, and she lowered her eyes. "I don't know what you want me to say."

"There's nothing you can say now. Your silence these last four years has said everything I need to know."

"I have said I'm sorry every way I know how. It was a mistake not to tell you, I admit that. But can't you see how difficult it is for me to live with this?" Would he make her pay the rest of her life for one lie of omission? A seed of anger began to take root inside her. "I won't keep begging you to understand me."

He leaned against the wall, his head turned up to the ceiling. "Then I guess that's that."

"I guess it is then," she said, her face drawing up like crumpled paper. She repositioned herself on the bed so her back was to him and he couldn't see her face. "I'm heading to Ganton for Christmas to spend some time with Mama and Eli. It's been a while and I need to see them."

She hadn't known that's what she wanted to do until the words spilled out of her. When she glanced back at Xavier, his face clouded with confusion and then hardened, his eyes darkening in spite of his laughter.

"You haven't gone home for any holidays since we've known each other. I had to *beg* you to have our wedding in Ganton, and even then, you wouldn't let me in the house. And now, you decide to go home for Christmas?" A hard laugh that turned into a snort escaped his lips. "I don't think I even know you."

Heat seared Ruth's face as if he'd pressed an iron to it. Tears pooled in her eyes, but she refused to shed them. How had they gotten here? The one man she thought she could lean on no matter what, the way she had with Papa, stood just a few feet away from her yet felt so far away.

Without a word, she left Xavier alone in their bedroom and stomped off to one of the guest rooms. Together, they had decorated it with a steel platform bed and a slate-gray accent wall. A gas fireplace added warmth. Xavier had said it would be a perfect room for Mama when she came to visit. Ruth had agreed quietly, knowing her grandmother would consider it excessive and would likely never set foot in their home anyway. Running her fingers along the threading of the duvet cover, Ruth took a few deep breaths. Next, she opened the curtains and peered out at the black night.

Their Bronzeville neighborhood stared back at her with all its growing pains, both beautiful and awkward at the same time. This place was usually all jazz, but sometimes blues, too, and late on nights like this, you could still hear the roar of race riots from the turn of the century and, in the background, the soulful sway of jazz in dance halls. Vacant lots stood stubbornly ugly next to sculptures and grand architecture, the Obamas' home in Hyde Park only a ten-minute drive away.

Ruth needed a sign, some guarantee that what she was about to embark upon would turn out okay. On good days, she had imagined her son loved and happy. But there were those nights, especially recently, when she woke up wet with sweat, thinking he was unhappy and struggling. She had no idea what she might find back home or if she would have a marriage to return to. But she saw now what she had to do. It was time for her to own up to her choices. The lies and the secrets had gone on for much too long.

She would go home and confront Mama. She would get answers about her son.

Seven

RUTH

As she crossed into Indiana, windmills turned as far as Ruth could see. Silos painted red and dusted with snow looked like fat peppermint sticks. Her damp palms slid on the steering wheel as she passed one mile marker after the next on the way to Ganton.

She had no desire to uproot her son, to snatch him from the soil where he'd been planted. Maybe that's why she had stayed away so long and hadn't made any effort to find him before now. Having a son was like holding a puzzle piece that didn't fit, no matter how many times you looked at the picture on the box. Still, not being in his life tore at something inside her, a rupture that time and marriage couldn't stitch together again.

Without any real plan, Ruth considered what she needed to do once she got to Ganton. First, she had to convince Mama to give her the name she'd withheld all these years "for all the right reasons." Her reasons. Her ideas about what was best for Ruth.

Shame stung her as she truly accepted how long she'd stayed away, and how she'd allowed herself to be bullied. Now, as she drove past the open fields of farm country, she remembered the life she'd once loved in Ganton. And there had been much to love, really. The water tower that grazed the sky, watching over them, tall and proud. The covered bridge she and Eli climbed up and lay on to get the best view of the stars at night. The rows of tall corn she crouched in as a little girl for games of hide-and-seek with her friends.

Driving into Ganton, Ruth noticed the frost skimming the top of the Wabash River, and she pulled her car over to the water's banks. She got out and walked gingerly across the ice to the river's edge where she and Papa had once strolled, her tiny hand enveloped in his larger, callused one. So many times they'd walked to his favorite fishing spot. She had often been impatient to feel that tug on the line and Papa would remind her, *Got to give it time, baby girl. They'll bite when they're good and ready*. They had fished together for years until Papa got sick.

Squatting, Ruth removed her glove and slid her left hand over the smooth ice that would melt in the spring. She remembered helping Papa pull the old lawn chairs from the trunk of his car, and then they'd sit here for hours in the kind of quiet that didn't need filling, just the two of them, without Mama or Eli. Pride shone in his eyes, her telling him about her good grades in science and math. That look he gave her was one Ruth drank down as if she'd been languishing in a desert. He'd say, *Study hard and get that piece of paper, girl. That's going to be your ticket to the big leagues someday. Then nothing can stop you. Papa is proud of his baby girl.*

Eventually, he became too weak to even walk from the bathroom to his recliner in the living room, let alone out to the Wabash River. Lou Gehrig's disease ravaged his nerve cells until they withered like leaves scorched by the sun.

She remained grateful he hadn't been alive to see her pregnant at seventeen. But during those nine months carrying her son, she stopped by the river when she was sure no one else would be around to "talk to" Papa and ask for advice. She needed his wisdom.

As she entered downtown Ganton, a few of the old family-owned stores stood as skeletons, hollowed out and emptied, replaced by big-box retailers on the outskirts of town. Chesterton Road cut through the center of town, but the street seemed smaller than she remembered, as if time had shrunk it somehow in the few years since she'd last visited.

Parking downtown, Ruth got out of her car. She trudged through the snow until she arrived at Lena's This 'n' That, a small shop, which fortunately looked just as tired as she had remembered it, with worn red-and-white-checkered curtains at the windows.

In high school, Ruth would stop by the store after school to see Lena, the white woman who owned it, and buy green apple Jolly Ranchers just to get away from Mama. After Papa died, Mama had no one to bathe and nurse, so the idleness coupled with grief consumed her, and she fussed over everything from a fork that still had food stuck to it after a washing to a layer of dust behind the TV that had been neglected.

We may be poor, but we're clean, Mama would admonish.

Lena had to be at least twenty years younger than Mama, but the two had been fast friends for a long time. Ruth paused outside the door. Did Lena know Ruth's secret? In a town like Ganton, where gossiping was as natural as breathing, you couldn't tell people to mind their own business. You had no business that wasn't theirs, too. But she couldn't bring herself to go to Mama's house just yet. They hadn't seen each other in four years and only spoke by phone every couple of months. What would she and her grandmother talk about? How would she get Mama to tell her who her son was?

The chimes jingled when she walked in the store. A few customers were milling about fingering knickknacks and comparing Christmas shopping lists. A young woman with eyes the color of blueberries and legs like twigs stepped from behind the counter.

"Hi. You're not from around here. Visiting someone?" Her bony fingers stroked beads on a necklace.

"I was born and raised here, but it's been a while since I've been back." Ruth heard the defensiveness in her own tone.

The girl bounced when she talked, like a wind-up toy. "Can I help you find something? By the way, your bag is really cool."

Ruth rubbed the leather of her Kate Spade bag and chastised

herself silently for not traveling with something more generic and nondescript. Less expensive.

"Thanks. I need two jars of blackberry preserves." Mama always spread preserves on her buttermilk biscuits Sunday mornings before church.

While the girl went to get the preserves, Ruth noticed a collage of photos on poster board near the cash register: a man, woman, and three kids who had to be theirs, judging by the similar wide faces, pale skin, and wheat-colored hair. Each set of children's eyes an exact duplicate of the others and their parents'. She marveled at the way the threads of their chromosomes were woven together in a quilt of connection. Somewhere was a child with Ruth's genes, her DNA running through him like a river.

"Those are the Wagners," the girl said over her shoulder. "It's terrible what happened." When Ruth looked confused, she continued. "They were using a space heater to keep warm and their house caught on fire. That's J.B. and Gabe right there." She pointed to two round-faced boys with big smiles.

"They were in the hospital for a few days, but they made it, thank God. So did Mr. and Mrs. Wagner. Polly, the little girl, was the youngest. She got out alive but ended up dying a couple hours later."

There were often news stories in Chicago about people tragically dying like that, too poor to afford heat. On a few winter nights back in the day, Ruth's family had gathered around the open oven to stay warm.

The cashier said, "They came in here all the time and Polly would sit by the register and punch in the numbers for me. My little helper."

"She liked fishing, too, I see." Ruth eyed a photo of Polly posing in a pink jumper in front of her dad with an openmouthed striper that was almost as big as she was.

"She sure did. Don't let the pink fool you. She caught that one herself, from what I hear tell of it."

Polly had, no doubt, like Ruth, learned patience from her father, the hours of waiting until that rod twitched in your hands. And she'd likely known the reassuring voice of a father who made you believe you could do anything. A Folger's coffee can sat next to the photos of the Wagners, with the label ripped off and lined notebook paper wrapped around it, taped, with the word *donations* scrawled in heavy black marker.

Ruth looked again at this mother and father in the photo and thought of how they walked through the world now with limp and idle arms, empty arms that had once held their Polly.

She never carried large amounts of cash except when she traveled, so she pulled a fifty-dollar bill from her purse and stuffed it in the can, ignoring the wide eyes of the girl behind the register as she handed over the jars of preserves.

"Is Lena here?" Ruth asked.

The blue-eyed girl gestured with her head. "I think she may be in the stockroom doing inventory. You can go on back." In Ganton, people seldom met a stranger, and they were trusting almost to a fault. Ruth missed that trust, living in a big city.

Stepping through the doorway into the dark back room, Ruth ran her fingers along the wall searching for a light switch. Nothing. The sharp edges of peeling paint nicked her fingertips. A heater hummed, but there was no other sound.

Something rolled across the floor and bumped up against her boot. A small scream slipped from Ruth's lips and that's when she saw a shadow move silently against the lower half of the wall in the darkness.

"Who's there?" she asked, willing her voice to stay steady.

No answer.

"Lena, are you in here?"

"Lena's gone."

The whisper ricocheted off the corner wall. Unsure where the voice came from, she backed up to leave the room and slipped on the wet floor, grabbing the side of a table to steady herself. Suddenly, the yellow light from a single bulb in the ceiling flooded the room.

She looked down to see a thin white boy holding a long light cord. He sat against the wall, his feet propped up on a box. He looked no more than twelve in his thick black-rimmed glasses that were too big for his narrow face. He wore an Indiana University sweatshirt that swallowed him. Patches of brown dirt coated the knees of his jeans, and Ruth noticed the rubber heels of his boots peeling away.

A ceramic jar lay at her feet. Her revelation turned on a giggle switch in the boy and he doubled over from the sheer force of it.

"That was not funny," she said, her voice squeaking like a bike chain that needed oiling.

"It was an experiment. I was trying to see how fast a cylinder would roll," he said, gesturing at the slight slant in the linoleum floor, "if there's no friction to stop it." He glanced at her boots and rolled his eyes as if she were a child slow to understand.

She knew that smug smile, or at least she knew the type. He probably peed in the neighbors' flowerpots for sport and in a few years would be smoking weed and car surfing in the school parking lot on weekends. He was pushing her buttons all right, but she evened her tone to let him know his tactics didn't work on her.

"What's your name?"

"Midnight."

Ruth twisted a thread from a loose button on her peacoat and wound it around her finger until it pinched her skin. "Sounds like a time of day to me, not a name."

The boy's face was the color of alabaster, a sharp contrast to his dirty dishwater hair. "Fat boys, they call Tiny. Me, I'm Midnight."

The tenor of his voice hung somewhere between boy and man, a tug-of-war between who he was and who he'd someday become. His small shoulders pulled back and he lifted his head, thrusting his jaw forward as if challenging her to doubt him.

"Well, I'm Ruth. Miss Ruth." She quickly added the title before her name. This kid needed to learn some respect. She couldn't be sure he'd heard her. He kept his eyes on the floor and hid the bottom half of his face in the collar of his sweatshirt.

Mama would say a boy like this was feeling himself, and she'd be right. A smart mouth wormed its way into boys, both Black and white, before their voices deepened or they grew peach fuzz. The Black ones wore their defiance like armor, weaponized against the slings and arrows of a world they couldn't control. But white boys entered the world carrying that arrogance inside them like a birthright.

"Does your mother know you're here?"

"What's it to you?"

Midnight threw every word like a grenade, obviously hoping for an explosion or at least a small grease fire. He stuck one finger inside a packet of peanut butter and licked it.

"I could have you arrested for breaking and entering," Ruth said.

Midnight's eyes grew wide, then they narrowed again. "Do it. Here's my phone."

The peanut butter had turned his teeth brown and gummy. He held up a phone in a white case that had his prints smeared all over it. He was probably a street kid who'd wandered in looking for food and found mischief. Ruth's son would be about the same age, and she hoped he'd turned out better than this kid.

Next, the boy picked up a pair of scissors and poked his right arm through his sweatshirt.

"Stop that before you hurt yourself." Ruth snatched the scissors from his hand.

He laughed, holding up his arm as if it weren't attached to his body. "I didn't even feel it."

Bumping his chair against a metal cabinet, Midnight kept his eyes on Ruth, his look daring her to reprimand him or call the cops. She wanted to tell him he'd never amount to anything with an attitude like that, but this kid wasn't worth a warning he'd never listen to anyway. Besides, small-town cops wouldn't take too kindly to a Black woman snitching on a little white boy.

"Where's Lena? The lady working out front said I could find her back here."

"I don't know. Guess she's out." This Midnight kid seemed perfectly at ease stirring up trouble in Lena's shop. It was Ruth who was on edge, and unfortunately, she could tell he knew this.

"When will she be back?"

Midnight shrugged, making a popping sound with his finger on the inside of his cheek. His indifference toward her cemented her fear that she knew nothing about how to relate to children.

Wanting nothing more than to get away from this obnoxious kid, she considered leaving the shop. But she wanted to see Lena and buy some time until she was ready to face Mama, so she hung around. Since she was getting nowhere fast in this conversation with Midnight, she tried the polite line of questions she used for her coworkers' kids on Take Your Child to Work Day. *How old are you? What's your favorite subject in school? What do you want to be when you grow up?*

Midnight sat up straighter in response to her last question.

"A microbiologist."

Tiny bubbles of spit popped up around his lips when he said the word, slow and careful to enunciate each syllable. She smiled. Kids in Ganton grew up to work at the plant during the week, bowl at Pete's one weekend, raid the junkyard the next. Something solid and resolute shone in his face, as if to convince her that if he sold you a dream, he was good for it.

A CHILD'S DREAMS COULD EASILY WILT AND DIE ON THE VINE. RUTH had learned this firsthand in Mrs. Thornton's third-grade class at Driscoll Elementary School. If you were Black and lived on the Grundy side of town, where Ruth had grown up, you went to Driscoll or the other public school a few miles away. The public schools in Ganton didn't require uniforms, but Mama had bought her granddaughter a navy-blue-and-white pleated skirt Ruth had begged for after seeing it on a long-legged white mannequin in a store window. Somehow, she got it in her head that smart girls wore plaid skirts with white ankle socks and black patent leather shoes. She never told

Mama, but that skirt in the window was the closest she could come to the uniforms she'd seen the Mother Mary Catholic school girls wear on the other side of town.

Ruth loved the knee-length skirt so much she wore it to school at least three days a week, ignoring the taunts of the other kids that she only had one outfit. Many of those children wore hand-me-downs from older siblings or Goodwill rejects, but that didn't stop their teasing. Papa said it had more to do with their envying Ruth's mind than her clothing.

At eight years old, Ruth cracked the spines of old science books held together precariously by Scotch tape, memorizing every obscure fact, which must have impressed the other kids, including Natasha Turnbull, her childhood best friend, who was a mediocre student at best. *You are soooo smart,* her friend said, making Ruth stand even taller with pride, especially having the most beautiful girl as her friend. Natasha had light skin and long wavy hair and wowed in anything she wore, so pretty she didn't need to wear pleats. And she knew it, too.

After Natasha received a string of failing grades, Ruth asked, "Did you get in trouble with your mom?" But Natasha just shrugged and said, "She's not home a lot, so she doesn't really notice. It's cool, though. She's always saying when you're pretty, you don't have to be smart."

Ruth thought about that for a long time and looked at herself in the school's bathroom mirror. Staring at her wide eyes that were too big for her long face, and her arms and legs that resembled skinny noodles, she knew then she'd have to focus on being smart. The good thing was she didn't have to work hard at it, as she was eager to learn about the life cycles of butterflies and frogs, and the five layers of the earth's soil. It was her research about soil that got her in trouble with Mrs. Thornton.

Ten minutes before the bell rang for recess one day, Mrs. Thornton told the class they would learn about soil layers that afternoon. Ruth had skipped ahead four chapters in her science book, reading at night by flashlight under her bedcovers long after everyone in her house had gone to sleep.

Anxious with excitement, Ruth stood up and blurted, "I can name the five layers of soil." Closing her eyes to focus on her memory and avoid the distraction of her classmates' faces, she recited, "Humus, topsoil, subsoil, parent material, and bedrock." Proud of herself for getting through the list without flubbing anything, she exhaled. Smoothing the pleats of her skirt, she smiled and waited for praise that never came.

Instead, her classmates looked from her to Mrs. Thornton, their mouths agape, expecting something Ruth had been too naïve to anticipate. Even Natasha buried her face in her hands as if Ruth had committed a crime. Their teacher's face flushed red and it took her a moment to speak. When she did, she pointed her knotty index finger at Ruth. "I'm the teacher, not you. Stop showing off and being disruptive."

The word *disruptive* was new to Ruth, but she knew immediately it had negative connotations based on the way Mrs. Thornton snarled when she said it.

"Another thing," her teacher added. "That skirt is in violation of the dress code. It's too short for school. I'll be sending a note home to your mother to let her know you can't continue to wear it."

Heat burned Ruth's face. She grabbed a fistful of her skirt and squeezed, suddenly self-conscious about her bare, skinny legs, feeling every eye in the class on them. With her long legs, skirts that fell below the knee on other girls were shorter on her. And besides, she'd seen some girls wear skirts midthigh. Why had Mrs. Thornton singled her out? Ruth ran from the classroom and hid under a staircase until the janitor found her and summoned the principal, who called Mama to come pick her up.

At home, Ruth stood outside her grandparents' bedroom, listening to them agonize over what to do.

Papa's baritone voice carried even when he tried to whisper. "She ain't learning a damn thing in that school."

Mama agreed. "Don't get yourself worked up. We both know these teachers don't care about educating our kids. They just babysit for the year and pass them on to the next grade. But what can we do about it?"

The next morning, Mama and Papa sat her down in the kitchen, both of them looking serious. "We need to talk," Mama said. "That school suspended you for a week for walking out of class without permission."

The punishment of not being able to learn for an entire week made Ruth physically ill. "I won't do it again, I promise. I won't talk about the soil, ever. Please let me go back to school."

Neither of them answered her right away. Finally, Papa said, "We're going to work it out, your grandmother and me. You're not going back there for long anyhow. You're going to Mother Mary next year." He glanced across the table at Mama, who looked as stunned as Ruth.

"Hezekiah, what on earth? You know we can't afford . . ."

Papa held up one hand that had begun to tremble slightly in recent months. "I said we'd find a way and we will."

And they did. The next school year, they enrolled her in Mother Mary, where the students were just a little less poor than the ones at Driscoll. A mostly white school where she didn't get in trouble for being smart. A school where every girl wore a pleated plaid skirt that skimmed her knees.

THE BACK DOOR TO LENA'S STORE OPENED, AND A GUST OF WIND blew in. A short, round older woman walked up swaying from side to side with a large brown box in her arms.

"I got it." Midnight ran toward her and wrapped one arm around the box.

"You'll hurt yourself. You can't carry this," she said.

With his knees buckling, he awkwardly tried to grasp it, putting the weight of the box on one arm while the other hung at his side.

"I told you to let *go*." Finally, the woman let the box drop to the floor. Her hair had grayed and thinned, and lines creased her face now, but Ruth recognized this was Lena. She looked the same, but worse, still wheezing and coughing, probably eating more casseroles than she should and smoking too many Newports. Never Camel or Virginia Slims or Lucky Strike. Always a Newport.

"Lena, it's me." Ruth waited as the older woman pulled her gloves off slowly and frowned, obviously scanning her memory for something familiar, but coming up short. "Ruth Tuttle, Ernestine's Ruth." She unwrapped her knit scarf and removed her hat. Ruth hadn't seen Lena since she'd come home that one time on summer break from Yale. And no one but family had been invited to the small wedding ceremony, not even Lena, who had become a good friend to her grandmother.

Lena said, "Well, I'll be . . . you sure are little Ruth Tuttle. Ernestine didn't say a word about you being back in town."

"She doesn't know I'm here. I want to surprise her."

Lena pulled her in for a hug and Ruth almost choked on the smoke smell that penetrated the woman's skin. Then Lena began pulling packs of Cobalt 5 gum from the box, plopping them on a table. As she moved about the small space in the back room, she wheezed, her breathing sounding like the whistle of a novice blowing into a clarinet.

The floor shone wet—likely from water that had spilled from the bucket sitting in the middle of the floor. Ruth realized that was why she'd slipped when she first walked in. Midnight slid on the floor now, his arms outstretched like he was riding a big wave of California surf.

"Patrick! What on earth? Why is this floor wet?" Lena took in the boxes on the floor that now had the mark of water stains.

First, fear flashed across his face. Then guilt. His expression reminded her of one of those poor milk carton kids, with big begging eyes that kept neighbors searching long after they'd gone missing.

"Answer me," Lena said. "Everything is wet. I can't afford to have any of my merchandise ruined."

The cashier with the blueberry eyes must have heard the yelling. She poked her head in the stockroom. "Is everything okay?"

"Go on and get back to work," Lena scolded. "What if a customer walks in and you're not at the register and we miss a sale? You know we can't afford that."

The young woman bowed her head, mumbled an apology, and hurried back to the front room.

Lena ripped open a pack of Newports and placed a cigarette in the corner of her mouth. "You still haven't answered me." She directed her attention back to Midnight. "I swear, if anything has water damage—"

"I'm—" Midnight began to speak but Ruth cut him off.

"It's my fault," she said. "It was dark in here when I walked in looking for you and I tripped over the pail of water. I'm so sorry. I can pay for any damages."

Midnight's eyes widened, but he didn't dispute her cover story. Lena waved her hand. "No. Don't be silly. I refuse to take your money. Accidents happen."

Ruth stared at Midnight until he made eye contact with her. She gave him one of those looks that said, *You owe me, and don't be surprised if I collect, even if you are just a kid.* He quickly averted his eyes.

Everything about Lena seemed more frantic and desperate than she'd remembered, and she felt sorry for this kid caught in the middle of all of it.

"You said you're surprising Ernestine, huh? I know she'll be glad to have you home for Christmas. Come on out here and sit down so we can talk. And, Patrick, go get some paper towels and clean up that water. Check those boxes and make sure nothing got ruined."

Midnight unrolled reams of paper towels, wrapping them around his hand, while Lena dragged two folding chairs into the store for them to sit on. It was obvious life had not been kind to Lena over the years, and she moved like a woman twice her age. She took a long drag on her Newport. Years ago, as soon as Lena turned her back, the kids from school would hold straws between their lips in mockery, blowing fake smoke into the air. Then they'd fake wheeze until they almost passed out. Ruth never joined in, since Lena was a friend to the family, the only one to bring chicken pot pies to the house when

Papa got sick. They returned the favor when Lena's husband, Neil, died young of a massive heart attack on the plant floor, a few years after Papa passed.

Losing their husbands bonded Lena and Mama more than ever. Maybe that was why this store was Ruth's first stop in town. When she couldn't talk to Mama, she turned to Lena, who knew how to take care of people, filling all those empty places inside you.

A symphony of jingles, explosions, and moans erupted from Midnight's phone. After making a dismal show of drying the floor, he'd followed them into the store and sat on the floor hunched over his phone, grunting every few seconds. Lena sighed in that exasperated way parents often do over some annoying habit they'd chided their kids about time after time.

"I can't believe that boy's thumbs haven't fallen off yet. Always playing some game about greed," Lena said.

"*Assassin's Creed*," Midnight said without looking up from his phone.

"Whatever it is. I tell you, that boy hears everything."

Ruth lowered her voice and scooted her chair closer to Lena's. "I found that kid hiding in the back room while you were out. How do you know him?"

Laughter that turned into a deep cough made Lena's body shake. "You have been gone a long time, dear. That kid is my grandson. Patrick's a good boy. Smart as a whip. Problem is he knows it. That combination can be trouble if you don't channel it the right way."

Lena had two daughters—Hannah, the older one, who was just a couple of years younger than Ruth, and Gloria, who had to be at least six or seven years younger than Ruth.

"Is that Hannah's son? He was just a toddler when I last saw him. I can't believe he's a grown boy now," she said, shaking her head. "You know, he told me his name was Midnight."

"These kids and their ridiculous nicknames. But yes, indeed, that's Hannah's boy. You know she passed a few years ago, so Patrick lives with me now."

Mama had told Ruth the sad news, and now Ruth felt guilty about not reaching out to Lena at the time to offer condolences. It seemed she was always guilt-ridden over something. "I heard, and I'm so sorry. I'm glad Midnight has you in his life."

Ruth glanced at Midnight and noticed his sweatshirt hanging off his shoulders, the red logo having faded to a dull pink. Electrical tape held together the frames of his glasses. In the distance, the screech of a snowblower grew louder, but Midnight stayed intent on his game, his mouth open slightly and his eyes locked on the screen of his phone. Eventually, he walked outside, scooping handfuls of snow and stuffing the snowballs in his sweatshirt pockets.

Now that Midnight was out of earshot, Ruth said, "I know you have that young lady working the register, but you should keep that back door locked, too. It's not safe for your merchandise or your grandson."

Lena tapped her cigarette with her index finger until gray ash fell from the bottom. "I don't pay any mind to robbers. Even with so many folks out of work, I haven't had a break-in yet. It's these gang-bangers I worry about trying to get their hooks into my grandson."

When Lena read the skepticism on Ruth's face, she puffed harder on her Newport. "These thugs don't discriminate between Black and white. All they care about is green, and they're coming from the big cities like Chicago over here to do their dirt. No offense or anything."

She was right. Balloons, stuffed animals, and poster board notes memorialized crime victims on many South and West Side Chicago streets. Yellow crime scene tape roped off manicured lawns on tree-lined blocks. Gang violence had almost become the city's shadow, walking with its residents everywhere until some grew numb to its existence. Even when they tried to step out of that shadow, it stalked them relentlessly. Ruth and Xavier lived in a zip code close enough to feel the heat from the flame but far enough away not to get burned on the regular.

Amid the threat of violence in the toughest areas, people still worked hard and raised families and launched businesses, and Ruth wanted to paint that picture for Lena to show her how both could be true at the same time. But she'd grown tired of all that obligatory educating. Even if gang violence had sunk its teeth into Ganton, Lena wouldn't move. Of those who left Ganton, most didn't come back, but the truth was, most people never left. Lena was born there and would die there.

Neither of them said more on the subject. Sitting in silence for a moment, Ruth watched a wispy cloud rise from Lena's cigarette.

"Ernestine told me you got married a few years ago," Lena said.

Ruth looked down at her gloves and rubbed the leather, thinking of Xavier. The way things stood when she'd left for Ganton caused her to seriously question the strength of her marriage. "Yes, I did. My husband had some commitments back in Chicago and couldn't make it this time."

Lena opened her mouth as if to respond but said nothing. She touched Ruth's chin, lifting it until Ruth met her eyes. "I for one am glad you're back home. You stayed away too long." There was something about the way Lena looked at her that said, *I know all about what happened long ago, but we'll pretend I don't.* Mama had been fiercely adamant about keeping Ruth's pregnancy secret. Was it possible she'd told someone?

"How's business these days?" Ruth said, eager to change the subject.

Growing up, there had been a steady stream of customers, especially around the holidays with people buying one-of-a-kind gifts for family and friends.

"People don't shop as much now that Fernwood has shut down."

"Shut down? What do you mean? The plant meant everything to Papa."

"They couldn't afford to keep the production here. Closed about six months ago. So many out of jobs now. Patrick's dad, Butch. Your brother. It's hard out here right now. Everybody's just looking out for their own, you know."

"Damn." Ruth closed her eyes to gather herself, recalling how Eli would come home after work with grease streaking his face. Over the years, Fernwood had laid off workers during lean times, but no one thought it would ever shut down for good. It's not like Mama would have called to tell her Eli was out of work, and Ruth *knew* Eli was too proud to have called her himself.

"Butch hasn't been himself since he got his walking papers. You know, losing your job isn't just about the money. It's like you lose everything. Everything that makes you who you are can be gone just like that." Lena snapped her fingers for effect. "All these car companies around the country are talking about filing for bankruptcy. And I don't know that Obama's going to do anything about it."

Hearing a white woman, even a family friend, make a subtle criticism of the incoming president who hadn't even taken the oath of office yet annoyed Ruth. It was like somebody talking trash about your crazy uncle. Family could mock and drag him all day, but nobody else could. Lena must have read her mind.

"I voted for him, don't get me wrong, but he promised change like all the rest that came before him. So, we'll just have to see. I'll believe it when I see it."

Ruth laughed to take the bite out of her frustration, hoping her words would come out restrained, minus any low-grade anger. "The man hasn't even measured the drapes in the West Wing yet. Give him time."

Lena had been good to her family. Her politics shouldn't matter, but Ruth couldn't help but wonder if she was like her colleagues at Langham who said one thing at work but did something very different behind the curtain of the voting booth.

Eight

MIDNIGHT

The ice grunted under the wheels of Miss Ruth's car, and the faster Midnight threw snowballs at them, the harder she must have mashed the gas pedal trying to get away. Her car swerved. He laughed. Granny couldn't see him from inside the shop, and he knew she'd have a fit if she saw him *acting out,* as she called it, but the diabetes made her eyes so blurry she once poured salt instead of sugar in her apple pie filling. Instead of going back inside, he stood there on the street and watched the car get smaller and smaller until it was an itty-bitty speck and then just part of the big blob of gray sky.

Midnight sat on the curb, the butt of his pants soggy from the snow. He heard steps and sniffles behind him, and that's when Bones ran up with his mouth open for one of Midnight's Reese's Pieces. Granny didn't like him feeding him candy, though. She said it made a dog's blood sugar drop, which made no sense because she insisted sweets made hers go sky-high. He counted out four Reese's, enough to stop Bones from begging but not so many to make him sick.

Bones hardly had any hair to keep him warm, and his thin skin felt slippery and rubbery, his bones jutting out in places like those raw chickens Granny had him hold by the legs while she seasoned them. The dog had followed Midnight zipping down alleys and through empty lots on the Pratt side of the railroad tracks. Nobody had ever claimed him, so he became the neighborhood's dog. The name Bones stuck. Every living thing needed its own name, maybe not the one it was born with, but one that fit. Granny wouldn't let Midnight take him home, though. *I have enough mouths to feed,* she said.

"Where do you think Miss Ruth is headed now?" he asked, and Bones shook his head, either to say he didn't know or to shake off the cold. Miss Ruth's skin glowed a dark bronze and she looked like one of those models from the clothes catalogs Granny got in the mail. She smelled sweet, too, like the perfume ads. What he didn't like was how she asked the same silly questions most grown-ups did. Even worse, she looked at him over the top of her glasses like the school principal did that time she gave him detention for putting thumbtacks on the substitute teacher's chair. Still, she'd covered for him and hadn't ratted him out. Nobody had ever done that for him before. Not ever.

THE SUN PEEKED THROUGH THE BLINDS THE NEXT MORNING AND Midnight wished it were still dark, so he wouldn't have to see the roach, small and black, on the kitchen floor right next to Auntie Glo's open pizza box from the night before. Once you got a roach in your house, you were stuck with it for a long time. They didn't die too easy. And as soon as you got rid of one, more came. He tiptoed across the kitchen tiles and raised his foot, then cursed under his breath when he realized it was just a stupid button from Granny's coat.

He fell back on the couch and let the springs bounce him like a trampoline. The spare room Granny had set up for him was so small it made his chest get tight and his mouth go dry, so he usually slept in the living room. The only cool part was that he could see the blink of the Christmas lights on the leaning tabletop tree Granny had put up after Thanksgiving. Burying his head in the pillow cushions of the couch, he banged his bare feet against the wall and tapped a beat to drown out the buzz of Auntie Glo's blow dryer and the bass from her speakers.

He pretended to be glad that school was out for winter break because every other kid was glad about it. But being in the classroom was way better than this. In more than a week, it would be a whole new year, but he'd still be in this house with people he didn't understand who didn't understand him.

A sour odor filled his nostrils before he heard the cry. His cousin, Nicky, toddled toward him on legs as wobbly as the ones on their kitchen table. The smell of a soiled diaper grew stronger the closer Nicky came, testing the sturdiness of his bowed legs with each step. Nicky reminded him of the way Daddy walked when he was drunk. Mom had always said Midnight would be the best big brother, and now he could see she'd been right. If his little sister had lived, he would've changed her diapers, too, and helped her walk and learn her first words.

At age one and a half, Nicky was often the first one up, and every morning, he wandered out to find Midnight, his cheeks red and puffy, eyes bright and searching. All he wore around the house was a diaper that drooped at the crotch when he dropped a load. Auntie Glo rarely bothered to dress him in much else, and she wore just a skimpy nightgown that was so sheer you could see her breasts through it. Mostly, she wore that when Daddy stopped by. Sober, he ignored her. Drunk, he stared a really long time. Once when Midnight invited his friends over to play video games, Auntie Glo walked through the living room to the kitchen three times, and their eyes got wider each time. He stopped inviting them over.

"I got you, little man."

Midnight carried Nicky with one arm and searched behind cereal boxes on the kitchen counter until he found a clean diaper. Auntie Glo had no sense of order and no appreciation for cleanliness. That's what Granny started saying three months ago, when she and Nicky moved in with them. He let out a frustrated sigh like Granny would.

"Hold on. Be still for me." Nicky was pink and doughy, and sometimes when Midnight held him, he pretended it was his baby sister and that Mommy stood right beside them and everything was the way it was supposed to be.

With Nicky's body wedged in the kitchen sink, Midnight ripped off the boy's stinky diaper with a quick jerking motion and wiped him with a paper towel he soaked in liquid Ivory. Nicky's arms and legs flailed, splashing water, some of it stinging Midnight's eyes.

After cleaning up Auntie Glo's son, he fixed himself a peanut butter sandwich and grabbed a gallon jug of water. He turned it up to his lips, ignoring Granny's voice in his head saying it's not proper to drink from the container.

Midnight heard a door open down the hallway and the pad of feet on the floor. Quickly, he wiped his mouth with the back of his arm and shoved the water back in the fridge.

"You're up early," Granny said. A pale light flickered down the hall and she walked into the kitchen rubbing her eyes. "Made your own breakfast, too, I see."

Midnight had lived with his grandmother for six months, ever since the day he watched Daddy whack Granny's knickknacks with his aluminum lunch box.

She'd said, *The day you married my daughter, I knew you were trouble. But she wouldn't listen.*

Bay horse head vases crashed to the floor and cracked, along with porcelain angel bells that still rang faintly after they hit the ground. Granny crumpled in the corner between the front door and the wall, deflating, like somebody had stuck a pin in her. The general manager at the plant had told Daddy and the others that they were shipping production overseas.

No one knew what to say to Daddy when he lost his job. After his big blowup, Granny found Midnight hiding in the bathtub. Without saying anything, she sat on the edge and put his head against her stomach and rubbed his hair the way Mommy used to do when he was sick.

This morning, Granny fixed herself a bowl of oatmeal and a scrambled egg, nothing sweet anymore. She said if you did something or avoided doing something long enough, it became a habit.

When Granny found out she had diabetes and had to start poking herself with needles every day, Midnight rummaged through her cupboards and checked food labels, throwing away anything with more than a few grams of sugar. He dumped chocolate hazelnut spread, Frosted Krispies, and pickle relish. She hid caramel nougats in the pockets of her housecoat, and he flushed those down the toilet after she went to sleep.

On the mantel was a picture of Granny in one of those big purple church hats tilted enough to cover her left eye. Must have been taken Easter Sunday, since that's the only time she went to church. His best friend Corey's folks took him to church a lot, but Granny had taken Midnight to get his first library card, and had taught him how to bake a lemon Bundt cake from scratch and how to change a diaper, insisting there was no such thing as women's work and men's work. The same summer she showed him how to thread a needle, she also made sure he could change a tire. He didn't mind not being taken to church like Corey.

"You know I saw you throwing snowballs at Ruth Tuttle's car yesterday." Granny poured unsweetened tea into a mason jar.

"I didn't do anything," he said, hoping to sound innocent. He didn't want to talk about Miss Ruth. He wanted to keep her all to himself for now.

"I'm not blind."

"Doesn't surprise me. This little delinquent didn't get home until ten o'clock last night," said Auntie Glo, who stood in the shadow of the hallway glaring at Midnight. Flaming red hair fanned her face and she stuck out her tongue with the silver stud piercing. Too lazy to make breakfast herself, she appeared whenever she heard Granny in the kitchen.

"It's none of your business what time I got home. You're not my mother," he retorted.

"Midnight, you know better than to talk back to an adult. Show some respect in my house." Granny leaned against the door frame, too unsteady to stand for long.

"Are you okay?" Midnight asked, concerned. Ever since his mother died, he worried about Granny dying, too. At night while she slept, he sometimes tiptoed into her room to watch her until he saw the slight rise and fall of her chest or heard her faint breathing.

"I'm fine, son. You know I just need to eat after I take my insulin. Now wash the dishes for me. I'll be in my room." Granny had already turned to head to her bedroom, carrying her breakfast with her.

"Gloria, come in here. We need to talk," she said.

Auntie Glo glared at Midnight and followed Granny, closing the door behind them.

The door was thick enough to support Midnight's weight when he pressed his body against it, but thin enough to hear some of what was said on the other side. Nicky sat on the living room floor and played with wooden blocks. He made noises, trying to get Midnight's attention.

"You got to be quiet," Midnight hissed, and put his finger to his lips.

Nicky yelled louder.

"I changed you. I washed you. I know you're hungry, but you got to wait. Now shush."

Midnight grabbed Nicky's pacifier from the countertop and stuffed it in his mouth. There was no time to rinse it first. Returning to his place against the door, he listened to the women talking. Usually, they complained about money, how Auntie Glo never had any and Granny didn't have enough left over after rent, utilities, and the expenses for the store.

"Business has been so slow lately, and I don't know how long I can afford to keep the store open. I sure hate to do it, but I don't have any other choice." Then Granny said something else that Midnight couldn't quite hear when her voice got softer.

"He's a pain, but where's he going to go?" Auntie Glo asked.

He couldn't make out Granny's answer. He pressed his ear as hard as he could against the door, but her voice was muffled.

The next thing he heard Granny say: "Butch isn't working and I'm already taking care of you and little Nicky. I just can't do it anymore."

"They made me cashier at Save A Lot," Auntie Glo said. "But it's not enough for me to get my own place yet."

"Yes, I know. Lord, I wish Hannah were here. Midnight needs his mother. I hate to uproot him and I know it's far, but I don't see another way."

A hard rock stuck in Midnight's throat. It hurt to swallow. Maybe Granny was sending him to join Daddy at Drew's apartment, even though she called it a hellhole. But it only took fifteen minutes to drive there, so it wasn't that far. Where else could he go?

Grabbing his coat, Midnight ran from the house, past the corner convenience store, across the snow-covered railroad tracks to Pine Top, the tiny section of town between Pratt and Grundy where dads tossed footballs on front lawns with their kids. Midnight heard shuffling behind him and there was Bones. When he slowed his pace, they ran alongside each other. A haphazard set of snow prints followed them, a record of the chaos neither could seem to outrun.

Nine

RUTH

Standing on this side of her childhood house, Ruth remembered leaving in her old Pinto at seventeen, with no baby, yet still heavy with her burden. When she had come home once on college break during the winter holiday, she had tried not to look at anything too long, moving in and out quickly enough to avoid any fresh stabs of guilt. One thing she did recall from that trip home was the house, its yellow paint faded and peeling in places.

Ganton had been cut off at the knees, folding in on itself, knocked down too many times to stand up straight again. A broken beer bottle and an empty Cheetos bag poked out of the snow next to one drive-way on the corner. Mama told her that house had become a Section 8 rental property with a revolving door of tenants who had no ties to the community or investment in its upkeep.

But the neighborhood held good memories, too. Ruth and Eli used to own these streets. Six years older than she, her brother did everything first: ride a bike, go to school, lose teeth and grow new ones. But long past the point of it being cool, Eli still hung out with his kid sister. They drew blue and yellow chalk lines on the asphalt for hop-scotch games and skipped down the street to chase the chimes of the ice cream truck. Back then Ruth didn't understand what it meant to be poor. Every house for as far as she could see stood tall and proud, one no better or worse than the one beside it.

What if Xavier had come with her on this visit? She pictured him at home in their living room with his feet propped up on the ottoman, watching football. Had she let her fears irreparably damage her marriage?

It had been four years since Ruth had been home. She only returned then with Xavier to be married at her home church by Pastor Bumpus, the preacher who had baptized her. A few hours in Ganton, just long enough for the ceremony, and that was it. She hustled Xavier out of town as soon as they said their *I do*s. It didn't matter that he wanted to see the house where she'd grown up. That house seemed so meager, and crazy as it sounded, she feared its walls might tell her story, revealing that she'd been a pregnant teenager.

Now the house was bathed in a warm, earthy brown. Ruth and Xavier had spent months poring over color wheels for their own new home renovation, and if she had to guess, this paint color had to be some variation of Moroccan Spice. There was no Christmas wreath on the door, but that wasn't surprising since Mama thought the holidays were too commercial anyway, only about the almighty dollar instead of the Almighty Himself.

Icicles hung suspended from the aluminum siding, one of them crackling before falling silently in the snow. After Ruth rang the bell twice, the front door grunted and then cracked open only as far as the short chain would allow. She remembered that space between the screen door and the main one, where flies went to die during the summer.

A face peered through the small opening before the door shut. As Ruth held the screen door open, the chain jangled and then the door opened fully, and Mama stood there with her eyes wide as a baby deer's.

"Child, what are you doing here?" Mama touched her granddaughter's face with one rough hand, gripping her chin tightly. "Is everything okay?"

Seventy-eight years in this world had taken a toll on Mama, her jaws drooping more than they used to, making the folds in her neck more pronounced. Her hair nearly all white and pulling away from her temples. How had she aged so much in the last four years?

"I'm fine, Mama. Nothing's wrong. It's almost Christmas. It's good to be home." Ruth bent to kiss her cheek.

Then a voice came from the dark hallway. "The chain is hooked to the flapper just fine, but I still can't get that dang toilet to flush." The deep voice probably belonged to a plumber, Ruth thought.

Mama was blocking Ruth's view and kept glancing back to the hallway, adjusting her housecoat. The man continued on about the toilet, his voice getting closer until he appeared there in the foyer. A light-skinned man in nothing but his boxer shorts and black socks that sagged at his ankles. His knees reminded Ruth of two golf balls.

An uncomfortable, almost guilty look flashed across Mama's face, as if she were a child who'd just stolen a cookie before dinner and had the evidence of crumbs on her mouth.

The strange man spoke first. "Um, um, R-R-R-Ruth."

His stammer jolted her memory. "Dino." He had been one of Papa's closest friends and had stuttered for as long as she'd known him.

Mama used to call Dino high yellow and joked that the only way he got any ladies was by being a pretty boy back in the day, with that wavy black hair that lay flat without gel. Now his back curved more than it used to years ago, his body betraying him as Papa's had. She hadn't even recognized him at first. "It's been a long time."

"It's mighty good to have you back in town," Dino said, his voice dragging like the sound of an audio recording playing at half speed. He looked from Mama to Ruth.

"Don't you have somewhere you need to be?" Mama said, flinging the belt of her housecoat to shoo him away. When he leaned over to peck her lips, she turned her head to sidestep the kiss and said, "Now stop with all that foolishness and get dressed and get on out of here." She wouldn't look at Ruth.

With a sheepish grin, he glanced down at his half-nakedness and headed toward the bedrooms.

Once Dino was out of earshot, Ruth said, "What's going on between you two?"

"Now you hush with that nonsense. Not another word. You know you're not too old for me to put you over my knee." Mama laughed nervously.

Ruth chose to drop the subject, but seeing Dino in Papa's house didn't sit well with her. Did he have a key to the house? More important, had he spent the night? The idea of another man walking on Papa's floors, sitting on his furniture, eating food from his fridge, and sharing a bed with his wife unnerved her.

"Take your boots off and put them here." Mama grabbed a newspaper from a nearby table and spread it on the floor of the foyer. "You know I don't like you tracking that mess through the house."

"I know." Ruth stomped her leather boots on the plastic runner to shake off the brown slush. "The house looks good, Mama. I see you had it painted." And to Ruth's amazement, she spotted a small, unassuming Christmas tree in front of the living room window.

"The church has a widows' ministry now. They sent a couple guys over to paint last year."

Mama's slippers scooted across the linoleum as she headed to the kitchen. Ernestine Tuttle was a big-boned woman but more lopsided than anything. Her breasts hung low on her belly with no butt to balance things out. The whole of her propped up on bird legs.

The kitchen was small and dimly lit, the table set for four like it had been when Ruth was growing up—a seat for herself, Mama, Papa, and Eli. As she was looking around, a sharp pain shot through her right leg when she banged it against the open oven door. "Shit! Ouch!"

"Watch your language. You not here two minutes and you already cussing. You know better than that in this house."

"Sorry, Mama, but why is the oven door open?"

"Trying to get some heat in here. Furnace went out a few days ago."

First the toilet and now the furnace, too. How was her grandmother living there with no heat in thirty-degree temperatures? Ruth thought about how little Polly had died after her parents used an alternative heat source.

"Why didn't you call me? I could've sent you the money to get it fixed." Her voice rose; she was frustrated with herself more than her grandmother. She had never sent money home, and the one time she offered, Mama had shut her down.

Her grandmother closed the oven door. "Never mind all that."

"Come to think of it, the landlord should be making all the repairs on the house. You should take him to court if he isn't. I have some lawyer friends who could advise you."

Mama waved her off. "I told you to leave it alone. I don't like getting mixed up with *lawyers*. Now let me look at you." Mama took a seat at the kitchen table and Ruth sat beside her. At the opening of her grandmother's robe there was a flash of green paper, and Ruth stifled a laugh remembering how Mama treated her bra like a bank.

The older woman's fingers glided across Ruth's twists, rubbing each patch of fuzz. "I'll make an appointment to get your hair done while you're here."

The renaissance of the natural hair movement had failed to impress Mama. In Ruth's sophomore year in high school, she begged Mama to take her to a place in Indianapolis she'd read about where a woman called Lady Simone locked hair. Instead Ruth ended up on the bedroom floor in a headlock between Mama's knees with a hot comb scorching the back of her neck.

"How are they treating you on the job?" Mama said.

"Just fine," she lied. "I'm developing a formula for our number-one detergent brand."

"I'm real proud of you. But you know they're not going to have you on that job for long with that wild hair."

"They hired me for my brain, not my hair. And my hair isn't *wild*."

"Now look. Don't let wild hair hold you back. They won't come out and say anything to your face. But you'll hear that your work isn't quite up to par anymore. You'll think it's something you did or didn't do. All I'm saying is don't give them a reason to start messing with you."

Ruth took her grandmother's hand into her own. "I know what I'm doing. My hair isn't a problem at work. Trust me." She laughed and added, "As long as nobody touches it."

"Don't you forget, we made a lot of sacrifices to send you to Yale so you could make something of yourself. We gave up a lot." What she left unsaid was the part about the baby born eleven years ago in this house.

A code existed in Mama's mind, one of expectations. She didn't care about impressing the neighbors. She never relied on Ruth's success to elevate her own stature. A practical woman like Mama believed in doing what was necessary to survive.

If it wasn't hair she fussed about, it was music. In high school, when Ruth would bounce in front of the mirror to some Biggie Smalls beat, Mama's voice was never far. *You better sit your tail down. That booty music won't get you into college or make you an engineer.*

Emerging from the dark hallway, Dino appeared in a pair of red-and-black plaid slacks and a tan overcoat. He slung a bag over his shoulder. An overnight bag. How often did he sleep here?

"You don't have to leave on my account," Ruth said, wanting him to stay so she could ask him a few questions about his relationship with her grandmother.

"No, he's ready to go." Mama practically pushed Dino toward the front door.

The man shrugged and threw up a hand to wave goodbye to Ruth. Even though her life had changed dramatically when she left this house and this town behind, she had just assumed Mama's world had stayed the same. But it hadn't. The secret about Ruth's baby hadn't been the only one the old woman had been keeping. As if anticipating a barrage of questions and eager to avoid them, Mama quickly busied herself in the kitchen, peering into the refrigerator. She hid her face behind the door of it as if to wall herself off from her granddaughter's probing, judgmental gaze.

"Are you hungry?"

"If you're cooking, I am."

Ruth pulled the two jars of blackberry preserves from her purse and handed them to her grandmother. "I thought you could use these for breakfast."

"You know I can. Thanks, baby." Mama put the preserves on a shelf in the narrow pantry. "I didn't know you were coming so I didn't cook, but I do have some chicken soaking in the fridge for tomorrow. I can fry it up now, though."

In a large aluminum pan, Mama poured flour and sprinkled in salt and pepper.

"How come Xavier didn't come with you?"

Ruth figured Mama would ask. Keeping her voice even, she said, "He has a new marketing campaign he's working on and couldn't get away."

"Not even for Christmas, huh?"

"No, it's a high-profile assignment, so he's extremely busy."

Mama had met Xavier the day of the wedding and hadn't seen him since. When she first laid eyes on him, she pulled Ruth aside and said his hands were too clean, too smooth, and way too pretty to be of any use to a woman.

Just before Ruth walked down the aisle, Mama whispered, "Baby, you sure he ain't got a little sugar in his tank?" It would take time for her to get used to a grandson-in-law who worked in a corporate office instead of the factory floor like most of the men Mama knew.

After dipping the chicken in buttermilk, they took turns coating each piece with the flour mixture before carefully dropping them in a deep pan of hot oil. The chicken sizzled, and hot grease leapt from the pan.

"I don't want you getting burned, so I'll take it from here," Mama said.

Ruth walked over to the oak buffet table where Mama used to display her granddaughter's perfect attendance certificates and report cards, but only when she got all A's. She swiped her finger across a layer of dust on top of the old record player that had gone silent when they laid Papa to rest.

Leather-bound books by James Baldwin, Zora Neale Hurston, and Richard Wright lined the shelf; she remembered Papa reading them to her as a little girl, along with the works of Du Bois and Douglass. Mama and Papa fed history to her and Eli, filling them with it as if they'd need reserve nourishment when the world left them withered, broken, and hungry.

On the wall above the buffet, Mama displayed framed pictures of Jesus, Martin Luther King Jr., and President Kennedy, the other Holy Trinity for old Black folks. But the faded portrait of Kennedy was missing, and in its place was one of President-Elect Obama, in a new ornate brass frame.

Standing in front of the photograph of the incoming president, Ruth felt a warmth wash over her. Her son would be growing up in a country led by a Black man. She hadn't seen her son since the day he still fit in the palm of her hand, and as much as she tried to forget at times, she couldn't help but resurrect dreams for him that had begun with soft whispers to her swollen belly and sometimes a silent wish made on a starlit night.

"Did you ever think you'd live to see it?" she called to Mama.

"See what, child?" Mama flipped the knob on one of the burners, and the boiling bubbles that had licked the rim of the pot of corn seconds before began to recede.

"Our first Black president. I thought about you and Eli on Election Day. Papa, too. I hate that he didn't get to vote for Obama."

"You live long enough, you're bound to see a lot of things. Good and bad."

"I know you're proud."

"Let's just hope they don't kill him. If he gets too high and mighty, they will. And my pride can't save him. Yours, neither."

"He'll be fine. The country's changing."

Mama walked over to the buffet, opened the top drawer, and

pulled out the Kennedy photo. "What happened to him?" And then she pointed to the pictures of King and Jesus. "And what about them? Hmm? If they killed Jesus, what makes you think they won't do it to a Black man in the White House?"

When Mama's mind was made up, there was no swaying her. Making her way to the living room, Ruth saw Papa's old brown recliner with the loose threads and white cotton puffs poking through the holes. Whenever Mama expected company, she would put a bath towel over the seat cushion to hide the rips and tears. Ruth slowly lowered herself into the recliner, nervous, as if Papa might see her and playfully run her off his favorite chair. Sinking into the upholstery, she let her fingers glide over the fabric of each arm.

Glancing up, she caught Mama watching her, leaning on the wall that separated the kitchen from the living room. "He loved that old chair. I told him he was going to die in that chair, and that rascal had the nerve to go ahead and do just that."

Shortly after feeding Papa his lunch, Mama had hollered a question to him from the kitchen. When he didn't answer, she found him in his chair, chin on his chest, dead. No matter how many years passed, this chair would always be Papa's. If you sniffed really hard, you could smell his tobacco and aftershave.

"It feels nice sitting here. Kind of like I'm closer to him, you know. After all these years, it's still hard to believe he's not going to come around the corner and tickle me until I get out of his chair." Her last few words caught in her throat.

"Oh, yeah. He loved clowning with you and your brother." Mama smiled.

"And with you, too." Ruth winked, but Mama ignored it.

Papa would come home from the plant with black grease on his hands and sink into this chair, waiting for Mama to walk by. Then he'd grab her from behind, leaving his fingerprints on her skin, and tuck her into an embrace she'd squirm out of, her giggle saying just the opposite, that she hoped he'd pull her closer.

Sometimes, they'd fire up the turntable and slow-dance to the Temptations while she and Eli laughed or covered their faces, embarrassed. Then other times Papa romanced Mama by swiping the latest issue of *Jet* magazine from the plant's break room, sticking it in his lunch pail to bring home for her to read about the stars of her favorite shows or some Harlem rapper bleaching her skin.

Now, Ruth scanned her grandmother's face for a glimpse of that woman, but she couldn't find her.

After Papa died and before those he left behind slunk off into their own corners of misery, they'd shared stories about things the old man used to say and do. Sometimes Ruth couldn't be sure if her memories were her own or someone else's.

By the time the sun set, Ruth and Mama were sitting down to a meal of fried chicken, creamed corn, green beans, and mashed potatoes. They ate without speaking, only the sound of their forks against the plates breaking the silence.

Ten

RUTH

There were few pictures around the house of Ruth's years at Yale, little evidence it ever happened except for Ruth's diploma. Whenever former classmates emailed old college photos, she cringed at the bowl-shaped mushroom hairstyles and the tracksuits they used to rock in loud colors. Students on campus wore oversized sweaters and slouchy, baggy pants. The only saving grace of late-nineties fashions had been that they helped her hide the leftover pooch she carried in the months after the birth of her baby.

When she got to Yale, no one knew her. The handful of kids from Ganton who did go to college stayed in-state. Her little corner of Indiana tethered Ruth to her past, to the possibility of questions she couldn't answer, forcing her to lie. But in Connecticut she could be somebody else. Start over. Create a new life.

Freshman year, she roomed with Emily Fontaine, a white girl from Greenwich. Ruth hadn't spent long periods of time with anyone white except for Lena back home. But Ruth soon realized that she didn't count. Lena wasn't like the white people she met at Yale.

Emily was petite, with tousled brown hair that she must have intentionally mussed to give it that careless look. She walked with her toes pointed outward, a sign that she'd studied dance. No one would consider her pretty in the purest sense of the word, but she had enough money to manufacture the illusion of beauty and make it look effortless.

The daughter of an anesthesiologist and a hedge fund manager, Emily came from money, like most of Ruth's classmates. Two older brothers had followed in her father's footsteps and worked on Wall Street. Ruth and Emily exchanged these obligatory, polite details when they first met outside their dorm and then had to begin negotiating how to fit each of their belongings into the cramped space of one dorm room.

After showering in the mornings, Emily would return to their room and flip her drenched hair forward and back, spraying water on everything within a two-foot radius.

"It's so weird. I never see you wash your hair," Emily said from time to time with practiced indifference that irked Ruth even more than if the girl had come right out and said, *I think Black people are dirty*.

Ruth could have told her she visited a salon in New Haven once a week for a shampoo and blow dry or roller set. But that would have led to a discussion on why some Black girls washed their hair once every week or, God forbid, two weeks, only serving to reinforce misperceptions. Ruth said nothing and just glared as Emily moved through the room with proprietorship as if it were *her* room and not *theirs*.

When Emily's friends visited, they sat on Ruth's bed and plied her with questions: *Where are you from? What do your parents do? Where do you summer?* She'd never heard anyone use *summer* as a verb. And it wasn't just the white kids who were elitist. Even the Black kids came off bougie as hell, recounting tales of their summers in the Hamptons and Links cotillions back home. Soon she realized this was how people distinguished themselves, figured out their place in the socioeconomic order of things.

These kids knew nothing about the real world. She wanted to say, *I created a life over the summer, thank you very much*. She wanted to tell them she had carried another human being inside her body, nourishing and growing it for nine months. Then she pushed it out into the world to live on its own.

She wanted to tell them that Papa had done backbreaking labor in a plant until he couldn't work anymore. That her grandmother had to button his shirts, feed him toast small bite by small bite, and lift him onto the toilet those last few months. When the bills piled up, Mama had to go back to work again at the Majestic Inn, picking up used condoms and cleaning beer-soaked sheets left behind by guests. Ruth had learned early on not to judge people by how they made their money as long as it was an honest living.

Just survive and make it through these four years. That's what Ruth told herself to stay sane. She attended the white keg parties and got her buzz on there first. Then she settled in for the night at the Black Greek ones where bodies pressed against each other in the darkness, sweat and weed thickening the air. Whenever Ginuwine's "Pony" came on, she'd be grinding in a corner with boys she'd seen on the yard or with townies, the local guys who infiltrated the campus's party scene. But if "Killing Me Softly" played in the DJ's rotation, she had to leave the party in tears because it reminded her too much of Ronald and what could have been. No one at Yale knew about him or the legacy he'd left in Ruth's life.

One of those tearful nights she came back to the dorm buzzed and saw Emily emerge from the communal shower naked. Smooth as wax paper, her flat stomach shimmering with fresh dew.

Ruth stared and, without thinking, said, "You are so beautiful."

Obviously mortified, Emily grabbed a ratty T-shirt from the bathroom counter and frantically slipped it over her head. "Oh my God, you're weirding me out right now. I'm flattered, but girls aren't my thing. Nothing personal. Really."

Ruth blinked, embarrassed she'd been so spontaneous. She didn't really think Emily was beautiful. Why had she said that? It was just that the girl's stomach transfixed her. Looking away, Ruth scratched her own midsection through her nightshirt, thinking of what lay underneath, the dimpling of flabby flesh and the stretch marks that itched constantly. Then she glared at her roommate.

"Look, I was just being nice. I don't get down like that, okay? And if I did, you wouldn't be my type. So, get over yourself." Nothing between them flowed smooth after that. They shared meager square footage and breathed the same air, nothing more.

Most days, Ruth couldn't stop thinking about her baby. She burrowed in the cathedral of books at the library, where she could lose herself in differential equations and probabilities, but she had trouble focusing. She wanted to fall in love with math again the way she had in high school, but the numbers became indecipherable and began to resemble a foreign language.

Doubt gnawed at her and panic crawled up her spine when she considered that the one thing she could always count on no matter what was slowly slipping away. Even as an unwed, pregnant teenager, she was still smart. Her mistake couldn't erode something so innate. All that changed at Yale, where she was often one of the only Black students in her class. It soon became apparent to her that an A in Ganton schools equaled a C in the prep schools these rich kids came from.

She couldn't flunk her classes and lose her scholarship, returning to Ganton a failure. Not after all her grandparents and brother had sacrificed to give her this opportunity. On one late night of studying, she dropped a quarter and a dime into a pay phone outside the library, then dialed her home number.

"Hello." Mama's voice croaked like she hadn't used it in hours.

"Were you asleep? Did I wake you up?"

Clearing her throat, her grandmother said, "No, baby. I was up. What's wrong?"

A deluge of tears gathered in the back of Ruth's throat. "Nothing's wrong. I'm fine, Mama."

Silence stretched between them for what felt like minutes but had to be only seconds. She heard Mama's heavy breathing on the other end and found it oddly comforting.

"If you need money, I can talk to Eli and have him send you a little bit. He doesn't get paid again until this Friday. So, you may have to wait till then."

"I'm good on money. I still have some left from what you all sent last time."

"All right then. How are your studies coming?"

From her backpack, Ruth pulled her quiz sheet from Multivariable Calculus for Engineers and stared at her failing grade under the light of a streetlamp. She crumpled the paper in her fist. "Classes are good. You know me. I love school. Things are fine. Look, I know it's late. I'm gonna let you go now."

"Ruth?"

"Yes, Mama."

"You deserve to be there just like those other kids. Don't forget that. I'm proud of you, baby."

Pressing the phone to her ear, Ruth cradled it, tucking Mama's words and her voice in her memory. Afraid her own voice would betray her, she gently placed the receiver back into its cradle.

Chemical engineering had a reputation for punching out those who couldn't cut it. Professors seemed to revel in this up-or-out approach to academia. When engineering students formed study groups, it was the Darwinian process of picking teams in grade-school gym class all over again. In the survival-of-the-fittest game, they chose Ruth last or simply left her out.

Desperate for motivation to fight, she conjured the memory she usually pushed to the corner of her mind because it was too painful to remember. Her baby boy's eyes and the disappointment she'd left in them. Walking away from him couldn't have been all for nothing. So, she found a tutor through the National Society of Black Engineers and burned that midnight oil, as Papa used to say when he took on extra shifts at the plant. Determined to not just stay afloat, but swim, she climbed from failing grades to solid B's in every class.

Ruth dug out Mama's Bible and flipped to the back, where she knew her grandmother kept photos that hadn't made it into the family photo album. A shot of Eli as a kid on his skateboard, jumping over a crack in the sidewalk. One of Mama's brother, Uncle Mitch, in his crisp white U.S. Navy uniform, smiling like he was excited to go off to war when he'd actually just been unlucky in the draft. Ruth found a few snapshots of herself when she couldn't have been more than three or four, cheesing for the camera, poking her tongue through a gap in her front teeth.

She riffled through the photos until she landed on a picture of her mother as a teenage girl. Mama and Papa had named their only child Joanna, after a woman from the New Testament whom Jesus had healed once and come to rely on as a traveling companion.

In this shot, Joanna wore a ratty fuchsia coat that could only be described as gaudy, flaring at the hips and stopping midthigh. If she was wearing a skirt, you couldn't see it, so she may as well have been naked from the waist down. A glaring, brassy necklace obviously on the cheap side sat on her neck catching the camera's light.

Mama and Papa had Joanna late in life, and from what Ruth could tell, they'd spoiled her, entertaining the girl's every whim, giving her a wide berth. Joanna had taken full advantage of her freedom and indulged in anything and everything she wanted, including crack cocaine.

It never made sense that Joanna chose that poison over her own children. How did a mother make that calculation? But who was Ruth to judge? You could say Yale had been her crack. The lure of it so potent she left her baby behind for it.

As a girl, Ruth asked her grandparents where her mother had gone. They always said she was sick and needed time away to recuperate. Leaving the door open for a miraculous, triumphant return someday. A prodigal daughter moment that never came, and Ruth began to wonder if her mother was even alive.

At school, students drew pictures of their mommies and daddies and explained their occupations as best they could with their childlike comprehension of the world. When Ruth received this assignment in

Miss Albert's first-grade class, she pressed the crayon hard on the dark green construction paper, drawing a brown outline of Papa. Big hands. Big work boots. And for his hair, she left part of it bare on top and colored in the sides with gray crayon. She used the same gray crayon to fill in Mama's curls that framed her face beautifully.

"Why isn't your mommy and daddy's hair black?" The loud, accusatory question came from Loretta Jenkins, a smart, wiry little girl who always wore three thick braids, one on either side of her head and one in the back.

"Because it isn't," Ruth answered her with a hint of defensiveness, without knowing why the distinction about hair color mattered, only that it did.

Knowing that Loretta's question had left Ruth off-balance triggered the other children to giggle, all their laughter directed at Ruth. Children didn't need details or context to understand differences and seize upon them.

Encouraged now by the other kids, Loretta piped up again, making her point plain. "They look old. Old as dirt."

Heat rushed to Ruth's head and she wanted to lob an equally hurtful blow back at the girl but couldn't think of a single thing to say with all those eyes on her and their laughter charging the air. She didn't dare tell Mama and Papa about it. She was too embarrassed. For them as much as herself. Instead, she confided in Eli. Loretta's brother, Kenneth, was in his class, and Eli marched right up to him the next day and socked him in his jaw. Hitting a girl was out of bounds and Eli knew this. Kenneth's innocence and ignorance of the whole matter was irrelevant, and when everyone saw his busted lip, Loretta kept her mouth shut for the rest of the school year.

Not until much later and after years of prodding did Ruth learn about Joanna's drug addiction. It began during the eighties crack epidemic and she was a textbook case: starting with marijuana as the gateway and then graduating to harder, more dangerous drugs. One of those stories that seemed a bit hyperbolic but parents told their kids anyway as a cautionary tale. It worked as a deterrent for Ruth, who swore off drugs. In that one area of her life, she could claim moral superiority.

It was a man—a boy, actually—that had been Joanna's downfall. Ruth often wondered whether Joanna had a Ronald in her life. Had she gotten caught up with a guy she thought she loved, someone who pounded away at her body until the pain went away? Mama and Papa would only say they didn't know the identity of Ruth and Eli's biological father.

You're better off without him, Papa used to say, sure that his love could fill the gap.

Mama usually dismissed the topic. *You don't need him, whoever he is. You got people. Not everybody can say that.*

But a little girl needed a daddy: the first man she would ever try to impress, a man who could spin her around and never let her fall, one who would set the bar so high that no other man could ever reach it.

For a long time, Ruth would look at men's faces wistfully, hoping that one of them would claim her as his own. She did this until she moved away from Ganton to go to college.

And then the object of her focus changed, and she began inspecting little boys' faces, wondering if one of them could be her child. Had her son done the same thing in search of her?

Ruth couldn't help but think of her husband, a good man who desperately yearned for children while a man like her biological father had ducked his duties. But then again, she had done the same thing. How was she any different from the man who had sired her? Whoever said the apple didn't fall far from the tree had been right, and the pain of that truth never dulled.

Eleven

RUTH

The rattle of what sounded like a busted engine outside grew louder. The sound was getting closer to their house.

"What's that racket out there?" Ruth pulled back the ruffled kitchen curtain and peered out the window. She couldn't see much of anything, though. The lights on the porch and the side of the house weren't working.

"Your brother's home," Mama said, without even going to the window or the door. She scrubbed a grease stain off a place mat and set a sparkling fork, knife, and spoon on either side of a plate.

The side door rubbed hard against the linoleum when it opened, and Eli's broad frame filled the doorway. Eli looked just like Papa, the way he stood, that scruffy black beard, those eyes that told what was on his mind before he ever said a word.

"Ooh, do I smell greens? So good makes you want to smack your mama." Eli winked and bent to squeeze Mama's waist. "Just kidding, Mama."

"Hmm. You know you don't smell any greens. I'll have turnip and mustards tomorrow with ham. Fried chicken tonight. Look who's here." Mama waved her dishrag toward Ruth.

Eli shielded his eyes with his hand and squinted, as if he didn't immediately recognize his own sister. "Who this? Do I know you?"

"Boy, quit playing," Ruth said, and ran into his arms. Time had a way of changing people, giving and taking away at the same time. Eli's body felt lean, yet his stomach had grown rounder. He'd let his hair grow out into a full Afro that appeared even bigger as it framed his thinned face.

"Nobody told me we were having a family reunion." Eli opened the refrigerator and grabbed a can of Bud.

"We're not. I wanted to surprise you all," Ruth said. A sickeningly sweet chemical odor oozed from Eli's body. "And you don't need a beer, big brother. You already smell like a distillery."

"A man's got to relax sometimes. Lighten up, lil bit. I know it's hard to do when you're still rocking those Clair Huxtable clothes ten years later."

Ruth rolled her eyes. "That wasn't even funny. You're getting off your game in your old age."

She and her brother slid easily into their half-joking, half-serious battle positions. It could only be explained as muscle memory and Ruth welcomed it, like salve on a wound she'd forgotten existed.

"Okay, enough, you two. Go easy on your brother. He's had a hard day. Sit down and eat, Eli, before your food gets cold," Mama said. She had kept the food warming in the oven. She didn't believe in microwaves. *All that artificial heat kills the taste of the food and the radiation causes cancer. I'm not ready to die before the good Lord calls me.*

Mama put a meaty chicken thigh and breast on Eli's plate, even though she had gently suggested earlier that Ruth take one of the legs. "He's grown. Why are you fixing his plate? I'm company and I had to serve myself," Ruth said.

"I'm the man around here, remember. And age first. Got to respect your elders, girl. Don't you know that?" Eli laughed with his mouth wide open and full of chewed chicken.

"If you were any kind of man, you would've fixed the toilet and furnace for Mama. And the porch light, too."

"You ain't back but two minutes and you already trying to boss folks around."

Ignoring her brother, she said, "Mama, I stopped in town at Lena's shop this morning. If it's just the lightbulb that needs changing, I could've picked up some for you earlier."

"If that's all it took, I would've done that a long time ago," Mama said. "But I bet Lena was surprised to see you."

"Oh, yeah. I met her grandson. Seemed like a bit of a brat. Running wild."

At the mention of Midnight, Mama and Eli exchanged glances. It was quick, but Ruth noticed.

"What's the story with that kid? Must be something the way you two are eyeing each other."

"Ever since the plant closed, Lena's been keeping him. Butch lost their place over on Laramie when he couldn't pay the rent anymore," Mama said.

There was something wrong with this caregiving that skipped a generation. An untold burden with a cost that couldn't be calculated. Mama and Papa had been substitute parents to Ruth and Eli just as Lena was now to Midnight. She wondered what these grandparents had forfeited, what dreams lay barren as they assumed the responsibilities of their children.

"Well, I say Midnight's better off not being under the same roof with Butch Boyd," said Eli. "He's a lowlife. He shouldn't have even been allowed to reproduce."

Eli had three children, twin boys and a girl, with his wife, Cassie. Ruth noticed that her brother wasn't wearing his wedding ring, and he hadn't yet mentioned her niece and nephews. It was obvious he didn't care for Butch, whom she vaguely remembered seeing around Ganton growing up. If he was as bad a guy as Eli made him out to be, she felt sorry for Midnight.

Mama heaped mashed potatoes on Eli's plate as if sustenance might improve his disposition. "Now I know you and Butch don't see eye to eye, but that's a horrible thing to say."

"All I'm saying is everybody ain't cut out to be a parent." Eli's words stretched into a drawl when he slurped his Bud between mouthfuls of chicken. His words also cut her with the sharpest precision.

In the early months of her pregnancy, Eli hadn't said much, but his smirks spoke louder than anything, telegraphing that with him dropping out of high school and her getting pregnant before graduating, it was a draw, with both failing to live up to expectations. Ruth saw a shadow of that same smirk on his face now.

Mama broke the silence. "You told me you wouldn't be able to make it home for Thanksgiving or Christmas again this year. I assumed you and Xavier were going to see his folks. But you're here. By yourself. You say he's busy working. What is it, baby? Why are you here?"

Why was she there? She paused long enough to filter her thoughts, determining what she could say that would adequately explain why she wanted to undo a secret their family had harbored for more than a decade.

Her fingers worried a nick in the table's wood. "I came back to find my son."

Eli coughed, choking on his food. Mama wiped her hands on a paper towel. "You know that can't happen," she said calmly.

"But things are different now. Xavier and I want to start a family. We just bought a new house. We're both finally making good money." As soon as those words were out of her mouth, Ruth wanted to scoop them back in. "I'm sorry, Eli. I know you're looking for work now that the plant's closed."

Her brother let his fork fall to the table. "I don't need your apology or your pity, lil sis. Me and mine will be just fine. It's you I'm worried about. You must have lost your damn mind talking about wanting to find your kid after all these years. You getting all high and mighty and cute now with your fancy job and house. Don't ever get it twisted. You have all of that because of what *we* did."

He pointed his finger at Mama and then himself. Afterward, he picked up his plate and took it to his old bedroom.

Ruth and Mama sat in a hushed silence, the smell of chicken grease still hanging in the air. Mama spoke first.

"You and Xavier can have as many babies as you want. But you can't undo the past and take that child back to Chicago with you. There are other people to think about besides yourself."

"I just want to make sure my son is okay."

"He's fine."

Ruth wouldn't give up that easily. Not now, when she'd risked her marriage telling Xavier everything. And she'd decided she wouldn't live her life any longer without knowing the truth. "What adoption agency did you go through?" She remembered the litany of questions Xavier had asked her. The ones she couldn't answer. "You were my legal guardian then, so I assume you signed all the papers?"

A strange look flashed on Mama's face, but she didn't say anything, so Ruth went on. "Did you meet the people who adopted him? I need to know who they are and where they live." Ruth dug her nails deeper into crevices in the wood. "Please."

"You ain't never laid eyes on him since you spit him out and now you want to lay claim to him. What sense does that make?"

Ruth wanted to say *ain't never* was a double negative that negated Mama's point, but all she said was "I'm not trying to *lay claim*. You took him from me. I had no choice. You didn't give me one."

"You're having regrets now because you don't like what you did. You can't live with it. But there's no going back. I'll tell you something else, young lady," Mama said, her voice getting tight. "You keep turning up the dirt, you bound to run into a snake one day." She held up one callused hand, grease smeared on her fingertips. "And it's going to bite you. Real hard."

When Mama got the last word, it chilled you down to your ankle bones. Froze you in place like cement. There was nothing left to say.

Mama turned her back and started raking leftovers into Tupperware containers. Then she ran a scouring pad over each burner on the stove until the dried sauces and gravies peeled away along with some of the stainless-steel coating.

Ruth sighed deeply and walked down the hall where the bedrooms were. Eli's door was closed. "Got Money," by Lil Wayne, blasted from the other side. Her hand lightly touched the knob. Growing up, a closed door meant he wanted privacy to listen to music, talk on the phone to someone of the opposite sex, or pleasure himself without interruption. She learned the last the hard way when she burst in once on her big brother lying naked on the bed with lotion and a towel beside him.

This time, she knocked first. When he gave her permission to enter, she found him standing in front of the mirror in his pajamas picking his Afro. Eli shouldn't be here in his cramped childhood bedroom. He should be in his own house with his wife and children, but this town, this country, this life, had cut him down to a boy again.

The one question that went unanswered because no one dared raise it was whether she and Eli even shared the same father. No one knew, and after some time, not knowing became easier. You could fill in whatever fantasy brought you peace. But she didn't need a DNA test to know Eli was fully her brother in every way that mattered.

"Hey," she shouted above the music.

Lowering the volume, he said, "What's good, lil bit?"

Ruth considered herself skinny, but not little and petite. Her long limbs flailed everywhere, and she wished to be more compact. Despite incontrovertible evidence to suggest otherwise, Eli's nickname for her made her feel small and cute.

A simple question, yet hard to answer. She didn't want to argue with him, not again. "I like your hair," she said. "I bet Mama gave you grief over it."

A laugh escaped his lips. "Yeah, she said something about how we weren't on a sixties picket line anymore."

Ruth sat on the edge of his bed and then stretched out on her stomach, beginning to feel comfortable again. She looked up to see Eli wagging his finger at her.

"Now, you know better than to get in the bed with your outside clothes on."

After a moment's hesitation, she glanced down at her sweater and leggings. Then she snorted and cackled uncontrollably. Admonitions from Mama could fill a book, and their grandmother had changed very little over the years. Except for one area of her life that left Ruth befuddled and unsettled.

Lowering her voice, Ruth said, "I saw Dino here when I first came home. He looked real comfortable. What's going on between him and Mama?"

Eli shrugged. "If it was anybody but him, I'd have some issues. But he's a good dude."

"Well, yeah, but what about Papa?"

"What about him? He's dead. Been dead years now." The blunt finality of those words stung and made Ruth wince. Eli had once held their grandfather up as an idol, but now he sounded dismissive about the man. Eli went on to say, "One thing I learned a long time ago is that you can't live your life looking back."

Now he was talking about her, and she took his reproach as a personal failing. Somehow, she had not lived up to Eli's expectations.

After Papa died, her brother had been the one she desperately wanted to impress. When she wore a new dress or tried a new hairstyle, she hoped he'd notice. Even when she got into Yale, knowing he'd be left behind, she smiled when he bragged to his friends about how smart she was.

Eli said, "So, you asking about Mama's love life. What about yours? Where's your husband?"

"I could ask you the same thing," she said. "Where's Cassie?"

He turned back to face the mirror, and in the reflection she could see his face fall in mock defeat. "Touché," he said, chuckling begrudgingly.

The two men remaining in her life had met on her wedding day four years ago at Friendship Baptist Church. She'd been nervous about her brother and her future husband meeting, wondering if they'd get along, hoping for Eli's blessing.

After the ceremony, they'd stayed in church chatting, the men soon bantering jovially about the close Super Bowl game between the New England Patriots and the Carolina Panthers.

"I seem to remember the Bears kicking some Patriot butt back in the day," Xavier said proudly.

Eli doubled over in laughter, almost popping his suit coat button. "Man, that was 1985. You still doing that lame Super Bowl shuffle?"

Ruth and Cassie kept a close eye on their husbands. As long as they were still laughing and didn't end up in a fistfight in the church, everything would be fine, Ruth thought.

"Now, if I was in the NFL, I'd really be ballin'," Eli said, pulling his arm back, tossing an imaginary football.

Xavier said, "A lot of those cats in the NFL and NBA lose that money as fast as they make it."

Pastor Bumpus rose from the pew and walked in circles, just like he did in the pulpit. "Don't make the mistake of following these ball-players. They're greedy. The Bible says no one can serve two masters. You cannot serve both God and money." He brought a closed fist to his lips and looked like he had the urge to preach.

In the middle of all of it, Ruth watched Mama in her ivory sequined suit, looking up at both men. The baby had complicated Ruth's relationship with her grandmother. Yet she could tell she enjoyed having her family and pastor together again the way they had been when Papa was still alive.

From her seat on a front-row pew, Mama said, "Well, all I know is some of these parents are trying to keep up with the Joneses, buying their kids all these expensive shoes with ballplayers' names on them. Some of the kids can't read their own names, but they're wearing four-hundred-dollar tennis shoes. Now that's crazy."

Xavier said, "You're right about that, Mrs. Tuttle. We can't build wealth by putting all our money on our kids' feet. But it's bigger than that. We need to start our own businesses. Eli, brother, look here. I hear you know your stuff when it comes to cars and mechanics. Why not open your own shop? Then get your kids involved so they can take it over one day."

The twins, Teddy and Troy, had loosened their ties and stretched out on the pew behind them. Cassie bounced Keisha on her lap, spooning applesauce into the little girl's mouth to keep her happy and quiet.

Eli surveyed his children as if seeing them for the first time, pondering each of their futures, and deeming it risky to dream too big. "I don't know about that, man. I don't have one of those fancy business degrees like you. Besides, soon as a Black man tries to make a big move, they chop your arm off. White man's got us by the balls, always has."

Realizing his language may have been a bit crude for the sanctuary, Eli mouthed an apology to Pastor Bumpus, who laughed it off.

Even on their wedding day, Xavier had been in teaching mode. "That's slave mentality, brother. Indoctrination. I know you can learn business, but you know cars already. I'm telling you to think about it. You never know how big it could grow. That's how the Ford family did it. In ten years, I expect to be driving a Tuttle SUV."

Eli grinned, his eyes twinkling. "A Tuttle SUV," he echoed. "I like the sound of that now."

When they left the church to head their separate ways, Eli whispered in her ear, "I like that dude."

If she couldn't have Papa's blessing on her wedding day, this was damn close.

At the time, many of her friends bemoaned the eligible Black male shortage: they were either emotionally unavailable, gay, in prison, or dating white women exclusively. Every magazine think piece reminded her she had a better chance of getting hit by a bus than finding a good brother. But Xavier had *put a ring on it* and Eli approved. She returned to Chicago believing she'd chosen wisely and well.

Now, she considered telling Eli about her fight with her husband, but he turned his music up again—too loud to talk over—and bounced to some hip-hop song she didn't know. That was her cue to leave, and she did.

Across the hallway was her old bedroom. She'd dreaded this moment and had avoided this room for as long as she could. The door stood open, enough for her to see the wood frame of her childhood bed with the four tall posts anchoring it. When she was a little girl, she'd played with dolls and read books on this bed. Mama was a practical woman not given to sentimentality, but she'd seen no need for wasting money on new furniture when Ruth left for college. So, everything looked the same, untouched by time.

Everything about it seemed sterile, and it was probably a guest room now. In spite of Mama's archaic rules about outside clothes touching the bed, Ruth sat gingerly and the springs squeaked beneath her weight. The room smelled of Pine-Sol, clean and airy. But no amount of freshening could wipe away what had happened here.

Twelve

RUTH

At seventeen, Ruth lay on her back, her hair matted like a bird's nest. It was oppressively hot that day and her thin pink nightshirt clung to her damp skin.

"I can't do this," Ruth cried from her bed.

"I don't see how you got much choice in the matter." Mama dipped a hand towel in a bucket of hot water, just as midwives used to do in those old black-and-white movies.

"It hurts so bad."

Pressure built in her groin, spreading to her stomach and back. This felt twenty times worse than her most intense menstrual cramps, the ones that had kept her home from school many days. Rocking back and forth on the bed, Ruth writhed on the sheet, riding each wave of pain.

"Women been birthing babies for thousands of years. No different this time." Mama's face had turned into a black cloud hovering over her. Still, Ruth pawed the air until she gripped her grandmother's arm, digging her nails into her skin.

"Please. I need to go to the hospital," Ruth begged.

Mama dabbed her forehead with a cool sponge. "Now, you know

better than that. You're going to be just fine. Trust me. Have I ever led you wrong?"

Ruth watched Mama looming above, her breasts swaying in her threadbare gown like two pendulums. Mama had been so careful to keep the pregnancy secret, and a trip to the hospital would expose their lie. She'd insisted that Ruth wear long tunic sweaters to cover her stomach and bright short necklaces that lured people's eyes away from her midsection. When she could no longer hide the obvious, Ruth stayed hidden in the house, feigning illness and completing her schoolwork at home those last two months of senior year.

The whistle from the nearby plant sounded, cutting the day in half. Work had ended, and it was suppertime. Eli's shift would've been over, but he had called in sick that day. Her brother always wore a baseball cap, even inside the house, but on this afternoon, he'd taken it off in reverence for what was about to happen. A crease lined his forehead as he looked down at Ruth.

"Come on now, lil bit. You got this," he said, holding to her ear a Sony Discman that played Erykah Badu's "On & On," which had been her favorite song that year.

But the music did little to calm the war raging inside her body. Her lower back seized up and the muscles twisted into one long braid of unbearable pain. It got so bad she even begged God to take her from this world and end her misery.

Mama covered her mouth lightly with her hand. "Now, you hush with that kind of talk. Don't play with God like that."

There were moments when the pain subsided, after one contraction ended and before the next one began, and Mama reminded Ruth of the pact they'd made as a family. As she dipped the sponge in a bucket of water on the floor, Mama's eyes never met Ruth's.

"Once you have this baby, you leave it right here with us. You go on to Yale like we planned and don't think any more about this child."

"It's not up to you or you." Ruth swung her head between her grandmother and her brother. "It's my baby. My choice. Actually, it's our baby. Mine and Ronald's."

Eli laughed, but it came out as more of a snort. "You don't even hear from him anymore. You think he's sticking around to raise a kid? Soon as he finds out, he's ghost. I'm telling you."

"You can't keep this baby," said Mama. "How are you going to go to Yale as the Black girl on scholarship toting a baby? I don't think so."

"Plenty of girls have kids and still go to school."

"I don't care about plenty of girls. I care about you. And if that's the way you want it, you might as well stay here in Ganton and go to community college. Your papa and I worked our fingers to the bone so you'd have a chance like this to get your education and make something of yourself. I bet your grandfather's turning over in his grave listening to your nonsense right now. We can't have a baby messing things up now."

"For months, all you been talking about is Yale this and Yale that," Eli chimed in. "You always bragging about being smarter than me, lil bit. So why you acting dumb now? We already settled on all this."

Ruth tried to steady her voice, knowing she was up against Mama and Eli, a formidable force when they got together and ganged up on her. "I don't have to go to Yale. At least not right now. Ganton Community College is perfectly fine. It wouldn't be forever." Her voice sounded shrill and foreign to her own ears because of the exhaustion that had overtaken her. Tears spilled from her eyes because she didn't know what she wanted and knew she'd been dreaming of life in the Ivy League, away from everything in Ganton that suffocated her.

A framed copy of her acceptance letter from Yale sat on the nightstand next to her bed. Eli picked it up and held it out to her. "Sis, I'm supposed to be the dummy in the family. But even I know you can't give up on this shot right here. That would be like being a number-one draft pick for the NFL or NBA and saying, 'Nah, I'd rather ball with my boys on the block.'"

The sticky air choked Ruth. The contractions had come again, faster this time.

"Do we understand each other?" Mama said, trying to pry a promise from her before the baby came.

Ruth had no energy left to argue. Sweat dribbled onto her lips and pooled on her chin. It tasted salty. "Yes. Okay. Yes."

Then everything happened fast. A fresh wave of pain overtook her body. She was caught in the undertow. Trapped.

Mama slid a plastic sheet under her bottom. It clung to her thighs. For a moment, Ruth thought someone was yanking organs from her body, one by one. The louder she wailed, the harder she squeezed Eli's hand, the way she'd imagined doing with Ronald. For the most part, she kept her eyes closed, but a few times she peered through the curtains of her eyelashes at Mama's face between her thighs.

"One big push now. Let's go," Mama said.

Pressure built in her pelvis again until she thought she might explode from the force of it. Then what felt like sharp nails ripped her insides apart. When she thought she might die there in her bed, her eyes shifted from Mama to Eli, memorizing their faces because she was sure she'd never see them again.

In an instant, though, the baby slipped from between her legs and all that pain disappeared as fast as if none of it had ever happened.

When Mama placed the baby boy on her slightly deflated stomach, Ruth's arms wouldn't move at first. They seemed wooden.

The baby slid in her hands like a hard-boiled egg. His black hair soft like the belly of a kitten. Thick white paste covered him, and his face was swollen, eyes scrunched in a cranky way like he wanted to smash the alarm clock. She could make out a small burgundy spot on his cheek that Mama would later tell her was a port wine stain, an abnormality of his tiny blood vessels. *Nothing to worry about. God marks some babies as special, that's all* is how she put it. Still, that baby was the ugliest thing Ruth had ever seen, and she found it hard to believe he had come from her body.

This baby's face would always represent a mistake she couldn't undo. It would haunt her. Somewhere deep inside, even back then, she knew this. After nine months of planning for how this little person would fit into her life, finally seeing him in the flesh, not as an abstraction, hit her hard. No matter where she went in the world, she couldn't escape what she'd created, and that scared her.

When Mama and Eli turned their backs, Ruth lifted the baby's head slightly, so her lips were close to his ear.

"I hate you," she whispered.

"I heard that." Mama dipped a washcloth in warm water and returned to wipe goo from the baby's eyes. "Don't say that to your child. You'll regret it."

The baby must have known they were talking about him. Had he heard what she'd said? He opened his eyes for the first time, like a light turning on, and she could feel his innocent milky-eyed gaze on her. She couldn't take her eyes off his.

The reality of her situation gnawed at her. She remembered the agreement with her family. If she kept the baby, she couldn't go away to college. Everything she'd worked so hard for would be lost and she'd be stuck in Ganton, a town that killed dreams before they took root. But if she let go of her baby, there would be a hole inside her that could never be filled.

"Give him to me, sweetheart. It won't do you no good to keep holding him," Mama said. She tapped her granddaughter's ashy knee. "Close your legs now. You gon' catch a fly up in there."

Ruth pressed her knees together, conscious for the first time of her indecent exposure to her grandmother and especially her brother. But she didn't let go of her son. His skin felt warm and sticky against her chest. She needed more time.

"He's mine," Ruth said, as if she were a toddler laying claim to a toy, and she hated how childish she sounded.

What she felt made no sense, not even to herself. This was more than a simple binary choice. She wanted her baby, yet she didn't. She loved him and hated him at the same time.

Eli had shrunk into the corner of the room, embarrassed maybe by seeing his sister in such a primal state, watching life come into the world for the first time.

The three of them had talked only in vague terms the past nine months, and Ruth hadn't thought far enough ahead, hadn't truly visualized the baby living outside her body, a living, breathing person who would require someone to care for him.

The baby fussed in Ruth's arms, squirming, and she held him tighter. "Where are you going to take him? Can't you just watch him for me here at the house until I come home for summer break?"

"No, it's been decided already. Don't worry about where he's going. He'll be just fine." Mama tugged at the baby's arm. "Let me have him, honey." The boy's eyes pleaded with Ruth. Turning her head away so she couldn't watch, avoiding his eyes, she slowly released her grip on her son, her own eyes hot with tears.

Eli held Ruth's arm firmly, as if she might spring from the bed to reclaim her baby. "Hey, sis, you ain't got to worry about nothing. Stop being hardheaded and let us fix this for you. We got this," he said.

Mama whispered, "I know you're mad at me now, but it's for your own good."

The linoleum floor creaked under Mama's heavy footsteps. The baby whimpered before the side door slammed shut.

Thirteen

RUTH

Ruth took her foot off the gas pedal and let the car move slowly through the streets of Grundy. After only one day and night back home, she had to get out of the house. The sky turned pale. It had emptied itself. But within minutes, snowflakes fell on the windshield and melted right away. The night was as confused as she was. The weather had always been unpredictable in this part of the country.

The car windows fogged, and Ruth jammed the defrost button. Winding her way through Grundy, she passed a faded malt liquor ad and empty lots with mangled signs for a braiding salon and a chicken wing joint.

Poverty didn't discriminate in Ganton, with Blacks and whites both getting their share of hard times. Her headlights shone on two young Black men with short braided hair jostling in the middle of the street. Just the sight of her people made her heart swell with pride. Still, when she heard their raised voices, she clicked the lock button on her car doors, a reflex she wasn't proud of, and she wondered if they were really jostling or maybe joking. How could she both love and fear her own people?

She wondered about the street her son lived on and hoped the house had heat that ran through the winter and working smoke detectors. She imagined a Black neighborhood like Grundy, where she grew up, a place where joy lived. Where people threw up a hand to wave when they checked the mailbox and piled into their Buicks for bingo and bowling on Saturday nights and church on Sunday mornings.

A few blocks over, stillness fell on Franklin Street, everything quiet except for the murmur of her car engine. Outside her window, she passed a building with a *Cold Meats* sign in front and a laundromat next to it. A small figure in a blue hooded jacket walked in front of the check-cashing store, kicking a mound of snow. The glare of her headlights caught his face. It was Lena's grandson. She hadn't forgotten that he'd pelted her car with snowballs. This boy's smugness irritated Ruth, and she drove past him. Her only mistake: looking in her rearview mirror. Regret dogged her almost constantly these days. A dustup of snow blew in Midnight's face. She put her car in reverse and rolled down the passenger's-side window.

"Midnight! Let me give you a ride."

"I can walk." She heard the defiance in his voice.

"It's cold and it's dark out here and this area—"

Even now, just as Black boys didn't walk the streets of Pratt, white boys didn't walk the streets of Grundy. Not at night. Not alone.

"I'm not allowed to accept rides from strangers!" he shouted with a smile.

"That's a good rule to follow, but it's freezing out here and besides, I'm not a stranger. We met yesterday at your grandmother's shop." Driving slowly beside him, she tried to keep her car going in a straight line while leaning over to yell to him through the passenger's-side window. "Please. Get in."

The wind picked up and Midnight staggered trying to push against it. He jerked the door handle and climbed in, his breathing hard and his long eyelashes dotted with snowflakes.

"Why were you walking the streets by yourself this time of night?"

Midnight curled his booted feet under his legs and reclined the seat. He ripped off his mittens and held his fingers with their reddened tips over the heat vent.

"I needed to get away to think."

Midnight was one of those kids the old folks would say had been here before in another life. She laughed, and his face became drawn, making it obvious he thought he was being laughed at.

"What have you been thinking about?" Ruth said.

He shrugged and didn't answer. She hadn't known him long, but it seemed Midnight stood on the outside of things, bitter, chafed by the unfairness of life. Yet his face also had an open, pleading countenance that she recognized in herself. He tried to mask his need with feigned indifference.

Midnight had to be around the same age as her son, and she wondered if they knew each other. Ganton was small, but what were the odds of that in a town of twenty-five thousand people? Besides, she had no idea what her own child looked like, so she couldn't describe him. Also, she felt sorry for Midnight and it didn't seem right to use him to get information. So, she stopped scheming in her head and tried to make conversation. The topic of the weather was always safe, if uncreative.

"Snow's really coming down hard. Nobody should be out in it."

"Daddy went to the plant every day in the snow, even when it was ten inches deep."

She heard the pride in his voice, same as Papa's. She also recalled the deep disdain her brother had for this boy's father.

"I can tell you're strong just like your dad."

"Can you drop me off at Granny's? My address—"

"316 Kirkland in Pratt."

Midnight raised his eyebrows in surprise. Pratt was one of the white working-class neighborhoods Mama told her and Eli to avoid as kids, even if Lena did live there. *Don't be caught over there after dark,* she'd said. Ruth had stayed home most high school nights, lying across her four-poster bed studying for AP exams. But Eli hadn't listened. One night, he came home with a bloodied, busted lip and a story about a couple of teen boys at a Pratt pool hall who fought him over which song to play on the jukebox. Come to think of it, Midnight's dad, Butch Boyd, had been one of those boys. Ruth wasn't sure how much had changed over the years. Now, she tried to shake off the jitters she felt about having to drive through Pratt, a Black woman with a white kid in the passenger seat. A white kid she hardly knew but still gave the benefit of the doubt. A courtesy too magnanimous for the Black kids on the street who reminded her of who she might have become if she'd stayed in Ganton.

"Why is it so quiet when it snows?" His voice rose from the darkness, startling her when she was getting accustomed to the silence. A bag of doughnuts Midnight had pulled out of his jacket pocket lay on the seat between them, and he reached for a glazed one with green sprinkles.

"The weather's bad, so not as many people are on the roads. I guess that's why it's quiet now."

The day of her wedding, she recalled Eli's young children asking why the sun was yellow and why water was wet and why the stove was hot. Maybe children never outgrew the *why* questions. Even the best answers led to an endless cycle of more *whys*.

"No. I mean snow is *always* quiet when it falls," he said.

"I give up. You tell me."

Midnight pushed his hood back away from his face and turned in his seat to face her. He licked his lips, outlined with sugar glaze and cracked from the cold.

"It's all about texture," he began, taking an exaggerated breath before continuing. "When you drop something on the hard ground, it makes a loud noise. But snow is soft, and it absorbs sound. Kind of like carpet."

Ruth suppressed a smile. "Yes, unlike rainfall. Raindrops fall at a higher velocity, so they make that slapping noise when they hit the pavement."

"How did you know that?"

"Science was my favorite subject in school."

That seemed to surprise and please Midnight. A blast of wind rocked the car like a tiny earthquake, and Ruth tightened her hold on the steering wheel to steady it. The motion knocked the phone out of

Midnight's hands, and it slid under his seat. When he bent to look for it, he bumped his head on the glove compartment.

"Ouch." He muttered under his breath, "Some people don't know how to drive."

"I heard that. I could have left you out there in the dark walking by yourself in a blizzard."

"It's not even that bad out here. I walk by myself all the time."

And why was that? she wondered. In every city, neglected children walked the streets looking for the love they either didn't get at home or rejected when it was offered. Lena nurtured almost instinctively, though.

The boy's gloved fingers fumbled with the radio controls, bypassing Top 40, jazz, and urban contemporary, which was the PC marketing code for Black music. He settled on a country station she knew had been Lena's favorite for years. Strains of guitar music filled the car, and when Midnight's head swayed from side to side Ruth turned up the volume and he sang along with his eyes closed.

"You know all the lyrics," Ruth said.

"Mommy loved Blake Shelton. She used to sing in the car all the time." The glow from a streetlight passed over Midnight's face, but it was blank, unreadable.

"I heard about your mom and I'm so sorry."

"She's been dead awhile. Died when I was seven." Death lived in Midnight's words, too. In the way he said them. No inflection in his tone. No sadness there, either. Ruth could only assume the more he said the words, the less they stung.

"I can only imagine how much you miss her," Ruth said.

"I wonder what it's like to be dead." He turned his face to the run-down row houses passing outside his window. "Granny said nobody's ever come back to tell us about it."

Snow fluttered in front of the car's headlights like confetti. Ruth clutched the steering wheel, dividing her attention between keeping the car from swerving and looking at Midnight.

"I still talk to her. And sometimes she talks back." He glanced at Ruth, as if daring her to dispute this fact.

"I talk to my papa, too. He was actually my grandfather and he died a long time ago, but I still miss him."

"Does he answer you back?"

"Well, I don't hear an actual voice. But when I have a problem I'm trying to solve and need to know what to do, I ask him. Then I get this overwhelming feeling that pushes me in the right direction, and I know that's Papa. When I still lived here, I'd go to the Wabash River to feel better. That was our special place."

This was the first time Ruth had told anyone about her talks with Papa. At home, when Xavier turned the lights out, she would lie on her side of the bed in the dark, shadows moving across the ceiling and horns honking on the busy street below, and silently tell Papa everything.

She swiped her cheek fast. Without looking at her, Midnight dropped his crumpled napkin on the console between them. It was brown, with the Dunkin' Donuts logo on it, and she felt the roughness of the recycled paper as she dabbed her cheek with it, leaving sugar crumbs stuck to her face.

Midnight said, "I go to the river sometimes with my friends."

Ruth cleared her throat. "Papa and I mostly fished there. You could look out as far as you could see and get lost in the water, the beauty of it, the stillness. Then you'd realize the river is bigger than any of your problems."

The kid didn't say anything, so she kept talking. "You know, my grandfather and your grandfather used to work together. Fished together, too."

Midnight tilted his head up like he was considering what she'd said. "Really?"

"Yeah, really."

"I never met my grandpa. He was already dead when I was born. Granny said I got my appetite from him."

Then he yelled. "Right here. You missed it." He twisted his

upper body and pointed behind him. "My street. Kirkland. It was back there."

Visibility was poor and she'd passed her turn. Forgetting the black ice beneath them, she slammed the brakes and the car skidded in the intersection. "Damn."

"You said a bad word." Midnight laughed louder than necessary.

"I'm sure you've heard worse on TV."

He looked surprised that he hadn't rattled her. The car churned the ice for a few seconds before turning around. The green house he pointed to seemed forlorn and sickly, with two rusted pickup trucks in the yard turning white in the snow. Lena's house had never been this run-down back in the day, but as a kid, she didn't have much to compare it with.

"Is anyone home?" Ruth said.

Midnight ignored her question and opened the car door to get out, but she stopped him. She took his phone from his hand, found his contact list, and typed in her name and phone number.

"If you need a ride in the next few days, call me. Don't walk these streets by yourself late at night."

He took his phone back and said nothing. He shut the door and trudged through the snow toward the house, then he stopped suddenly and ran back to her car. Had he forgotten something? She rolled down her window. A blast of snow rushed her face.

With his eyes squinted and mouth twisted, Midnight held on to her door and said, "How long can a cockroach live with his head cut off?"

The absurdity of the question itself and the fact that he ran back to her car to ask it stunned her into silence for a second. Then she said, "I don't know, but I do know you're going to freeze if you don't get into that house."

"You don't know the answer," he said triumphantly, and grinned as he ran sideways pushing against the wind gust.

A young woman with an angry face and pink hair rollers framing her head appeared in the doorway and yanked him by the arm.

That had to be Gloria, Lena's younger daughter, the one who got into enough trouble for Mama to predict she wouldn't amount to much. With a quick glance back in Ruth's direction, Midnight jerked free of his aunt's grasp and the door closed, leaving Ruth to wonder about Midnight and what life was like for him in that sad little green house.

Fourteen

MIDNIGHT

Corey's house on Hill Top was a ranch-style bungalow with a front porch, and Midnight preferred it over the house he used to live in with Daddy. It reminded him of the midday sun, bright yellow with white shutters and flowered curtains at the kitchen window. Sometimes, he pretended his mom was inside making heart-shaped pancakes for breakfast before school in the mornings and singing Blake Shelton songs while Daddy worked in the yard. Now, Mom's face dissolved into that of Miss Ruth. Every time he looked at her name and the number that she'd stored in his phone last night, a rush of warmth flooded his body and he caught himself smiling.

At the side of the driveway, Mr. Cunningham bent at the waist, digging his shovel in the ground and lifting snow off the walkway. Mr. Cunningham was a short, solid guy with dark skin and rounded shoulders whose brow always seemed folded like a paper airplane. Even though he'd shaved his head bald, you could still see the shadow outline of hair on both sides. Sebastian said the Cunninghams were older than most kids' parents, and that's why Mr. Cunningham had gone bald already.

"Think fast." Pancho whipped a football toward Midnight, whose knees plunged into the snow, trying to catch it with his left hand, his other arm practically useless. He missed.

"I wasn't ready, dork." Midnight pawed the snow with his gloved hands, the uneven terrain of the snow working against him, making it tough to find equilibrium. Then he muttered under his breath, not sure if he wanted Pancho to hear him or not, "Plus, the trajectory of the ball was all off."

"You catch like a girl." Pancho must have heard him.

"Yeah, a baby girl, bebita," Sebastian took birdlike steps with his chest poked out. He was half Black, half Puerto Rican, basically a light-skinned Black boy with curly hair until he opened his mouth and the words came fast from the back of his throat, his *r*'s rolling.

Midnight's bum arm made him the butt of jokes sometimes. His whole body burning with humiliation, he said, "Shut up, you spic. Just shut up." He'd heard Daddy call some of the Hispanic guys from the plant that name behind their backs, and he'd sneered when he said it.

Sebastian's eyes narrowed to dark slits. He obviously knew the word. Corey even stiffened but stayed quiet. After hesitating a second, Sebastian said, "Your mama," picking at Midnight's deepest wound. He pointed at Midnight with one hand and held his belly with the other, falling back in the snow, forcing laughter. "Your mama's so stupid she took a spoon to the Super Bowl."

Sebastian's giggles trailed off and everything went quiet.

"Leave him alone," Corey said, scooping the ball, tossing it away from his body, and then getting under it for a smooth catch. Midnight called Corey his best friend, but at times he didn't know for sure how he felt about him. Corey dominated Little League, and Midnight could never even make the team. Whatever it was, that uncertainty circled Midnight's head sometimes like a gnat that wouldn't go away no matter how many times he swatted at it.

"I can take care of myself." Midnight knocked the ball from his hands.

"What's wrong with you? You better quit trippin'." Corey elbowed Midnight's ribs.

Whether he asked for his protection or not, Corey had always given it. Somehow, that made Midnight feel weaker. He knew Corey thought he owed him something after what happened the summer after third grade, when they became friends.

Nobody knew who or what started the fight that day in the open land off Sheldale Road. You could say the fight found them. Usually, you could blame it on the heat, nothing better to do, or maybe a sugar rush from too many Starbursts. But this one felt different from the start.

It was hot and all the boys—too many to count—ran around with no shirts on, the sun blazing on their backs. Mom had died the year before and Daddy had closed himself off, so Midnight spent more time wandering on his own looking for something to get into. Running from his rage. Or maybe running to it.

In the open field just outside Pratt that was soon to be a gravel pit, boys hurled rocks at each other, a stream of pebbles spitting dust clouds in the air. One boy stood out, with a strong arm and determined look. The maroon splotch on his cheek stayed there even when he rubbed it with the back of his hand. Like war paint. He had perfect aim. Recognizing him from school, Midnight knew he was smart and popular and that his name was Corey, but they'd been in different classrooms that school year.

It didn't take long to see that a couple of boys were aiming for Corey. Spotting a jagged rock in a pile of gravel, Midnight squatted to pick it up and hurled it at the boys going after him. Evening things out. Making it a fair fight. He imagined Daddy smiling, proud of him for the first time in a long while. Patting him on the back for being a fighter.

A brief look of shock crossed Corey's face when Midnight began helping him. They fought the enemy side by side. The other boys were bigger and older, their red-hot faces twisted in anger as they lobbed rocks at Corey and Midnight. Midnight laughed every time he and Corey put the right spin on a rock and it hit one of those jerks in the mouth.

"Go back where you came from," a husky boy with a bruised, bloody jaw shouted. His brown hair spiked like blades of grass.

"Make me," Midnight shouted, unsure where he was supposed to go, adrenaline jittering in his veins.

"Nobody was talking to you," the boy said, making it clear his command had been for Corey.

"So?" Midnight said.

"So shut your mouth."

Another kid piped up, pointing at Corey. "Yeah, go back to Africa."

One of the seven continents, Midnight recalled from social studies class, but he didn't know much else about it. Corey was from Indiana, not Africa, so none of it made sense. But the air had a charge to it and nothing needed to make sense.

Other boys crowded around them then, waiting, eager to see if the fight would take a more interesting turn. Soon, the commotion got the attention of the whole neighborhood. Scruffy-faced grown men in wifebeaters showed up swinging baseball bats, vowing to defend their kids. Women waved their arms and screamed. Then, out of nowhere, a gunshot blasted the air. Midnight whipped around to see who'd fired the shot. A tall Black man stood a few feet away, a gun pointing to the sky.

"You leave that kid the hell alone, or I swear—" the man said, a crazed look in his eyes. Everybody scattered like roaches, not waiting for him to finish his sentence or make good on his threat.

Corey stood frozen, looking up at his defender, as scared as anyone. Then a switch must have flipped inside him, because he dropped the rocks he'd been holding and started running.

"This isn't over," one of the older white boys yelled.

Once Midnight caught up to Corey and they'd put a few blocks between them and the open field, he said, "That guy with the gun was kind of nuts, huh? You know him?"

Corey shook his head. "I don't know him."

"Did you see all the blood on that kid's face?" Midnight said.

"Yeah." Corey slung his T-shirt around his neck and looked at the dusty insides of his hands like they weren't his own. "I didn't mean to make him bleed like that. He and those other boys just kept saying stuff and then they started throwing rocks at us. I just hope I don't get in trouble with my mom and dad."

Midnight shrugged. "But it was fun, right?"

"I guess. Well, I need to head home," Corey said, vigorously wiping his hands on his jeans.

Wiggling his toes in his sandals, Midnight felt restless, energized by the fight, not ready for the day to end. "It's not that late."

"I still have to go."

"Okay."

He watched Corey walk down the street and disappear behind a storefront.

Midnight ran home to tell his father about how the fight had gone down and the rocks he'd thrown at the biggest boy out there. He left out the part about the gunshot, in case Daddy used that as a reason to dole out punishment instead of praise.

"You did, huh?" Daddy slouched in his chair, his eyes on the TV.

"Yeah. It was a huge deal. You should've seen everybody there. I found this rock that was sharp on the edges and I threw it as hard as I could. Just at the right angle to hit his face." His words came fast.

Daddy glanced away from the flicker of the TV screen to take in Midnight's mussed hair, the spots of dirt on his face. "How does the other kid look?"

"Bloody. Really bloody. You should've seen it. Blood coming out of his nose and mouth. I think his eyes, too." As he talked, the story grew.

Daddy's lips twitched, as close to a smile as he got these days. "That's my boy. Way to give 'em hell, Patrick."

Midnight's heart grew to three times its normal size, and he thought it might burst.

Now, on the front lawn of Corey's house, just like that summer years ago, they were hopped up on adrenaline, this time with hurt feelings, too, their blood racing. Nobody wanted to be weak or to even be called weak. As if reading each other's minds, Corey and Midnight lunged at Sebastian like synchronized fighters and pounded him with kicks and punches. Not to be left out, Pancho jumped in, throwing blows at anyone in close range. Midnight pulled hoods, stuck his fingers in mouths and up noses, kicking at legs and backs and faces.

"Enough. Cut that out." The booming voice above them belonged to Mr. Cunningham. When he stabbed the snow with his shovel, the boys flew apart like bits of debris after an explosion.

"What the hell's going on here?"

The boys looked down at the snow, at their hands and feet, anywhere but at each other or Mr. Cunningham. When their bodies finally sighed like factory machines at the end of a shift, the only sound was their heavy breathing.

"Sorry, Daddy. We were just fighting over a stupid girl. That's all," Corey lied, not looking at his father.

"Son, girls aren't stupid. Don't let me hear you say that again." Mr. Cunningham's eyes scanned all of them. "And next time, remember that real men settle disputes with their words, not their fists."

By this time Mrs. Cunningham stood on the porch in a brown wool coat wrapped tightly around her with the hem of her white flannel nightgown hanging below it. Everything about her seemed simple, like she'd walked out of the pages of their social studies lesson on the Pilgrims, except she didn't wear the white collars and cuffs or cover her hair with a bonnet. She looked the part of a librarian, which made sense since she worked part-time at the library. She looked as if she wanted to say something but thought better of it.

"It's all right, Verna. They're just being boys." Mr. Cunningham gave them a sharp look that telegraphed, *This better be the end of the fight.*

Soon, the boys huddled side by side on the porch, sipping cocoa with whipped cream floating on top. They were eleven now, too old for sleepovers, but the cream reminded Midnight of one time he stayed over at Corey's house and Mr. Cunningham let them lather their faces in shaving cream while he taught them the proper way to shave.

Just as he always did, he asked each of the boys, "Are you saving your allowance money?"

Midnight nodded and said yes like always, not wanting him to know he didn't get an allowance anymore now that Daddy wasn't working. Mr. Cunningham patted his head and said he was glad to hear it, that he was proud of him for developing a savings habit early.

He had a fancy title, vice president or something like that, approving loans at the Heritage Bank, so he appeared in pictures in the *Ganton Beacon*, cutting ribbons and presenting big checks to people.

Somewhere far off a car moaned trying to push its way through the ice. The tree limbs shook, skinny and naked, trembling under the wind. When the Cunninghams went back in the house, Corey grabbed a handful of snow and packed it between his hands.

"I want it to always be winter with snow every day," Corey said.

"How come?" Pancho said.

"I don't know. It's fun to play in," Corey said.

"It never snows down south in Loos-i-ana, though," Sebastian said, glancing at Midnight, stirring waters that were just beginning to settle after the storm.

"Why are you looking at me?" Midnight said.

"I don't know. I heard stuff."

"Like what?"

A neighbor's snowblower sputtered in the distance.

Pancho snapped his head back and forth between the boys as if he were watching a prizefight.

"You're always starting something. Geez." Corey pulled his arm back and threw his snowball, watching it land with a thick thud in the hedges.

"Well, my mom said Midnight's moving to Louisiana." Sebastian put his mug of cocoa to his lips and blew into it hard enough for bubbles to overflow the rim, like a small volcano erupting.

A raw feeling tugged at Midnight's gut, a scab ripped off a sore that hadn't even started to heal. Granny hadn't said where he might have to move. Or he just hadn't been able to hear over little Nicky's cries.

"Your mom's lying then." Midnight wanted to scream or maybe disappear into the mounds of snow.

Sebastian spoke softly, muttering under his breath. "Well, if my mom's lying, then your grandmother must have been lying, too. She told my mom at the post office."

Louisiana. Hearing Sebastian talk about Granny's plan made it real, and it turned his stomach. With a stick, Midnight made lines in the snow, saying nothing. What could he say? Leland Ford moved to Indiana from Louisiana in the middle of fourth grade. He talked funny and told stories about his daddy teaching him how to kill things there—deer, ducks, and wild alligators—anything that moved. But that wasn't the bad part. Daddy had taken Midnight hunting before and that didn't scare him. The stories Leland told, though, were about all the things down there that hunted *you*, like deadly spiders and rattlesnakes.

In social studies class, they called Louisiana part of the Bible Belt, maybe because people there read the Bible a lot even on days other than Sunday. Granny kept a Bible on her nightstand, but he rarely saw her open it. She kept it next to her whiskey, or cough syrup as she called it. The few times he tried to read it, he got stuck when people with weird names begot other people with even weirder names.

THE FRONT DOOR TO COREY'S HOUSE OPENED AND MRS. CUNNINGham beckoned them inside for lunch. Following behind Sebastian, Midnight kicked a dusting of snow onto the boy's jeans as they marched up the porch steps. This house reminded him of ones he'd seen on TV. It always smelled good, too, like whatever Mrs. Cunningham was cooking. This time, she served beef stew. The boys ate quickly, and she refilled their bowls with extra helpings of carrots and potatoes. While everyone looked at Mr. Cunningham as he told another corny joke, Midnight buried his face in the bowl and licked it.

A few times, for no reason at all, Mrs. Cunningham gave Corey sloppy kisses on his cheek and he giggled, then scrunched up his face and wiped it off with the back of his hand.

"Stop, Mom," Corey said.

Sometimes his friend didn't get how lucky he was to still have a mother who embarrassed him. After lunch, the boys played in the snow until the sun scooted behind the clouds and a red line of dusk streaked the sky. Sebastian and Pancho headed home before the streetlights came on so they wouldn't get in trouble, and the Cunninghams called Corey in to do some reading before supper. It didn't matter what time Midnight got home. The pills Granny took made her fall asleep too early to notice much, and Auntie Glo was probably deep in a pot haze by now.

Walking along the railroad tracks back to Pratt, Midnight turned his face up to the dimming sky, opening his mouth to catch the snowflakes. He cursed each streetlight that popped on. Maybe if he slowed down, they would, too.

Fifteen

RUTH

Municipal buildings often smelled of old paper and bad plumbing. The county clerk's office emanated the same musk, Ruth discovered the minute she walked in. Signs and arrows in this building pointed to where a couple could apply for a marriage license and file for divorce. Happy, hopeful beginnings and sad, bitter endings right there, side by side.

She and Xavier had been so excited to receive their license to marry. Tess's and Penelope's signatures appeared as witnesses, even though they themselves couldn't marry in the eyes of the law or even God, as some believed. While she and Xavier remained at an impasse regarding her son, she put her faith in that license, proof of their legal obligation to each other as husband and wife. A contract he couldn't easily break.

The morning she'd left Xavier to come to Ganton, he zapped a frozen waffle in the microwave and she ate a premade yogurt parfait from the supermarket. Each of them chose quick, easy breakfasts. Somehow, the silence that day cut deeper than angry words. Her eyes burned with tears thinking that the institution of marriage might have meant more to her than to him. In the three days she'd been away, they hadn't spoken or texted.

The weatherman on the radio had warned about the temperature dropping just below freezing, but it felt like a sauna in this building. Ruth unwound her wool scarf from around her neck and fanned herself with a flyer she picked up on county ordinances.

Under her coat she wore a conservative navy pantsuit, remembering that Xavier always chose the color blue for ad campaigns when he needed to convey trust and stability. Even though she had just come for information about her son and his adoptive parents, some part of her felt the need to prove to the government that she could be entrusted with the care of a child.

As she surveyed the room for the right clerk window, she sensed someone watching her. A thumping buzzed in her chest like an alarm. She pulled her twists to her cheeks to obscure her face. She felt a light tap on her arm and, letting her hair fall from her fingertips, she slowly turned around.

A woman with piercing green eyes and wiry brown hair stared back at her. She jerked the safety harness strapped to a little girl's chest. The contraption reminded Ruth of a dog leash and she swore she'd never use one with her own child. A chunky girl in a Colts jacket who had to be no older than fourteen stood with the woman and little girl, but slightly off to the side, as if she didn't want to acknowledge the association.

"Homeroom," the woman said, snapping her fingers.

"What did you say?" Ruth asked.

"Homeroom. We were in the same homeroom class freshman year. I'm Kaylee. Remember me?" The woman grinned as if she'd achieved a personal victory, having solved the puzzle of how they knew each other. Her leathery, weather-worn skin resembled that of a woman twice Ruth's age. The old cliché about aging that Black don't crack proved true once again.

Putting this woman in a time machine and imagining her much younger, Ruth had a vague memory of Kaylee playing in the marching band. "Yes, I remember now."

Ruth also recalled that Kaylee was one of several girls who had gotten pregnant freshman year. This wasn't an unusual phenomenon at Pratt High, the public school where Ruth ended up going. By this time, Papa was long gone and so was the money to continue her private school education.

Kaylee raked one hand through her hair, absently pulling at a tangle. "Haven't seen you around here since high school. You must've moved away. I would've loved to get out of here, maybe go to Ohio where my dad's side of the family lives, but then my high school boyfriend and I had a kid sophomore year, so you know . . . You remember Bobby Chesniak from school, right?"

The name sounded familiar but Ruth couldn't place him. She nodded anyway.

"Anyhow, this is Olivia." The teenager's face contorted in disdain and she rolled her eyes heavenward, obviously wishing she could be anywhere other than here in the clerk's office with her mother and baby sister.

"And this here is Mandy. She's in her terrible twos now and gets into everything if I'm not watching." Kaylee gestured to the leash as if to justify its use. Mandy was sucking on a lollipop that had turned her lips bright orange.

Ruth had stopped about three feet from the adoption records window but didn't want to move any closer until Kaylee walked away. "Well, looks like you have a beautiful family. Good seeing you again."

Kaylee put one hand under her chin like she was thinking. "Your little one's probably not all that much younger than Olivia, huh?"

Dread grabbed Ruth by the throat and almost strangled her. "I don't know what you mean."

"I know a lot of girls had babies in high school. For some reason, I just thought you had, too. I didn't mean anything bad by it."

Ruth shut down her speculation. "No, you must have me confused with someone else."

Even saying those words sent Ruth into a spiral of guilt as she once again denied her son's existence. In obscure moments like these, Mama's Sunday school lessons came to mind, and Ruth thought of Peter, who denied Jesus before the rooster crowed three times. She had told this lie many times before, but always to people who just casually asked if she had children. But this was different. Kaylee had known her back in the day, and Ruth couldn't be sure whether she was fishing for confirmation of something she believed to be true.

Kaylee looked confused but not uncomfortable enough to stop talking. "Sorry, guess I was wrong. Good you didn't get mixed up with anybody from high school. I'm married to a great guy now, someone from a couple towns over. Bobby walked out on us, the bastard. That's why I'm out here in this cold trying to collect child support from his sorry ass. You can't just make babies and then walk away from your responsibility. That's not right. You know what I mean?" Kaylee waited for affirmation.

Pain seized Ruth's heart and her knees buckled under Kaylee's proclamation. She couldn't meet her eyes. This woman she barely knew had exposed Ruth's own abject failure as a mother. *Responsibility*. Whether it was walking away from her child or staying silent while her grandmother walked away with him, it all added up to Ruth shirking her duty as a mother. She was no better than Olivia's deadbeat dad.

Mama had predicted Natasha would be the one to get pregnant in high school. *Mark my words. She'll be next.* But it was Ruth who got caught, not her best friend. Looking at Kaylee now, stuck in this town with a kid by a man who had walked out on them, she saw clearly for the first time the life Mama had been trying to save her from.

Inching away from her old classmate, Ruth said, "Yeah, you're doing the right thing making him pay. Good luck. Nice seeing you again."

When Kaylee and her daughters left the building, Ruth considered following behind them. Maybe coming here had been a bad idea. Local government operated like a massive machine, churning out reams of paper with little humanity involved. It seemed too officious and dulled by routine to bend to her pleading for information. Still, she had to try.

On her drive to the center of town, she had practiced what she'd say to whatever paper-pushing bureaucrat she encountered, as well as how she'd say it.

I'm here to obtain copies of adoption records for my files, please. Deferential, yet firm and confident. While she continued to rehearse in her head, a woman's voice emerged, so high and tinny it sounded as if it might break, like a thin thread pulled too tightly. "Next. May I help you?"

The clerk behind the partition had loose reddish curls framing her round face. Some would call her attractive, in that matronly way that comes with the natural rounding of age.

By now three more customers had lined up behind Ruth. She ran her fingers along the braided leather strap of her purse. "Yes, please. I'm trying to find my son."

That's not what she'd practiced saying, but now that she'd said it, the woman on the other side of the Plexiglas window almost let her perfunctory smile slip. "Your son? This isn't the police station and we don't take missing-person reports here. What is it you need, ma'am?"

That extra title of respect rarely used on a woman Ruth's age only meant that the clerk had grown impatient. On the woman's desk was a framed picture of a little girl with bangs and two long red braids. Her granddaughter, perhaps. Ruth thought of asking about the child as a way to build rapport with this woman, but she could tell it would be futile.

Ruth leaned closer to the opening in the window and whispered, "My baby was given up for adoption in 1997. And now I need a copy of the adoption records."

The woman sighed. "All adoption records in the state of Indiana are confidential."

Ruth swallowed the panic rising in her throat. "There has to be some way to find and contact my son."

The woman shoved a piece of paper at Ruth through the partition. "Here. This is the Adoption Matching Registry Consent Form. Fill this out front and back and mail it to the Indiana State Department of Health. The address is on the bottom of the form."

She had obviously repeated the steps to this process a thousand times. Glancing at the form, Ruth scanned the list of requirements:

FULL NAME OF THE ADOPTEE'S FATHER
ADOPTEE'S NAME AFTER ADOPTION
FULL NAME OF ADOPTIVE PARENT 1
FULL NAME OF ADOPTIVE PARENT 2

There was no way Ruth could fill this out, since Ronald had no idea that she'd ever been pregnant with his child. But she couldn't admit that to this clerk. She could predict the assumptions this woman would make: *There goes another Black girl having babies out of wedlock.*

Regret poked at Ruth. Even if Ronald hadn't wanted a relationship with her, he had a right to know he'd fathered a child. Maybe she'd been selfish in withholding this information from him. What if he had stepped up and assumed his responsibility as a father? She sighed. Too many years had passed and she couldn't undo the decision she'd made.

Ignoring the hard foot-tapping of the man in line behind her, Ruth squeezed the paper and waved it in front of the sliding glass window that the clerk had now shut a few more inches.

"I don't know my son's name or the names of the people who adopted him. I can't complete this form because I just don't know."

Without looking up from the papers on her desk, the clerk returned to her memorized script. "This is the form. The adoptive parents would have to also be signed up with the registry for you to be matched and for you to contact each other. If the adoptive parents haven't signed the child up for the registry, you can't get any information. And don't expect to hear anything from the state anytime soon. They're real backed up over there. It could take more than twenty weeks to process your request."

Twenty weeks. She couldn't wait five months. Her spirit flagged like the sputtering motor of an old beater car. Glancing over her shoulder at the people in line behind her, Ruth wondered if their quests were as impossible as her own. The clerk scribbled notes and stamped documents. Ruth didn't move, silently begging the clerk to have mercy on her and help her figure out what to do next.

Finally, the woman looked up and smiled too hard, showing too many teeth. "That's the form. Fill it out as best you can. Next!"

When Ruth backed away, she bumped into the man behind her in line. Her eyes lingered on the registry consent form. She wanted to spit on this official piece of paper and its absurd requirements. Government had so many gatekeepers to keep you from the truth. To keep her from her son.

INSIDE THE COCOON OF HER CAR, WITH THE WINDOWS ROLLED UP, Ruth let out a primal scream, releasing some of the tightly coiled tension inside her. When she powered her phone up again, it beeped. Maybe Xavier had texted or left her a voicemail message. She wished he were there to hold her hand, massage her shoulders, and whisper reassurances in her ear.

The missed call had been from Tess, though, not Xavier. She dialed her friend's number and she answered on the first ring. Tess sounded almost breathless, as if she'd bounded across the room to pick up her cell.

"It's about time you called me back. Okay, girl. I got the hookup on tickets to one of the Obama inauguration parties in D.C. But we need to order now. Are you in? Please say yes."

The fervor over Obama's election seemed so long ago. As proud and hopeful as she was, Ruth had already crashed after the high of that night. All she could think about now was her baby, finding him and then . . . She didn't know what then.

"Ruth? Are you there? Did you hear me? Hellooo?"

"Yeah, I'm here, back home in Ganton."

After a brief pause, Tess stammered, "Oh. Okay. What's going on? Are things all right?"

Ruth felt an overwhelming need to unburden herself and tell

someone the truth for once. And who better than Tess, who had kept her own secrets, having waited until after graduating from law school and joining a top firm to come out to her family. By then, she was self-sufficient and could handle their rebuff financially, if not emotionally.

"I've been keeping something from you, from everyone. I only just told Xavier a few weeks ago." Ruth exhaled loudly. "The summer after my senior year in high school I had a baby and I left him behind. I have no idea what happened to him. I'm back home now to find him."

Tess let out a low whistle. "Okay, wow. Okay, what do you need? You know Penelope and I have your back. How can we help?"

There was no judgment in her friend's voice. None. Ruth's throat tightened, a bottleneck of tears trapped there. Tess understood.

"I just need to find him. I need to make things right." She paused. "And I need to make things right with Xavier. He's upset that I didn't tell him the truth a long time ago."

She waited for Tess's reaction and possibly any indication of Xavier's mood lately.

"He'll be all right. Give him time. He loves you," Tess said.

"Yeah, I know he does," Ruth said, not fully convinced of that anymore.

"How can I help?" Tess said.

"I never signed any papers, and Mama and Eli are not talking. They won't share the adoption papers or give me any names. I'm sitting outside the county clerk's office and they gave me this form to fill out and it's asking *me* all the questions I need answers to." Everything came out in a rush of breath. Ruth pulled at her twists.

Immediately, Tess went into attorney mode. Her job primarily involved going after companies for monopoly leverage and price fixing. Adoption law was not her specialty, but she was a lawyer and, more important, a good friend. "What year was it that you had the baby?"

"1997. In August."

Ruth heard Tess typing furiously on her laptop. After a minute,

Tess said, "Okay, 1997 is the year the Indiana Putative Father Registry law went into effect."

"Did you say *punitive*, like punishment?"

"No, *p–u–t* . . . *putative*. From what I'm seeing here, from 1997 on, any unmarried father has the right to register that he may have a child out there born around a certain time. If he registered and the lawyer didn't give him a chance to weigh in at the time the adoption took place, the whole adoption could be upended."

Once again, Ruth felt guilty for withholding information from Ronald. She cranked up the heat and blew into her hands to warm them. Rationalizing her decisions made the most sense right now.

"Mama was so careful to be sure no one knew I was pregnant. And even if Ronald suspected something, he wouldn't have wanted anything to do with me or the baby." She watched melting snowflakes slide like tears down her car windows, reliving their breakup, feeling foolish all over again.

But then she remembered Kaylee and how she alluded to Ruth's having been pregnant in high school. Mama used to say, *Nobody in this town can hold water*. Did Ronald know they shared a child? She hadn't told him, but maybe someone else had.

"Okay, so you didn't sign any papers," Tess said. "You say your high school boyfriend didn't make a play for the kid. If he didn't, that leaves your grandmother, who was your legal guardian. However, it doesn't sound like she had guardianship of your baby. And even if she did, parental rights supersede those of the guardian. This was still your decision to make about what to do with your child."

The cold of the afternoon, or maybe a sense of dread, crawled under Ruth's skin. It coursed through her as she listened to her friend confirm her suspicions. Something wasn't right. And she knew it. Then Tess offered another unthinkable possibility.

"You know how we do, especially the old heads. In a small town. Or down South? They'll give the baby to family or a neighbor to raise and it's all hush-hush. You just never know."

Dropping her cell phone on the car seat, Ruth just barely heard her friend's voice. Had Mama handed her baby off with no paperwork? If so, without a legal document, Ruth could still claim her son. Not that she was sure that's what she wanted. She didn't know what she wanted. But if, just if, she chose to be a mother to her baby, there was a good chance she still had rights to her child.

Sixteen

RUTH

The next morning, Mama's house creaked like old people's bones, a bit rusty and resettling with the fluctuations in temperature. As much as Ruth wanted to confront Mama and demand answers, it was best not to tip her hand and let Mama know her suspicions. Somehow, she needed to find proof that the handover of her son had been off the books.

When Ruth walked down the dim hallway toward the kitchen, she heard a scraping sound. Sunlight streamed through the narrow kitchen window and illuminated Mama kneeling on the linoleum, grating a bar of soap like a block of cheese, her fingers knotted from arthritis. Her lips pressed together and the veins in her forearms bulged with each scrape. That fresh, clean smell reminded Ruth of her cotton church dress flapping in the summer breeze on the clothesline next to Papa's work shirts.

Mama poured washing soda and borax into the five-gallon bucket of cloudy white water.

Standing in the doorway to the kitchen, Ruth cleared her throat.

Without looking up from her work on the floor, Mama said, "Morning, Ruth."

"You know I can get you a deal on detergent through work. You don't have to do this."

"No need," Mama said, breathing heavily as she continued her soap-making.

Strangely, it made sense. The woman who had forced Ruth to give birth at home in a little room of shame like some scene out of the 1950s didn't believe in store-bought laundry detergent.

Ruth thought of the stories parents told their kids about scrappy childhoods, walking five miles to school in the snow wearing shoes with holes in the bottoms. Skepticism kept Ruth from fully buying into that as a kid, especially when more than one grown-up had the same hard-luck tale. And today, no one besides hipsters and home-schoolers would believe her if she told them her grandmother made her own laundry soap in the twenty-first century.

"I work on these formulas. You only need to use a little bit of detergent. You could save yourself some money and not have to do it by hand."

Mama stirred with more vigor, her breaths coming faster with each rotation of the giant wooden spoon. She stopped to wipe her forehead with the back of her hand. Then she smiled up at Ruth.

"Oh, listen to my chemical engineer talking. I love it, but don't forget I was washing clothes before you were born, Miss Thing. I don't need you schooling me on it now. And before I forget, look what I left for you on the kitchen counter."

Beside a scrub sponge and a water glass sat a roll of toilet paper. Ruth asked, "Why is the toilet paper in the kitchen?"

"Because somebody doesn't know how to hang it on the roll right. I got up and went to the bathroom this morning and like to have a fit. You know it goes over, not under. Didn't we teach you that?"

Ruth wanted to laugh, but she didn't dare do it with Mama's scolding eyes boring into her like she was nine instead of twenty-nine. When they first married, Xavier hung the toilet paper the wrong way and Ruth didn't want to fuss over little things. Instead of nagging over something so minor, she joined him by going rogue with the toilet paper rolls.

"You tell her, Mama." Eli walked into the kitchen wearing a blue-and-white pin-striped suit. He tugged at the tie choking his neck.

No one said a word. Too shocked to craft a smart comeback, her mouth opened in amazement. Her big brother had worn a suit to her wedding. Yet he hadn't even worn one for his own nuptials, having skipped the ceremony and taken Cassie to the justice of the peace instead. The only other time she'd seen him in a getup like this had been Papa's funeral.

"What? Y'all never seen a brother looking clean before? You need to get out more."

"Very nice. I'm impressed. Where are you headed?" Ruth said.

"Sam's Club. They're hiring for an inventory clerk. See how I'm matching the store colors? Look and learn, people."

Mama put her hands to her face. "You got an interview. Praise the Lord."

"I got to go or I'll be late." Eli brushed his lips across both of their cheeks before heading to the door. But before he left, he tossed a set of keys on the kitchen counter.

"Why did you have my keys?" Ruth said, confused.

"You didn't see your engine light on?" Eli shook his head, disappointed.

That warning indicator had come on the night she drove Midnight home, but she'd been too preoccupied to do anything about it. "I guess I need to take the car into the shop for service."

"I already got you, lil bit. Your spark plug's bad. I put in a new one. The car's probably been starting slow and running rough, right?" When she nodded, he said, "Oh, it's gon' purr like a kitten now."

Without looking up from her bucket, Mama said, "That was mighty nice of you, son."

"Yes," Ruth said. "Yes, it was. Thank you, Eli." Affection for her big brother squeezed her chest. As much as he and Mama exerted control over her life, they loved her fiercely. Before he walked out, she said, "Hey, Eli."

"Yeah?"

"Good luck today. You got this."

He winked. "They don't even know."

When they heard Eli pull out of the driveway onto the street, Mama turned to Ruth. "This is the best news we've had in a long time. Have you been watching your brother's eyes? He had locked himself away in there and nobody could free him. The old Fernwood plant gave five hundred of them their walking papers. It's been six months and I prayed he'd come out of that funk he was in, but he hasn't been the same man since."

No one had needed to tell Eli he'd work at the plant someday. Everyone simply knew it, with the certainty of new mornings dawning and darkness eclipsing the day. The Monday after his eighteenth birthday, Eli reported for his first shift at Fernwood, making batteries on the assembly line. In the nineties, life was good, and even in Ganton, people had a little change jingling in their pockets.

Practically every day for five years while she still lived at home, her big brother reported for duty, sometimes flaunting a particularly generous paycheck after a grueling week of overtime work or a cost-of-living increase. Most of his money went for parts for his own car and the thirsty women who inevitably liked to sweat brothers with good jobs.

"I can't help it if the ladies love Eli," he'd say, smiling smugly.

However, over time, the U.S. economy soured and so did Eli's idealism about the work that had sustained the Tuttles for generations. Racism on the plant floor, poor work ethic for some, and just time itself dulled the luster of Ganton's crown jewel. Eli had put in seventeen good years, almost half his life at this place.

Now, with Fernwood closed for good, it seemed as if the town's beating heart had stopped. Ruth had been reading up on it. Not only were people not buying as many cars in a recession, but fuel prices had risen, and the American automakers couldn't keep up with the new demand for fuel-efficient models. Car buyers were turning to Japan and Europe for fuel-efficient imports.

But understanding what had happened didn't make it any easier seeing her brother suffer. She could tell it was taking a toll on Mama, too.

"One drink at Wally's turned into two and three and . . ." Mama's voice trailed off and she shook her head, as if she could shake off whatever demons had taken hold of Eli.

"That's rough, but he has a wife and three kids to support. I didn't want to ask in front of Eli, but where are Cassie and the children?" Ruth said.

Mama dried her hands on the skirt of her apron and pulled a framed photo of Eli and his family from the buffet table. "He's still married to her on paper. But she found out that while she was working every day, he was hanging over a bar stool talking nonsense. So, she told him to get himself together or get out. I thought she could've given him more time. But these women today have no mercy on a man trying to make it out here. Now she's cut back on how often he gets to see his kids. I know that's been killing him."

"Marriage is supposed to be for better or for worse," Ruth said absently.

"Are we talking about your brother or you? What's the real reason Xavier didn't come with you?" The intensity of Mama's gaze forced her to meet her grandmother's eyes.

As convincingly as she could, Ruth said, "Everything's fine between Xavier and me. Really. He's juggling a lot of major work assignments right now. It's stressful, but he's on the executive track and I'm proud of him."

"Well, he's one of the lucky ones." Ruth heard the pain in Mama's voice when she thought about Eli. The helplessness. "It's hard out there trying to find work with a record, you know."

"But that drug offense was minor, and besides, it was a long time ago. I have a couple lawyer friends in Chicago. I can talk to them about how we can get that expunged from his record."

"It's not that simple," Mama said, wiping imaginary dust off a framed photo of Eli.

One of the darkest times of their lives had been when Eli did time for misdemeanor drug possession. It was the nineties back then, when the war on drugs should have been renamed the war on Black men. There seemed to be a bounty on the head of every brother. It made no sense that Eli was there, even if only for a few weeks, in the same place with murderers awaiting trial. Side by side with guys who had put bullets through people's heads. They'd expected Eli to serve a much longer sentence—two years—and Mama had moaned day and night that her grandbaby couldn't live in a cage another day. *Get back, devil, get back. Only you, God, can break the shackles and set him free.* Through some miracle and maybe Mama's petitions to the Lord, Eli got out fast, but Ruth always wondered what scars lingered inside her brother, invisible ones he never talked about.

Mama never took her eyes off Eli's photo. "He was back in jail just a few years ago."

Her words shot straight through Ruth's chest. "What are you talking about?"

"Don't you dare bring this up to your brother. He should never have brought out that gun, even if he was just trying to keep the peace."

"Gun?" Ruth shouted, finding it impossible to believe Eli would get himself involved with guns.

"Nobody got hurt. It's over now and I don't want to talk about it." To emphasize her point, Mama got up, put on her coat, and left the house, claiming she had errands to run.

Mama never said it, but Ruth knew she'd wrestled with her own regret over Eli's not having a man to look up to after Papa died. She tried and failed to be mother and father to him and overcompensated for that failure.

So many times, Ruth had wanted to scream, *What about me?* She knew Mama loved her. Deeply. But as much as folks refused to admit it, mothers loved their children differently. Even before Papa died, Mama made a distinction between her grandchildren.

When Eli threw a football through the living room window as a kid, Mama laughed at the shattered glass and seemed almost triumphant, as if some milestone of raising a boy had been reached. A few years into Papa's ALS, he asked Ruth if he could just that once pour his own milk over his bowl of Raisin Bran. He was too weak, trembling too much, to hold the carton steady. It was hard to believe this was the same man who had taught her and Eli how to hold and fire a gun during hunting season. But Ruth hadn't wanted to deny her grandfather that sense of control. She handed him the carton and he dropped it, spilling milk all over the kitchen floor. *Look what you've done*, Mama yelled at Ruth, accusing her of using poor judgment. Those memories stayed with Ruth, and yet reflecting on these slights years later seemed small and petty. There was no fairness scale that could right the wrongs from childhood.

SHORTLY AFTER MAMA LEFT THE HOUSE, THE DOORBELL RANG. When Ruth opened the door, she found Pastor Walter Bumpus standing in the doorway. He was wearing a long black overcoat, dress slacks, and a wide-brimmed hat he lifted from his head in a show of greeting. As a short man who wore everything oversized, he often looked like a child playing dress-up in his father's clothing. A blast of cold air rushed in behind him.

The pastor's face betrayed him, a brief look of shock flashing there at the sight of her. He hid it quickly, though, with a toothy grin that exposed his blue-black gums.

"Ruth Marie Tuttle. It's been a long time." No one called her by her whole name, except for Mama, and it usually meant she'd done something to earn some reprimand as a kid. In spite of his small stature, the senior pastor of Friendship Baptist Church consumed every room with his rich baritone, which could fill a stadium with no amplification necessary.

"Good morning, Pastor. It's good seeing you again."

After removing his gloves, he took both of her hands in his, and they were cool, yet soft as a flower petal. "I haven't laid eyes on you since the day I married you and Xavier. In the Bible, even the prodigal son came home to a forgiving father and a huge feast."

Ruth bowed her head, shamed. She knew preachers were just

men and women, mere flesh and blood, with no greater connection to God than anyone else. But if the Lord had called this man to ministry, maybe He had anointed him with divine understanding. As a little girl, he had submerged her cloaked body in the baptismal pool, and she couldn't count the many times he had come to their table for Sunday dinners.

Sliding her hands from his, she wondered what he could see beneath the shield of her skin. Did he already know her teenage sin?

They walked to the living room and he sat on the sofa, patting the empty spot next to him. She chose the love seat opposite him, irrationally worried that he could see her sin and it would reveal itself more in the morning light streaming through the window.

"Mama's out for a bit, but I'm sure she'll be back soon," Ruth said, glancing at her watch.

Pastor Bumpus stretched one arm across the back of the couch and crossed his legs. He was obviously in no hurry. "Never mind that. You know we take care of the widows at Friendship, so I just stopped by to say hello to Ernestine like I always do. It's a pleasant surprise to see you here. I am glad you made it home for Christmas and that we get to talk." After a beat, his lips curled into a small smile. "My, my, my. You look more and more like Joanna every day. Beautiful."

At the mention of her mother's name, Ruth cringed. They shared genetic material—DNA floating in their blood—but she wanted the similarities to end there. "With all due respect, Pastor, you're wrong. We're actually nothing alike."

He leaned forward and perched on the edge of the sofa, his hands extended outward, palms up. "Are you a praying woman, Ruth?"

Slowly, she said, "I guess so. I talk to God sometimes."

That answer sounded inadequate. No one had ever asked her that before. Ruth lived a dual identity, raised up on religion but schooled in science. Experts drew a solid line between the two, their differences irreconcilable. She wasn't sure what to believe. Still, she had prayed her entire life. She prayed for prom dates and promotions. She prayed for Papa to live. She prayed for green lights at intersections when she was running late. She prayed for the Bulls to make three-pointers in the final seconds on the shot clock. She prayed for lemon Bundt cakes to rise. She prayed for the pregnancy test she took at seventeen to be negative, negotiating with God that she wouldn't be a repeat offender if He let her off one more time.

Sometimes she prayed for her son, that he was okay, that she hadn't irreversibly damaged his future when she walked away like Joanna had when she left Ruth and Eli behind. God considered each petition on its merits, she figured, and sometimes ruled in her favor. Sometimes not.

She felt Pastor Bumpus's eyes on her. He said, "We all fall short of the glory of God. Joanna did. I do. You, too. We all do. That's why we have to pray for God to turn every wicked thing into something good. You think of Joanna leaving you and your brother behind as abandonment. Maybe it was. But God knew better. Her leaving allowed you to have a chance at a better life being raised by Hezekiah and Ernestine. Look at you now. An esteemed Yale graduate."

His voice rang triumphant. Why was he even going there when she hadn't mentioned her abandonment issues? Had Mama told him how resentful she'd been about Joanna's disappearing act? Pastor Bumpus leaned back again as if to get a better view of her, admiring God's handiwork.

On Sunday mornings when she was a girl, he would invite her and other star students to the pulpit for special recognition, reading to the congregation from their report cards, listing all their good grades and reciting teachers' praise. The first time, it had embarrassed her, but then it became a motivator to earn nothing less than A's in every subject.

Then the acceptance letter from Yale arrived, offering her a full scholarship. The church hosted a celebratory luncheon after service to honor her as well as a boy cellist in the congregation who got to play a concert with the Chicago Symphony Orchestra. How would Pastor Bumpus look at her now if he knew her secret?

She couldn't tell him her story, but she also couldn't stand the way he'd elevated her undeservedly. "You don't know my whole story. I've made mistakes. Big mistakes. There are things I can't undo. I needed my mother."

Her voice cracked around the edges. She thought of her Catholic friends at Yale who sat in little booths behind a curtain, confessing their sins to a priest, liberated by the anonymity of it all. But she couldn't tell Pastor Bumpus everything. She wanted to say that if she'd been raised by her mother, maybe she wouldn't have turned to Ronald for love. Maybe she wouldn't have gotten pregnant.

Pastor Bumpus closed his eyes and lifted his hands above his head, reaching heavenward. "Listen to me carefully now. You thought you needed a mother. But the Bible says in Philippians, 'My God shall supply all your needs according to His riches in glory in Christ Jesus.' The word of God is as real today as it was yesterday."

The cadence of his voice rose and fell in a rhythm, and Ruth felt a sermon coming on. And as much as she had revered him since childhood, she remembered he had limitations, too, just like everybody else.

That time she came home from college for a brief visit, the church was in an uproar over his alleged mishandling of congregants' tithes and offerings. Word in the pews had it that Pastor Bumpus had taken tens of thousands of dollars in donations earmarked for the church mortgage and used it as seed money to fund a children's recreation center. Apparently, he hadn't come clean with the members and some questioned his financial stewardship. *We have to keep our children busy and off these streets,* he'd said in his own defense. It was a worthy cause, and many in the church refused to condemn the pastor's good work, while others blasted his dishonesty and dubious methods. She didn't know which side to come down on and chose to stay neutral.

When he opened his eyes at the end of his prayer, Ruth was standing above him with his coat over her arm.

"It was wonderful seeing you again, Pastor. I'll tell Mama you stopped by."

She meant no disrespect, but she couldn't pray away this problem. Not now. Not yet.

"I'm always here for you and your family. Remember that," he said, rising and taking his coat. She walked him to the door.

With Pastor gone, Ruth sat alone with thoughts of Joanna. As a little girl, she would close her eyes as tight as she could and try to remember her mother—her eyes watching, her hands holding, her mouth kissing her. Now, as an adult, she grasped for bits of information and images floating past in the dust storm of memory. But that picture in her mind remained out of reach. Her mother had disappeared just after Ruth's third birthday. She had missed so much. Ruth making honor roll every year. The science fair trophies in fifth and sixth grades. Perfect report cards all through junior high. Her induction into the National Honor Society. The birth of Joanna's first grandchild.

Sometimes when Ruth tried to picture the woman raising her son, she pictured someone like Joanna: unrefined, irresponsible, and even uncouth. Thinking of her child's mother as a villain made it easier to dislike this woman she'd never met, to dismiss her the way she had her biological mother. At the same time, this logic made her feel guilty for delighting in the idea of someone bad raising her son.

So much in Ruth's life had been defined by Joanna—her presence and her absence. Ruth had made a vow to never become the girl the world expected her to be, the one who slept around and got pregnant by a guy who walked away. Yet that's exactly who she had become. Her mother's daughter. Her greatest motivation to excel in school and become successful had been the driving desire to reverse that fate.

Seventeen

MIDNIGHT

Midnight buttoned his white dress shirt and smoothed the creases of his black funeral pants, the ones Granny kept on a wooden roller hanger. She didn't allow shoes in the house and the socks he'd worn all day stunk like his boots. In the clothes dryer, all he found were mismatched socks, those that survived the sucking vacuum of the air vents. So, he took off the ones he'd been wearing, cranked the window open, and draped his socks over the sill to air out. When he sniffed them a few minutes later and deemed them acceptable, he tucked the ends of the socks under his toes to cover the holes.

The Tuttles were coming over for spaghetti dinner that night. They hardly ever had company, and surely nobody as special as Miss Ruth. A smile snuck up on him and he didn't know where it came from. Only that he wanted dinnertime to hurry up.

Midnight stood beside Granny, who leaned over a steaming pot of marinara sauce, stirring, licking the spoon, and stirring again. When she finally noticed him in his dress clothes setting the table, her mouth opened and then she shut it, saying nothing. Every night since he'd found out he might be shipped off to Louisiana, he set the table for dinner. Forks on the left, knives and spoons on the right. If he arranged the place settings properly and filled the glasses with ice, maybe Granny would notice how useful he was, helpful even, and change her mind about sending him away.

The first thing Auntie Glo did when she came in the kitchen was laugh at Midnight and say, "Who died? You look ridiculous." Even her insults couldn't dampen his mood, and he smiled back at her, for once not having to fake it.

"Leave him alone," Granny said.

As soon as Midnight heard a car pull into the driveway, he flung open the front door. Mrs. Tuttle came in first, her large body bent forward, her heavy breasts swinging when she walked, like the trunk of an elephant, and he worried she might topple over. She held on to her son Mr. Eli's arm for support. Miss Ruth came in last, and Midnight actually smelled her perfume before he saw her. He banged his good arm on the kitchen counter trying to move away from the door, pretending he hadn't been staring.

At the dinner table, he sat next to Miss Ruth, and when they said grace, her long fingers squeezed his, the way Mom's used to when he got his shots at the doctor's office before school started. Not since Mom died had he felt such comfort, reassurance that he'd be okay. After the blessing, he felt Mr. Eli's eyes on him, something unspoken passing between them whenever they saw each other.

"What did you ask Santa to give you for Christmas?" Ruth said, spooning green peas onto her plate.

He hadn't believed in Santa Claus for years and neither had his friends. He figured Miss Ruth didn't have kids of her own and didn't know too many. But he couldn't disappoint her. "I asked Santa not to send me to Louisiana."

"Patrick!" Granny's face got tight and she pressed her lips together.

It was Mrs. Tuttle who spoke next. "Now, what do you know about Louisiana, young man? I bet you've never been," she said.

"Mama, leave him alone. Maybe he read about it in school," Miss Ruth said, sipping her lemonade.

Mrs. Tuttle waved her fork, spaghetti dangling from it. "Stop defending this child. That's what's wrong with kids these days. They don't take the time to learn. They don't know how to appreciate the South. Now, take Mississippi. That's my home." She leaned in, the table squishing her big breasts. "It's beautiful. Have you ever sat under a magnolia tree and sipped lemonade on a hot day? Or ran your fingers through black soil that grows the food you eat, that grows the cotton they used to make that nice shirt you're wearing right now? Huh? You tell me."

He wasn't sure if he was supposed to respond or whether this was one of those questions grown-ups asked where the answer was understood, but not spoken. By the way she looked at him, though, he figured she expected an answer. "No, ma'am," he said, his eyes on his plate, thinking the peas reminded him of little eyeballs.

"What are they teaching you in your history books, young man? What do you know about Louisiana?"

"The people from there talk kind of funny, I guess," Midnight mumbled, his eyes still on his plate.

Mrs. Tuttle laughed without smiling and it sounded more like a cough, and he could hear the phlegm in the back of her throat. "How do you think you talk? You sound funny, too."

Her face turned serious again. "Louisiana gave us jazz and all that good Cajun and Creole cooking. That's culture, child." As she ate, sauce dripped onto her chest, but she didn't notice.

Granny said, "All right now. Food's getting cold on your plates while you're doing all this talking."

With his mouth full, Mr. Eli said, "Everything's good, Mrs. Dureson. Tastes like more."

Granny liked it when people ate her food and asked for seconds. Soon as he said those words, she brought out a fresh bowl of spaghetti, spilling sauce when she plopped it on the table. She grabbed for her napkin and frowned. "Now, Midnight, you know better than to put paper towels out here instead of our cloth napkins," she said, frantically dabbing red stains.

A slow, sneaky smile crossed Auntie Glo's face as she bounced little Nicky on her lap and fed him applesauce. "He never learns. No home training. So lame."

Midnight stuck his tongue out at her. He had put out what they always used for dinner, the Brawny towels Granny had the coupon for: two rolls for the price of one. Jamming his toe against one of the table legs, he said, "Sorry."

Miss Ruth patted his arm, and while he could barely feel her touch through his shirt, his heart slammed against the walls of his chest. She said, "Don't worry about it, Lena. I use paper towels all the time. They're preferable over napkins. They don't disintegrate in water and they absorb a whole lot better." Then she looked at Midnight. "Do you know why that is?"

"I don't know," he said, disappointed that she sounded like one of his teachers and frustrated with himself for not knowing the answer, especially since it was a question about science, his favorite subject.

"The paper is woven together loosely. That allows liquid to move easily among the fibers," Ruth said, unfolding the paper towel next to her plate and placing the square on her lap.

Then he remembered. "One time my friend Corey and I did this experiment with kitchen sponges. We had a whole bunch of different kinds like natural and artificial and we had to see which ones could hold the most water."

Interrupting his story, Granny asked if anybody wanted refills on lemonade. Before anybody could respond, the front door opened, and he heard Daddy's voice. "Smells like I'm right on time."

In a low voice, Mr. Eli said, "I think I just lost my appetite."

Granny pulled an extra chair from her bedroom and pushed it up to the table. "Have a seat, Butch. You're late, but there's plenty."

"You didn't tell me he was coming." Mr. Eli folded his arms across his chest and glared at his mother.

Daddy sucked the air from the room. "My family, my house. If you don't like it, leave."

Granny chewed her bottom lip and dumped more food on every-body's plates, as if that would make them act nice. She left the table momentarily and returned with a bottle of Scotch and placed it on the table in front of Daddy. Maybe to keep him calm. He tipped the bottle and chugged as if it were a jug of milk.

It got so quiet that all Midnight heard was forks tapping against teeth. This time when Granny got up, she grabbed the remote and turned on a news channel. The anchor said something about car companies getting bailed out, but Midnight had heard of that happening only when somebody went to jail. Like the time Drew got arrested for reckless driving and Daddy bailed him out.

Miss Ruth cleared her throat and said, "Well, this is good for the automakers. I think Obama's got a plan to fix things, and who knows, maybe Fernwood will be back in business."

No one agreed or disagreed with her, and Midnight didn't know enough to have an opinion. He'd heard a bit about the election in social studies class. Miss Hightower called it historic but told the kids they weren't allowed to say who their parents had voted for.

"No way," Daddy said. "I'll believe it when I see it. These big auto manufacturers make all this money on the backs of the little guy then can't pay their bills. Hey, I can't pay mine, either. Is Obama gonna bail me out?"

Mr. Eli shook his head. "You dumbass. The big guy creates jobs for the little guy. They win, you win."

Every time Daddy and Mr. Eli raised their voices in disagreement, Miss Ruth changed the subject to something less toxic, like how toned Michelle Obama's arms looked in sleeveless dresses. She'd also read that Barbara and Jenna Bush had given Malia and Sasha Obama a fun tour of the White House, where they all jumped on the beds and took turns sliding down a solarium banister. That story made Midnight miss the baby sister he never got to meet.

Moving away from talk of politics, Granny said, "Well, Christmas will be here in a couple days. I hope business will pick up. Too many people buying gifts on eBay. How are small businesses supposed to make it?"

Daddy bit into a crunchy slice of garlic bread. "Ask Eli over here about eBay. He's been stealing tire sensors and gear sticks from the plant and putting them up on eBay for years."

Midnight's mouth went dry. Nobody spoke at first until Mrs. Tuttle put her hand on Mr. Eli's arm. She said, "Let it go. Just eat."

Ignoring her, he slammed his hands on the table. "You want to talk about stealing? You stole from Fernwood every damn day when you came in to work an hour late and then took six smoke breaks. If they hadn't laid you off first, they would've fired you. Your hands are dirty up in here. Trying to point fingers at me."

Daddy jabbed his index finger in Eli's face. "I'll point at you anytime I want. What's dirty is what runs in your veins. I remember hearing about your grandpappy using the old rubber band trick to get a machine to work. I bet people died on the road 'cause of him cutting all kinds of corners to meet specs."

Something Midnight couldn't name charged the air and he waited for the next explosion. Miss Ruth reminded him of a block of stone, her body stiff, rigid with rage. He could see it in her eyes. He worried she might slap Daddy. Maybe she should. Why did he have to always ruin things? When she finally spoke, her voice was scary low. "You keep Papa's name out of your mouth."

A kitchen chair scraped the linoleum. Mrs. Tuttle gripped the sides of the table to brace herself as she stood. "This has gone on long enough. Lena, thank you for dinner. I know you were trying to do a good thing, getting our families together again, the way it used to be when our husbands were still alive. But things have changed. I won't have my husband, God rest his soul, disrespected like this." She shot a glance at Daddy, who looked away.

The color drained from Granny's face. She pleaded, "Come on now. Ernestine, please sit down. My son-in-law can be a bit of an ass, I know. But I consider you one of my oldest and dearest friends. Besides, I cooked all this food. Can we just eat? Please."

The anguish made Granny's face draw up like a dried-out grape. He worried about her bad heart. Did hearts wear out like old factory machines? He couldn't lose her, too. Silently, he begged Mrs. Tuttle to do what Granny asked and stay. Slowly, she lowered herself back into her seat.

Then little Nicky screamed and pounded the table. Everyone turned to see his square mouth opened wide, revealing pink gums. Midnight reached across the table to gently press a pacifier to his mouth and the child grabbed it, holding it between his lips.

Miss Ruth said, "What happened to your arm?"

Midnight's shirtsleeve had lifted just enough to expose the scars he tried to keep covered. Granny's eyes flashed from Daddy to Mr. Eli and then to Midnight.

He shrugged. "It happened a long time ago. It's no big deal."

Lightly touching the shiny pink skin on his forearm, she said, "It is a big deal. It looks painful. Does it still hurt?"

He shook his head and she let it go. They all began twirling their spaghetti on forks while he thought back to that day three years ago.

THE BOYS JUMPED HIM THE DAY AFTER THE FIGHT AT THE NEW gravel pit. He had been sitting on the curb of his street trying to build a fort with sticks. The smell of grilled meat wafted from somebody's cookout nearby.

Midnight never saw the boys coming.

They descended upon him, knocking his glasses from his face, and everything became a blur. They ripped his T-shirt as he lay on his side, his cheek scraping asphalt. Cool liquid splashed his arm. Only later, at the hospital, would he learn it was lighter fluid.

"This is for being such a punk-ass traitor," one of the boys yelled before lighting the match and tossing it at him.

The fire's heat was so intense, he thought his skin had peeled away. Still, in the fog of losing consciousness, he heard Corey's voice. "Stop. Stop."

At the hospital, the doctors said he'd suffered third-degree burns and was lucky only his arm had been burned. He was also lucky Corey had shown up when he did and screamed for help.

Granny cried at his bedside while Daddy looked for someone to blame. "How do we know that Corey kid didn't set Patrick on fire? Huh? Tell me that. Maybe he got scared, his conscience got to him. He called for help when he thought he might get in trouble for what he'd done."

The pain medicine kept Midnight too groggy to tell Daddy any different. Word of what happened spread around town, and so did Daddy's accusation. Eli Tuttle kept defending Corey even from behind bars. He'd gone to jail for shooting that gun in the air when the white boys attacked Corey the day before. Maybe he stood up for Corey because they were both Black. People in Ganton chose sides, lining up behind whomever they believed.

A week later, doctors told Midnight the skin on his arm would heal, but the burns had snapped his nerve endings and it was possible he would never regain feeling in his arm. The thought of never swimming or playing baseball or tossing a Frisbee made him want to die.

Only when he slept could he forget about everything he'd miss out on forever. And whenever he was awake, he and Daddy argued about what had really happened.

"Those boys had been saying mean things to Corey that day, and I was just helping him." Corey had been too traumatized to identify the boys and none came forward, so no one got in trouble for setting Midnight on fire.

"You should never have gotten mixed up in that in the first place."

At night, when Daddy's plant shift ended, he came home and washed Midnight's arm with mild soap and then rubbed on antibiotic ointment. Sometimes he felt a slight sensation in his arm, but most of the time, nothing. But strangely, Midnight instantly felt closer to his father than he ever had since Mom died. He smelled the cigarette smoke on Daddy's breath, the chemicals from the plant on his clothes. Lying on the bed, his arm stayed numb, but his heart vibrated with feelings he couldn't explain.

When Daddy changed his dressing, he told him he forgave him.

It was absolution Midnight hadn't asked for. He said, "It's okay, son. You're still young, don't know any better."

He wrapped a gauze roll around Midnight's arm and held the ends down with tape. "You didn't have a clue you were fighting on the wrong side of the war."

Eighteen

RUTH

On the drive back home after dinner at Lena's, they passed the fence of the old Fernwood plant. In the glow of their headlights, she read the sign: *This facility is closed. NO TRESPASSING.* She could still picture Papa and Eli walking out at the end of their shifts carrying their lunch pails, their hands leathery, dirt under their fingernails.

Eli didn't come home with them. He wanted to be alone. There were so many questions she needed to ask him. She couldn't stop thinking about what Butch Boyd had said at dinner about him stealing and her grandfather cutting corners at the plant. Eli had fired back at Butch but hadn't refuted any of the man's accusations.

Ruth took a detour and stopped the car when they got to the Wabash River, the one place where she most felt Papa's presence. Here, she could think and wait for her grandfather's spirit to make everything clear again. A sheet of ice covered the river. Snow dusted the windshield. Mama sat next to her, quietly wringing her gloved hands. Ruth couldn't ply her grandmother with questions without the old woman taking it as a personal affront, a dagger straight through the dignity of their family. Pulling as close as she could get to the river's edge, Ruth put the car in park and let the motor idle.

She pulled out her phone to see if she had any messages or missed calls from Xavier. After a stressful day at the office, he often played racquetball at the East Bank Club, where he could yell and whack the ball loudly to let off steam. He hadn't tried to reach her, so that's probably where he was. She knew she could just call him, but she wanted him to get in touch with her first.

"I'm tired. Why did you stop here?" Mama asked.

"I don't know. I guess because this is where Papa took me fishing every summer. I just started thinking about all the memories here and of him working at Fernwood, too."

"Sure are. So many good ones, too. Baby girl?"

"Yes, Mama?"

She lifted Ruth's hand from the steering wheel and squeezed it hard. "You know your grandfather and your brother. You've known them all your life. They're good men. Trust in that."

Fernwood had provided jobs for most of the men in the Tuttle family. The plant did the same for those living in other midwestern cities who came to Ganton, alone at first, without their wives and children. Once they got hired on, they stayed with relatives, sleeping on rollaway beds, cots, couches, and even floors. Then, when they had worked enough shifts to save money, they bought or rented shotgun houses of their own and sent for the rest of the family to join them.

Every morning, Papa rose before the sun came up to press his shirt and pants, even though the dress code allowed for latitude, with some workers wearing wrinkled T-shirts and raggedy jeans. Adorning her grandfather's head like a crown, that Fernwood cap, even on his days off.

Sitting at the kitchen table eating her Cheerios, Ruth would sometimes snatch his hat and try it on. The cap swallowed her tiny head, its brim falling to her nose. He'd lift it gingerly, just enough to see her eyes, and they'd both laugh. She missed their game of peekaboo.

Sobering, Papa would impart some life lesson. *A man's got to take pride in his work. Do a good job. Do right by the company and that company will do right by you.*

That's why Ruth couldn't reconcile that steward of values and virtue with someone who would cut corners and put people's lives at risk. It didn't add up.

BACK AT THE HOUSE, RUTH SAT IN PAPA'S RECLINER, TURNED THE pages of one of the old photo albums, and handed a loose photo to Mama on the couch next to her.

Mama squinted as if the sun were in her eyes. She peered at the image of her late husband as a young man in overalls, looking cool as a summer breeze.

"I know you miss Papa and that you were always faithful to him. But I've noticed that you're getting close to Dino." Ruth stopped there and studied Mama's face to gauge whether she'd gone too far.

"Dino's a nice friend to have, but he's no Hezekiah."

"I know. I wasn't comparing."

Ruth was certain that if Papa had lived, Mama would have smiled more, had a reason to fix her hair, polish her nails, and wear the dried-out foundation that Ruth had stumbled upon in the medicine cabinet.

Turning the pages of the album, Ruth stopped at a photo she'd never seen before, of a little girl around eight years old with two pigtails on either side of her head, in a plaid dress with bobby socks and scuffed Mary Janes. She turned it over and read what was scrawled on the back. *Ernestine, 1938.*

"Now, that was a long time ago." Mama took the photo from Ruth and pulled the album onto her lap. She ran her pruned fingers over the plastic covering. "Seems like another lifetime."

"Where was this taken?"

"In Mississippi. McComb. That's me in front of my school. One room for all the grades. It was segregated, nothing but colored."

Mama often talked about the Jersey cows and the butterfat milk they produced and how they endured scorching hot days. She relayed tales about her father readying bales of cotton for the textile mills, coming home with stories of how it was so hot he felt his skin melting, sliding right off his body. *Just a new kind of slavery,* he'd said.

"Look at you," Ruth said, a bubble of affection for Mama rising inside her. Just thinking of her grandmother as a little girl, innocent and full of wonder, made her whole body warm. "I know you were ready to get out of that dress, so you could go play."

"I jumped rope half the day in that outfit. There's one song I made up actually from stories I heard the old folks telling," Mama said.

"Do you still remember it?"

> *They brought us here on ships . . .*
> *Then tore us up with whips.*
> *God say nothing to fear . . .*
> *But cotton still king here.*

Ruth imagined her grandmother's voice vibrating in her throat and slicing right through the thick Mississippi air.

"I know times were hard for Black people in those days, but at least you had some fun," Ruth said.

"Yes, we had good times all right. But all good things come to an end, as they say. I don't think I ever told you about my cousin Alfonso. He was just like a firefly. Alfonso moved so fast you had to catch him before he lit someplace else." Mama slid her hand between the pages of the photo album and pulled apart the ones that stuck together. She pointed to a boy about twelve or thirteen, in tan overalls and a brown derby hat pulled low over his eyes.

"He was a pretty boy. He'd be right there when we jumped rope and all the girls would chase him around. One day he was showing off for us and jumped in the air, clapping his shoes together. I tell you he was a mess. This one time he lost his balance and fell in the dirt and it caked to his backside. But he got up dancing and the girls ate it up." Mama laughed while gazing at the photo of her cousin.

"I bet he was something else. I wish I'd known him," Ruth said.

"He would've gotten a kick out of you and your brother. Sometimes, I wish he would have made less of a scene, less of a spectacle, you know. Anyway, that day, the girls were cackling and screaming when Alfonso went to the bathroom at the general store to clean himself up. He wasn't paying any mind to what he was doing, and he started to open the wrong door. He realized his mistake quick and headed for the colored bathroom. But by then these three white men had walked up. I'll never forget that one who said, 'Did I see your nigger hands touch that door?'"

Mama spat the n-word like it had a sour taste. Ruth had grown up hearing from her grandparents about whips and police dogs and fire hoses spraying Black folks, but it always felt like an ancient tale. Like something she had read about in history books or watched in documentaries. Something older people used as leverage to prove that people her age had it easy. Or rhetoric they hoped would motivate them to take advantage of opportunities that had been hard won. Ruth didn't know if she could bear hearing more of the story, as she felt like a child inching closer to a flame, not sure if she should touch it or not.

"Those men kicked dirt in Alfonso's face and walked away laughing about it. He stood there and took it. What else could he do? That night he was supposed to come over to our house for supper. He loved Ma's greens and cold-water corn bread. We were all sitting around the table talking about Sunday school lessons and the price of lumber coming down. But Alfonso never showed up."

Mama tilted her head up to the ceiling and closed her eyes. The living room felt small and tight, with a pall of melancholy covering it.

She went on with her story. "Then we heard some commotion outside, and my father went out to check. There was Alfonso running fast, zigzag-like, with these white men chasing him. Then he just turned in circles, his hands stretched out, his eyes glowing in the dark. Those men were everywhere, and he was trapped. Pa walked right out there and stood in front of Alfonso and told those men to take *him*, do what they needed to do to him instead of his nephew. But they didn't pay that no mind. They said this was the little nigger that tried to use the white bathroom and he needed to learn a lesson."

"I can't imagine." Ruth rested her hand on Mama's thigh.

Papa used to tell stories about the civil rights marches decades later that moved through Chicago to support the striking Memphis sanitation workers. He said he drove up there to march with them holding a sign that screamed in bold letters *I AM A MAN*. Every time he talked about it, Ruth thought there was something screwed up about a world where a man needed to carry a sign to remind the world and maybe even himself that he was indeed a man. She honestly couldn't fathom what they'd endured in Mississippi in the 1930s.

Mama continued. "They wrapped a long rope around the tree where we had just picked walnuts the week before. It had rained not too long before. You know, one of those summer showers that's over before you know it. So the ground was wet. All those men made a big circle around Alfonso. He'd turn one way to try to run and then the other. Every time, he'd kick up mud and it would splash on his pants. He reminded me of a caged animal, and I figure that's how they saw him. It's about what they thought of him. You can't think nobody's human and do that to them. I stood in the doorway with Ma and Mitch and we watched them hang Alfonso."

Ruth's breath caught in her throat and she looked down at her hands, which were clenched in fists. "Dear God. I don't know what to say."

Watching her grandmother, she imagined that little girl in pigtails from the picture, and anger welled inside her until it spilled from her face in hot tears.

"What did you do?" Ruth said, her voice barely a whisper.

Mama's mouth twitched, and her words emerged hard and gravelly. "What could we do? Not a damn thing right then unless we wanted to be hung next. We just stood there real still until it was over. I'm telling you this story because of your son and what I said to you when you brought him into the world." She leaned back in her chair.

Ruth wondered how that lynching long ago could be connected to her child. "I don't understand," she said.

"That next morning after they hung Alfonso, my folks made your uncle and me pack our suitcases and we all headed to the train station. They'd had enough. You hear the old folks who used to say they were sick and tired of being sick and tired? We left Mississippi and came here to Indiana and stayed with family that had come before us. We didn't have much else but a hope and a prayer. And each other. But it was a fresh start, and that's what we needed."

Mama looked around the dimly lit room as if she were appraising the value of everything in it and had settled on a low figure. "Sometimes leaving is the best way. The only way."

What could Ruth say to that? Surviving Yale and Langham seemed small and inconsequential compared to what Mama had seen and endured. There were so many unanswered questions that Ruth needed her grandmother to answer.

She went to her bedroom to get her purse and returned to sit beside Mama again. "That breaks my heart, and I get why you had to leave. I even understand why you wanted me to leave Ganton without my baby. You wanted what was best for me. But now, I'm back. I'm here. I need you to help me with this."

Pulling the crumpled paper from her purse, she handed her the registry consent form. Mama stared at the paper but didn't move.

"Here. Take it."

"What is this?"

"Just read it, please."

Hesitantly, Mama took the form. Fear crossed her face as she read.

"What is it? Tell me what's got you so spooked right now."

"Where did you get this rubbish?" Mama threw the form on the floor.

Taking a deep breath, Ruth said, "The county clerk's office. I need to fill it out if I have any hope of reconnecting with my son."

The way her grandmother looked at her, Ruth wouldn't have been surprised if Mama had gone outside and yanked a switch from a tree to whip her, had it not been such a bone-chilling winter day. Even as full-grown as Ruth was.

"Mama. Please. That day, when you left with the baby, where did you go? Nowadays you can drop a baby off at the hospital or fire station, no questions asked. But there was no safe haven law back then. You had to take him somewhere." Ruth moved close enough to smell the Jergens lotion her grandmother lathered on her arms and legs after her nighttime bath. "Where, Mama?"

Her eyes glazed over, unreadable. "I took him to Jesus. He's with good, God-fearing people. That's all that matters."

Ruth swallowed past a hard lump at the base of her throat and tried to ignore what sounded like mockery from her grandmother. "This whole thing was off the books, wasn't it? There were no adoption papers, were there?"

Mama didn't answer, and Ruth took her silence as confirmation.

Nineteen

MIDNIGHT

Izzy bummed loosies off people and she usually scored a whole pack of cigarettes by nightfall. Her blue-gray eyes crossed each other and sometimes she stumbled over her own feet. That's how she got the name *Dizzy Izzy*. And when she opened her mouth to talk to you, her tongue poked through the gaps where her missing teeth should have been. Pancho said people with no teeth gummed the inside of their jaws, and he knew this since his great-grandpa did it.

Every other Friday, Izzy camped out in front of the gas station. It stayed busy on Fridays. Granny always said the money from payday must be burning holes in people's pockets.

"Can you help me out? I just need a couple dollars to get me something to eat," she said, telling a lie, since everybody knew she only wanted cash for cigarettes.

They didn't like to get close to Izzy because she smelled like rotten meat left out in the hot sun for weeks. But that didn't stop Corey from moving closer and saying, "I'll get something for you to eat. Be right back." He had money because he still earned a weekly allowance for doing chores around the house and sometimes just for bringing home good grades.

Two guys in red bandannas leaned against the outside wall of the gas station, one of them pouring Red Hots in his mouth. Midnight recognized them as local gang members, or at least that's what people said. And he knew people could be wrong. The one who wasn't eating elbowed his friend and pointed to the boys. They moved in front of the door, blocking the entrance. When Pancho tried to push his way between them, the taller one stood with his legs spread wide and said, "Hey now, where are your manners?"

Both men wore Air Jordans that looked new enough to have just come out of the box. Red with chunky white soles and thick tongues. Their matching red laces undone.

Once the guys tired of taunting them, they stepped aside and even opened the door for the boys to walk inside. That small gesture of civility resembled respect, and it made Midnight and his friends walk taller, maybe even strut into the gas station.

Greasy hot dogs rolled on a grimy rack and nachos covered in orange cheese sauce sat under the harsh glare of a heat lamp. A thrill surged through Midnight as they bumped into each other in the narrow aisles. Just the mere anticipation of the mischief they could find here made his blood jitter even before he knew what form it might take.

Sebastian plucked a bag of dill pickle chips off a display and tossed it across the aisle to Corey. "Think fast."

Everybody knew Corey had the best arm in town and that's why he had gotten the reputation for being the greatest pitcher in Ganton Little League history. Not bad at catching, either, he leapt off the floor and snatched the bag from the air, bumping into an old lady as he landed. "Oh, sorry," he said. She rubbed her hands along the front of her coat like he'd spilled something on her.

Never having an idea that didn't live in somebody else's head first, Pancho scooped three Snickers bars and hurled them at Midnight in rapid succession. "Think fast," he said, parroting Sebastian.

The first candy bar sailed past him and slid across the floor.

With one bum arm, Midnight's reflexes had slowed. All the video games he played helped, but he knew he'd always be one step behind his friends.

Focusing intently, he managed to catch the other candy bars and clutched them against his jacket.

A delivery guy wheeled in a stack of cases of Diet Coke on a panel truck. Midnight grinned at his buddies before he jumped on and pushed off on it like a skateboard. The other boys' eyes widened in amazement.

Even if they had been on the witness stand with their right hands raised to God, they couldn't pinpoint for sure which of them had knocked over the tiered display of Funyuns. When the yellow bags of onion rings tumbled, one after another, to the floor, a large, red-faced man appeared in front of them. The name stitched on his striped gas station shirt was *Dale*.

"What the hell is going on here?" he said, breathing hard. Sebastian and Pancho started backing up slowly. "Don't you dare try to run away."

When Corey stooped to pick up as many of the fallen bags of Funyuns as he could, the wet soles of his boots squeaked on the floor. Dale snatched the onion rings from his hands. "Were you trying to steal from my store, kid?"

"No, sir," Corey said.

"Open up your jacket."

That request from Dale must have confused Corey as it did Midnight and the other boys. All of them stayed silent, glancing at each other, unsure of what was going on, only understanding it wasn't good.

"Did you hear me? Either you open your jacket, so I can see what you stole, or I'm calling the cops."

Other customers in the store had stopped their shopping to stare. Without thinking, Midnight said, "He didn't steal anything."

He couldn't help but remember the day those older boys set him on fire, yet Daddy and other people accused Corey of doing something he didn't do. Some people in this town would never give Corey a break.

"Will you just be quiet?" Corey said under his breath, the fright on his face surprisingly more intense as Midnight defended him.

Dale kept his angry eyes on Corey, who pulled loose the snaps on his jacket. The zipper got stuck and Corey pulled hard until his coat opened. When Dale was satisfied there were no hidden bags of Funyuns, he said with a growl, "Get out of here. All of you."

Sebastian and Pancho ran to the door, but Corey walked slowly as if he knew Dale was still watching him. Midnight, who followed behind, turned back to the gas station owner and said, "Told you so."

Corey turned around. "Will you *shut up*?"

Once they were back outside, Izzy stood on the curb with her hand outstretched, her toothless grin spreading. Corey dug into his jacket pocket and pulled out a ten-dollar bill. When he held it out to her, she glanced from his face to his hand and back again to his face.

"Here," Corey said, almost shoving the bill into her hands as if he were anxious to get rid of it.

"Oh, thank you. What's your name?" Izzy said, her eyes following Corey, but he'd already turned away from the store.

Midnight grabbed Corey's jacket sleeve. "How come you let that guy in the store talk to you like that?"

"Yeah, you just let him get away with it," Pancho said.

When they reached the street corner, Sebastian put his fists up to his face. "I would've kicked his ass. You know that."

"Me, too," Midnight chimed in.

Spinning around to face Midnight, Corey pushed his chest. Lightly at first. Then harder. "You are so dumb sometimes."

"What did I do?"

"You kept pissing him off. You play too much."

None of this made sense to Midnight. Corey overreacted whenever he thought he might get in trouble at home or school or anywhere. "So what? You didn't steal anything, so who cares if he gets mad?"

"Just shut up. You don't get it."

A strange quiet followed them like a shadow. Midnight thought about what Corey said, but he still didn't understand.

THE COLD BLISTERED MIDNIGHT'S FINGERS. IT BIT HIS FACE AND snatched his breath. But it also brought him closer to Daddy, and that made freezing his butt off worthwhile. While he was out of school for Christmas break, he tried to spend as much time with his father as he could. Besides, Indiana cold beat Louisiana, where you sweated all the time in the heat.

"How much you paying for the day?" Daddy said to a large man in a navy down jacket and a Colts hat. He grabbed one of the shovels and handed Midnight a metal dustpan that was easier to manage with one hand.

"Depends on how much work you do, Boyd. Twelve fifty an hour. Got all of Pratt to cover. Street team can't get it all," the man said. He carried a clipboard in one hand and a hot drink in the other. A trickle of steam rose from his cup.

Snow had been falling all week, the heavy kind that stuck. Granny hadn't even opened the store one day this week after seven inches covered their street, making it impossible to even get her car out of the driveway. The plow truck hadn't shown up until the next day.

"Bet I can outlast you, Boyd." That dwarf-looking guy, Loomis, with the limp, was always talking tough, even though his right leg was shorter than his left.

"Keep it up and I'll dunk your pointy head in the toilet next time." Daddy punched him playfully and then put an arm around his shoulders, and they stumbled in the uneven snow.

The three of them worked steadily, Midnight trying as hard as he could to keep up with the men. Trails of filmy vapor carried their onion and cigarette breath, and they cursed as if they didn't see Midnight standing there. They bragged, about either women or money or cars or all of it.

"You know they got a seven-day cruise going to the Bahamas.

I'm taking Shirley with me on a honeymoon," Loomis said, hobbling after Daddy in the snow.

"Your first trip better be to the justice of the peace, don't you think?" The force of the windblown snow and his laughter made Daddy hold his side.

By now, other men hired to shovel for the day had joined them, and Daddy pounded his shovel in the ground to get their attention. He held the handle like it was a microphone. "Forget the Caribbean. I'm saving up to go to France someday. I met a girl from there a long time ago when I was driving trucks long distance. She offered to show me around to the places tourists don't know about."

Midnight had seen Daddy with a few women after Mommy died, but he suspected he might have been lying about this one. Something about the way his mouth twisted like when he talked to the electric company, the cell phone people, his boss when he'd been late to work, or Drew around the first of the month.

But usually, when Midnight was in school, he saw Daddy only twice a week, so much of what he knew about his life now he pieced together from what he heard him say to other people. Some of it must be true.

"Is that right now, Butch Boyd? You had a French girl?" Loomis tapped Daddy's shoulder. "I think I'll stick with Ganton women. At least they shave their pits." He stepped back to avoid the jab of Daddy's shovel handle in his ribs.

That laugh of Daddy's was like a safe that Midnight didn't have the combination to anymore.

When his father shoveled snow, he attacked it like it had done something bad to him and he had to make it pay. He jabbed at each mound with the blade and scooped it up, tossing it aside like chicken bones. "Bend at your knees," Daddy said to Midnight.

"Like this, right?" Gripping the handle of the dustpan, Midnight pricked the snow, but it was packed too tightly for him to make a dent.

"Try pushing it. Lean into it more." And that's what he did, just like Daddy said, throwing all his seventy-three and a half pounds on it. "You got it, Patrick. That's my boy."

His back ached a bit, but there they were, side by side, snot dripping from their noses, grunting with each scrape of the asphalt. Midnight's glasses slid to the tip of his nose and he pushed them up.

A strong wind whipped around them. While Midnight staggered, Daddy stood up to it, feet spread apart, like he could fight it with his bare hands. He grabbed Midnight and pulled him close. Daddy's coat smelled of gasoline and sauerkraut, kind of like a fart, but he buried his cheek deeper in the space between Daddy's arm and rib cage.

Once the wind died down, Midnight pulled back. It was like when the doctor had told Granny about her diabetes. One slice of apple pie was okay every now and then, but you had to know when to stop. Too much of it could hurt you if you weren't careful. Same thing with getting too close to Daddy.

Midnight made small circles in the snow with the dustpan. "Um, so I was thinking about going out for Little League next year."

If he joined the team, they'd be counting on him for games and he wouldn't be able to move to Louisiana. All his friends played baseball, but after he got burned, he gave up on the idea. He might have missed out on his shot, though. During training, he watched Corey, Sebastian, and Pancho run, pitch, catch fly balls, field ground ones, and bat.

Before Midnight got burned, Daddy had coached him on weekends, determined to see his son start at the best infield position. *Soft elbows. Stop locking those knees. Watch the ball. Get ready for it before it comes to you.*

His father's gaze, following every move, had burned like a flame at his back. Midnight's head tightened like it had a rubber band pinching it.

Now, Daddy swiped his nose with his jacket sleeve and rested his arms on the handle of his shovel. His breaths came loud and fast like he'd been running.

"Leave that baseball crap to those who can't do any better. I told you to focus on science. You won that science fair last year, right?" The sun's brightness blinded Midnight, but he squinted up at Daddy's face, which was unreadable.

"You'll be a doctor someday. Treat cancer. Save guys like Elroy Richards. Hell, find a cure for it. Get some letters behind your name, in front of it, too. We need some good doctors in this town. And in this family."

Daddy's eyes weren't on him anymore. Instead they focused on something far off that he couldn't see, some future picture he was drawing in his head as he talked. Then, as if he remembered Midnight was still next to him, he laid a gloved hand on his shoulder. "Forget tryouts. You're bigger than baseball. Remember that."

Daddy expected him to do big, important things someday. But he also wondered if Daddy didn't think he was good enough to play baseball. At least not with only one good arm.

"I read about this guy, Pete Gray. He was an outfielder in St. Louis and he played in the majors with only one arm."

Daddy laughed. "That's one guy. And how long ago was that? The forties? And the Browns were the worst team in the league. So bad they folded and became the Baltimore Orioles."

Midnight's shoulders slumped. "Okay, but I know I can do it. I can be like Corey. He gets good grades *and* he plays Little League. Mr. Cunningham said it's important to be well-rounded."

Daddy frowned and immediately Midnight knew he'd said the wrong thing. "I've told you before that I don't like you hanging around that kid so much. No need to go over to Hill Top or Grundy to find friends. Plenty of good kids right here in Pratt."

"But why?" Midnight said.

"I'm your father, I don't need a reason. But I have plenty. I heard that Corey kid was causing trouble at the gas station today. I also understand there were some low-life thugs hanging around. I don't want you mixed up in that. When Lena first mentioned you going to Louisiana, I didn't like the idea so much. But if you can't keep your nose clean, that's where you're headed." Daddy yanked his shovel from the snow mound and began the walk back to his truck.

Helplessness settled so deep in Midnight's bones, he barely felt the cold anymore. Desperation buzzed around him, and he frantically searched for a way to control what seemed to be out of his hands.

He kicked the dustpan as hard as he could, making it skitter across the road. And then he ran to catch up with his father.

Twenty

RUTH

Ruth hadn't seen her high school best friend since twelfth grade. Even though it had been a long time, she believed their bond withstood all those years of separation. The year Ruth had the baby, Mama kept her quarantined in the house and pretty much made her walk away from all her friendships, including the one with Natasha. But now, with Mama stonewalling her, she needed to talk to Natasha, the one person who kept it real no matter what.

In one of her attempts at a put-down, Mama had casually mentioned that Natasha had stayed in Ganton and did hair at A Cut Above, a salon where you could get sew-ins, twists, braids, rod sets, relaxers, as well as fish dinners from a gaunt, well-dressed man in penny loafers.

"Get your fried catfish right here." Ruth heard him before she saw him, his voice potent with strong lung capacity, reminding her of those vendors who hawked ice-cold beer at baseball games. With all the years that had gone by, she couldn't believe he had remained there giving the same sales pitch. He and those smelly fish dinners hadn't crossed her mind in forever, but his presence—consistent and familiar—made her smile.

The moment she walked in she smelled hair sizzling in the jaws of a flat iron like bacon frying in a skillet, and she noticed one stylist braiding with the precision of someone crocheting an afghan. The scent of singed hair from an old-school press-and-curl filled the air.

At a workstation in the far corner by a window, Natasha brushed loose hair from the nape of her client's neck and then curled a few stray locks in the front. Perhaps she felt Ruth's eyes on her. When she looked up and spotted Ruth, her face lit up with a smile and then just as fast went dark, transforming into an impenetrable mask.

Ruth gripped the straps of her purse, pressing the bag to her chest like a security blanket. An awkward discomfort descended upon her as she stood in the middle of the salon looking lost.

Natasha had intentionally turned away from her, but why? With trepidation, Ruth walked slowly to the stylist chair where her old friend spritzed holding spray that tickled Ruth's nostrils.

"It's me, girl. Surprise?" Ruth said, adding an upward inflection to her words, turning them into a question.

"Ruth. I didn't know you were in town." Natasha's tone stayed neutral, drained of any emotion, good or bad. In spite of her friend's indifference, her voice still sounded the same, as if it had been dipped in warm brandy. She kept her eyes on her client through the mirror, brushing gel onto the woman's edges.

Sensing her visit might have been a mistake, Ruth backed away a few steps and said, "I know you weren't expecting me and I see you're busy. I don't want to take you away from your customers."

Finally, turning to look at her, Natasha said, "I've got twenty minutes before my next client. I need to mix her color anyway. Come with me."

After bidding her client farewell, she led Ruth into a narrow supply closet.

"Sit here." Natasha pointed to a stack of brown boxes labeled *shea butter oil,* and Ruth bristled at the command but obeyed. Jars and bottles of leave-in conditioners, shampoos, and detangling lotions lined the walls.

Natasha pulled off her decorative scarf and shook her head, waves of sandy-brown hair falling like a river. It was all hers, not because she had a receipt as proof of purchase, but because it grew from her head like that. In the early grades, all the girls swore Natasha must have had more than just Black blood in her. She had to have been part Indian, they surmised, with her golden-brown skin and dark eyes dotted with flecks of bronze.

At recess, Natasha's body glistened from the Vaseline her mom used to coat her skin, guaranteeing Natasha wouldn't be one of those ashy kids people whispered about.

"What is it? I can tell you're angry with me," Ruth said.

Natasha, with her back to Ruth, squeezed a tube of orange hair color and let the liquid flow into a plastic bowl of purple dye, the mixture turning a deep russet when she stirred it.

"You don't get it, do you? Everything is still all about you."

Ruth watched her friend's hands at work. The mixing process reminded her of the hydrocarbons, whitening agents, and perfumes she blended to make detergent on her job. She smiled in spite of the distance between them, thinking of how Natasha hated chemistry in high school, how she cursed the Bunsen burner and whined about having to memorize the elements of the periodic table. Now she mixed solutions with the finesse of a chemist.

"*Eleven* years. That's how long it's been since I've seen you. You ghosted me senior year. First, you started acting funny, and then you wouldn't take my calls or answer the door when I stopped by. So forgive me if I don't jump up and down at the sight of you and kiss your ass after all this time."

What could Ruth say to that? Any excuse she gave would sound lame, woefully insufficient to repair the tear in their once durable bond. "You're right. I did everything the wrong way."

Natasha rinsed her hands and sat on a box opposite Ruth. As if a dam had broken, years of hurt and resentment gushed from her like rolling waters. "Was it when you got into Yale? Is that when you decided to cut me loose? You needed to upgrade, I guess. I wasn't good enough for the bougie new friends you would make. Just tell me the truth. No need to bullshit anymore."

Ruth's chest caved as if her friend had bludgeoned it with her truth. "That's not how it was."

"You were always the perfect one. The good girl with the good grades who got into all the good colleges. I was just the good-time girl with mediocre grades and no planned future. You know what I kept telling myself? That none of that mattered 'cause we were tight. We were *girls,* ride or die." Natasha covered her face with her hands. "I was the fool. You played me."

Drained and tired of carrying the lies, Ruth jumped in. "There was nothing perfect about me. I was hiding from you and everybody else. I've been hiding my whole life. Even now." With downcast eyes, she said, "I was pregnant senior year. I had a baby."

Silence sat between them, the air charged with Ruth's revelation. When she raised her eyes, she saw Natasha stunned, mouth agape, absorbing what she'd just heard. "Pregnant? I didn't know, girl. I had no idea."

"No one knew," Ruth said. "Mama had me in hiding and I took my classes at home. Gave birth there, too."

Natasha propped her legs up on the shea butter box and crossed them with Ruth's, making a tic-tac-toe board of sorts, just like no time had passed between them. Something loosened inside Ruth. "You could have told me. You didn't have to go through that all by yourself."

"I had Mama and Eli in my ear telling me what to do. To keep this secret. That a baby would mess up everything, hold me back. I was too young to know what I really wanted."

For a moment, an ease settled between them in the tiny supply closet and they were teen girls again, sitting on Natasha's leopard-print bedspread eating Crazy Bread from Little Caesars. For the first time since she'd been back home, Ruth didn't feel a desperate need to run away.

Natasha said, "Okay, can I ask you something? I know it had to be Ronald Atkins's baby, 'cause you didn't sleep around like that. So, did you tell him?"

Ruth's stomach knotted at the mention of her old boyfriend's name. She struggled to speak. "I never told him."

Natasha leaned forward and put a hand on her shoulder. "I didn't like who you were when you were with him. You were afraid to move or do anything without his approval. Then he started talking to other girls while you were still together. I wanted to cut him or at least get his Social Security number, so I could jack up his credit someday."

Ruth laughed through the tears that choked her.

"He took your spark, girl."

That's when Ruth remembered why she had stuck close to Natasha, a girl some dismissed as flashy, a bubblehead, a chickenhead, or *fast as popcorn,* as Mama called her. A girl whose curves made Ruth's body look like a bag of bones, all arms and legs dangling and tripping over each other. But if Natasha cared about you, she had your back. Even as a young girl, she would have clawed a grown man's eyes out if he messed with one of her friends. And as bright as her glow was, she knew when to recede into the shadows and let you stand in the light.

"Anyway, I came back home to find my baby," Ruth said. "Well, I guess he isn't a baby anymore. He's eleven."

A puzzled look settled on Natasha's face. "You don't know where he is? Didn't you give him up for adoption?"

That question would forever stump Ruth and haunt her. "Mama took him right after he was born and to this day she won't say what happened. I'm here to finally find answers. You mentioned Ronald. I never told him about the baby, but you know how this town is. He could have still found out somehow. Do you know where he is?"

When she came home to Ganton for her wedding, she had looked over her shoulder, afraid she'd run into him. Now she needed to know if he had registered with the state as the baby's father. If he had, there was a chance she would be able to find her son.

Natasha said, "Girl, his sorry ass ain't claiming nobody's kid. Ronald's been over in Iraq for a while now. Army, I think. I'm hoping Obama will bring the troops back home. I got cousins over there.

What are they fighting for when the real war is right here with people losing their jobs and their houses? It's ridiculous."

Ruth pictured Ronald in fatigues leaning on a tank with desert dust swirling behind him. In high school, he had never been particularly patriotic, and she always assumed he'd get a job at the plant like Eli and Papa.

"I had no idea he was over there. I hope he makes it back home safely," Ruth said absently.

A new sadness and regret swept over her. It hit her that Ronald could die fighting somebody else's war and never even know he had a son. Not that she had much faith in him stepping up to do the right thing and being a father to their child. Ruth thought of her own father, which she rarely did—a nameless, faceless creation of her imagining, a man she'd been forced to build and design in her mind. Either her mother didn't know who had impregnated her or she hadn't bothered to inform him. There was a man out there with her DNA who didn't know she existed. His absence had left a hole in her that could never be filled.

Natasha pulled her back to the present moment. "What's your plan? I wonder if your kid is still here in Ganton. If he is, I probably know him. We'll find him together. I got you, girl."

A heaviness Ruth didn't know she'd been carrying lifted with her friend's offer to help. She didn't have to do this alone. It also hit her that after all these years of holding on to her secret, she'd told three people about the baby in the past month. Xavier had been the hardest to tell, and her honesty might have doomed her marriage. They still hadn't spoken since she'd left Chicago; it was the longest they'd ever gone without speaking. But Natasha had been supportive and nonjudgmental. If Ruth had confided in her a long time ago, things might have been so different.

Tess had been helpful, checking with one of her National Bar Association friends in Indianapolis who handled adoption cases. He told her that for every adoption decreed by an Indiana court, the State Department of Health needed to furnish a record of adoption for the child. This was added to the Indiana code in 1997, the same year Ruth gave birth.

"I don't have much to go on." Ruth sighed. "Maybe it was all off the books or maybe not. He could have been adopted, and if so, there has to be a record of it. I'm sure there are plenty of adopted kids in town. How do I find which one is mine?"

In dramatic fashion that reminded Ruth of the spontaneous Natasha she'd known growing up, her friend lifted her hands, streaked red and gold with hair dye. "You know what? I don't really remember the details, but a few years after you left Ganton, there was this scandal in town. A lawyer got arrested for some shady shit. He did all sorts of illegal stuff, but I know there was some kind of adoption fraud. Now, I'm not saying it's connected to your baby, but you never know."

Ruth tried to hide her terror. It had never occurred to her that there had been anything nefarious about her son's adoption. She'd heard stories about people selling babies on the black market, but that only happened in the movies and in news stories overseas. Not here in Ganton. And as churchgoing as Mama was, she'd *never* be involved in something like that.

Natasha opened the door of the supply closet. Her next client would arrive soon and she needed to restock her chair area. She had no idea she'd just turned Ruth's world into a spinning top, leaving her to consider that her son might have inadvertently become a pawn in some crime.

Ruth followed her friend back out to the salon, where stylists and clients moved about, women getting their hair done before the upcoming Christmas holiday. Natasha called the entire room to attention and wrapped her arms around Ruth.

"Ladies, this is Ruth. My bestie from day one. She's a doctor in Chicago, y'all."

In a low hiss, Ruth corrected her. "Engineer. Not a doctor."

Waving her off, Natasha said, "Same thing."

To some people, it really was the same thing. Either you'd made something of yourself or you hadn't, and that was all that mattered. Ruth was acutely aware of how different her life was now compared with those of everyone in the room. But even with a six-figure salary, she was still the same person. A twinge of panic still hit her when she would come home to a dark apartment after a thunderstorm before she remembered that she'd of course paid the electric bill that month.

To her surprise, people cheered as if starved for good news, drinking in a success story. When Natasha hugged her, Ruth smelled the citrus scent of her gum and she thought of how they were scolded by their teachers for gum-smacking.

Whispering in her ear, Natasha said, "We're so proud of you. And I'm here for you, girl. Let me know if I can help, okay? You got this."

ALONE IN HER CAR, RUTH TURNED OVER IN HER MIND WHAT NATAsha had said about a lawyer who was arrested for adoption scams a few years after Ruth gave birth. Pulling out her cell, Ruth ran a Google search and a series of results appeared. She slid her finger over the face of her phone, scanning headlines and the first few paragraphs of several news stories.

A South Bend family had sued an adoption agency for not disclosing the violent past of a child the couple adopted from India.

A think piece claimed the world orphan crisis was nothing but a myth. The neediest children were sick, disabled, or too old by the standards of Americans seeking the perfect baby. There just weren't enough healthy, adoptable infants available in third-world countries for the Westerners clamoring for them.

Had her son gone to one of these hopeful or even desperate families? Or had he been an ornament, a decorative conversation piece for some ostentatious social climber? That possibility turned her stomach. She thought of the elegantly coiffed white women she'd seen strolling city streets with Chihuahuas and Yorkshire terriers peeping from their purses. They even adorned their dogs with sweaters and topknot ribbons like little girls. These had to be the same type of women who adopted Black babies from Africa and toted them around as accessories.

She kept searching online, scrolling past the most recent stories, and found in the *Indianapolis Star* an account of an attorney named Stanley DeAngelo, who'd gotten busted several years ago for bribery, extortion, and tax fraud. Apparently, he and his law partner had misused client information to enrich themselves.

Just as she was about to exit out of the article and move to the next one, she noticed that DeAngelo had been implicated in numerous cases of adoption fraud stretching from Ganton to Indianapolis. One case centered on a teenage girl who gave birth about twenty miles from Ganton and promised her baby to a couple who never got the child. DeAngelo absconded with all the money the couple had paid during the girl's pregnancy. According to the article, he had drained the bank accounts of several other hopeful couples who wanted babies, but never got them.

Ruth couldn't imagine the pain those couples must have felt. And what happened to the babies? She searched for other articles and found a few local news sources that repeated what was said in the *Indianapolis Star* article. Could this DeAngelo have been involved with her son's adoption? She couldn't find news about any other shady adoption stories concerning a lawyer with ties to Ganton. Maybe it was this guy. If everything had been legit and legal, Mama would have said so. But her haunted eyes and tightly sealed lips made Ruth suspect there was more to the story.

Ruth leaned back in her seat and rubbed her temples. DeAngelo had been convicted in 1999, just two years after Ruth had the baby, and he went to prison for falsifying adoption records and the other crimes. Her stomach churned thinking of her family's possibly having gotten involved with somebody like this.

The photo in the article showed DeAngelo in a gray suit, white dress shirt, and red tie, posing in front of a bookshelf, maybe his law library. He had a pinched nose and a cleft chin. More than likely a publicity headshot from his practice.

On the Indiana Department of Correction website, she typed "Stanley DeAngelo" in the offender name search field. The results came up a moment later: *No information found.* There was an option to search by the offender's number, which was useless because she didn't know it. This man could have answers about her son's identity. She had to find another way to track him down.

Twenty-One

MIDNIGHT

A late holiday afternoon with no homework or chores stretched before the boys, long and tempting. Sebastian went bowling with his family and Pancho went Christmas shopping with his aunts, leaving Midnight and Corey to scratch boredom's itch.

Midnight tried not to think about what Daddy had said about sending him away. His father hadn't said to never play with Corey again. Just not so much. Not to get in trouble. Today didn't count as *so much* or *trouble*.

Outside Leo's auto shop, they tried to hold their balance sitting on their lumpy backpacks. After pushing each other off a few times, it got old fast.

"We can play video games at my house," Corey said.

Midnight scooped a handful of snow and stood to smash it into a stop sign. If he and Corey just ran into each other out playing, they couldn't help it. But if he actually went over to his house right now, that would mean he planned it and Daddy would say he'd broken the rules.

"Nah, I have a better idea," Midnight said.

He spotted a green dumpster nearby, flipped it on its side, and opened the lid. Holding his breath, he dove in headfirst.

"What are you doing? Are you crazy?" Corey said.

Going deeper into the trash heap, Midnight waded through half-eaten subs, ripped tire rubber, an empty pork 'n' beans can, carburetor cleaner, pizza scraps, and a bolt cutter.

A bolt cutter. Yes. That would work. Its jaws were worn down, likely from years of use and repeated sharpening. With his good hand, he shoved it in his backpack.

"What's that for?"

"You'll see. Let's go."

Midnight's fingers and toes tingled as he ran through downtown to the outskirts of Ganton. When he licked his lips, he tasted his own snot and then spat in the snow. His breathing pounded inside his head. Corey kept pace with him, his body small, athletic, and lean enough to run for miles without panting. The next thing he knew, Corey had passed him, but slowed down since he didn't know where they were headed.

"We're almost there."

"Where?"

A few dozen feet later, they came upon an old fence that wrapped around a large piece of land. They heard a low rustling.

"What's that?" Corey said.

"It's just the wind."

"Where are we?"

Snow covered a heap of scrap metal about twenty feet high. Something hot and primal raced through Midnight's body. A high he couldn't explain, but he felt it every time he did something risky.

"It's the junkyard. Daddy brought me a bunch of times last summer. You can find lots of cool stuff."

"But it's winter. Nobody's even here."

Midnight smiled and pulled the bolt cutters from his bag. "I know."

A padlock hung on the fence's gate to keep intruders out. Midnight gripped the brass body of the lock. "Help me out," he called to Corey.

"You're breaking in. We're gonna get in trouble," Corey said, his eyes widening.

"I come here all the time with my dad. No big deal. Just help me hold this. They're like big scissors." Together, they wrapped the bolt cutters around the lock and squeezed until they heard the crunching sound and it split in two.

Midnight pushed the gate open and walked onto the lot. "Are you coming or what?"

"You might not get in trouble. But I will. Remember what happened at the gas station?" Corey kept looking around like he was expecting somebody to leap out from behind an old car.

"What's this got to do with that stupid Dale thinking somebody wanted to steal his stale Funyuns?"

"You don't get it."

"I don't get why you're such a scaredy-cat sometimes."

Corey rolled his eyes. "It stinks out here." He covered his nose with his arm.

"Guess I'm used to it." The smell of garbage and toxic fumes hit them whenever a strong wind blew, but everything stunk after that dumpster dive.

For somebody not too excited about coming, Corey was already a few feet away wiping snow off a car, his navy-blue mittens doing double time as snow continued to fall.

"What you got?" Midnight said.

"A muscle car. One of those old Mustangs. Wonder if the engine's still in there." Corey grinned like he did when he caught a seventy-five-mile-per-hour fastball.

Midnight checked under the hood. "Nah, it's been stripped already."

"Let's see if we can find some more cool cars," Corey said, running ahead. "Come over here and look at this one."

Midnight slowed his pace, a prickly feeling starting in his feet like little needles stabbing them. From a distance he saw Corey brushing snow off a red car with a white stripe down the middle. "Yeah, that's a Firebird. Definitely a nice muscle car." He said it the way Daddy would've.

"So why are you way over there?"

"Wait. I can't feel my toes." The tingling sensation Midnight experienced moments ago had turned to numbness. These boots had lasted him two winters, but now they had holes in the soles.

"Let's sit in this one for a few minutes to get warm." Midnight pointed to a Mustang with black leather covering the inside. Nothing warm about it, but it beat being outside in the bitter cold.

Hopping in next to him, Corey unzipped his jacket. He must have been hot while Midnight still couldn't feel his toes. Then, he put his feet up on the dashboard, his knees up against his chin, and Midnight noticed his eyes were closed. Corey wore brand-new, waterproof Timberlands. Watching Corey like that made him think about what Daddy had said once about the Black temp who'd been hired to replace him when the company had temporary layoffs a few years ago.

"I think Black people have it better than white people," Midnight said, opening the glove box and rummaging around until he found a straw. The words didn't sound quite right when he heard them floating in the chilled air of the Mustang.

"That's just dumb."

"Makes sense to me. Black people are taking over everything." He let the straw dangle in the corner of his mouth like Daddy did with his Marlboros.

Why had he ever thought the way Corey walked and talked was cool? Or that anybody wanted hair so stiff it never moved? Even the name Midnight sounded as stupid as Daddy always said it was.

Corey picked up two McDonald's ketchup packets from the glove box, rubbed them between his hands, and then stuck them in his armpits to warm them. After tearing off the tops of the packets, he squirted both in his mouth at the same time.

"Now that's dumb," Midnight said.

"Not as dumb as what you said about Black people."

"Whatever."

"We only get one month out of the whole year, just February. And it's the shortest month."

"But white people don't even have our own month."

"Uh, March, April, May, June, July . . ."

"Oh my God. Check this out." When Midnight reclined his seat, he saw something that made him forget all about who was taking over the country. A tattered page torn from a magazine poked out from beneath the seat. He pulled it out and held up a picture of two pink breasts.

"Are those really . . . ? They're huge." Corey leaned in so close that Midnight could smell the ketchup on his breath.

"I know. Have you ever seen real ones, like, up close before?"

"No. Have you?"

"Yeah. Sometimes, I watch my auntie Glo when she's in the shower. Hers are really little and weird-looking, kind of like those plastic dropper bottles we use in science class."

Corey laughed, and they groped under their seats to see if they could find more magazines when they heard a loud ding.

"That's probably my dad," Corey said. "He wants to go over my decimal multiplication homework." He zipped his jacket and pulled his hood over his head, still thumbing through the message on his phone. "And then Mom wants to quiz me on vocabulary words."

Midnight rolled his eyes. "We're not even in school right now. It's Christmas break."

"I know. They still give me work to do. Not for a grade or any- thing. When I finish, we still have to decorate the tree."

The tree. How stupid it had seemed when Corey told him they'd driven forty-five minutes outside of town to buy a Christmas tree. Mom had liked the smell of real trees, but they always found one in Ganton. Pines or firs with soft needles. Daddy didn't decorate at all anymore, and he couldn't now if he wanted to, since he stayed in Drew's apartment. Granny just put up the same fake table tree every year, with the spinning Elvis in a Santa suit on top.

"Your parents are so strict."

"Yeah, and I'm gonna be in trouble. I should have been home hours ago."

Before getting out of the car, Midnight stuffed the magazine page into his jacket pocket. The feeling was coming back to his toes, and he wiggled them to get the blood flowing. Their footprints were still visible, a road map to quickly get them back to the fence where they'd come in.

About ten feet into their walk, they heard something rattling.

"Let's go," Midnight said, and sprinted, wiping his fogged glasses with his mittens and adjusting his backpack straps on his shoulders. Corey bolted ahead of him and made it to the fence first. He pulled on the gate, but it must have gotten stuck in the snow.

The jangling sound got closer and Corey clawed the chain link, using his upper-body strength to pull himself up. Within seconds, Midnight was there, too, and found his foothold on the fence, but with one arm struggled to pull his body to the top. Before he had a chance to look back, he heard the growl.

Halfway up the fence, Midnight glanced down and saw the little yellow eyes of the German shepherd glowing in the dusky dark, searing into his backside. He clutched the fence wiring. Any slight stumble could end with him being supper for the junkyard dog. Bones had taught him enough about dogs not to stare and make him think he was challenging him. He looked up instead.

"Give me your hand," Corey called to him from the top of the fence.

The dog barked, and Midnight froze, his body disobeying his mind, which told him to keep climbing.

"A little bit more and you got it."

Looking up, he saw Corey's outstretched hand. The dog lunged at the fence. Midnight lifted himself up another few inches and clasped Corey's hand.

The dog's growls and barks rumbled in his ears as he threw his backpack over the fence and with Corey's help propelled himself to the other side. He landed with a thud onto the snow's cushion, his breaths coming in short grunts.

"We made it." Corey dropped to the ground, too, lying on his back.

The dog was still running and jumping on the other side, fangs bared, lunging at the fence. A trickle of blood oozed from Midnight's wrist where he must have scratched it on the fence. He licked the blood and then grinned at the dog, sticking his tongue out at him because he could.

At home that night, Midnight found Granny at the kitchen table going over the books for the shop. Her fat fingers snaked the length of a piece of paper filled with lines and numbers. Auntie Glo and Nicky must have been out visiting one of her weird friends.

Without looking up from the paper, Granny said, "I made you chicken teriyaki with rice. No skin on the chicken. Doctor says we got to eat healthy."

"Yeah, okay," he said, not hungry, the adrenaline from the day at the junkyard still filling him. From the smell of the house, Granny had already had Kentucky Fried Chicken for dinner. No greasy bag in the trash. She must've hidden it in the big bin out back, but he knew. Still, he didn't mention it.

She put away her books and calculator and began setting up the Monopoly board on the kitchen table. They started playing and he watched Granny's eyes follow the tokens on the board.

"Never put all your eggs in one basket," she advised. "Invest in a lot of different properties. One goes bad, you still got others."

"Did you and Mom ever play?" he said, taking out a cash loan early in the game.

"Oh, yeah. I taught her this game and everything else about money."

He wondered if Daddy would've known how to manage his money better if he'd played Monopoly. In the first round of the game, Midnight sold and mortgaged all his property and ended up in bankruptcy. Even though he knew it was just a game, his loss made him ashamed. When he thought she wasn't looking, he snatched six hundred dollars from the bank.

"I saw that," she said. "Cheaters never win, Patrick."

Even with her bad eyesight, she noticed everything. He thought about Corey's dad working at the real bank with all that money every day and for the first time realized the Cunninghams were likely very rich.

He said, "Granny, do you wish we lived at the Boardwalk? I do. We could own it and charge people a ton of rent. We'd stay on the top floor."

She rubbed her eyes and wiped the crust that collected in the corners. "I've never had a lot of money and I've made it through. I never stole a dime from anybody."

Midnight didn't know whether or not to believe her. He didn't smell any *cough syrup* on her breath, so maybe she was telling the truth. "If I was poor and really hungry, I think I'd steal food."

"It's never right to steal, I don't care how bad off you think you are."

"You mean like what Daddy said Mr. Eli and his grandfather did at the plant?"

Granny stacked the play money, put away the tokens, and folded the board fast. "Don't let me hear you bring that up again. Butch should never have said that. He has a temper sometimes and doesn't know what he's saying. You misheard part of it, so don't go repeating it. We don't know what anybody did or why."

Following him to the couch, she waited for him to get settled for the night and then sat on the edge by his feet. She opened a fresh pack of Newports and put a cigarette between her lips.

"I remember when Daddy wasn't mad," he said.

Gazing out the window, she turned away from him to blow out a ring of smoke. "You're too young for memories," she said. "You're supposed to be out there making memories, not looking back on them like some old man."

Whenever it got quiet and dark outside, those times he had nothing better to do, thoughts from years ago rattled around in his head. He couldn't shake them. "What color were Mommy's eyes? Do you remember?"

He watched Granny's flabby neck jiggle when she swallowed. "They were kind of like a chameleon, I guess. When the water at the river had that deep blue color to it, her eyes matched it. But when she'd be out playing as a kid and get blades of grass stuck in her hair, her eyes looked green to me. I guess she had that kind of beauty where you didn't know what to expect or when. Always a nice surprise."

Those times when Granny still put him to bed at night, he thought just maybe she'd live forever, but then light came in from outside—the moon or maybe just a streetlight—and it showed him all the things he never noticed in the daytime. Like how her skin bent and folded. The way her eyes had dulled over time like a light-bulb burning out. What would happen to him when she died? She told him not to worry about it, but he knew it could happen. And if Daddy couldn't take care of him anymore, who would?

"Am I really going to have to go to Louisiana?" He looked away from Granny, terrified of her answer.

She patted his knee. "I can't say for sure right now."

Closing his eyes, he faked sleep until he heard Granny tiptoe away. Miss Ruth's face appeared in his mind, and he wasn't sure why, but he allowed himself to picture what it might be like to live with her. They'd conduct paper towel experiments and she'd learn the lyrics to Blake Shelton songs. He'd ride in her Infiniti on summer days with the top down, and it wouldn't matter that Daddy called her a traitor for driving something other than an American-made car.

He tucked those thoughts of Miss Ruth into the part of his brain that helped him sleep and usually guaranteed good dreams at night. But still, he tossed on the sheets and couldn't get comfortable, his mind twisting around Granny's words about him moving to Louisiana. *I can't say.* Her words played over and over in his head and he kicked the covers violently, yet nothing drowned out the sound of her voice. *I can't say.*

He got up and crept down the hall to his bedroom. Kneeling, he ran his fingers along the rough carpet under his bed, pushing aside pencils, notebooks, and an old bike helmet. Finally, he made contact with his dusty old nursery rhyme book from when he was a child. He pulled it out, flipping through the pages until he found the slick, slightly bent photograph. Lying down again with a flashlight, he studied his mom's face until his eyes burned. He'd snuck the picture out of Granny's album months ago. It was the only candid shot of him and his mom—the two of them at the Indiana State Fair sharing a cloud of fluffy, sticky-sweet cotton candy. In the photo, a glob of it was stuck to her nose and she was trying to lick it off. The picture came out a bit blurry because Daddy had tilted the camera laughing so hard at how silly Mom was being that day. The memory made Midnight smile, and he held on to that feeling, lying under the covers with the photo on his pillow, until everything inside him dulled to a low, pleasant hum and he fell asleep.

Twenty-Two

RUTH

A haze of cigarette smoke hung in the semidarkness of Wally's Tavern, stinging Ruth's eyes. She couldn't stop thinking about DeAngelo and how he could be the missing link, the compass leading to her child. In a town as small as Ganton, people had to know him, especially if he'd duped so many out of money and had been at the center of multiple adoptions gone wrong. Maybe she could inquire subtly without tipping people off about her own son. And if anyone would know, it would be Wally. She'd been around enough bartenders to know that they heard all sorts of strange things in their line of work and kept many confidences.

Her eyes adjusted to the shadows and she made her way to the wraparound bar, the sticky floor gripping the soles of her boots. It was two days until Christmas, and a string of lights hung above the bottles. She remembered people saying Wally kept them up all year.

An older man with a slight bend to his back leaned on the bar holding a wad of cash. When Ruth got closer, she recognized him.

"Dino, what are you doing here?" As soon as she said it, she realized how obtuse her question sounded. He lived in town, and even if he didn't, this was a public place and he had every right to be in the tavern.

He smiled wide, exposing the gold crowns that capped his back teeth. "Well, I'm actually here to p-p-pick up some garlic wings for your grandmother."

Hopefully, Dino didn't see the surprise on her face. She would need to get used to having this man around. Recovering quickly, she said, "Mama loves her wings. Spicy and breaded, right?"

"You know that's right."

Wally emerged from the back with two Styrofoam containers of food and handed them to Dino with a plastic bag. How long would Dino be visiting with her mother that evening? Ruth had been staying at Mama's house every night for almost a week, and he hadn't been back to the house since she first arrived. But would he stay the night this time, and if so, would she be interrupting when she returned to the house? In the college dorms, her roommates always left a ribbon on the doorknob or some other sign to indicate they had overnight company. But this was new territory—her grandmother—and she didn't have a clue how to navigate it.

Dino touched her wrist. "I've been thinking. Your grandmother's been working hard around the house lately and I thought it might be nice for her to get away. Not too f-f-far, mind you. Maybe Chicago for a weekend. Something nice downtown, you know."

Mama didn't do a lot of frills. She was a no-nonsense, frugal woman. But perhaps Ruth had no idea what her grandmother liked these days. Once she married Xavier, their calls became less frequent, and as more time passed, the distance became just as comfortable as the closeness they had once shared.

She tried to picture Dino and Mama wining and dining in some swanky hotel on the Magnificent Mile and she couldn't. And the way he said it, it appeared Dino was asking for her permission, her blessing. She had no right to forbid it.

"That sounds like a wonderful time. Maybe Xavier and I can make some hotel and restaurant recommendations."

Dino exhaled, as though he'd been holding his breath the whole time. "Yes, I'd like that."

He looped the plastic bag with the wings around his wrist and sat a wide-brimmed hat atop his head. "I'll be seeing you."

The bells on the front door jingled when Dino walked out. Ruth took a seat on the end bar stool and watched Wally hang glasses by their stems on a long rack behind the bar. Two of his kids went to high school with her, and his oldest had played basketball with Eli. Everyone knew Wally. He was a fixture here in Ganton, but she'd left town before reaching the legal drinking age.

"What can I get you, pretty lady?" he said, and she couldn't tell whether he remembered her.

"Right now, I'm just curious if you know this guy. I read about him in the paper." She held her cell phone out to him with a photo of DeAngelo's mug shot.

Leaning across the bar, Wally glanced at her phone. "I can't place him right now, but I can't say I don't know him, either."

Disappointed, Ruth said, "That's fine. It was worth a shot."

"Wait, let me see it again." This time, Wally took her phone and brought it up to his face. Twisting his handlebar mustache, he frowned.

"You recognize him," she said.

"Oh, yeah. I didn't at first. But yeah, of course I know him. Wish I didn't. That's the lawyer, DeAngelo, who got locked up in that whole baby deal. Took advantage of some good people. He was just in here about a month ago. Made sure to come in when we were slow, if you know what I mean. Didn't have to see too many people."

Ruth looked past him to the bottles of liquor lining the wall. "So he's out of prison and here in Ganton?" Her heartbeat quickened, and she recognized the fear now that she was getting closer to the man who might have the answers she'd been looking for.

"He did his time at Terre Haute and now he's got a place over on Wayland, just outside of town. Out in the middle of nowhere. A lot of folks wanted to wring his neck for what he did, so it's safer for everybody that he keeps his distance."

Terre Haute. The federal prison. She'd been using the database for state correctional facilities. That's why his name hadn't turned up in her search. Not once did Wally ask why she cared to know about DeAngelo. She got the feeling he enjoyed showing off his knowledge of legendary Ganton characters—criminal and otherwise.

"Oh," added Wally, "if you're looking for your brother, he's back there at the card table." So he did remember her.

She hadn't been looking, but Mama had been right about Eli spending most of his time here now that he was out of work. In a far corner of the bar Ruth eyed the card table where the best bid whist players were crowned. She spotted Eli sitting with several guys and a few women who used to work on the line at Fernwood. She vaguely recognized the older ones and lamented how it'd been months since they'd lost their jobs. Still, they carried the smell of plastic on their skin from their days at the plant.

"Rise and fly, my people, rise and fly," said Freddie, an old man with skin like dry, shriveled autumn leaves. If you lost, you had to get up and go so the next player could have your seat in the game.

If any of them held anger in their hearts, they either hid it or released it here. Cards slapped the table and people talked smack because they took this card-playing thing very seriously.

"Don't mess with this bitch," Eli said as he slammed a queen of spades on the table.

Eli had learned bid from Papa. Many of the whites from Fernwood had played bridge, euchre, or rummy until they caught on to bid under the tutelage of Blacks at the plant.

"Ruth Tuttle. Is that you over there? Your brother didn't tell me you were home for Christmas." Gwen, who had worked as an equipment tester, had to be in her sixties by now, but she still looked good, as most Black women did with age, all the years settling in her hips and on her face making her appear strong and assured, not old. She had put three sons through college with her plant job.

"My brother's getting forgetful in his old age. Good seeing you, Gwen."

Smiling, Ruth rested her hands on the back of Eli's chair. He grunted and she checked out his promising hand. He had partnered with Gwen for bid, and in the smoky shadows of the bar, Gwen's eyes followed his and right away Ruth could tell from the way her tongue ran over her top lip that she had the big joker and she was letting Eli know they were about to grab another book.

The table shook when Gwen dropped that last card, the big joker. Eli howled after their win and rammed his fist into his chest, bellowing a warrior's chant. After a few more games, Eli took a seat at the bar.

"I'll have what he's having," Ruth said to the female bartender, who had to be freezing in her low-cut tank top. Reindeer antlers sat atop her head. Ruth slid onto the stool next to her brother.

"You still here? Why?" he asked.

"I'm in a bar." She glanced at her wristwatch. "It's nowhere near closing time and I want a drink." The bartender passed her a Bud. Martinis and margaritas were her usual drinks of choice, but on her brother's turf, she drank what he drank.

The high from his bid whist win had been short-lived, and she watched it wear off like an old Band-Aid that refused to stick. He rubbed his thumbs over the condensation on his beer bottle as if that bottle were his only friend. She wanted to gather him to her and cradle his head against her chest, but she reminded herself this was a grown man, her big brother, not a child.

"Get your drink on, then," Eli said. "I hope you not a lightweight anymore. We'll see if you can hold your liquor."

Glancing down to the other end of the bar, Ruth eyed a bald guy in a tight muscle shirt licking his lips and looking at her like she could be a steak dinner and he hadn't eaten in weeks. Eli positioned himself to block the man's view, the way the church mothers draped a handkerchief over a young woman's lap to cover her legs when she wore a short skirt.

Nursing her beer, Ruth thought about all the brothers out of work, filling their hours here at the bar, some of them lured to criminal enterprises. She remembered Lena talking about gangs planting seeds in Ganton.

Turning to her brother, she said, "I hear gangs are cropping up here doing drug deals and recruiting kids to help them." Just saying those words made her fearful for her son.

Cocking his head, Eli said, "Who did you hear that from?"

"Lena. She's worried about Midnight."

"Look, she don't know what's going on. I heard about kids at that gas station over on Main getting hassled. But trust me, nobody's pushing weight right there in the open. And they ain't messing with little white boys like Midnight, either." He chuckled. "Real gangsters know that gas station is hot as hell with cops around somewhere."

She trusted her brother's take on it, knowing he'd paid for his own mistake dabbling in drugs. Still, she didn't want her son anywhere near this kind of activity. "You said kids are getting hassled?"

"Yeah, you got these wannabe gangsters. In this town, there ain't shit to do sometimes but pretend you the Nino Brown of Ganton."

"I wonder if Midnight's been approached."

"I don't know, but I do know that if Butch Boyd knew how to raise his kid, he'd stay out of trouble." The mention of Butch's name reminded her of that disastrous dinner at Lena's.

"Surprised Butch isn't here playing cards, since so many from the plant are here today."

Disgust crept over Eli's face. "Better not show his face."

She wanted to ask her brother about the outrageous claims Butch had made, especially about their grandfather. She had believed in Papa just as she had Santa Claus and the tooth fairy. Even a few years after she discovered both to be mythical, she pretended to still believe, because somehow, she needed larger-than-life legends to steady her in the real world. She wanted to know what Eli thought, but she couldn't risk him exploding here in public. Not with so many former plant workers nearby.

"Why do you and Butch hate each other so much?"

"A man doesn't just hate another man for the hell of it. There's always more to it. That more usually has something to do with a woman. A woman that was his or one he wanted to be his. I know that's what you're thinking, but it's never been like that between Butch and me."

"Okay, it's not about a woman. What is it about then?" The last time Ruth remembered the two scuffling had been at a Pratt pool hall as teenagers, arguing over playing heavy metal or hip-hop on the jukebox. But that squabble didn't last.

Eli ran his hand over the top of his head. "We're just different and we don't mix. That's all I got. Anyhow, don't want to ruin my buzz."

"What's really going on with you, Eli?"

"I'm good."

"How did that interview go?"

"It went."

"Does that mean you got the job?"

He tilted the bottle back and took a big gulp. "They said, 'Can you lift fifty pounds?' I said, 'Yes, sir.' They said, 'Can you work nights and weekends?' I said, 'Yes, sir.' Then they said they needed somebody who could track inventory online using Microsoft Office applications. 'Can you do that?' And, well, that was the end of that. Game over."

Frustration clouded his face, resignation pressing his shoulders until they slumped. The same set of grandparents had raised them both in the same house. The same Ganton schools educated her and Eli, and yet her flower bloomed while his never made it beyond a bud.

"You have to reframe your thinking. Even if you don't meet every requirement, walk into those interviews like you're at the spades table about to run a Boston on everybody. You need a winner's mindset."

He laughed. "You must've learned that shit in college. Psychology, right? Some book about a hundred ways to get inside the mind of a broke brotha? Am I right?"

The bottle of Bud swung in Eli's hand when he talked. Ruth threw up both hands in surrender, hoping he'd see she had come in peace.

"Look, I'm sick of you feeling sorry for yourself. You're not the only one with problems. I haven't told anyone this, but there's a guy on my job that I trained and now he's getting better, high-profile assignments."

"Damn. Them white people be tripping. Sorry about that, sis. But at least you still got a job."

"How are you so sure they're white?"

Eli twisted his mouth into a smirk as if he didn't need any confirmation. Her eye roll must have told him he'd guessed correctly.

"Hey, Eli?"

"What's good, lil bit?"

"Do you ever feel like life is getting ahead of you, like you can't control what happens anymore? I mean, it's your life, but somebody else is pulling the puppet strings. Nothing is the way it used to be or the way it should be." She knew she wasn't making much sense, not even to herself. Her thoughts jumbled in her head.

Eli glanced at his phone. "I know where I should be right now. On the plant floor. The smell of hot steel all around me. All those machines coming alive in my hands just like a good woman. I can still hear the buzzing and other sounds in my head. Sometimes, they wake me up in the middle of the night. It's like they teasing me, you know."

Even the memory of the plant made his face glow, and then that flame was extinguished just as fast. Ruth ached for her brother to regain everything he had lost.

"Cassie should be by your side through this thing. She's your wife, the mother of your children. One thing I can say about Mama is that she stuck by Papa when he got sick. She hung in there till the end."

Eli took a swig of his beer. "Mama's a soldier, man. Ride or die. Now, Cassie. She took it real good in the beginning, rubbing my face, whispering sweet words in my ear. You know how y'all women do. Talking 'bout how she loves me more than biscuits and gravy and I would always be her husband no matter what. That's what she said until the bill collectors started calling. Then I started smelling some other brotha's sweat on her."

"I didn't know," Ruth said, her hands tightening around her bottle. She thought about Xavier and how she'd really handle it if he got demoted at his company, or worse, let go. You like to think you know yourself and those closest to you, but you don't until you're tested.

"Like I told Cassie, she saw my lack, not my love. Then she had the nerve to try to keep my kids from me." Eli smashed a peanut shell in his fist and his whole body shook, as if to shed the memory.

He'd never opened up to her like this before, but then again, she'd been a kid most of the years they'd spent together. Men kept their hurt tucked away deep on the inside. If it rose high enough to spill out of them, they ran it off on the basketball court, drowned it in a bottle, or buried it deep inside a woman. But they rarely talked it out.

Ruth gripped her brother's arm and forced him to look at her. "Don't let that happen. Fight for my niece and nephews. I know how much you love them, and I've seen the way they look at you. Like you drew every star in the sky by hand."

He made a gurgling sound as if he were speaking underwater. "There's nothing like having your kids in your life. When I miss weeks with mine, it's like years, you know."

Keeping her eyes on her beer, Ruth said, "I know it's not the same, but I've tried for eleven years to convince myself that I could just go on with my life not knowing anything about my son. I was fooling myself."

Eli threw his head back. "Here we go. You still digging, ain't you?"

"Does the name Stanley DeAngelo mean anything to you?" She studied his face.

Unexpectedly, he nodded. "Yeah. A lawyer. Kind of shady. That cat had a reputation for being a fixer. Bribing judges and shit. Made problems go away, if you know what I mean. Got locked up for some years, I think. Why?"

Papa's legacy helped Eli get his job at Fernwood. Still, even a misdemeanor followed you. What if her snooping blew this adoption fraud case wide open and people started asking questions because she came to town asking them first? Even if it was long ago and for a minor offense, Eli already had a criminal record, and now she knew he'd done time on gun charges. If he were implicated in another crime, would anyone ever hire him again? But she needed answers.

Swiveling on her bar stool to face her brother, she said, "Did DeAngelo have anything to do with my baby?"

He appeared genuinely surprised by her question. "What? Hell, no. Let me tell you. Mama took care of the adoption. I don't know what lawyer she went through, but I can't see it being him. She not crazy."

She believed Eli when he said he knew nothing about a connection to DeAngelo, but her intuition nagged at her. "Okay. Maybe. Maybe not." She nibbled on a few peanuts underneath the cracked shells on her brother's napkin.

Alcohol lubricated her brother's tongue, this she knew. He used to let secrets slip all the time—once revealing a foreclosure on an uncle's swanky new house, another time exposing a cousin's extramarital affair. Right now, he was just drunk enough to tell her the name of her son.

"Who are they?" she asked.

"What are you talking about?"

"The people raising my son. What are their names?"

Eli paused, maybe to consider the question, and Ruth could tell he knew her son's adoptive parents. "Mama and Papa, they're our blood, but they're not our biological parents. But they were the ones who were there all those years for me and for you. That's real family. That means something. The people raising your son? They're good people and he's *their* son. You can't change that."

In that moment, Ruth felt like she was paddling upstream against a strong current. The closer she got to her baby, the larger the waves got, and she didn't know how to swim through them.

"You talk about family. I'm your family. I'm your sister. Yet you won't help me."

Eli swished his beer like mouthwash. She could see the muscles in his neck straining. "All I did was *help you*. I helped you keep your dirty little secret so you could go off to college and make something of yourself. So you could do something with your life and not end up like me." He stretched out his arms, swinging the bottle.

Ruth tensed on her bar stool. "You're drunk and you're unemployed. That's why I'm not going there with you right now."

She watched barely contained rage pass over Eli's face, tightening and twisting it until each swallow of beer stilled him. Ruth fought differently with her brother as an adult. Their quarrels as children could be excused by youthful innocence and were often smoothed over by some new preoccupation the next day. But now, they knew how the world worked and their barbs carried a more potent poison. They knew better, yet they kept hurting each other anyway.

Twenty-Three

RUTH

The front door to Lena's house sat ajar, only a sliver of dark space visible. Ruth pushed it open. The text from Midnight had been urgent, and she'd rushed over from the tavern. Midnight's message read: please come. granny is sick.

Lena suffered from high blood pressure and diabetes. Mama said that sometimes Lena came home from work too tired to stick herself at night with the insulin needle. She was still relatively young, but the stress of trying to keep the shop in business had taken its toll. *A slow death* was how Mama put it.

The house smelled of mildew and cigarettes now. Ruth rotated in a full circle in the living room, taking in the stacks of unopened mail, coupon clippings, and credit card solicitations covering the dining room table and the floor.

"Lena. Are you in here? Midnight! Lena!" she called.

Silence.

On the mantel above the television sat an eight-by-ten photo of Midnight as a baby in Hannah's lap. For the first time, Ruth noticed her straight nose. Square jaw. Sandy hair. Her chromosomes passed down to Midnight.

It didn't seem fair that this woman had been snatched from her son's life. Standing behind them in the photo was Butch, with a fresh crew cut, his lips turned up in a smile that almost made him look handsome instead of perpetually angry as he usually did.

A clicking noise came from one of the bedrooms down the dark hallway. Midnight appeared, bumping a small red suitcase against the wall. He smelled like sweat and whatever food had crusted on his shirt. Maybe lasagna or leftover spaghetti. Ruth pulled him by his arm into the living room, the roller bag clattering after him, scraping the baseboards.

"Tell me what's going on. You had me worried to death when you sent that text about Lena. Where is she?"

"She's okay now." Midnight plopped on a chair, crumpling the unopened mail beneath him. "I needed to tell you something and I didn't think you'd come."

Need poured from his slender body, desperation stretching out like a hand bobbing above the ocean's crest, like a swimmer begging someone to pull him up before he drowned. Ruth leaned against the wall, her arms folded, vacillating between hugging and shaking him, and, in the end, she settled on neither.

He twisted the handle of the luggage. "Are you gonna tell Granny I lied to make you come?"

The suitcase he carried fell open, socks and underwear tangled with turtlenecks and T-shirts in a tumble on the floor.

"You must've wanted me to come over here to give you a ride to the bus station," Ruth said, gesturing toward the open suitcase.

"Huh?"

"I assume you're planning a trip." Her gaze swept his belongings strewn across the floor. From the looks of it, he planned to run away from home.

He just shrugged.

"Where's your grandmother?"

"She had to work late. Doing the books." The ritualistic way he said it, she knew Lena must've told him that many times before.

"And your auntie?"

"Gettin' high somewhere, I guess. Little Nicky's at the baby-sitter's."

When Midnight rattled off all the reasons that he found himself home alone at night, she heard no sadness in his voice. And that had to be the saddest part about it. He didn't expect more, and any indignation he might have felt had been wrung out of him.

"Have you had dinner?"

"Nope."

Ruth made her way to the kitchen, where she found a loaf of white bread, sugar, eggs, and a carton of milk only one day past the expiration date. She sniffed and detected a slight sour smell along the rim but decided it would do.

"It's too late for breakfast," he said, pointing to the eggs she was cracking into a bowl. "It's suppertime."

Midnight rested his elbows on the counter, and she handed him a whisk.

"French toast for dinner is special in a way. It's breaking the rules, kind of like when you eat dessert before dinner."

He seemed to accept that explanation, even be pleased by it. She didn't know how to cook too many dishes, and relied on Xavier for most meals, but luckily, she'd watched Mama enough to remember how she did the French toast. While she heated Crisco oil in a skillet, Midnight mixed. The ripples made by the whirling liquid seemed to entrance him, and he beat it faster and faster. Ruth smiled, thinking about how Mama's arm fat would jiggle every time she beat anything while cooking.

"What are you smiling about?"

"Just thinking I might have to take you home with me. You're even better than my electric mixer at getting rid of lumps."

He whipped even harder, getting so carried away that some spilled over the side of the bowl, but she didn't bother to wipe up the mess.

Something about this scene in this kitchen fed a fantasy for Ruth. Finding Lena's apron stuffed in a drawer, she put it on, tying it at the waist. She practiced moving around the small kitchen as if she belonged there, humming while she dipped half slices of bread in the mixture.

In this moment, cooking with Midnight at her side, she felt like a mother. Comfortable. Sliding into it as if she'd been doing it forever. The pan sizzled when she dropped the bread slices in the hot oil, and she delighted in having this young boy at her hip while they watched each piece turn golden brown.

"Do you know how to make heart-shaped pancakes?" Midnight asked the question when they sat down to eat.

"You don't like your French toast?" Had the edges come out too crisp or the center undercooked and squishy? Maybe she'd added too much milk or used too few eggs.

"It's good. I was just wondering about heart-shaped pancakes, though. Corey's mom makes that for him all the time."

"Oh, your friend you do science experiments with. Well, I've never tried any fancy shapes. Maybe next time."

Midnight helped her clean the kitchen, mopping up gritty sugar and egg off the countertops. When they finished, she pointed to the clothes surrounding the open suitcase. "Put these away."

He picked up a turtleneck and sloppily folded it. "I'm going to Louisiana. Granny said so."

"Maybe it's just for a short visit."

"No. To live. Forever."

Midnight's words fell like stones.

This kid exaggerated, stretching the truth until it ripped in two from the pulling. Believing him took extraordinary leaps of faith that he hadn't earned with her yet. But he'd hinted at this during dinner the other night, and Lena hadn't denied it or clarified her intentions.

"Did your granny give you a reason?"

"Not enough money to feed another mouth. That's what she said. I guess we have cousins there I can live with. Nobody wants me here." He gestured to the empty suitcase. "Might as well leave now if they don't want me."

Everything Midnight said about the move seemed on the nose and intentional, as if he thought she might have influence with Lena. All kinds of businesses had grown sluggish in this bad economy. People like Eli and Butch lost jobs and struggled to find new ones. But were things bad enough for Lena to consider shipping Midnight south? Anything Ruth said would have sounded hollow, so she sat silently on the couch. She couldn't promise him that his future didn't involve a move south.

He had a lost look about him, and she could tell he moved through life rudderless, without his mother to anchor him. Out of the corner of her eye, Ruth caught Midnight staring at her. Of everyone he knew in Ganton, he'd called her, practically a stranger. But she understood it. Sometimes, when you met a nice person who showed you a little attention, that person became a placeholder for your mother.

"You look a lot like your mom," she told him, glancing at the mantel portrait, grasping for the right thing to say.

He shrugged. "I was just a kid when we took that picture." She had to laugh because Midnight spoke as if he were an old sage looking back from the other side of a long life.

"I bet you miss her a lot."

"One time she went to McDonald's every day for like a month so I could get all eight of the Transformer figures in the Happy Meal. She wouldn't let me eat all the fries 'cause they're bad for you, but I got to keep the toys." His eyes lit up so bright when he told that story, but they burned out fast and he got quiet again.

On impulse, she said, "Put your coat on. Let's go get ice cream for dessert."

"Seriously?" Midnight launched himself from the couch, punched the air in delight, and bolted for the door. "Corner Diner has the best ice cream."

The light from the diner glowed in the night like a firecracker against the dark sky. Midnight swung the car door open before she could turn off the ignition. Ruth got out and followed him quickly to the front door, her childhood memories the wind at her back. After a BLT or an open-faced roast beef sandwich, they always ordered dessert, chocolate ice cream in a waffle cone for Eli and strawberry in a cake cone for Ruth.

At the entrance to the diner, Midnight hung back, skittish like a horse that just got spooked. She held the door for him, and he dragged his feet going inside. She wasn't sure why.

There were very few customers that night so close to Christmas, and Ruth figured people were out doing last-minute shopping or having pre-holiday celebrations. Midnight chose a stool at the counter and Ruth sat down next to him. A middle-aged woman with a boxy body and a horizontal straight line where her lips should've been stood behind the counter looking as if she'd been expecting them even before the jingle of the door. Her green cat eyes got fat as egg yolks the minute they walked in.

"Menus?" she asked, holding one out to each of them.

"No, just ice cream for us, and I think we both know what we want," Ruth said. On the drive over, they had reminisced about their favorite flavors and how they'd evolved over the years. The diner prided itself on serving throwback treats, like the Popsicles she and Eli used to get from the ice cream truck as kids.

When Midnight gave his order for a peanut butter swirl sundae with chocolate syrup, the waitress began writing on her notepad, but her gaze stayed on them, as if telling Midnight to blink twice if he was in danger.

"Is this your sitter?" she asked Midnight.

"No," he said in a small, fearful voice.

"I was just wondering." Her unsettling surveillance suggested they'd broken some unspoken rule by being there. Or being there together. They always went for the mammy caricature.

Ruth forced a fake smile. "I was wondering, too, whether you're serving ice cream today or an inquisition." At that, Midnight smiled for the first time since they'd arrived.

Color drained from the server's face. "I didn't mean any harm. I was born and raised right here in Ganton and didn't recognize you. That's all."

"Well, I guess we have something in common after all." Ruth beckoned Midnight to leave the counter and follow her to a booth away from the woman's prying eyes.

A few tables away, an elderly couple ate cheeseburgers, laughing at some shared joke. A mom and dad tried to wrangle three little kids who were entertaining themselves by tossing tater tots at each other.

She'd missed out on those parental rites of passage, but now she sat opposite Midnight, who dangled his chocolate-dipped cherry over his mouth and flicked his tongue at it, watching it swing from its stem. Ignoring her own melting Popsicle, she watched him, but didn't correct his table manners. She wanted to ask if the server had given him trouble before, but she didn't. He seemed relaxed and happy now.

This time she had a taste for a raspberry Popsicle, since it reminded her of ones that she and Eli used to get from the ice cream truck. Once she finished, she held the stick between her thumb and index finger. "Watch this."

She blew on it hard as if she were extinguishing birthday candles. The stick disappeared and then came back when she blew into the air again.

"What the heck?" he said.

She laughed at his open mouth and wide eyes. "It's magic. When I was a few years younger than you are now, the ice cream man did this trick for us every week and we'd watch his hands and mouth closely each time trying to figure out how he did it. But it happened so fast and he never shared his secret with us."

"So how did you figure it out?" Midnight looked under their table to see if the mechanics behind the magic hid there.

"I tried everything I could think of for weeks, and finally I asked my fourth-grade science teacher and she showed me. If I let you in on the secret, you can't tell anybody else." She leaned in close to him across the table.

"I won't tell, I swear."

"It's an illusion. The idea is to flip the stick with your thumb and middle finger. Put tension on it like this, making sure it's lined up perfectly with your hand and wrist."

She reached for his arm to demonstrate, and it sank limp and heavy in her hand. Quickly, with his other hand, Midnight pulled his sweatshirt sleeve down to cover it. Gently, she lifted the sleeve and exposed the deep red discoloration of his skin. Dry. Waxy. When she looked up at him, his head dropped. "You can tell me what happened. Who hurt you?"

At first, he hesitated. She waited until he began to speak. "Some stupid boys. They were messing with Corey and fighting him. Just 'cause . . . he's Black. But I helped him. And then they got mad at me and set my arm on fire."

She shuddered, picturing the flames lapping at his skin, alive and crackling, singeing it until it peeled from his bones. In a country enlightened enough to elect a Black president, its original sin still infected so many, even children. "I can't imagine what you went through. Corey is lucky to have a friend like you."

"I guess. A lot of people blamed Corey even though it wasn't his fault." Midnight rotated in his seat, pointing his body in the direction of the woman behind the counter. She sprayed glass cleaner on the outside of the display case while shooting furtive glances in their direction.

"Forget about her. You did the right thing and it cost you a lot." She patted his arm. "Not many people have the courage to stand up to a crowd and defend someone who's been treated unfairly."

"Your brother did."

"My brother, Eli? I don't understand."

Midnight shrugged as he often did. "Lots of people picked sides and everything. Eli—I mean Mr. Eli—was the main one who took up for Corey and tried to make Daddy stop saying all those mean things about him. And the day of the fight, Mr. Eli stopped the whole thing when he shot that gun in the air."

Ruth fell back against her seat. It felt as though someone had vacuumed the air from her lungs. She struggled to breathe. Her mind raced faster than the rest of her body could catch up.

Midnight's friend Corey. Could he be? Could he be her son?

Still rattled, she forced herself to think. Eli wouldn't risk going back to jail for just anybody. But he would do it for his nephew.

"Are you okay?" Midnight stared at her, likely confused by the rush of emotions playing on her face.

"Yes, I'm fine," she said, looking beyond him.

She scrambled to think of the few offhand references Midnight had made to his friend. It seemed Corey excelled in science just as she had, but she couldn't remember much else. Was it really possible that all this time, her son had been right here in Ganton, as she'd suspected?

"You don't look fine," Midnight said, waving his hand in her face.

"I should get you home. It's late," she said quickly. "I don't want your grandmother to worry."

Back at Lena's house, no one was home yet. Midnight told her he slept on the couch sometimes and asked her to tuck him in. A strange request for a boy his age, but she recognized how needy he was, desperate for affection. Guilt consumed her, playing mother to this boy she barely knew while some other woman tucked her own son—Corey?—in at night.

When she and Natasha were girls, they used to play house, lining their baby dolls up on the couch to do their hair and dress them for outings, baking their meals in play ovens, and then putting the dolls to bed at night. Back then, they were playing games with no consequences for missteps and misunderstood feelings. But this was no game, and Midnight wasn't her baby doll.

She sat next to him as he lay on the sofa, his head resting in the curve of her arm. That shock of hair against her elbow surprised her, slick and smooth against her skin. Soon, Midnight's eyes closed, and she heard the slow, steady breathing of his sleep.

The moon hung low outside the window. Heavy winds rattled the front door. Doubt crept into her mind. How could she be sure that

Midnight's friend was her son? Maybe this was a coincidence and she'd read too much into what he had told her. Still, she couldn't reason herself out of the certainty she felt deep in her bones. She wanted to find Eli, beg him to confirm what she thought she knew. Would he acquiesce?

Mama had worked so hard to keep her son's identity from her. Yet now, she was impotent, stripped of her lies and secrets, everything that had emboldened her self-righteousness for years. Ruth would confront her grandmother, fling the truth in her face until she cowered for once.

She ached to call Xavier and tell him what she'd just learned. That she was almost certain that she knew her son's name. But would this draw them closer or create more distance between them? She couldn't be sure.

Ruth carefully lifted Midnight's head, placed a couch pillow under him, and propped up his legs, covering him with the jacket he'd tossed over the back of the couch.

Planting a soft kiss on his forehead, she whispered *thank you* and slipped out of the house without waking him.

Twenty-Four

MIDNIGHT

The next day, Midnight and his friends, their toes sore and numb from kicking tires in an empty lot and playing at the rec center, weren't ready to head home yet. It was Christmas Eve and they were hopped up on Ring Dings and grape soda. Their energy needed a place to unravel and run free.

"Watch this," Midnight said, holding a stale piece of leftover Halloween candy corn like a dart and releasing it with the snap of his wrist. What he'd lost in strength in one arm he made up for in the other. He watched the curve of the candy as it left his hand and then ducked behind an industrial garbage bin when it hit a woman limping along on a cane. She didn't notice a thing.

"Oh, snap. You hit that old lady," Corey hissed over his shoulder.

"Wait. Check this out," Pancho said, as he grabbed the candy bag from Midnight. He aimed and missed the city worker salting the road.

Sebastian laughed. "Man, your pitch needs work. For real."

And that's how the game started. Targets weren't created equal. As messed up as it was, tagging old people and little kids earned you bonus points.

Old man for four points.

Old lady for six.

A baby stroller got you eight points.

Anyone in a wheelchair for ten.

Crouching behind the dumpster, they took turns aiming the candy corn and ducking for cover before their victims caught them. They stifled snorts when a pimply-faced kid in a Santa hat rotated in a complete circle trying to figure out what had poked him on his cheek.

By the time they emptied the bag of candy corn, the streetlights had come on, and they moved across the alley's edge and made shadow puppets with their hands. The boys' laughter ricocheted off the walls of the old drugstore and they forgot their curfews.

"I learned a new magic trick last night," said Midnight. "I can make stuff disappear."

He remembered Ruth's hands gliding across the Popsicle stick.

And then he remembered the flash of her ring.

A husband. Midnight hadn't thought of Miss Ruth as someone's wife, even though her diamond ring sparkled like the Wabash River under the glare of moonlight. If she had a husband, then she might also have kids. He thought that if she did, she'd have them with her, but as much as he wanted to know for sure, he hadn't asked. In a state of ignorance, his fantasy about her as his own mother, a second mother, took root and blossomed.

"Okay, are you just gonna stand there and stare into space or show us?" Sebastian said.

"I can't. It's a secret."

Corey exhaled loudly. "Then why did you bring it up?"

"'Cause I wanted to."

"Can you make yourself disappear?" Sebastian said, a stupid little grin spread across his face.

"No, but your dad disappears all the time, and I bet he won't be home for Christmas," replied Midnight, agitated.

Sebastian often complained that his father worked late hours at a food-processing plant a few towns over and got home long after everybody else in the house went to bed.

"At least my dad has a job and he lives with us."

"Shut up."

"Make me."

They stomped in the slush, splashing the dirty melting snow on each other's pants legs, and hardly noticed two men at the entrance to the alley who had been in shadow, wearing red bandannas on their heads and loose-fitting jeans hugging the middle of their hips. In the grocery store or at the mall, Granny would tell boys and grown men both to pull up their pants. *Have some respect for me if not for yourself,* she'd say.

"What's going on, fellas?" asked the shorter, beefier one.

"We're on our way home," Midnight said, backing up a few steps. The men looked familiar. These were the same guys from the gas station who had opened the door for them.

"What's the hurry? Let's talk man to man," said the taller one.

The sky had completely dimmed, and Midnight thought about something Corey had said to him years ago about all of them being the same color in the night. But when he looked at these two men and his friends, everyone except him shared the same brown skin— some lighter, some darker, but all brown. He dropped his head and stuffed his hands into his jacket pockets, covering his whiteness as best he could. Something glowed in the shorter guy's hand. Thinking it could be the blade of a knife, Midnight sucked in a quick breath.

"I like these guys. We got the United Nations right here," the short guy said, nudging his friend.

"More like a bag of Skittles."

The smaller one seemed to be in charge. "Where are my manners? Have some. Chocolate's good for you."

No one moved, and Midnight realized the silver in his hand was the foil wrapper on a Hershey bar.

"Hey, little white boy." The short one moved closer to Midnight, laughing.

Sobs gathered in Midnight's throat, and he swallowed hard to force them back down.

"Leave him alone." Corey stepped between him and the man.

Midnight had long known his whiteness stood out next to his friends' Blackness. One hot July afternoon, Midnight had joined the other boys on the stoop outside the payday loan store. His hair pasted itself to his face and neck. Sebastian scooted away from him. "Y'all white boys smell like wet dogs," he said. Midnight had wanted to get up and walk away—no, run off—but he refused to let the others think Sebastian's insult had bothered him. Later, when he told Granny, she had said it had nothing to do with being white. The problem, as she put it, was that Daddy let Midnight's wet clothes sit in the washing machine until they stank like mildew.

Corey had kept his eyes lowered that day, focused on rubbing a shard of glass from a broken Coors bottle gently against his forearm just to see how hard you had to poke to break the skin. "My dad said we all bleed the same no matter what color we are," Corey told the group, and it sounded like something Mr. Cunningham would say with his firm voice and kind eyes. And with that, Corey had shut them up.

The two gangbangers, who seemed a little high, moved on from Midnight's whiteness to Corey's burgundy-ness. "I know you. You're the big baseball star. What happened to you? You spill a gallon of Welch's grape juice on your face?" The short one took his index finger and ran it across the birthmark on Corey's cheek and then inspected his finger. The taller man bent over and laughed, grabbing his knees.

Corey jerked his head away from the man's grasp. The birthmark on his face had been the butt of jokes in school one year, and every kid in class, Midnight included, had picked on him until they got bored and people stopped caring. But these guys hadn't earned the right to make fun of Corey's face.

"That wasn't funny," Midnight said. The words didn't sound as tough as they had seconds before when he had rehearsed them in his mind.

"Check out the mouth on this one." The shorter guy advanced on

Midnight and said, "You ready to join the Kings of Comedy, huh? Let's hear you tell a joke."

Midnight stared at the ground, his heart beating wildly. The men circled them and chuckled. The boys moved closer to one another, their jacket sleeves touching. What did these guys want from them? Money? Sixth graders didn't have any. It had to be something worse. Much worse. Auntie Glo said one of the local gangs wore red bandannas and they scored points sometimes based on how many people they killed.

The shorter guy stood in front of him now, so close Midnight could smell the chocolate on his breath. "Why so jumpy?"

Glancing over his shoulder at the length of the alley, Midnight tried to calculate how fast he would need to run to make it to Plymouth Street and then around the corner to head to Pratt without them catching him.

"You need to relax, little dude. I'm Bo," he said, extending his hand, dry white spots between his fingers. "And this is my boy Larry, or L-Boogie as we call him."

Midnight glanced up and then stared at the ground again.

"We'll forgive you all for your lack of manners," Bo said when none of the boys shook his hand. "You see, I have a business proposition for you."

Midnight made a mental note to look up the word *proposition* if he ever made it home.

"I bet you all like Jordan high-tops. Am I right?"

Midnight didn't intend to, but he looked down at his boots, slick and rubbed raw from overuse. Granny had bought them two years ago and they now pinched his cold toes. She had promised him new ones for Christmas.

"Yeah, they're cool," Pancho said.

"That's right. They're real nice. Better than what you getting for Christmas, I bet," Bo said, kicking up his expensive gym shoe. A wide, diamond-studded watch hung from his wrist. "You can have all this, too."

"How? What do we have to do?" Sebastian asked.

"A little bit of this and that. We pay you. Once we see your work ethic, we'll show you how to run a business and make even more money." Bo licked the chocolate stuck to the foil wrapper.

"He's right. But it's more than business. We're family." L-Boogie stepped closer to them, running his tongue over his teeth. The white vapor of his breath filled the space between them in the alley.

"I can do some jobs for you." Sebastian stood straighter, preening as if Dale from the gas station had offered him a summer job.

"Yeah, me too. How much you paying?" Pancho asked.

"Will you shut up?" Corey told Pancho and Sebastian under his breath.

"I'll be real disappointed if we can't do business," Bo said, drawing *real* out into two syllables.

No one spoke at first, and then L-Boogie and Bo told them they'd be in touch soon, that they knew how to find them. Then the men looked at each other and laughed so hard their knees buckled. Midnight didn't know what that meant but he figured it wasn't good.

A shot of cold air ran along the insides of Midnight's legs and he realized he'd peed on himself. As soon as the men turned out of the alley, he ran toward home without saying goodbye to his friends or seeing where they went. The night air, cars, storefronts, and naked trees whizzed by. He ran past Obama/Biden yard signs until the string of McCain/Palin ones began. He ran until he couldn't hear anything but the echo of his footsteps in his head.

A block from his house, with his lungs full, he hugged a stop sign and banged his head lightly on the metal pole. Sure, he liked to get into a little trouble every now and then. Mostly just to prove that he could. And because it was fun when there was nothing better to do. But he wasn't the sort of kid to join a gang or sell drugs for one. Why did Bo and L-Boogie choose him?

WHEN HE FINALLY MADE IT HOME TO GRANNY'S, HE SAW A COUPLE of cars lined up on the street and Daddy's truck parked outside. The engine still clicked and crackled, telling him his father had just arrived. Midnight didn't want to see anybody right now, not with a bomb exploding in his chest and piss in his pants. Nobody could see him like this. Especially not Daddy. Before Midnight turned the key in the lock, he heard laughter and music. Opening the door just a crack, he peered inside.

Just like on Super Bowl Sunday, the smell of chicken wings, brats, and beef brisket hit Midnight's nose the moment he walked in the house. During Christmas week, people set aside unpaid mortgages, overdue bill collector notices, and job ads to be merry and not miserable for once. In the kitchen a couple of Daddy's buddies were egging on Loomis, who held the Elvis tree-topper like a microphone, crooning off-key about being nothing but a hound dog. He knew Granny invited Daddy's friends to the Christmas Eve party just to be nice. Running through the living room, he saw Marsha from the credit union, Kimmie the interstate toll-taker, and a couple of people who regularly came to the store.

He ran past everyone and into the bathroom, where he stripped off all his clothes as fast as he could. In the shower, he stood there for a long while letting hot water pour over him, feeling the pee and pressure of the day roll off him like sludge.

After he finished, his skin blazed red hot and the mirror was completely fogged up. He toweled off, and using his forefinger, he wrote *I hate my life* on the mirror. Then he opened the door and sneaked into his bedroom to put on clothes.

When he emerged from his room, he saw Granny and Daddy in the hallway, their faces contorted in anger.

Granny exhaled loud as a muffler exhaust. "Butch, you know the rules. You get him Mondays and Fridays, and that's it."

Grinding out each word, Daddy said, "It's Christmas week and I want my son staying with me."

"You can't just swoop in at Christmas and make up for everything you haven't been doing. It doesn't work like that. Putting on a big show once a year isn't enough. I'm not saying it's your fault you're out of work and can't do everything you used to, but you can't even afford to buy him anything for Christmas."

Dumb presents didn't matter to Midnight, and right now all he wanted was for them to shut up. Every few weeks, they had this same argument, and admittedly he sometimes enjoyed it because he liked being talked about and fought over, but tonight he was tired.

He walked up and stood next to his father. "I want to go with Daddy," he said.

Daddy smiled, and Midnight knew it was aimed more toward Granny, rubbing it in that she'd lost this round. Being with his father at Christmas wouldn't be so bad, and it might make it easier to re-member holidays with Mom and the normal life they used to have. He could taste the fear from earlier that night, and his legs trembled, Bo and L-Boogie's laughter still taunting him. The last time he'd felt truly safe had been with Mom, and he needed that feeling again now more than ever.

Twenty-Five

RUTH

Ruth clapped and slapped hands with Natasha as they sat cross-legged on her friend's bed.

Mama's in the kitchen burnin' that rice,
Daddy's on the corner shootin' that dice.

They sang their old schoolyard rhyme to the tune of "Rockin' Robin" over and over, as if they could blast themselves back to the little girls they were growing up in Grundy.

Natasha's three-year-old daughter, Camila, bounced at the foot of the bed waving her Princess Jasmine doll. The little girl with the wavy hair like her mother's shouted *tweet tweet* along with them.

"Oh my God, girl, I don't think we've done that since eighth grade," Ruth said, falling on her back trying to catch her breath.

"But wait," Natasha said. "Was it your mama stink or your breath stink? There was more to the song. How did the rest of it go?"

"I don't know, but it's pitiful when we just start humming because we can't remember the words. We are getting old." Ruth sighed.

"Speak for yourself. I am still fly," Natasha said, tossing her hair from her right shoulder to her left.

Camila bounced on the bed screaming, "Again, sing it again!"

It had been a surprise to learn Natasha was a mother, too. She'd married Luis Irizarry, the boy they'd known from shop class in high school. He had stood out as being exotic, like any Puerto Ricans in Ganton, since most people in town were either Black or white. Ruth hadn't realized how diverse the world was until Yale, where she roomed with the granddaughter of a Korean war bride her junior year and briefly dated a young man from Mumbai who led a climate change initiative on campus.

Ruth put a hand on Camila's shoulder. "She's a beauty, just like you."

"Yes, she is. Now you know I love the brothas, but I wanted my babies to have some hair I could get a comb through. That's why I married a Puerto Rican man."

Ruth laughed awkwardly, but her friend's words stung. She hadn't detected any hint of self-hatred when they were growing up, but maybe she'd been too naïve to notice.

"You are wrong for that." Ruth ran her fingers through her own kinky twists and had to admit there were days she wished for a smoother texture, for hair that didn't break a thin-toothed comb the first day she used it. But she said, "I'm happy nappy, thank you very much."

"Your hair looks fine. I would like to trim those ends for you, though." Natasha pulled one of the corkscrew tips of Ruth's hair.

"You better keep your scissors away from me."

Natasha laughed and said, "What I do want is to see this husband of yours. Come on now. You been holding out on me."

Smiling shyly, Ruth pulled up a photo on her phone of Xavier at an Urban League gala in downtown Chicago. That night, he'd rocked a black fitted Tom Ford tuxedo.

Natasha's eyes bucked. "Well, yes, we can."

"Stop, you are so silly."

"What? I'm just saying you out here making Obama-level marital moves."

When their laughter settled, Ruth tried to achieve cool nonchalance, not wanting her voice to betray her giddiness. "Do you know a boy named Corey?"

"Of course. Corey Cunningham. His friend Sebastian's got people that know some of Luis's people. They may even be kin. You know how that goes. Why?"

Ruth took a breath, but Natasha caught on quickly.

"Wait, you're not telling me . . . ?"

Ruth hesitated, knowing that when she said it aloud, it would feel real. Softly, she said, "I think Corey could be my son. My baby."

Not to be left out, Camila put her hands on her pajama-clad hips and repeated *my baby* while strutting across the bedroom floor.

Natasha gripped Ruth's hand. "For real?"

"I think so." She told her friend about her conversation with Midnight and relayed how Eli had stood up publicly for Corey, even going so far as to get arrested.

Natasha sat up straight in the bed. "Okay, you took Patrick Boyd out for ice cream? I don't get it."

From the outside, Ruth could see how strange that might seem, and she suddenly felt the need to defend herself. "First of all, he likes to be called Midnight. And you know my family and Lena's have been tight for years, so I guess we just got thrown together a few times since I've been back in town. The real news is about Corey, not Midnight."

"I know, I know. Well, if this is true, we got to go."

"Go where?"

"To his house."

The way Natasha said *to his house* tickled and scared her all at once. She spoke the words slowly and deliberately, as if Ruth were having trouble comprehending. Her friend had always been the spontaneous one, boldly telling boys she had crushes on them and borrowing the school van for a joy ride. Growing up, Natasha's spontaneity often pushed Ruth to move when her natural inclination would have been to proceed with caution or just wait.

Ruth stood and paced in a small circle at the foot of her friend's bed. She nervously ran her fingers over the buttons of her cardigan as queasiness rocked her stomach.

The small pleasure of repeating Corey's name aloud to herself had felt oddly comforting. But until now, Ruth hadn't allowed herself to carefully consider the last name of Cunningham or the people who belonged to that name, the people raising her son, and the house where they all lived together on some street right here in Ganton. The euphoria Ruth had felt knowing her son's name after all these years was starting to fade like a narcotic wearing off.

"Pump the brakes. I haven't decided yet what I'm going to do." Ruth fell onto the bed again, with her hands covering her face.

Natasha stretched out beside her with Camila bouncing on the bed. "I hear you, girl. I didn't mean to push."

Ruth exhaled. "I just need more time. Also, I did some research online based on what you said about that lawyer getting arrested for adoption fraud."

Propping on her elbow, Natasha said, "What did you find out?"

"I think I know the name of the guy you remember from the news. Does 'Stanley DeAngelo' ring a bell?"

Natasha massaged her forehead. "Girl, you know I'm bad with names. I just know there was a shady lawyer in town who got caught for all kinds of crimes."

"Yeah, I looked into it and DeAngelo kept coming up in my search. Well, he's out of prison now. He got out a year ago and is living over on Wayland. I can't help but think he was involved with Corey's adoption. If so, did he do this whole thing off the books?"

Natasha shifted her position on the bed and absently stroked her daughter's hair. "I get it. You need to know what's up, and if it wasn't legal, maybe you got some options."

The implication of Natasha's words settled within Ruth. If the adoption was indeed fraudulent, she might have rights to Corey as his biological mother. But for now, she only wanted to focus on getting to know her son and learning about his life.

"This is all so new and I'm just trying to figure it all out. Now, tell me what they're like. The Cunninghams." Using their last name and avoiding the word *parents* was the easier way to talk about these people who were raising her baby.

"They're all right. They got good jobs. They're good people. Live over on Hill Top. Let me put it like this. They're like a knockoff version of the Huxtables."

"I'm glad. At least Corey's not being raised in Grundy." The scream of a passing police siren punctuated Ruth's statement and she immediately regretted her words. Natasha rolled away from her on the bed and sat up.

"What the hell's that supposed to mean? You're in my house right now. In Grundy. Your grandmother and brother live in this neighborhood. You were raised right here in Grundy."

"I didn't mean it like that."

"What did you mean, then?" Natasha said, indignation baked into her raised voice.

Camila climbed onto her mother's lap and waved the doll in her face. "What's wrong, Mommy?"

"Nothing, sweetheart." She rested her forehead against her daughter's and smiled. "I'm just wondering if Mommy's friend knows where her son goes to school now."

Pretending she didn't detect the sarcasm in Natasha's voice, she said, "Where?"

"Driscoll. *Right here in Grundy*. The school that wasn't good enough for you back in the day."

The public school that used to get all the raggedy books and secondhand furniture, where she and Natasha had met. The one her grandparents pulled her out of to send her to the Catholic school, where it was okay to be smart and girls wore pleated skirts every day.

"Are we really going to get into it over grade schools right now?" Ruth said, anxious to change the subject.

Her friend closed her eyes. "Things were just so different for you and me. I can't pretend that it doesn't matter. And look at you now. Your big fancy city life."

Natasha's parents both worked for the city utilities company, but they had never married. Her father wanted and tried to be part of Natasha's life, but her mother wouldn't let him. Growing up, Natasha rarely talked about her future, whereas Mama and Papa, though they'd only finished high school, pushed Ruth hard. They told everyone she'd be a doctor someday, and Papa was sure of it when she took such care dispensing his baclofen for spasms and methotrexate for joint pain.

"That was all a long time ago," Ruth said. "What I do care about is that Corey gets the best education possible."

"Driscoll's changed a lot. It's not like when we were there. They started bringing in kids like Corey from Hill Top and some whites, too, put a little money into it, and now it's actually a pretty decent school."

"That's good to hear," Ruth said.

Pretty decent wasn't good enough for her son, but she didn't say anything, not wanting to offend Natasha any more than she had already. Ruth kept her eyes on Camila when she finally spoke. "What do you wish for Camila? When you think of her living anywhere in the whole world, what do you imagine? Can you picture that place? Can you see it?"

Natasha closed her eyes and ran her fingers through Camila's hair.

"Remember that group called The Future Is Girl? We were like eight or nine years old and they took us to that big house in Indy with the leather sofas and chandeliers. Even the faucet handles in the bathroom were gold. When you looked out the windows, the grass was the greenest I'd ever seen, all of it the same height, and there was no end to it."

"Yeah, it was a country club." Ruth had almost forgotten that field trip for *at-risk* girls, where skinny white women in capris served them asparagus roll-ups and fried oysters and then watched them like lab rats to see if their palates could appreciate fine food.

Natasha's eyes widened. "That was a country club? All these years, I thought one of those ladies owned that house." She laughed. "Anyway, I never forgot it and I always imagined I lived there. Once I had Camila, I pictured her living there, too."

"I hope Camila redecorates. That striped wallpaper made my eyes hurt, and those golden dog statues were ridiculous."

They groaned at the memory and sat quietly, letting the past wash over them. Suddenly, Natasha nudged her with her knee. "Sit up. I just remembered the rest of the words."

"What words?" Ruth said.

"To the rhyme, girl."

Once again, they played the hand-clapping game, laughing so hard it seemed obscene to indulge themselves this fully.

> *Brother's in jail raisin' hell,*
> *Sister's on the corner sellin' fruit cocktail . . .*

THEY PARKED ON THE STREET OUTSIDE THE RECREATION CENTER, where many of the kids went to socialize while school was out for the holidays and their parents were at work. Many in town now credited Pastor Bumpus for working to get this facility off the ground in spite of his questionable methods.

Just an hour ago, it seemed reasonable to take time to process everything she'd discovered. But the more she talked with Natasha, the more excited she became. After eleven years, what sense did it make to wait any longer?

They decided sitting outside Corey's house felt indecent for some reason. Stalking him at the rec center somehow felt more appropriate. Since Midnight would likely recognize Ruth's Infiniti, they'd taken Natasha's car.

Camila entertained herself in the back seat, loudly singing the *Sesame Street* theme song. Whenever she took a break to sip her apple juice, Ruth could clearly hear strains of laughter and squeals from the kids on the other side of the fence. The children chased each other, tumbling in the snow, and they became a blur, one kid indistinguishable from the next. Without ever having seen a photo of Corey, she wondered if she'd recognize him, if there would be a maternal buzzer that would sound in her body to alert her.

"There's Sebastian. He's the one in the black jacket with the red stripes on the arms. Look at him go," Natasha said. "You should see him running bases."

But Ruth couldn't focus her eyes on Sebastian. She had a familiar tightness in her chest like she was losing air, the same feeling she had when the doctor told the family Papa would eventually die from ALS. It was that dread, the fear of what was certain to come next, that wouldn't turn you loose. After blinking a few times, she saw that right on Sebastian's heels was a slender white boy, and Ruth recognized the way he moved with sudden stops and starts. "Midnight?"

"That's Patrick . . . my bad . . . Midnight, always hanging around the Black and brown kids. He thinks he's Black, Lord help him. Cracks me up. Always wearing hand-me-downs. White people kill me trying to be Black when it works for them. Just pitiful."

"Don't say that. He's been through a lot. I think he's just trying to get some love wherever he can find it," Ruth murmured, keeping her eyes on Midnight darting around other kids, his feet kicking up sprays of snow. She surprised herself with her quiet yet solid defense of a boy she hadn't known very long. When he turned to face the street, Ruth slouched in her seat, hoping he hadn't spotted her.

Natasha gripped her arm tight and said, "There he is. That's Corey. The one in the yellow hat."

Ruth sat up straighter in her seat. She was staring at a stranger. She was staring at her son. How could both be true at the same time?

A marble grew in her throat, threatening to cut off her airway. Her forehead pressed against the car window, which had grown foggy from her breath, and she wiped it fast. Still, that window separated them. She yanked off her gloves and laid her hands flat on the glass. If she couldn't have skin-to-skin contact with her baby as she had the day he was born, this would have to be enough.

Her eyes followed the boys, who were flipping and tumbling in the snow. Corey climbed a high mound and rolled down the slope with elegance and ease. He exuded gracefulness and athleticism. He was everything she wasn't. The other boys followed his lead and seemed to pull from his energy. He stood at the center of things, not apart from the others as she had in middle school.

She hadn't expected Corey to be so slight. But Natasha acknowledged he was small for his age. If he'd been born in a hospital, she'd know his birth weight. How big should an eleven-year-old boy be? Ruth had no idea what was normal for his age.

She heard Natasha's voice next to her but kept her eyes riveted on the playground. "That's your boy. You loved him from the beginning. He's here in this world because of you."

This boy could be hers. It was very likely that he indeed was. Ruth stayed quiet watching the boys run, jump, and tumble, their bodies descending in the snow and rising again.

Averting her eyes, Ruth sighed. "I still don't know that I feel like a mother."

"Look, there's no one way a mother is supposed to feel." Then Natasha lowered her voice and glanced back at Camila, who was now jamming to music through her headphones. "Sometimes, I wish I hadn't had a kid. What could I have done in these three years if I'd been free to come and go as I pleased, no kid to tie me down? This little girl drives me crazy sometimes, but I love her to pieces. Love can be complicated and messy. Believe that. Stop beating yourself up."

The kids on the playground kept screaming, and before long Camila was begging Natasha for a Rice Krispies Treat. Ruth tried to cancel their noise and isolate the sound of Corey, only hear his voice rising above the others. Of course, that was impossible.

Ruth scanned the playground until she spotted Corey again, and she watched him until a whistle blew to end the outdoor activities and the children filed back inside the rec center.

When she saw him disappear into the building, she couldn't help but think of him vanishing with Mama on the other side of her bedroom door all those years ago. She had an overwhelming urge to run into the rec center screaming his name—some action, something— all the things she now wished she'd done the day he was born.

Twenty-Six

RUTH

After leaving the rec center, Ruth rewound and replayed the image of Corey on the playground over and over. A private memory she could enjoy alone in her own mind, even as she sat across from Eli in the living room. It was Christmas Eve, and they were lounging on the couch, binge-watching back-to-back reruns of some nineties sitcom. A couple of cans of Bud sat on the TV tray next to the couch. Eli sat expressionless, not reacting to any of the punch lines or laugh tracks. She and her brother had said very little to each other since the night at the bar.

His words had cut into her. She thought of the sacrifices he and Mama had made so she could have a chance at doing something with her life. The way they'd protected her reputation. How had she never thanked them for that? She'd gone along with the lies all those years because she worried about what other people would think of her. How that one slipup could forever tarnish the image she'd clung to like a lifeline.

"When I got pregnant, what did you think? I mean, what did you really think of me?" After Papa died, she knew that Eli considered it his duty to stand in for their grandfather and preserve her reputation. "Did you think I was a ho?"

Some sort of spell broke, because Eli almost rolled off the couch laughing at the hopefulness in her voice. "Nope, one baby don't put you at ho status. You still a corny-ass nerd, though."

When he turned his beer can up to his mouth, Ruth saw Eli at ten years old guzzling whole milk from mason jars, at thirteen draining orange juice straight from the jug, and then at eighteen, when they were barely speaking to each other, throwing back Gatorade before basketball games. He caught her staring and she gave him a goofy smile, one of those smiles that she hoped meant no matter how old they got or how much they hurt each other, they'd always be brother and sister.

She wanted to tell Eli how the guilt of leaving behind her son had eaten away at her. That the truth might have ruined her marriage. But she also wanted to tell him how excited she was that she'd figured out who her son was, or at least she was pretty sure she had. And most of all, she wanted to thank Eli for protecting Corey, for sacrificing his freedom for her son. But the words stuck in her throat, and before she could untangle them, she heard the sound of Mama's slippers.

"Cut these lights off. You're not paying the light bill here." Mama flipped the wall switch and unplugged the small Christmas tree by the window, leaving the house in darkness except for the flicker of the TV. Ruth shared a quick eye roll with her brother while Mama's back was turned.

"And get those filthy boots off my couch," Mama said to Eli, her voice buzzing in the room like a housefly.

"Stop trippin', Mama. Relax," he said.

The TV screen went black and Ruth could see in the dim room that Mama was holding the remote. Eli opened his mouth to protest but closed it. Growing up, they both knew that look on Mama's face meant she was serious.

"Scoot over," she told him, turning on one lamp after realizing the room had gone dark.

Eli unlaced his Timberlands, tossed them on the floor, and threw his legs over the back of the couch so she could sit down. The popping from the furnace provided the only sound in the room. Someone from church had come by to fix it, and now the house radiated heat.

Perched on the edge of the sofa, Mama pulled her nightgown above her knees, exposing stretch marks and dimpling on her thighs. Her face looked tired, lines of age and stress creasing it, and Ruth knew she and her brother had put more than a few of them there. Maybe time away with Dino would do her some good after all.

Mama glanced at Ruth. "You've been mighty busy since you've been home, staying out till all times of the night. Hope you're not still meddling about that boy."

Ruth considered stalling or lying outright. She still wanted to find out if or how that lawyer factored into everything, and she needed more time. But she couldn't hold back any longer. "It's not meddling when it's my son. I've found him. I know that Corey Cunningham is mine." A heavy weight lifted from her when she said that. She took a deep breath and waited, watching their faces closely.

Mama and Eli stared back at her, motionless. Mama spoke first, in a quiet voice. Too quiet. "What was that you just said?"

"I said—"

"I heard what you said. I want to know what in God's name got into you." Mama stood and hovered over Ruth, who got to her feet, too. Then her grandmother bent over and her hand came down like a brick and smacked the coffee table. Mama's body shook. "I told you to leave it alone. You never listen. As much as your grandfather and I have done for you. All we sacrificed and you just throw it away like trash. Is that what you think of us? Of yourself?"

The wall clock chimed, the pendulum swinging back and forth. The knot in Ruth's belly tightened.

Mama turned to face Eli, who was still stretched out on the sofa. With accusation in her voice, she said, "Was it you? Did you tell her about Corey?"

Ruth covered her mouth with both hands, hearing Mama finally admit the truth. Eli stared at the ceiling, shaking his head. "I didn't say a word, but she was gon' keep pushing until she found out that boy's name."

"I don't care how much pushing she did. We had an agreement,"

Mama said. "And besides, you know how Ganton is. Word will get around that we're making trouble for the Cunninghams, and you know Harold Cunningham is a big deal downtown at the bank. And you've been in jail twice now. What good is that going to do you when you're trying to get somebody around here to hire you? Huh?"

Ruth turned to her brother. "I know what you did to protect Corey. You went to jail for it. Thank you." Eli acknowledged her gratitude with his eyes but said nothing.

She had known this moment would come, an inevitable reckoning when she would need to stand up to her grandmother. Even if it meant lighting a match to her rage, or worse, becoming the source of her greatest disappointment.

"I've lied to everyone all these years, even my own husband. What's worse is I've lied to myself. No more. I'm not a child. I let you manipulate everything because you said you were doing it for my own good. Now I get to decide. Me and no one else."

Her words landed hard, crashing onto the living room floor.

"That boy has a mama and a daddy. He has no idea he's adopted. Have you thought about that? If you care anything about him, you won't turn his life upside down." Mama fixed her granddaughter with a stare, long and steady.

Something Ruth couldn't name sat heavy on her chest. The truth was she hadn't thought that far ahead, beyond knowing her son's identity and making sure he was all right. Now that she had his name and had seen him, what would she do about it?

"All I know is I'm tired of the secrets in this house. I'm tired of keeping quiet about everything. There's a lot of messed-up stuff in our family and we just pretend it's not there," Ruth said.

"Child, if you don't quit talking in circles . . . You got something to say, spit it out." Mama sat on the couch again, folding her arms over her chest.

Ruth glanced at her brother and then said, "I want to talk about Butch Boyd." Eli seemed fidgety all of a sudden, like he was ready to spring from the couch and walk out of the room.

"Butch said something about Papa cutting corners at the plant. He made it sound like he'd broken the law. You two told me not to believe it, but you never looked me in the eye and said there was no way Papa could do something like that."

A part of Ruth felt sorry for Mama, watching her recoil as if she'd been slapped in the face.

"People always talk shit on the line, especially Boyd," Eli said. "Papa never did nothing wrong."

Mama held up one hand to quiet Eli, and it seemed like she was trying to swallow around something hard in her throat. Looking straight ahead, she took a couple of long breaths and then spoke as if she were narrating a movie in her mind. "The first time they asked Hezekiah, he said no. Came home and told me the line supervisor wanted him to pass a lot of parts through real fast. They needed him to keep things running."

Ruth couldn't believe what she was hearing. "Mama, I'm sure they had quality control engineers come by and check to make sure everything met standards. If cars went out with bad parts in them, that's dangerous."

"It's those engineers who sign off on stuff when they know it ain't right," Eli jumped in. "That was way above Papa's pay grade. So, it wasn't his fault."

Mama worried the seam of the sofa's slipcover. The woman always so sure-footed, certain of everything, bold in every proclamation she made, searched for words.

"Your grandfather was no saint," Mama began, finally looking at Ruth and Eli. "He did cut corners like they say."

Leaning forward on the couch with her elbows on her knees, Mama put her face in her hands. "We almost lost this house when they went up on the rent. When he first got sick, he could still work, but he was on a lot of prescription drugs. You remember. We used every penny he made for medicine. Those supervisors out there knew about it and they took advantage."

"Aw, man," Eli said, jumping to his feet. "I always heard stuff.

You know how people talk. But I didn't know they did Papa like that. I would've handled it for him." He pounded his closed fist into his other hand.

"Settle down now," Mama said. "Everything your grandfather did was for the two of you. We saved up any extra money we had after all the bills and kept it in a special fund." She looked at Ruth. "Your scholarship didn't cover books or your dorm room fees."

Another sacrifice to give her a better life. At Yale, she worked out at the campus gym that had a pool and a sauna. A chef prepared themed meals in the dorm. When she turned it over in her mind, it felt like too much, a burden.

Ruth looked back at her grandmother, stunned. Mama said, "Remember when your grandfather pulled you out of Driscoll and promised you'd never have to go back? That fall, you had a spot at Mother Mary, that Catholic school."

Ruth shook her head. "No, no, no."

"Yes. He did what he had to do to give you the best education possible. That wasn't free. None of it."

If only she'd known at the time, she would have told Papa it wasn't worth it. The price was too high.

"That's what parents do," Mama continued. "They don't think about themselves. They put the children first."

Without coming out and saying it directly, Mama was calling her selfish, not selfless like her grandfather. All because she wanted to know her own son. But Ruth refused to accept that label, knowing now that a lifetime of lies never added up to anything good. A lifetime of doing the wrong things for the right reasons. A lifetime of lies that started small, like a nick in the windshield, then eventually shattered the glass.

Twenty-Seven

MIDNIGHT

Midnight woke up Christmas morning at Drew's apartment and he breathed in the usual smell of onions and armpits. Being there wasn't so bad, and Bo and L-Boogie wouldn't be likely to find him there, although maybe gang members took off work on Christmas like everybody else. He lay still on the couch under the coat Miss Ruth had covered him with at Granny's. It still carried her flowery scent and he put it over his head to get a better whiff.

"Ho, ho, ho." Drew came through the front door carrying a case of beer in green packaging with red ribbon tied around it. This would be the only festive thing in the whole place. Other than that, it was just blank white walls, one beige leather couch, and a beanbag in front of the TV.

Daddy stumbled in from the bedroom in sweatpants and a T-shirt. "I thought you were staying the night with Nadine," he said, turning on the TV.

"I did, buddy. Nadine's spending the day with her family. It's now ten thirty in the morning. On Christmas." Drew added that part in case Daddy had forgotten. "Oh yeah, month's almost over, Boyd. Don't forget you still owe me December rent."

"Yeah, yeah, I know. I told you I'd pay you." Daddy was still sleepy, barely opening his eyes or mouth.

"I thought you and I could kick back and celebrate," Drew said. Then he finally noticed Midnight. "I got some Hawaiian Punch, too. Pretend you're on a warm beach somewhere. You like Hawaiian Punch?"

Midnight nodded, imagining the Cunninghams sitting around their live Christmas tree opening presents in their pajamas, drinking cocoa with marshmallows. At least that's the way Corey had described it to him last year, like something out of a TV commercial. He hated the way his friend bragged without really bragging, making extraordinary things sound routine.

Daddy sat next to him on the couch and a news story came on about Christmas tree farms, blaming a tree shortage on the recession. And then a mention of the newly elected president who would be inaugurated next month.

"They all think they're better than us," Daddy said, pointing to the screen, maybe meaning Obama or the woman and man anchoring the news, her in a red sweater and the guy in a black suit with a red tie. Or perhaps all of them. "Think we're trash."

Midnight wanted to ask Daddy what the news anchors had against them, but he thought better of it since his father tendered beefs with all sorts of people, even ones he'd never met.

The doorbell rang and Granny walked in with two gifts wrapped in gold foil, with a red ribbon stuck to the top gift. In her other hand she carried a sack of groceries. Even though she tried to hide it, he saw her glare at Daddy before setting eggs and a loaf of bread on Drew's kitchen countertop.

"Patrick, have you had breakfast yet?" Granny asked, slipping out of her boots.

Midnight shook his head. "I'm hungry. Can we have French toast?" he said, thinking of the time he and Miss Ruth cooked breakfast food for dinner.

Ignoring his specific menu request, Granny turned to Daddy. "He's a growing boy. He needs three square meals."

"Damn holidays." Daddy slid his hand over his face and wiped the sleep from the corners of his eyes. "Can't find any decent restaurants open."

Within minutes, Midnight smelled butter heating in a skillet and then heard the crack of eggshells. Soon, they were all sitting on bar stools at Drew's kitchen counter eating fried eggs and cinnamon raisin toast.

After breakfast, Granny handed him the two packages wrapped in gold foil. Midnight took them and read the gift label: *Merry Christmas! To Patrick, From Granny & Daddy*. He glanced up at his father, who shrugged, obviously just as curious as Midnight to see what the unwrapping would reveal.

He tore at the paper around the first box with frantic fingers and found two new Nintendo games he'd been wanting. Screaming in delight, he kissed Granny and Daddy and even Drew, whose face flushed.

"Glad you like it. Merry Christmas," Granny said, beaming. "Now open the other one."

In the second, larger box, he found a pair of brown snow boots. Holding them to his nose, he inhaled the smell of leather and some strange chemical they must put in new shoes.

"Cool."

He knew money was tight and that she had likely delayed payment to a supplier for the shop just to buy the boots and those games. Even in his euphoria, he made a mental note not to forget what she'd done.

"Okay, brush your teeth and wash up good before you start playing."

After Midnight finished in the bathroom, he rummaged through Daddy's dresser drawer for a rechargeable battery he remembered seeing there. He heard Granny and Daddy talking in the hallway and swore they'd just mentioned a gang. When they got closer to the bedroom, he scrambled under the bed to hide.

Daddy came in and plopped down on the mattress, which squeaked and dipped just above Midnight's head. From his vantage point on the floor, he could see his father's crusty white heels, his toes sinking into the carpet.

"I don't know about any gangs, but I do know he's hanging out with the wrong people," he heard Daddy say. "Christina from the diner told me he was in there the other night with some strange Black woman. She described her right down to her fancy coat and purse and boots. Bushy hair. Fit Eli Tuttle's sister to a tee."

Midnight fidgeted in his hiding place. He heard Granny sigh. "You don't need to be worried about Ruth. She's like family. I know you and Eli don't see eye to eye, but that should have nothing to do with her."

"Don't want her around my kid. I don't like it. Don't like it at all."

Dust traveled up his nose and Midnight stifled a sneeze. The one person in this stupid town who looked at him like he was really somebody was Miss Ruth, and Daddy wanted to take her away from him, too.

He heard the flick of a lighter and then smelled smoke from Granny's Newport. "Keep your voice down before Patrick hears you. Besides, she's just back in town to get to know her own son. Ernestine's beside herself about it, but you can't control your kids when they're grown."

An ache shot through Midnight. He almost forgot to breathe.

"Who the hell is her son?"

After a long pause, Granny said, "Corey Cunningham."

That hit Midnight like a kick to his gut. He barely heard anything else. His brain froze. *Miss Ruth was Corey's mom. Corey was her son.* It didn't make any sense. Corey's mom was Mrs. Cunningham. He forced himself to lie still, to not make any sound. His stomach was an elevator dropping twenty stories in two seconds.

Only snatches of conversation filtered through the fog in his mind. Different versions of the same word kept coming up. *Adoption. Adopted.* Corey was adopted. What did that mean? In fourth grade, a girl named Jessica Seeley told everyone she was adopted and that it meant she had four parents to love her instead of just two. She said her new mom and dad picked her out of a whole nursery full of babies and chose to take her home. At the time he thought it sounded pretty cool, but now it just seemed greedy. Midnight barely had one parent, and he wasn't sure that one even loved him sometimes.

A bubble of happy that had been growing in Midnight's heart popped. How had he been so stupid? He hadn't even had time to decide exactly how he felt, whether he wished Miss Ruth were his mom or his girlfriend.

The only thing he did know was that when Miss Ruth looked at him, only him, and asked him questions, he felt special. To her, if to nobody else. Nobody except Mom had treated him like that before. When she died, he had given up on hoping for much of anything.

If Miss Ruth thought he mattered, maybe he really did. He couldn't have been wrong about her, about everything. If this was true, though, that she was only around him to get to know Corey, it had all been a lie.

Twenty-Eight

RUTH

Before the sun came up on Christmas morning, Ruth lay in bed with her eyes closed but her mind racing, fully awake with all the feelings she hadn't had time to feel until now. The anticipation for meeting Corey one day soon skittered in her veins, and when she imagined it, she got scared. Then came the longing to be close to her grandmother and brother again. People said you could be lonely in a house full of people, and whoever said that spoke the truth.

Her phone vibrated on the nightstand and right away Xavier's name appeared. She picked it up, and in her haste, her fingers went limp and the phone fell to the floor. She scrambled to scoop it up and said hello loudly before realizing it was a text message, not an actual call.

Merry Christmas, Ruth.

She reread the text over and over and waited to see if he typed more. He didn't. She analyzed every word, how he had called her by her first name instead of *baby* or *honey* or *sweetheart* like he usually did. The use of a period instead of an exclamation point. Did that mean Xavier greeted her on Christmas out of obligation instead of genuine affection?

Matching his tenor and tone, she texted:

Merry Christmas, Xavier.

She had so much to tell him, but she couldn't say over a text message that she'd found her son. In their four years of marriage, they'd never been apart before, and she missed his uneven breathing, the warmth of his rough thighs brushing against hers in bed at night. These stiff sheets didn't carry his scent, and she struggled to conjure the exact smell of him. And that laugh of his that sounded more like a hiccup with its guttural stops and starts. His absence made the whole world unsteady, teetering on its axis, everything precarious.

At times like this, she wanted to ask Mama how she and Papa had held their marriage together for so many years. Through losing their daughter to addiction, raising two grandchildren, a terrible illness, and probably a host of other things that had chipped away at their union, secrets they'd both take to their graves.

She could easily call Xavier. After all, this was Christmas. She *should* call him, she was the one who'd left. But she was afraid. If this time apart had convinced him to end their marriage, she didn't want to know. She couldn't bear to know. If he couldn't forgive her lie and make peace with it, how much of a marriage did they really have?

She heard Mama banging pots and pans and knew how preoccupied she could get with her cooking. Nothing had changed to dissolve the tension in the house, but Mama believed in carrying on the act of living, no matter what. Ruth walked down the hall to the kitchen.

Pecking her grandmother's cheek, Ruth said, "Merry Christmas."

"Merry Christmas, baby." Mama stood over the stove turning strips of bacon in popping hot oil.

Ruth breathed in the rich, savory odor and stepped out on the front porch for some air, the cold stillness hitting her instantly. After a minute, she couldn't take the chill and came back inside. "Everything seems more quiet out here than I remember."

"What do you expect? It's Christmas," Mama said, chuckling under her breath. "Nothing's stirring this early but trouble."

Mama fussed with the knobs on the stove and then greased a pan for biscuits without turning around. When Ruth noticed the jar of blackberry preserves she'd bought sitting out on the table, she smiled to herself.

The front door swung open and she heard the light thuds of little feet running through the foyer.

"Merry Christmas, Mama!" "Merry Christmas, Mama!" "Merry Christmas, Mama!" In rapid succession, her niece and nephews echoed their greetings and hugged her grandmother. Then they looked up at Ruth and said hello shyly. They hadn't seen her since her wedding, four years ago, and Teddy and Troy had been just four years old then, and Keisha just one. Four years was a long time for little kids. She might as well have been a stranger to them. She knew their limited relationship was her fault; there was more she could do as aunt, even with the distance.

Eli filled the cooler in the garage with ice, and Cassie, who had planned to leave after saying hello, decided to stay. She gave Mama a smile and then took a spot next to Ruth at the sink, helping her coat catfish with cornmeal so it would be ready to go in the FryDaddy later in the day.

Feeling protective of her brother, Ruth said in a soft voice, low enough for only Cassie to hear, "He's been through a lot and he needs you by his side. He'll never admit it, but it's true."

Cassie nodded without saying anything, and when Eli joined them in the kitchen, the two shared a kiss. Obviously, the holiday spirit had had an effect on them. When Ruth looked from one to the other, they just shrugged, as if to say it was wintertime and estranged couples got cold and lonely, too. Would it be that simple for her and Xavier to patch up the tear in the fabric of their marriage and reclaim that kind of intimacy again?

When the Tuttles gathered like this, you could usually count on interaction in extremes. Either everyone laughed until their bellies ached at memories and old stories that had been retold hundreds of times before or someone said something out of order that stopped the merriment cold. Eli's children forced you to smile even if you didn't want to, as they played with their new toys and ran through the house like it was the size of a football field instead of a matchbox.

As everyone ate breakfast, Teddy, his mouth full of biscuit, declared, apropos of nothing, "Our new president is Black." This simple statement of truth from an eight-year-old loosened the diaphragms of everyone at the table and their bodies erupted with laughter. She had no idea children that age processed race and its significance.

For Mama, this, like most things, was a teachable moment. "All you kids, big ones, too, need to thank those young folks in Pike County, Mississippi. Otherwise, you wouldn't have a Black president. When I was just a girl, SNCC did its first voter registration drive right there in McComb."

Ruth and Eli found each other's eyes and silently telegraphed how aggrieved they were to have to hear this story again. Mama had told them this Black history fact many times over the years. While she didn't live there long, Mama had been mothered by Mississippi as much as her own mother. "I see you two rolling your eyes," she said, glancing from Ruth to Eli.

"Sorry, Mama," Ruth said, spooning scrambled eggs onto her grandmother's plate.

"My father and his sisters and brothers did some backbreaking work in McComb. You kids have it good today. So good you can think about turning down jobs even when you don't have one," Mama said.

Eli stiffened, the muscles in his neck pulsing. He obviously knew what Mama would say next, while the rest of them looked confused.

"Yes, I'm going to tell it. Eli got a call yesterday about a job they got open at the crime scene cleanup place. I know it's not the easiest work, son. You're likely to see some things you wish you could unsee, but at least it's money coming in."

Everyone looked at Eli and Cassie wrapped her arms around his neck. "Praise God, baby. Yes!"

A man's dignity, his self-worth, was often tied to how he made his money. A rock that anchored him in the world. Eli needed this. Ruth knew Cassie had bought the kids' Christmas gifts this year, and that had to make him feel like less of a man.

"That job sounds promising, big brother."

He managed a half smile. "It pays pretty good, just like most jobs people don't want to do. That's why garbagemen make a lot of money."

Ruth could hear the defeat so deeply embedded in his voice that even the hint of good news couldn't camouflage it. But she heard hope, too, or maybe that's what she wanted to hear.

Then Keisha pulled Eli by the hand, leading him into the living room, where a few wrapped gifts had the kids' names on them. He sat in Papa's recliner, the seat closest to the tree, and Keisha jumped on his lap.

"Okay, go, Daddy."

Eli couldn't be grumpy for long with his little girl smiling up at him. He played along with a befuddled expression on his face. "What? What you want me to do?"

She sighed dramatically with the air of a grown woman. "How many times do I have to tell you it's your job to play Santa since he's stuck in traffic delivering toys to other people's houses?"

Everyone laughed and watched Eli hand out presents one by one to his daughter and sons and then smile with satisfaction at their oohs and aahs. Mama and Cassie planted themselves on the couch patiently showing interest in Barbies and Pokémon action figures.

Ruth thought back to seeing Corey romp in the snow. What was Christmas Day like at his house? How many gifts would he unwrap, and which one would be his favorite? She would never know his family traditions.

There had been times over the years, especially after Papa's death, that Ruth dreaded entering this house, hating everything from the slant to the smell of it. She had attached almost every grievance in her life to someone here. But on Christmas, everything came into focus more sharply and she saw them all with new eyes—their flaws and their beauty—and she chose to appreciate them because, in the end, they were family.

Twenty-Nine

MIDNIGHT

*C*orey's *real mom.* That was the thought that had been running through Midnight's head on repeat after he heard what Granny said. His skull ached with a thousand tiny needles poking it. He had slipped out of Drew's apartment without anyone noticing. Outside, he let the cold air wrap around his face and hush Granny's words in his head. He tried to breathe deeply, but his throat closed as though a fuzzy tennis ball had lodged there. He had to get away, somewhere, anywhere, but he didn't know where.

When he made his way downtown and stumbled upon Bones, he didn't rub his belly, and he had always rubbed his belly. He'd even rubbed his belly after Diane Romero beat him up after school last year, and when Rusty Flanagan stole his science homework and copied the answers. He pet Bones even after he realized he might never play Little League. But not this time.

He couldn't stop thinking about Miss Ruth covering him with his jacket when he fell asleep. He yanked it off and threw it into a slushy puddle of melted snow. And to think he'd blown air into his cupped hands before he talked to her to make sure he didn't have stinky breath. He thought of all the dumb things he'd told her and kicked his coat. Dirty snow water splashed his face.

"Little man is mad at somebody. What did that coat do to you?"

Midnight turned around to find L-Boogie, the tall, quiet gang-banger from the night before, the one who walked with a limp, an invisible string pulling the right side of his body. He still wore a red rag, this time tied around his neck as a scarf. Midnight had thought if he ever saw him again, he'd be scared, looking for an escape route in case the guy wanted to cut up his body into tiny pieces like the serial killers he saw in the movies, but he didn't feel afraid. He didn't feel anything.

"I'm not mad. She—" He cut himself off.

"Uh-oh. Woman problems already. These females can be a trip."

Midnight shrugged, unsure how to respond.

"Well, looks like you going to war with that coat. Somebody pissed you off bad. Tell me who and I'll take care of 'em for you."

For a second Midnight thought L-Boogie might mean it, until he laughed. Then Midnight laughed, too, soft like a pot of water on low boil.

"Where's your little crew?"

Midnight shrugged. "We don't hang like we used to." That wasn't exactly true, but maybe it would be.

L-Boogie rubbed his cheek like he was thinking. "You don't need trick-ass friends. You need family."

Midnight rubbed his arms. It was still chilly out and he needed his coat, but it floated in a puddle at his feet. L-Boogie took off his leather bomber jacket and wrapped it around Midnight's shoulders. "Put this on. Come on in here and I'll buy you something to warm you up."

They sat across from each other in a booth at Dunkin' Donuts, one of the few places open on Christmas, and Midnight ran his fingers across the soft black leather of L-Boogie's coat. He dipped his glazed doughnut hole in his cocoa the way Daddy did with his coffee.

"Tastes good that way, right?"

"Yeah. Thank you. This jacket must have cost a lot of money."

"Let me teach you about economics, son. Supply and demand. You produce a product that people really want to buy, and they'll pay top dollar for it. That's how business works. I'm a businessman. That's how I afford to have nice things." He rolled his tongue over his teeth and made a sucking sound with his lips. "Let me tell you another thing. I don't go into business with just anybody. Got to be family. You remember Bo? You met him."

Midnight nodded. "You're related to Bo? You all don't look alike," he said, thinking of his baby sister, wondering if she would have had sandy hair and blue eyes like he did.

"Closer than blood. We not into that funny shit, now, but we cool. Like brothers. I didn't have my father around when I was growing up. Don't even know that nigga's name."

L-Boogie gave Midnight a serious look and leaned across the table.

"Don't get no ideas now about repeating that word, though. You hear?"

Daddy had used that word before, when he talked about Eli Tuttle getting better shifts at the plant. But he'd said it different, the way it came out of his mouth wasn't the same, and Midnight knew it was a bad word. Granny flipped off the radio in the car whenever a song with that word came on. He didn't understand why, but every time he heard the word, his blood curdled like milk left outside in the heat.

When Midnight realized L-Boogie was waiting for an answer, he said, "I hear you."

L-Boogie pulled out his cell phone, swiped his left thumb across the screen, and stopped on a picture of a kid in a wheelchair, a boy with a round face and no neck holding a bright orange balloon that said *Get Well Soon*. In the photo, nurses bent over and stooped to his level, smiling for the camera, but the boy stared blankly.

"That's my cousin Duron right there. He's a poet now. I put some of his rhymes to music and he might get a record deal. Anyway, some dude busted a cap in him six years ago. Shot me, too." L-Boogie raised his shirt to show a thick, ropy scar on his belly.

"Duron can't feel a thing below his waist."

Midnight touched his own arm and thought about the nerve damage and how it could be permanent.

L-Boogie continued: "When Bo heard about it, he helped our family pay for some of the operations and went in with me to buy him this chair. My auntie didn't have to come out of her pocket for nothing. Bo knew she didn't have the money and he stepped up as a man. He's like a brother to me."

He reared back in the booth, stretched one arm across the back of the seat, and took a slow sip of coffee, making a slurping sound. "Looks like you could use some real brothers, too."

L-Boogie's mouth was on the cup, but his eyes stayed on Midnight, and it was like he was silently telling him something important. As if he knew things about the world Midnight couldn't possibly know. Midnight studied L-Boogie, trying to figure out what he meant without coming out and asking him. Some things he knew for sure. No one in Ganton wanted him around unless they could use him. Tolerating him just to have someone to be the butt of their jokes. Being nice to get information. Midnight had never wanted a baby sister until he almost had one. And he had never wanted a big brother until he figured L-Boogie was offering to be one.

"You feel me?" L-Boogie asked.

A doughnut hole bobbed in Midnight's hot chocolate and he swirled it around with his tongue and nodded. "I feel you."

Thirty

RUTH

The Sunday after Christmas, Ruth walked up the stairs to Friendship Baptist Church and heard a strident chord from the organ echoing from the windows, the melody as familiar to Ruth as an old nursery rhyme, but still slightly out of memory's reach. Red poinsettias lined the entrance to the church. Two Black women in stark white suits and white pillbox hats stood stiffly, like dance club bouncers, holding programs in their white-gloved hands, all puffed up with false power. They frowned when Ruth approached.

She ran through a mental checklist:

She'd showered that morning.

Her hair was freshly flat-ironed.

She'd popped a spearmint Altoid in the car.

She'd stomped the brown slush from her boots before entering.

Neither of the women looked familiar, which wasn't unusual since she hadn't been back here since her wedding. Their eyes traveled the length of her body, but they said nothing.

"Good morning," Ruth said, and reached for one of the programs.

"Every morning the Lord gives us is good," one of the women corrected her, smiling, but showing no teeth.

The church filled quickly, and within minutes Natasha appeared by Ruth's side, holding Camila by the hand.

"Your hair's looking fly, girl. Who did it?" Natasha laughed at her own shameless plug and attempt at humor. She'd flat-ironed Ruth's hair for the service so that Mama couldn't complain that her grand-daughter had scared away the saints and even the sinners.

"You are a magician, but I'm going back to my natural style as soon as service is over," Ruth said, taking in the congregants, most of whom were dressed in their Sunday best and likely still rocking relaxers.

This church had raised her, and she remembered sitting in Mama's lap in the choir stand and waiting long after service was over for Papa to be done taking care of deacon business.

Keisha was to be baptized today, so many in her family sat in reserved seats up front. The girl stood by one of the front pews in a long white chiffon dress, her arms extended out from her sides while Mama tied a lilac satin bow at her waist. Her thick hair, pulled into a bun, sat high atop her head. Cassie licked her fingers, then smoothed her daughter's edges.

Keisha wriggled in her mother's grasp, tripping over the hem of her dress, squirming to free herself from the pageantry of her bap-tism. Sitting on the pew, Teddy and Troy reminded Ruth of a young Eli, fidgeting in their suits, tugging at itchy shirt collars, and kicking the back of the seat in front of them.

Ruth was dressed in her Tahari charcoal pantsuit, which she often wore to client meetings. Elegant and classic. She thought it would be perfect for church, but now, glancing from Mama and Cassie to other women in the church, Ruth noticed they all wore skirts or dresses, most with hems at the knee or below. That must have been why the ushers had given her the evil eye. Since she hadn't set foot in this sanctuary for years, she'd forgotten its customs, its rules for how to be a proper lady in the world and in God's house.

A man slightly bowed in a brown suit walked over. *Dino*. "It's g-good to see you," he said, and Ruth nodded.

Natasha piped up. "I hear you and Mrs. Tuttle are thinking about a little getaway to Chicago. I love seeing older people still being *active*."

Dino's face reddened and Ruth jabbed her friend's ribs, immediately regretting that she'd confided that piece of gossip.

The organ's melody floated through the sanctuary and Ruth looked once again to Mama, on the second row with Cassie and the kids, and then back at Dino, who still seemed flustered. Pulling him to the side and away from Natasha, she said, "Thank you for taking care of Mama for me."

The lines between Dino's brows smoothed and water floated in his yellowed eyes. Not wanting to embarrass him further, she patted his shoulder and walked away. As Ruth moved down the aisle toward the front of the church, she heard her name shouted loud enough to be heard over the praise and worship music. "Mrs. Ruth Tuttle Shaw."

Before turning around, she recognized that voice and the familiar title he had used to introduce their union the day he married her and Xavier.

"Good morning, Pastor." When Ruth hugged him, her arms got tangled in his billowing purple robe. Neither of them mentioned his visit to the Tuttle home and the way she had unceremoniously escorted him out.

"It's mighty good to see you," Pastor Bumpus said, holding her hands in his. "I know how mightily the Lord has blessed you and your husband. Xavier, a marketing executive. And you, an engineer." The pastor paused to smile and shake his head slightly in awe at the word *engineer*. "Oh, what a mighty God we serve."

Most late-night comedy shows had a hype man to warm up the crowd before the main event. Pastor Bumpus was his own hype man, or if you heard him tell it, he'd probably say he was a front man for Jesus himself. Ruth recognized the signs. The minister was getting her ginned up for something.

"You know God is testing Ganton and the whole country with this recession we're in. Friendship just started a building fund. There are a lot of souls for us to save and we need a bigger house of worship to do it in. We hope you'll see your way to bless us as God has blessed you." Pastor reached into his robe and pulled out a donation envelope that he slipped into her hand.

A chord from the church organ punctuated his ask of her. A church ritual she had forgotten, and she bristled at Pastor's brazen solicitation for money. Still, she accepted the envelope from him and found her seat next to Natasha, who had chosen a seat on the same row with Mama and the rest of Ruth's family. As teenagers, the girls always sat next to each other, either stifling laughs or throwing shade at somebody.

Waiting for the service to begin, Ruth turned in her seat to look at the front door, checking to see whom she might still recognize all these years later. Mother Hayes, who had to be pushing ninety by now, walked in, leaning heavily on a cane. Her hat game had remained impeccable throughout the years and she stunned in a turquoise skirt suit with rhinestones and matching pumps. Mother Hayes had mothered Natasha and many of the girls in the church when they needed a firm hand.

Looking around the room, Ruth tapped her foot nervously. Natasha had said the Cunninghams never missed Sunday service, and Ruth was anxious to see them. It's why she wore eye makeup, and truth be told, it was the real reason she had let Natasha style her hair.

In the vestibule, Ruth spotted a white man talking animatedly with Pastor Bumpus. This was odd because, as far as she was aware, everyone knew that eleven o'clock on Sunday morning was the most segregated hour in America. That especially held true at Friendship Baptist, the oldest all-Black congregation in Ganton.

The man looked vaguely familiar—sixtyish, with a narrow, sunken face—but he didn't have that hungry look of politicians who swarmed Black churches at election time.

She elbowed Natasha. "Hey, check out that white guy talking to Pastor. Do you know him?"

Her friend turned in her seat. Squinting to get a better look, she said, "Hmm. That guy has been popping up here the past few months. I don't know what his deal is, but you know Ganton's growing now.

All kinds of developers come by the church trying to get Pastor to sell so they can build town houses and shopping centers."

In Ganton, they knew your name at the hardware store and the butcher shop. Neighbors came over to check on you if they hadn't seen your curtains move in a couple days. While Ruth hadn't lived here in more than a decade, she couldn't imagine somebody bulldozing it beyond recognition. Some storefronts had gone out of business a long time ago, leaving patches of vacant land as reminders. But even the ghost of what Ganton used to be felt enough like home that Ruth couldn't fathom not preserving it.

The service began and Pastor Bumpus took the pulpit, preaching about second chances, something Ruth prayed for when she remembered to pray. God extended His generosity to many in biblical times, and Pastor listed one by one the names of sinners, those redeemed and the ones the Almighty Himself might have determined irredeemable.

"Adam and Eve believed the lies of a snake. Rahab prostituted herself. David committed adultery. Reuben slept with his father's concubine. Solomon had a sex addiction. And Moses murdered a man."

With each example, Pastor's voice rose and so did the people, leaping to their feet to applaud and shout *amen* and *glory* and *hallelujah*. They did what Ruth couldn't always manage to do in her measured, analytical life; they gave themselves over to something more powerful than themselves.

While everyone closed their eyes and bowed their heads in prayer, she looked around again, scanning the congregants for Corey. The room was nearly full, but she couldn't see any boys who looked like the one she'd seen playing with Midnight that day at the rec center. Sweeping her gaze back the other way, her eyes landed on that same white man she'd seen earlier with the pastor, his arms folded, frowning. Their eyes met and she looked away, embarrassed that she'd been staring. He wasn't one of her old teachers, so where did she know him from?

Keisha joined three other children and five adults at the baptismal font, each wearing long white robes, their heads cocooned in white turbans. As the organist pounded the keys to "Take Me to the Water to Be Baptized," Ruth saw Eli rush up the aisle, his eyes wide and expectant. He was late, but at least he showed up for his daughter.

Suddenly, it came to her how she recognized the man. It was from the photo in the *Indianapolis Star*. Stanley DeAngelo, the shady lawyer who got out of prison last year. When she turned to look at the pew where he'd been sitting, he was gone. Had she imagined it? No, she had seen him, she was sure of it.

While the congregation sang, Ruth nudged Natasha. Under her breath, she said, "That man I saw earlier talking to Pastor was Stanley DeAngelo."

"What? How do you know it's him?"

Surreptitiously, she dug in her purse for her cell. Being an old-school church, Friendship Baptist didn't allow the use of phones during service. Hiding it in her bag, she quickly did a search and found the article about DeAngelo's arrest. When his photo finally loaded, she leaned over to Natasha and said, "I knew it. That's definitely him."

Why had this convicted felon shown up here? What had he been discussing with her old pastor? Her mind raced, and a memory surfaced of Mama saying she'd taken the baby to Jesus. Had she brought Corey to Pastor Bumpus?

The Cunninghams' absence from church began to make sense. They likely knew she'd be here today with her family. Maybe Pastor tipped them off that she was in town.

After performing the marriage ceremony for her and Xavier, Pastor Bumpus had encouraged them to start a family. It was entirely possible he'd always known the truth about her son. She'd never suspected, but she hadn't been looking, either. He had a history of coloring outside the lines, making legally questionable decisions for what he considered good reasons, like the funding of the recreation center. Dozens of church members had left the congregation after he'd mishandled their donations.

A hush fell over the sanctuary and she forced herself to focus on her niece gingerly descending the steps to stand in the water. Pastor held a white handkerchief over Keisha's nose and mouth and then dipped her in the baptismal pool. The congregation's singing and clapping drowned out Keisha's sputtering cries. Mama threw her head back and lifted her hands in praise. "Thank you, Jesus," she murmured.

The immersion in water, the cleansing of one's soul, meant you were burying your old life, with all its malevolence and mistakes, to rise into something new, something better. As much as Ruth wanted to believe that better days lay ahead, she left church more confused than convicted.

Thirty-One

RUTH

Back at the house, she took off her suit and wriggled out of her bra and pantyhose, needing her body and spirit to be lighter, unrestrained. In the bathroom, she stuck her head under the faucet and let the water fall over her freshly flat-ironed hair until each strand shrank back into its natural state.

She took out her phone and began composing a text message to Xavier. You won't believe what just happened at church. I saw this crooked lawyer who may have worked with Mama on Corey's adoption. I think Pastor's in on it, too. Her thumb hovered over the button to send it, and her held breath felt hot in her throat as she imagined Xavier reading it.

Then she remembered that he had no idea who Corey was because she'd neglected to tell him about her son's identity. Too much needed to be explained. Shaking her head in frustration, she deleted what she'd typed.

The smell of mushrooms and onions filled the house, and she could hear Mama and Cassie clanking pots and pans getting Sunday dinner together. They would eat as a family to celebrate Keisha's baptism. The kids kept bumping into Ruth's closed bedroom door and she figured they were playing with their Christmas toys. The house literally hummed with their happiness, that unrestrained bliss of youth. Someday life would chip away at the bliss and make the children as guarded and jaded as she'd become.

After some time had passed, she heard the kids watching videos with Eli in his room, and that's when she quietly stepped into the hallway and walked a few paces to Mama's room. She closed the door behind her.

Her body moved in an automatic gear, outpacing her head. She had no idea what she was looking for exactly, but there had to be something that traced the adoption, illegal or not. And perhaps linked Mama to DeAngelo.

This room had been off-limits to Ruth and Eli growing up, and they'd obeyed, staying away, always speculating about what their grandparents kept hidden here. Just being in this room seemed subversive. The blood pumped through her veins stronger now. She ran her hand over the rings of wood on the dresser and pulled the top handle. The drawer was stubborn, and she yanked hard to get it unstuck. The drawer screeched and Ruth froze. She crept to the door and put her ear to it but didn't hear any footsteps coming, just the sound of her niece and nephews.

When the dresser drawer finally opened enough, she reached inside and found an old pair of eyeglasses, a set of keys, and a denture case. She ran her hand along the inside and pulled out a laminated card with the name *Hezekiah Tuttle* on the front with a tiny, grainy photo of Papa. It had *Fernwood* printed in bold letters at the top, and she immediately recognized it as her grandfather's work ID. She had so many questions to ask him, and staring at his photo reminded her of the futility of that wish.

Wiping away a tear, she went over to the closet and found rows of boxes on the shelf. As she expected from an older woman, Mama kept lots of papers.

She pulled down a few boxes and sat on the bed. Rent receipts. Tax returns going back decades. A pang of guilt stabbed her. She shouldn't be snooping in Mama's room, yet she felt compelled to keep going.

"Dinner's almost ready! Get washed up!" Mama yelled from the kitchen, startling her.

She had to be quick. Opening the last box, she couldn't believe what she found inside. Stacks and stacks of her report cards, from Driscoll Elementary to Mother Mary and Ganton High. Mama had saved them all.

The shuffling of feet outside the bedroom grew louder and she heard Teddy and Troy arguing over who got to use the soap first to wash their hands. This was no time to reminisce.

She riffled through the papers, uncovering church donation statements and, in a separate folder, Papa's death certificate. She brought it to her face to take a closer look and then reached back in to see what was beneath it. She gasped.

A record of adoption for a male child born in August 1997.

At the top of the page, the Cunninghams were listed as the adoptive parents. Name of attorney: Stanley DeAngelo. Her stomach seized. She felt like she'd been kicked.

She had been right. This was her proof that he'd been the one to handle the case.

She focused her eyes on the page and saw what was filled in for the names of the biological parents:

FATHER: *UNKNOWN*
BIRTH MOTHER: *ERNESTINE TUTTLE*

Ruth's hands flew to her mouth. How could this be? Why had DeAngelo listed Mama as Corey's birth mother? A bitter taste coated her tongue and she thought she might vomit.

"Ruth, are you coming? I said dinner's ready!"

Quickly, she put the boxes back on the shelf and shoved the folder under her arm and ran back to her own bedroom. With her phone, she hastily took a photo of the adoption form and texted it to Tess, asking her to discreetly share it with her attorney friend for help understanding what this all meant.

How would Ruth face her grandmother? A woman who had broken her trust and lied to her repeatedly. She had wanted to believe that DeAngelo duped Mama, an unsuspecting, innocent old lady. But was that the case?

Mama carried plates of piping-hot smothered chicken and candied yams to the dining room table and poured tall glasses of iced tea. When she laid eyes on Ruth's hair, she seemed taken aback but said nothing.

Keisha kept up a constant chatter about every detail of the baptism: how cold the water was, how it stung her eyes, the way Pastor's hand smelled like fish when he covered her mouth and nose.

Mama wielded a heavy hand with the Lawry's seasoning for her smothered chicken. Family raved about it, but now it tasted like paper, and Ruth moved the meat around in her mouth until it turned to mush.

"What's the matter, Ruth?" Mama asked. "Eat your supper."

What was it about women of a certain age who always commanded people to eat? *Eat,* they said. Lena had done it when Butch raised a ruckus at dinner the other night, and now Mama issued the same command. As if stuffing them with food would satisfy a hunger that food couldn't reach, a starving that was actually soul-deep. Teddy and Troy competed in a fierce battle of thumb wars but weren't allowed to leave the table until they ate every green bean on their plates. Eli helped himself to seconds of Mama's famous chicken. When they finished eating, Cassie took the kids to Eli's old bedroom to watch YouTube videos. Silently, Ruth helped Mama and Eli clear the table and stack dirty dishes in the sink.

Ruth's phone pinged. She glanced down and saw a text from Tess. A sharp pain seized Ruth's whole body. According to her friend, DeAngelo would've needed her grandmother to apply for a birth certificate, pretending to be the biological mother, and list it as a home birth.

So, Mama had knowingly lied and said *she* had given birth to the baby. That made her an active participant in this sham, not an unwitting victim.

"Mama?" Ruth said, her voice deceptively gentle.

"Yes, baby?" She put an orange crusted pot in the sink to soak.

"You've been lying to me."

Eli kept his eyes on the utensils he was drying, apparently sensing the trouble bubbling up in the room. Mama looked wounded, but quickly regained her composure.

"I'm not sure what this is all about, but I know it can wait until after we've finished cleaning up," Mama said.

Ruth clutched her cell phone tightly and held it up. "You should look at this." Her eyes locked on Mama.

"Finish washing those glasses. Now's not the time."

"I am not a child who has to follow your orders," Ruth said. "Look at it."

She had never raised her voice with her grandmother like this before. The sharp edge to her tone cut through the room. She pointed to the image of the adoption consent form.

Mama cupped her mouth with her hand but didn't speak. Eli turned the phone so he could see the screen, and after reading the adoption form, he let out a low whistle. "Naw, Mama, you didn't get mixed up with this DeAngelo dude, did you? Say it ain't so."

"It is so. This is the proof. My grandmother not only consorted with a criminal to keep me from my child for eleven years, but signed a legal document swearing *she* gave birth to my baby." Ruth ground out the words.

Finally able to speak, Mama said, "Everything I did was for you, because I love you."

"You call this love?" Tears rolled down Ruth's cheeks. "You have no idea what love is." Eli squeezed her shoulder.

Mama twisted the sponge in her hands. Her eyes fixated on the kitchen window. While her physical presence was there, she must have traveled someplace else in her mind. Her lips parted and then closed and opened again, as if she didn't want to speak but something beyond her control compelled her.

"After Hezekiah died, I didn't know how to make up for everything he used to do for you kids. It wasn't just about being a provider, either. He always said we were better together, and he was right, as usual. I walked around so lost for so long. Mostly I turned to God and sometimes the man of God, Pastor Bumpus.

"I was trying my darnedest to give you kids the best start in life I could. Eli, when you got arrested for dabbling in that dope, I almost lost my mind. They cage our boys, shackle their possibility. Put a lock on their dreams. But not you. I wouldn't let them do that to my grandson. Pastor introduced me to Mr. DeAngelo. I gave him a little piece of money and he talked to one of those judges and they sent you home to me.

"I thought God only gave us one big storm as a test, you know. Once we passed it, we were good. I was wrong. When you got pregnant, baby girl, I saw every dream we had for you rotting and dying off. You were smart as a whip from the day you were born. You could have been anything you wanted to be in the world. But not with a baby. So, I took him to the church. Pastor Bumpus said there was a couple that was new to the church that had been trying for years to have a baby and couldn't. He had me talk to Mr. DeAngelo, who told me what to write on those papers. I knew it wasn't right in the eyes of the law. Maybe God's, neither. But it was the right thing for your future. And that's all I had my eyes on."

Mama shrank before them, not quite broken, but deflated like an old tire from Leo's auto lot. Ruth eyed her brother, wondering if Eli was considering how his grandmother had bought his freedom.

Quiet hung over the kitchen until the phone shattered the silence. It stunned Mama, who hesitated before answering.

She frowned at whatever the person on the other end told her. "Oh, dear Lord" was all she said.

"What is it? What's wrong?" Ruth asked.

"It's Midnight. Lena said he's run off."

Thirty-Two

RUTH

Late into the evening, Ruth tossed in her bed and listened for the house phone to ring with news about Midnight. They'd told Lena to call with an update, no matter the hour. At one and two and three in the morning, nothing, and finally she drifted off to sleep. Just before daybreak, garbage trucks rumbled nearby and she could hear other sounds of the street waking up. Like something shot out of a cannon, Ruth sat up in bed, remembering all over again her conversation with Mama and that Midnight was missing.

Without saying much to each other, Mama and Ruth dressed and met at the front door to head over to Lena's place.

Only a few streetlamps lit this end of Kirkland Avenue, which made it scary to imagine Midnight wandering out there all alone. Unlike in Chicago, darkness had always descended upon Ganton like a heavy blanket, so total and complete you sometimes couldn't see your hand in front of your face. They had waited until the first hour of daylight—the only respectable thing to do in Mama's mind—to knock on Lena's door.

They stood awkwardly in the doorway, together yet apart, acutely aware of the bomb that had just detonated in their family the previous afternoon. Midnight's disappearance offered a new preoccupation, a distraction for them, postponing the inevitable conversation.

The door stood open, and right away the stench of scorched meat met them. Inside, Lena was making tracks from the couch to the kitchen counter, the floor tiles wailing under the weight of her anxiety.

"Come on in," she said, a Newport wedged in the corner of her mouth. "I burned my roast last night and it still smells, so I opened the door to get some air in here. Wasn't paying attention to what I was doing after I realized Patrick was gone."

Lena's eyes held a wild terror in them, and Ruth had to look away to avoid seeing the palpable fear. Before they'd even taken off their coats, Eli arrived, anxious to do what he could to help. He faced Midnight's grandmother like a soldier reporting to duty. "He's coming home. Don't you worry." Drawing strength from her brother's resolute voice, Ruth held on to his words, letting his confidence extinguish her fear.

Mama went through Lena's cupboards until she found a glass and a bottle of whiskey. "Worrying won't bring him home any faster. You just need to get your mind and your nerves right." She poured a small taste for Lena. Something to take the edge off.

On the women's usher board at church, Mama joined the other sanctified folks in preaching against the sin of alcohol consumption. Yet she excused Eli's overindulgence and was now serving whiskey as a sedative. Ruth added this hypocrisy to the running tally she was keeping.

Ignoring her grandmother, Ruth said, "What can we do?"

Lena held the glass to her lips with both hands and drained it. "I don't know. He hasn't called or texted or answered his phone. If anything happens to him . . ."

Ruth rubbed Lena's back through her threadbare pale blue nightgown. Sharp pain squeezed her chest. "I should have mentioned this before, but Midnight called me over here one day before Christmas. He had packed a suitcase. Didn't say where he was planning to go, but I convinced him to put away his clothes and the suitcase."

Lena looked stricken. "I didn't know you'd been here. He didn't say a word. Yes, you should have told me."

"I'm so sorry I didn't."

Lena ran into one of the bedrooms and returned pulling the red suitcase Ruth had seen Midnight with that day. She fumbled with the latch until it fell open, empty. "I checked his closet and his dresser drawers. His clothes are still there. Maybe he didn't run away. What if somebody snatched him off the street?" Her voice became more strident and agitated as she spoke.

One of the bedroom doors opened and closed. Midnight's aunt Gloria appeared in a loose-fitting sweatshirt that stopped just above her knees. She balanced her son on her hip. "Now, who would kidnap him? That little pain in the ass. You know he likes to pull pranks. He'll be home when he gets hungry." In spite of her dismissiveness, Ruth glimpsed worry shadowed in her eyes, too.

"Have you called the police?" Ruth asked.

Lena puffed on her Newport and walked to the open front door to blow out the smoke. She craned her neck looking down the street, as if Midnight might suddenly appear. "I waited a couple hours at first because, you know, he's a kid and he always stays out later than I'd like . . . but that's boys for you. When it got late and I couldn't get ahold of him, I called the cops. They came over and asked a lot of questions and took one of his class pictures with them." She took another hard drag on her cigarette.

Midnight had left behind his suitcase and clothes, but that didn't mean he hadn't run away. If something triggered him, he might not have planned ahead. Ruth could still hear the despondency in his voice. In a child's mind, everything was magnified and world-ending. Why hadn't Ruth grasped the depth of his despair? She had been so overwhelmed by how Midnight had inadvertently revealed her son's identity. That was all she could think about then. She replayed their conversations from that day on a loop in her head until the words they'd spoken got scrambled in her mind.

Eli stood in the middle of the living room stretching his hamstrings as if preparing for a race. Immediately, she could tell that blood and adrenaline were pumping hard in him and he was ready to do more than just stand there talking. "All right now. Let's get focused on finding him. If the police won't, we will. What had Midnight so riled up he wanted to run away?"

Ruth ran her fingers through a tangled knot of hair, a nervous habit she had. "He didn't say a lot and I didn't want to push him. But he did tell me he was upset about having to move to Louisiana and he didn't want to go." She felt guilty knowing she was betraying Midnight's confidence. But finding him and bringing him home safely had to be the top priority.

Lena's face reeked of apology. "I wasn't trying to get rid of him. God knows I wasn't. Money's just been so tight lately. I knew that was on his mind, but I didn't think he'd worked himself up that badly." She rummaged in her purse, tossing aside Chapstick and a bottle of aspirin, until she found another cigarette.

An engine roared, and all heads snapped in the direction of the sound. A truck pulled up in front of the house and she recognized it as Butch's. All eyes focused on it, waiting to see if Midnight would emerge from the passenger side. They huddled in the doorway, no one moving until that truck door opened. It didn't. The air thickened with their disappointment and deepening fear.

"I looked every place I could think of, but nothing," Butch said as he made his way up to the house. The cold had reddened his runny nose and he breathed heavily. When his eyes finally settled on Eli, he stiffened.

But Lena stopped him short. "Don't even. Not today. Not now. Did you check Leo's lot and the junkyard? What about the rec center? You know he likes to hang out there."

"Checked all those, went up and down the aisles at Walmart," Butch said. "Stopped in practically every gas station and no sign of him."

Lena said, "Can you hand me my phone? I need to try the Cunninghams again. I haven't been able to get ahold of them. I know Sebastian and Pancho are home, but I'm not sure about Corey."

Every synapse in Ruth's body fired. She knew Corey and Midnight were good friends, but she hadn't considered that her own son could be missing, too. She kept her eyes on Lena's face, wondering what the Cunninghams were saying on the other end of the call. Mama moved closer to Ruth, as if sensing her alarm. But the only comfort Ruth wanted was to know Corey was safe in his bed.

A fresh wave of anguish distorted Lena's features as she locked eyes with Ruth. Mama had told her about Corey's birth, Ruth knew it. A tight knot lodged at the bottom of her belly.

"The Cunninghams have been out searching for Corey, too . . ." Her voice trailed off.

Dread coursed through Ruth's blood. Moving away from the others, she walked over to the living room window. Almost instinctively, she wrapped her arms around her stomach, where Corey had lived when he was at least physically part of her body. She couldn't lose him again. Not like this. Mothers everywhere waited up nights for their children to come home after school or by curfew or to return from war. That wait had never been hers until now.

Eli, sensing Ruth's fear, put his hand on her shoulder.

Still gazing out the window, she said softly, "I'm grateful for what you did that day when you fired your gun. You protected him."

"I been doing it his whole life. Corey doesn't really know me, but I've got his back. Always." Squeezing her shoulder, he gently turned her to face him. His eyes bored into hers. Black pupils. Red around the edges from lack of sleep or too much alcohol the night before. Maybe both. "He's with good people and they take good care of him. But I'm his uncle and I make sure he's okay. I never let anything happen to him."

Eli had been her protector from day one. Balled fists making her bullies cower. A sure voice vanquishing the monsters under her bed. And now he had become an invisible shield for her child. His very own superhero. Relief swept over her like a monsoon rain.

She nodded, momentarily unable to speak. When she found her voice again, she asked, "What's he like?"

"Your kid? Smart. Guess I have to admit he took that after you. Good-looking, though, like me." He winked.

Resting her head on her brother's shoulder, Ruth laughed and imagined her son growing up to look like his uncle someday.

"I hear he's something of a baseball star. Is he really that good?" She glanced up at Eli.

"He's got a good arm on him. And if he makes it to the major leagues, you best be sure I'll let him know we blood."

They laughed at that, and only now did she realize it had been a mistake to stay away so long. Corey should know his family, but what if it was too late? She felt helpless and needed to do something.

Walking back to the kitchen, she said, "All right, let's make a list of all the spots the boys typically go to hang out, and I can start searching. I know you already hit a bunch of them, Butch. What have we missed?"

"We can split the list," Eli said. "I'll drive in my car and look around, too."

Grabbing a notepad from the kitchen, Ruth began scribbling the names Lena rattled off. *Save A Lot, the baseball field, Corner Diner, the McDonald's behind the old Concord Mall.*

According to the thermometer on the windowsill, it was thirty-six degrees, a bit warmer than previous days, but Ruth worried that Midnight's jacket, the one she had covered him with the other night, was too thin.

She checked her phone to see if he had texted. Nothing. She decided to send him a message.

I'm worried about you. Let me know where you are. I will come right away. I promise.

FOR MORE THAN AN HOUR SHE DROVE TO THE SPOTS ON HER AS-signed list, plus every nook and cubbyhole of Ganton she could think of. At each place, she asked, *Has Midnight been here?* With some people, she had to provide additional details beyond the boy's nickname, clarifying, *Lena's grandson, Patrick. Butch Boyd's son.* In a small town, people either knew you or at least knew of you. Reluctant to verbalize her deepest fears, she sometimes added, *It's possible he's with Corey Cunningham.*

At one gas station in the center of town, a hulking, bearded man who appeared to be the owner scowled at the mention of the boys. "That little punk. He and his little thug friends haven't been in here lately. If you ask me, they're all trouble, and I don't like trouble." Ruth flinched at the characterization of her son as a *thug.* The man's gaze swept over her in a way that told her he placed her in the same unflattering category.

She left the gas station deflated. Her car moved slowly through Grundy, in the neighborhood where she'd found Midnight wandering aimlessly late at night. At least the heavy snowfall had subsided a couple days ago. Still, she worried for his safety even more now than she had that day.

Her phone buzzed, vibrating beside her on the passenger seat. She pulled over to look and saw it was a text from Midnight. Her heart lurched in relief.

overlook point at wabash river

Wabash River. Why hadn't she thought of the river before? She considered calling him, asking if Corey was with him, but didn't want to say anything that might spook him. Overlook Point was about a fifteen-minute drive from the bank where she'd stopped to check her phone. She considered texting Lena to let her know she'd heard from her grandson. But she figured Midnight probably ran away over frustration with Lena's threats to ship him off to Louisiana. If so, hearing from his grandmother could set him off and send him on the run again. Besides, Lena and Butch were even farther away from Overlook Point than she was right now. Shifting the gear out of neutral, she sped toward the river.

Thirty-Three

MIDNIGHT

Daylight came up slowly, like thin veils being lifted. The ice that glazed over the Wabash River had ruptured, and jagged sheets of it floated like puzzle pieces. The blurry fog cleared, and everything was making sense, finally fitting into place. L-Boogie's jacket swallowed Midnight and he pulled it over his face, breathing in the smell of the leather. Midnight had decided not to run away. If it hadn't been for L-Boogie, he might have repacked that little red suitcase and thumbed a ride somewhere, anywhere that wasn't Ganton or Louisiana.

Corey lay opposite him on his back, the wet ground beneath him. They were only about a foot away from the river. Corey tossed a baseball above his head from one gloved hand to the other. The way he was lying there, fully open and exposed, made Midnight think that Corey was unafraid. He didn't fear Midnight's having any power to ever hurt him the way his very existence had hurt Midnight.

Corey wound the ball between his legs without dropping it. His arms perfect, not like Midnight's. Looking at his friend's profile, he noticed that the curve of Corey's nose resembled Miss Ruth's. Corey had no idea Miss Ruth was his mother. He was sure of that. What if Midnight told him? That would shut him up and wipe that smug look off his face. But he'd never believe him.

"You got any snacks in there? I'm hungry." Corey pointed to Midnight's backpack.

"No," Midnight snapped, and shoved the bag behind him.

"Stingy."

"Whatever."

"I bet you don't know how the man on the moon cuts his hair," Corey said.

"How?"

"Eclipse it."

Midnight wanted to laugh because it was funny, but he coughed instead. "Okay, I got one. What's a tornado's favorite game to play?"

"What?"

"Twister," he said with a laugh.

Eager to get away from Granny and Daddy after what he'd overheard, he had texted Corey Sunday morning and found out his family was skipping church, which they hardly ever did. For hours, they goofed off all over town and ended up staying out all night, sitting in a Denny's booth and then the twenty-four-hour Walmart in town. At one point he heard Daddy in one of the Walmart aisles shouting his name. They ducked out before he spotted them and headed to Taco Bell. When Corey's allowance money ran out and they couldn't afford to order more food, they decided to go to the river.

As usual, Corey had whined about making the Cunninghams worry, but Midnight told him he'd had an important meeting with L-Boogie and could only discuss it face-to-face.

In reality, he needed more time to think about what he wanted to do. They came here, where they often swam during the summers. It was fun to see the water crusting with ice, the smoke rolling off it.

Corey turned onto his stomach. "C'mon already and tell me the big secret."

L-Boogie had said you needed to test people to see if they were real friends, to know if you could trust them. He'd said, *You set the limits and see what they do. You are in control. Always.* When Corey agreed to stay out all night without calling or texting the Cunninghams, Midnight figured he could count on him. *Your own blood ain't always loyal. But when you find one who can be loyal, that's a real one right there,* L-Boogie said.

"Okay. I guess I can tell you now about the *proposition.*" Midnight loved the way his lips and tongue moved around that word ever since he'd heard Bo say it in the alley that night.

Corey propped himself up on his elbows. "What is it? This better be good."

"I told you it would be good, didn't I?"

"Just come on with it. You've been holding out long enough." Corey tried to act cool, but Midnight knew he'd been jittery with anticipation. They'd been on the run almost twenty-four hours.

Midnight licked his cracked lips and let the white vapor from the cold seep from his mouth like cigarette smoke. "We're gonna go into business with L-Boogie and Bo. All we have to do is sell candy for school. They'll take care of everything else. We could make hundreds of dollars. Isn't that crazy?"

Corey was sitting fully upright now, his brow scrunched in a frown, eyes wide with fear. "Yeah, you're crazy. I don't want to sell anything. I don't want anything to do with those guys."

"It's like a big business with grown-ups. Don't be such a baby."

"I'm not a baby."

"You are, too."

"Am not."

Midnight sat up straight. This put him in a better position to make his point. "If you could make a lot of money, what would you buy?"

"How much money?"

"Like a million dollars."

"I don't know."

"C'mon. What would you spend it on?"

"Maybe a different baseball glove for every day."

That seemed like a stupid way to spend a million dollars, but Midnight didn't know what he'd do with that kind of money, either.

One time Granny said the state paid people to take care of kids nobody else wanted. Maybe the Cunninghams raised Corey as their own son because the money was good. Maybe that's why they were rich, and Corey didn't really care about money.

"Well, if we sell a ton of candy then we can buy anything we want. Baseball gloves and whatever."

When Midnight first heard the proposition from L-Boogie, he wondered if it might be too good to be true. But the more he looked at L-Boogie's gold watch, his leather jacket, and the Jordans, he became a believer. Corey shivered and kept the lower half of his face buried in his coat collar. His voice was muffled. "I don't know. We could get in trouble. My mom and dad made me promise I'd stay away from those guys."

Midnight sat cross-legged, his knees bumping up against Corey's. He looked him straight in the face. "Well, you may not want money, but I do . . ." The wind picked up and sounded like a train barreling through town.

"Money for what?"

"Money to move somewhere other than where Granny wants to send me. Or money to help Daddy get a new place for just the two of us." Saying those words and hearing them carried by the early-morning wind made them seem truer than when he just thought about the idea of moving.

Corey rocked back and forth on the ground with his hands shoved in his coat pockets. "That's nuts. Just talk to your granny. I bet you won't have to go."

Easy for Corey to say. He lived on Hill Top, where people didn't worry about money like they did in Pratt. Whenever he spent his allowance and wanted more money for salt and vinegar chips, the Cunninghams just gave it to him.

Corey pulled out his cell phone and got that panicky look he always did when he thought he was breaking somebody's rules. "I got to go. My mom and dad are gonna be really mad this time. They'll probably ground me for a week." He looped the straps of his backpack around his arms and struggled to pull it up around his bulky down jacket. "Look, if you need money, I can just ask them to give you some."

"I don't want your mom and dad's money." If only Corey knew

they weren't his real mom and dad. Midnight considered telling him so but decided to keep his mouth shut. For now.

"Then why are you complaining all the time? Go on and move if that's what you want."

In that smug way of his, Corey always let you know he had more than you did and probably always would. Midnight unzipped his backpack and pulled out his airsoft pellet gun, the one he'd taken from Daddy's truck. Corey was good at a lot of things, but he wasn't the best at everything. Definitely not the best at this.

Corey's eyes got big. For a second, the shock of seeing the gun must have stolen his voice. His mouth hung open, but he didn't say anything. At least he'd stopped whining about his mom and dad and getting in trouble.

"What the hell, Patrick? Where did you get that?" Corey leaned back, falling to his elbows and looking from the gun to Midnight.

He'd called him *Patrick,* the name nobody used except Daddy, Granny, and his teachers.

The weight of the gun in Midnight's good hand bent his wrist.

"It's mine."

"Did you steal your dad's gun?"

"No. It's my new pellet gun. Not a real one. Duh. My dad did show me how to shoot a real gun before, though."

Corey inched backward as Midnight waved the gun in zigzag lines, aiming it nowhere and everywhere.

"Guns are supposed to be locked up. That's what my dad said."

"I told you it's not real, dodo. We're hiding our real ones from the government 'cause Daddy said Obama's gonna take away everybody's guns."

"Obama didn't say that."

"You don't know."

"Neither do you."

The wind had settled to a dull whisper. Midnight let the airsoft rest on his knee.

Corey fumbled with his phone and said, "I'm calling my mom."

"*My mom. My mom,*" Midnight repeated in a singsong voice, and waved the gun to match the melody. He should tell him about Miss Ruth, let him know the truth. Tell him his parents weren't really his parents. Make him wonder for once what it felt like to not be sure who really loved you.

"Shut up," Corey muttered.

"I bet you can't shoot this." Midnight knew Corey had never fired a gun before, real or fake. The Cunninghams wouldn't even buy him a water gun when they were little.

"Maybe I don't want to. Guns are stupid anyway."

"I dare you." He held the airsoft out to his friend, who kept his head down but eyes on the gun. "Only if you're not scared."

"I'm not scared."

"Prove it."

"Give it to me." Corey snatched it by the barrel and right away crossed his thumbs on the pistol grip and pointed his index finger toward an imaginary target.

"You're not holding it right." Kneeling next to him, Midnight heard Daddy's instructions in his ear. He wrapped his good hand around one of Corey's, positioning his friend's fingers on the pellet gun. *Don't pull the trigger, squeeze. You should squeeze it like you're making a fist.*

Corey got the hang of it fast, like he did everything else, and now clutched the gun with the same confidence he did a baseball bat, as if he'd done it a million times before.

Then Corey hopped to his feet and aimed it at the icy ground, the trees, the sky, everywhere. *Pow. Pow.* A wildly alive look came over his face and he moved like he had firecrackers in his pants.

A grin spread across Midnight's face and he momentarily forgot his anger, forgot that he knew the truth about Miss Ruth. Whenever you watched somebody do something for the first time, it felt good. Especially if it was something you'd done before. Like you were doing it again for the first time, too.

But he reminded himself of what Corey had taken from him, how he had ruined everything in his life, from his bum arm to Miss Ruth.

He didn't know for sure, but Miss Ruth didn't seem to be the kind of lady who liked guns very much. He bet that when she saw her *son* shooting a gun, she would be pretty upset. He took out his phone and texted her. He knew she would come.

But as he watched Corey run along the river's edge firing the airsoft, he got the urge to do something even bigger.

The summer after fourth grade, Mr. Cunningham had spent a lot of money on a new pitching glove that Corey bragged about constantly. To break it in, Mr. Cunningham baked it in the oven like a steak and ran over it with his car. Corey carried that stupid glove everywhere and wouldn't stop talking about how soft the leather was. When Midnight couldn't take it anymore, he'd slipped the glove out of Corey's bag one day and nuked it in the microwave for five minutes, until the rawhide melted. After that, Corey had to play baseball with a regular glove like everybody else.

Now, Midnight had another big idea. Blood rushed through him just thinking about it. He took out his phone and began dialing when Corey called out to him.

"Boom and you're dead," Corey shouted from up the river, the barrel of the gun aimed right at Midnight.

"Quit pointing it at me. If you hit me, *you'll* be dead."

"Sorry! Look at me! Did you see that?" A black-capped chickadee skidded across the river when Corey fired a pellet close to it.

"911. What's your emergency?" Midnight had been so caught up watching his friend that he didn't realize the call had connected already. The lady operator sounded calm and official, just like the ones on TV.

He didn't know what to say. He hadn't planned this part. Lowering his voice a few octaves, he tried to sound like Daddy. "Um, I'm calling to report a guy with a gun at the river."

"Wabash River?"

"Yes."

"What's your exact location?"

"Um, the Overlook area."

"Okay, are you in danger right now, or are you in a safe location?"

"Yeah. I'm okay. I'm safe."

"A unit is on its way."

Midnight's heart raced, fear and thrills rushing through him at the same time. Corey had never gotten detention at school and the Cunninghams hardly ever grounded him, but this time he'd get in trouble, for sure.

The popping sound rang in his ears.

Corey ran toward him laughing with the pellet gun. "Do you want to take a turn now?"

Shaking his head, Midnight said, "No, that's okay. I get to play with it all the time."

"Okay."

Corey raced back to the river's edge, sliding on the ice, still firing the airsoft.

It felt like barely a few minutes had gone by when he heard tires screeching, the sour smell of exhaust filling his nose.

Excitement curled in Midnight's belly as he anticipated what might happen next. In school, if a kid screwed up really bad, the school officer pulled him out of class while everyone stared and echoed, *Oooh, you're in trouble.*

Suddenly, a man's voice yelled, "Drop the weapon and freeze!"

Two men appeared dressed in black. Badges on their belt buckles shining like searchlights. The cops had come fast.

They ran up to where Midnight was still sitting on the ground. Both had their guns drawn and pointed at Corey, a few feet away.

Corey didn't blink. He just stood there motionless, his arms wooden, holding the pellet gun out in front of him.

"I said drop your weapon, now."

Midnight's belly flip-flopped and his mouth went dry. He waited for the police officers to tell Corey he was in trouble and they were calling his parents.

But they never did.

They just kept their guns aimed at his best friend.

Thirty-Four

RUTH

Seeing the Wabash River resurrected Ruth's childhood, all those summers here by Papa's side, his hands—rough and scraped raw from hard work—guiding hers along the fishing pole. She'd always felt safe here.

Warning signs along the riverbank urged caution and in bold red letters on white placards said, *Thin Ice. Keep Off. No Skating.* That still, glassy river, so immense and beautiful, could be deceptive. Midnight's text had asked her to come to the river, but it didn't sound dire, thankfully.

She hoped they hadn't wandered onto the ice. Every worst-case scenario flooded her brain.

She got out of her car and picked her way through the brush toward the water. Each footstep she took thundered in her ears. The crunching sound she made on a patch of ice caused her to jump.

Something rustled nearby and then she heard a man's voice. Her head jerked in the direction of the sound. In the distance, she spotted two small figures under the spotlight of the rising sun. *Corey.* He and Midnight were together. Two larger figures that had to be adults faced them. A patrol car nearby. She almost sobbed with relief. Police officers had found the boys and they were safe. She ran toward them.

"Hey!" Ruth yelled, stumbling over the rocky terrain.

When she got within a few feet of the officers, she saw they had their guns pointed.

At Corey.

Dread gripped her and her legs wobbled. A strange noise escaped from Corey's lips like his voice had gotten trapped in his throat and was trying to break free. His outstretched arms, holding a gun, appeared stuck in that raised position. Why did he have a gun? It didn't make sense.

Her primal need to protect him overrode everything. Her body lurched forward in front of Corey, placing herself between him and the cops' guns.

"Get out of the way, lady, before you get yourself killed!" shouted the white cop.

"He's a child! Don't shoot!" Ruth screamed, choking on the cold air.

They stood there in this slow-motion standoff. To Ruth, it seemed like she was yelling behind a wall of soundproof glass, because the cops didn't lower their guns even an inch.

The other officer had light brown skin and he looked familiar to her, but she couldn't place him. Her eyes pleaded with him to understand, to stop pointing his gun at her son. But he stared at her blankly, showing no recognition.

"Miss Ruth." Midnight's voice.

She couldn't look at him. Her eyes darted back and forth between the cops holding the guns. She said, "Stay out of the way, Midnight."

"You don't care about me. All you care about is Corey because he's your son."

He's your son. How did Midnight know? Her mind scrambled to climb out of its fog when she heard a thud behind her. Corey had dropped the gun. She felt it smack the ankle of her boot.

The officers ran over, pushing her aside. The brown-skinned one snatched the gun from the ground, and the white officer told Corey, "Put your hands behind your head."

This time, Corey listened and, moving like a robot, did as he was told. Ruth had flashbacks of the bucket boy on the el in Chicago. That same fear shot through her, much more magnified now.

The cop patted his shoulders, under his arms, along his rib cage, and then between his legs until he reached her son's ankles.

Corey whimpered, and she glanced down at his face, his eyes squeezed shut, with thick black lashes curled upward like silk drapery covering a window. Just the way she remembered them the day he was born. A sharp stab of regret hit Ruth when she remembered whispering, *I hate you*, just before he'd opened his eyes for the first time.

The white officer kicked the back of Corey's knee, buckling it until it bent, and Corey fell to the ground. Ruth knelt beside them and put her face next to the officer's. "Why are you doing this? He's just a boy." She tuned her voice to peak performative articulation. "This has been a terrible misunderstanding. This is an eleven-year-old child. Let's be sensible here."

Ignoring her pleas, the officer finished his pat-down and determined that Corey didn't have any hidden weapons on him. "You can put your arms down now," he said, and Corey had to be told again before he lowered them.

"You're Ruth Tuttle, aren't you?" said the darker-skinned officer.

She nodded and then she remembered. The name on his badge was *Jenkins*. Kenneth Jenkins. The boy Eli had socked in the jaw defending her honor back in grade school.

Officer Jenkins asked, "Is this your son, and did you buy him this gun?"

"I'm—he's, well, he has parents. They're not here." She lowered her voice as if Corey couldn't hear, but of course he could. He stiffened by her side. "I don't know where he got the gun."

"It's mine," Midnight said in a shaky voice. "It's just a toy gun. No big deal."

"We see that now. But it is a very big deal. This wasn't on the gun," said the white cop, whose badge read *Griffin*. He bent down to pick up the orange muzzle tip.

"My daddy removed it when he took the gun apart to fix it. I guess it fell out in my bag. I tried to put the orange thing back on, but I couldn't . . ." Midnight's voice trailed into a barely audible whisper by the end of his sentence.

Ruth hadn't thought about the type of gun it was when she saw Corey with it, but she knew her son wasn't dangerous. "Yes, it's a toy. He's only eleven years old. Why are you treating him like a criminal?" Tears stung her eyes.

Officer Griffin fixed her with a harsh glare. "This kid seems a hell of a lot older, and these pellet guns look just like the real thing."

With his slight build and baby face, Corey appeared young for his age, not older, but before she could say anything, Officer Jenkins added, "We responded to a call about a guy out here at the river with a gun."

Midnight fidgeted and buffed a chunk of ice with the toe of his boot. Ruth grabbed him by the shoulders. "Do you know anything about this?"

Without looking at her, he mumbled under his breath.

"Speak up," she said.

"Yeah, I called 911, but I was just playing. I didn't mean for it to be a big deal." His shoulders shook and he sniffled. "I guess I was mad."

She withdrew her hands from his coat as if she'd touched a hot flame. Covering her mouth, she said, "You were playing? *Playing?* Corey could've been killed! How could you be so reckless?"

The police radio squawked, and Officer Jenkins spoke into it, letting someone know the situation was under control. But this day had moved far beyond anything they could control. She felt like she was sinking into a pit of helplessness.

"You're Butch Boyd's kid, aren't you?" When Midnight nodded, Officer Griffin said, "I'll have a talk with your dad. Calling 911 is serious business. Not a joke. You hear me?" Midnight nodded again.

Turning to face Ruth, he said, "In the future, they need to play with these in a safe, controlled location with special protective equipment. Not out here on the river. And this gun can't be used until it's fixed, with the orange tip put back on properly. If the wrong person had seen Corey out here swinging that gun around, things could've turned out real different." She didn't like the way he said *real different*, reminding her how this all could've ended. Ruth's limbs shook, and tears leaked again from her eyes. If she hadn't shown up when she did, those cops very well might've shot her son.

After collecting everyone's phone numbers and addresses, Officer Griffin confiscated Midnight's gun. "Patrick Boyd and Corey Cunningham. We've been on the lookout for you two." Stepping away from them and putting his phone to his ear, he said, "I'm gonna have the station get in touch with your parents to let 'em know you're safe so they can come pick you up."

Ruth turned to face Officer Jenkins. "I'll wait with them until their families get here." He nodded, and both officers returned to their police car but didn't pull away, obviously waiting until the parents arrived.

Corey rolled into a tight ball on the ground, the curl of his body a tumbleweed. Ruth knelt beside him in the cold, wet earth and pressed one hand against his back.

He recoiled at her touch. "Don't touch me! Who are you? I'm not your freakin' son." He hurled the words at her like bricks, and they landed heavy on her heart.

Then he turned his anger on Midnight. "They could've killed me. You lie. You always lie." Corey spat the words at his friend.

This was the first time Ruth had really heard her son's voice. The deep yet soft timbre of it. He got to his feet and pushed Midnight's chest. Midnight just stood there, drained of his earlier bitterness, as if waiting for a harder, more punishing blow. As if he deserved it. And he did.

Corey kept going. "That's why your granny's makin' you move. Nobody likes you. Nobody wants you around. You play too much." He turned to Ruth. "He's a liar. I know who my mom and dad are." He searched her eyes for confirmation, to make Midnight's words

from earlier untrue. Just as the one storm had settled, another gathered strength.

All that time she had spent agonizing over whether she wanted to
be his mother, and she hadn't stopped to consider that he might not
want to be her son.

Ruth surrendered to the inevitability of the truth and whatever
followed. Looking up at Corey, she said, "It's true. I'm sorry, but it's
true. You were adopted, and . . . and I'm your mother."

Thirty-Five

RUTH

A haunted look flickered in Corey's eyes.

"You all lie. All of you." Snot ran from his nose, mixing with tears.

Ruth studied the curve of his mouth, the slope of his nose, and recognized the Tuttle family resemblance. The burgundy birthmark remained, a smudge on his cheek. She resisted the strong urge to touch it. As if he could read her thoughts, Corey turned away from her and curled into a fetal position on the cold ground, resting his head on his backpack.

She moved closer to her son. She had no idea what to say, some-how, after all these years, totally unprepared for this moment. "I was seventeen when I had you. Not much older than you are now. I was afraid."

"Just leave me alone, okay? I don't know you, lady. I don't want to know you."

She had to make him understand. Pressing her hands to her cheeks, she kept talking. "I'm sorry. I didn't know what to do, and when you were born my grandmother made sure you went to a good family. Maybe I should have fought to keep you, to be a mother to you, but I didn't. Now, I can't change that. But you have an amazing life with wonderful people who love you, and I'm not sorry about that.

I can't tell you how proud I am of you," she said, her voice choked with emotion.

Corey covered his ears. "I don't want to hear it. You're not my mom!"

"Hey, Corey." Midnight reached for his friend's arm.

"Get off!" Corey shouted.

Midnight's chest caved as if he'd been struck. "Come on. Don't be mad at me. Okay?"

Why had he done this? Part of her wanted to analyze what drove him to be so reckless with the gun, reckless with the police, and reckless with the truth. But her head ached, and she couldn't process anything more.

Corey's voice crackled like a bonfire, lifted by the wind. "I hate both of you."

Ruth folded her gloved hands under her chin as if she were praying. For the past eleven years, she'd imagined this moment, meeting her son for the first time. Not once did she predict the raw pain she saw playing across Corey's face.

Butch had been driving in the area searching for Midnight, so he showed up first. He surprised her by saying "Thank you," but Midnight stayed silent and shuffled behind his father toward the truck. The police officers got out of the patrol car and came over to talk to Butch about what had happened.

Corey stayed motionless on the ground, but when he saw the Cunninghams' car pulling up, he ran toward it. He stopped short before he reached the sedan. Ruth imagined he felt torn now, unsure of who he was and where he actually belonged. She blamed herself for the agony that rendered his body rigid with uncertainty.

The man and woman who emerged from the car seemed hesitant, too. Scrambling to her feet, Ruth stood erect, brushed dirt from her jeans, and tried to smooth her hair. She figured her eyes were red-rimmed from tears and lack of sleep, and she wondered what impression she was making on the adoptive parents of her son.

Mr. Cunningham had a deep brown complexion with a gray-

speckled mustache. Worry lines creased his forehead. Mrs. Cunningham, who was a few shades lighter than her husband, had her hair
pulled back in a tight French braid. She wore little if any makeup and
a dress or skirt that hung below her houndstooth coat.

She spoke first. "Corey, honey," she said tentatively, inching
toward him.

As if a spell had broken, he ran into the woman's arms, sobbing.

"You're safe now, son," Mr. Cunningham said, putting a protective arm around the boy's shoulders.

Son. That word shattered something inside Ruth. Mrs. Cunningham's cheeks flushed, and above Corey's head, she met Ruth's eyes.
The ripe scent of fear emanated from this woman.

From what she could tell, the Cunninghams appeared to love
Corey. And he loved them. She saw it now in the natural way they
cleaved to each other and moved as one. Everything made sense all of
a sudden. Corey had traveled through Ruth, but he wasn't hers. The
certainty of that realization stunned her, and instead of bringing her
peace, it made her ache for what she didn't have, for what should have
been hers all these years.

Thirty-Six

MIDNIGHT

The vacancy sign at the Oak Creek Motel blinked red. Midnight couldn't ever remember the *No* lighting up. He knelt on the bed and pulled the blinds apart to see if he could spot Daddy outside having his morning smoke before the sun came up. All he saw was the motel clerk tossing a big black garbage bag into the dumpster and then scratching his balls through his pants. Daddy had gotten a room there after Christmas, when Drew put him out for not carrying his load. Maybe a move to Louisiana wouldn't be so bad now, a chance to leave everything behind.

While he had his face pressed to the window, he heard the turn of the door handle. As soon as his father walked in, Midnight caught a whiff of sickly sweet weed.

Daddy looked pissed. "If you ever pull a stunt like that again, I'll put a bullet in you myself."

Only one day had passed since everything happened at the Wabash River, and already he knew nothing would be the same again. Daddy wouldn't stop talking about it. Midnight stood between the two beds, the air stuffy in the tiny motel room. "I said I'm sorry."

Ever since that morning, people watched him and whispered, smiling too hard when he caught them staring. He hadn't heard from Corey and doubted he would see him until school started again next week. Sebastian and Pancho must've heard what happened, and they hadn't texted him. Usually the four boys met up on New Year's Eve to set off fireworks and listen to the crackle and boom in the night air. But he knew he'd be ringing in the new year alone.

Even Bones stayed away. Granny said somebody had finally taken him to the shelter, which made Midnight sad. It meant he wouldn't be around anymore. It occurred to Midnight that Bones might get adopted just as Corey had, and he felt the strange stirring of jealousy over a dog. How would his new owners know he liked his belly rubbed in small circles with a light scratch, not too much fingernail?

Daddy plopped down on one of the beds and Midnight held his breath to block the smell. "The last thing I need is the cops hassling me. You know they still haven't given me that airsoft back. You had no business taking it from my truck. Next thing you know the feds will be on my ass about my real guns. Goddamn it, Patrick. What the hell were you thinking?"

Midnight looked down at his socked feet, the left pressed on top of the right. He lost his balance and reached for the arm of a chair to steady himself. "Guess I wasn't thinking."

"Damn right, you weren't. Good thing I've got a buddy down at the station. They were talking about charging you with delinquency for making a fake 911 call. You're lucky they didn't haul you off to juvie."

Midnight wanted to scream that juvie would be better than this ratty motel with the peeling walls and the nasty brown stains on the bedspread. But when Daddy got like this, you had to let him go until he stopped on his own.

LATER THAT AFTERNOON, AT GRANNY'S SHOP, MIDNIGHT SAT NEAR the door waiting for Granny to finish up for the day. People were taking advantage of the after-Christmas/New Year's Eve sales on baskets of jellies and jams, and wool sweaters that gave him static shock.

There was nothing Granny couldn't get some sucker to buy, not even an old miter saw of Daddy's. She rested her hands on her hips and looked up at a man twice her size. "That's as low as I'm going. Not a penny less. I'm telling you, this thing will cut through baseboards like butter. Either you want it or you don't." People said Granny could sell shoes to a man with no feet. And she probably could.

A moving van idled at the end of the street, and when he leaned against the shop window, he saw J. B. Wagner from school stumble over a pothole. He carried a tube TV with the cable cords dragging behind him. After J.B.'s little sister, Polly, died in that fire, his folks had cleared ash from the roof and gutters and mopped up the soot, but every time Midnight walked by their house, the air hit his nose and it always smelled of death.

Granny had said, *Too many bad memories in that house, and you can't wash them away.*

J.B.'s neck stayed scaly and red from burns that hadn't healed. The kid should've worn a turtleneck to hide them, the way Midnight wore long sleeves to cover his scars. Midnight pretended he didn't see him when he walked in the store. "We're moving today," J.B. said.

Midnight licked the peanut butter from a Reese's off his thumb. They had both lost their sisters, but that didn't make them friends. "Yeah" was all Midnight managed to say.

"My dad got a job at a dairy in Crawfordsville."

When Midnight didn't respond, J.B. said, "So everybody from school says Corey tried to shoot some lady and the cops with your gun."

A wad of spit rose from Midnight's throat and filled his mouth. He wanted to shoot the projectile at J.B., but he swallowed it. "Shut up and leave me alone. You don't even know what you're talking about. I thought you were busy moving."

"We are. It's just that I heard stuff. Sebastian's mom said you and Corey might have to go to jail."

Nobody was going to jail, but in a way, Midnight wished he could pay for what he'd done with something other than bad dreams that chased him from night to day.

But none of that was any of J.B.'s business.

A Coors beer can rolled onto the street and a car zoomed by, crushing it flat. Midnight stared hard out the window at the mangled aluminum, keeping his eyeballs real still until he couldn't see J.B. anymore, even with his side vision, then he felt J.B. move away after he got tired of being ignored.

Midnight wandered to the back of the shop and found Granny closing up the register. She put a hand on his shoulder and asked, "You doing okay?" The last couple of days, he'd caught Granny staring, watching him more closely than before. And she touched him lightly, as if he might break.

He mumbled an "okay" and watched her finish up around the shop. When she was done, he followed her out to the car and they sat in silence on the drive to her house.

Midnight set the table as Granny heated up the roast chicken, mashed potatoes, and fancy peas. She told him to use their good dishes, a sign she was trying too hard, and that usually made him nervous. She even asked him to put out the cloth napkins, instead of the paper towels Miss Ruth had said were plenty absorbent.

When he had come home from the river Monday, Granny hugged him so hard he thought his bones would break. Then, in the next breath, she screamed at him. *What were you thinking? You could've got yourself and Corey killed out there. Don't you ever, ever, ever do that again.*

Now, he knew what she'd tell him over dinner. When something you had expected for a long time happened, it fell like a peanut falling in the snow, making no sound at all.

She would ship him off to live with his cousins in Baton Rouge. He'd go to a new school. Make new friends. Maybe it wouldn't be so bad to start over. Maybe even be given a new nickname by those who knew nothing of Midnight and his old life.

Granny took long, slow drinks of tea. Glancing up at the photo of him and Mom on the mantel, she said, "I miss Hannah every day. She was my firstborn. I can never get her back, but I have you now. You know, I've been thinking about some things."

"Like what?" he said, waiting for it, even choosing to welcome it with parted lips.

She glanced up at him. Her shoulders rounded as if somebody had strapped a fifty-pound sack to her back. "I'm selling nearly everything in the shop. I'm gonna have to close it." He heard the sadness in her voice.

"So, I'm moving to Louisiana." He said it for her, so she wouldn't have to.

With his fork, he squashed the lumps in the mashed potatoes.

"Let me add a little sour cream and butter to them," she said, whipping the potatoes with the serving spoon. "That should make them nice and creamy."

She continued. "I got a new job at Save A Lot, where your auntie Glo works. Cashier for now, but they know I've run my own shop for years, so they're talking about making me a store manager. Less stress. Money's not bad. So, nobody's moving anywhere. I want you to stay right here with me."

Granny shuffled to Midnight's side of the table and wedged her hips onto his chair. He smelled the Jergens face cream she used to smooth out her wrinkles. Squeezing him hard, she said, "I promise you this. We're sticking together as a family. We'll do just fine right here in Ganton. All of us."

He'd longed to hear those words. But now, he stared at his plate unblinking, watching potatoes ooze between the prongs of his fork.

"What about Daddy?" he asked.

Granny sighed. "He's still looking for work. I think he's checking into that dairy in Crawfordsville to see if they're hiring. But he'll figure it out. Don't worry."

Nothing felt solid and sure anymore. Midnight leaned his head back on the kitchen chair. Miss Ruth's face haunted him, the deep disappointment he'd put there frozen in his memory. She had been the one to tell him she felt closer to her grandfather at the Wabash River. That place sounded magical in her voice, and maybe that's why he'd gone there in the early hours of Monday morning. To find some magic.

Midnight wanted to start over, but how could he do it here in Ganton? How could he face Corey at school and all the other kids who knew what he'd done? For the first time, he wished he were J. B. Wagner in his family's Chevy following the moving van, leaving all he'd loved and lost in a trail of exhaust.

Thirty-Seven

RUTH

Ruth found herself on Verna Cunningham's doorstep New Year's Eve morning, facing the woman in her wrinkled nightgown. Verna's eyes were tired, empty, as if she were long past crying. Ruth didn't want to cause any more upset than she already had, but she needed to talk to the woman raising her son. The memory of the hurt and shock in Corey's eyes still haunted her, and she braced herself for facing him again.

Verna opened her front door wider and stepped back into the house as if she were expecting Ruth—an unspoken invitation, or just resignation. The severe, single braid Verna had worn when Ruth saw her at the river now hung loose and undone on her shoulder. She walked to the kitchen and Ruth followed her. An Obama yard sign leaned against the kitchen wall. Verna removed a reminder note stuck with a magnet to the refrigerator door.

"There's a school trip in a couple weeks to the Children's Museum in Indy. The permission slip is due Monday," Verna said, sitting at the counter typing hurriedly on her laptop.

"I hear they have some nice exhibits there. I'm sure Corey will love it." Ruth didn't know exactly what to say or even where to stand in this woman's home. She kept expecting her son to come around the corner any moment.

Apparently sensing her unease, Verna said, "Harold and Corey went to pick up groceries for dinner tonight. They won't be back for a little while."

Nodding, Ruth swept the kitchen with her eyes, taking in the matching yellow curtains and canisters, imagining her son growing up here in this cheery, storybook home Verna and Harold had made. She wondered which of the four kitchen chairs was Corey's, but she didn't ask.

Mothering bloomed in houses like this, where the scent of gingerbread wafted through the air, and Ruth suspected it came from something freshly baked and not an air freshener. She tried not to be too conspicuous, her eyes consuming this strange house that Corey could probably navigate blindfolded.

Ruth thought about Xavier and pictured the two of them with a family of their own, baking cookies, hustling little ones out of the house for school in the morning. Xavier in cahoots with the kids, cracking corny jokes and conspiring with them to do something indulgent while she remained the practical one.

Finally, Ruth said, "How's he doing?"

Leaning back in her chair, Verna said, "Last night he started screaming. When I went in his room, I could tell he was having a nightmare."

"Everything that happened at the river was terrifying." Ruth paused before saying, "I didn't mean for him to find out about me this way. I didn't even know who or where he was until a little over a week ago."

Verna held up a hand to stop her. "I thought about this day so many times. I pictured it. What you would say. What I'd say. But I knew this day would come. That you'd show up at my door. But I always thought it would be me or Harold who told Corey he was adopted."

Unsure of how to respond, Ruth looked down at her hands and said, "I know it was hard for him to hear the truth that way. I'm just glad I showed up at the river when I did."

Something fiery flared in Verna's eyes. "Don't expect my gratitude."

"No. No, I'm not expecting anything."

"You came to town and befriended Midnight, playing mother to him. He's a fragile boy and you got him all worked up. Those cops could've shot and killed my son. Corey told us about Midnight daring him to fire that gun and then calling the police."

"I had no idea Midnight knew the truth, and I didn't realize how angry and resentful he'd become." Ruth chose a chair next to Verna's, slowly lowering herself into the seat. The two women sat quietly, avoiding each other's eyes.

This time when Verna spoke, her voice registered low and soft, the kind you had to lean in to hear. "When Pastor Bumpus told us about the baby, I'd just had my fourth miscarriage. Some of it was from stress probably. You never know for sure, though, why your body betrays you." She twisted the tie from a bread bag around her index finger.

Had the Cunninghams been desperate enough to participate in a fraudulent adoption just to become parents?

Verna's eyes hardened and she looked directly at Ruth. "That boy is ours in every way that matters. We are the only family he knows." Her words sounded like a preemptive strike in case Ruth wanted to reclaim her son.

In a reflective tone, she said, "I'll never forget when Pastor placed Corey in my arms for the first time. It was hot that day when he brought him here to our house. I still swaddled him in a blanket, and Corey kept his eyes on me, followed me everywhere. That night, I told Harold he had the air-conditioning set too high. I didn't want Corey to catch pneumonia."

"What about your husband? How did he feel about raising a child that wasn't his own? Biologically, I mean." Xavier's words replayed in Ruth's head, his assurances that he could have handled the truth and loved Corey as his own.

The corners of Verna's mouth turned up slightly. "I swear, the minute Harold laid eyes on Corey, he said, 'That boy's got my nose and my chin.'" Verna laughed at the memory. "The older Corey gets, the more people swear they look alike, and Harold just smiles and doesn't tell them any different."

Ruth looked at this woman, trying to read her face, wondering how much she knew about Corey's adoption. "Do you worry, though, that everything could be upended?" She paused before saying, "I know about Stanley DeAngelo and what he did."

Tess's friend said criminal laws in Indiana had changed and crimes were reclassified after 1997. Still, he suspected DeAngelo would be guilty of forgery or counterfeiting for having Mama sign adoption forms falsely claiming to be the birth mother. He also felt certain that DeAngelo had committed a federal crime by defrauding a state institution. That meant Mama and the Cunninghams could be culpable for their involvement in the crime.

Verna pinned Ruth with a steely stare. "I know you probably think Corey's adoption is phony. But we have papers. They're still legal papers. We signed them." Her eyes pleaded with Ruth to believe her.

"So you're saying that in the eyes of the state, this was a legitimate adoption?"

"Yes, that's what I'm saying. Mr. DeAngelo met us at Friendship, in Pastor's office. Harold and I knew there was something fishy about a woman Ernestine's age having a baby. When we questioned Pastor, he admitted that you were the actual mother, but you were young, too young to raise the baby yourself, and wanted your son to have a good life. And we wanted to be parents so badly." Verna bit her lip.

Ruth felt a surge of indignation rise within her. "But I didn't say I wanted anything. I had no say. I had no idea where my grandmother had taken my baby."

Surprise flashed across Verna's face, and she quickly tried to hide it. "I'm sorry for anyone who got hurt in all this. When Mr. De-Angelo went to prison for conning those other people, Harold and I got scared. But in all these years, nobody's come around asking questions or stirring up any trouble for our family. Until you."

The ticking of a grandfather clock in the living room echoed in the background. Ruth pressed her fingers to her lips. "I don't want to cause any problems for you or Corey. One thing I'm sure of now is that you love my son and he loves you. I don't want to mess that up. I won't interfere."

Worry and anxiety seemed to drain from Verna's body. She nodded. Then she got up and moved to the staircase, motioning for Ruth to follow. Ruth had never imagined what Corey's bedroom looked like, but now they stood in the doorway. Baseball trophies crowded every flat surface, dirty gym shorts hung from the lampshade, and video game cords and comic books poked out from beneath the bedspread. She derived some pleasure from seeing a glimpse of untidiness in the Cunningham home.

"I tell him to put all this stuff away before somebody trips over it," Verna said quickly, placing a baseball glove on a shelf in the closet.

Every detail of this room reminded Ruth of all the small moments of mothering she'd missed with her son. His first tooth coming in. Stomachaches and scraped knees. The Little League games. Cupcakes for school on his birthday. Time—and one lie on top of another—had robbed Ruth of all that.

Verna pulled a laundry basket from under Corey's bed and began tossing shirts and socks and pants into it.

Ruth's voice caught in her throat. "This isn't easy for me, but I'm grateful to you for loving him."

Verna nodded. "We'd do anything for him. Corey can be too trusting and naïve for his own good sometimes. His dad and I had the talk with him last month."

"Oh. Corey's been thinking about girls already?" Ruth whispered, as if someone could hear them. "And sex?"

Verna laughed. "All boys think about that at some point. But no, I mean the talk about how to carry himself as a Black boy in these streets when his dad and I aren't around."

Sunlight streamed through the curtains of the small window. *A Black boy's life wasn't worth two dead flies,* Mama always said.

Verna continued: "My biggest worry has been that he'll grow into one of those Black men that white people fear and then kill because of that fear." What she left unspoken was that his small, young body triggered that same fear.

"I'm sure you told him not to argue with the police." Ruth's thoughts returned to the morning at the river and to the bucket boy in Chicago. She thought of Eli getting stopped for carrying weed. Even Xavier wore suits sometimes on casual Fridays to avoid getting hassled. A wave of nausea passed over her as she began to comprehend the constant worry the Cunninghams had trying to keep Corey safe.

Verna looked up toward the ceiling and exhaled. "Always be polite. Don't talk back. Keep your hands—"

Ruth finished her script. "Out of your pockets. Make sure they're visible. Stay alive."

"We tried to prepare him, but see? It still didn't matter. His *best friend* handed him a gun and set him up."

Opening the closet, Verna stood on tiptoe to reach the top shelf. She brought out a framed photo of Corey and Midnight hoisting a science fair trophy high above their heads. Both boys smiled brightly.

Ruth's heart plummeted all over again wondering how Midnight had learned the truth.

Lines of worry and life experience furrowed Verna's brow. "First it was gangbangers coming after Corey and his friends. Then Midnight. If Midnight were Black? He'd be in juvie right now. And you know if Midnight had been the one holding that toy, the police never would've pulled out their guns to begin with. But my boy. My sweet boy scared them. How could they point their guns at him?" Her voice stretched like a frayed rope ready to break.

Ruth nodded and her own voice quaked as she relived her fear. She recalled staring into the barrels of both guns, bracing for bullets. "I've also been thinking about these local gang members. How big of a threat are they?"

"Harold and I reported them to the police. Apparently, Ganton doesn't have any organized, official gangs. Not yet, anyway. Those guys are Bo Thompkins and Larry Baisden. Their families go way back, I guess. They've done some small, petty crimes and police say they have their eye on them. But apparently, befriending neighborhood kids isn't illegal. It's Midnight I can't get over. He's a nice enough kid, been to our home many times, but he has no idea. He doesn't know what it means to be a Black boy in this country."

"You have so much weighing on you as a parent. I can't imagine."

"My son is everything to me. Everything . . ."

Tears must have flooded Verna's throat. She couldn't go on. Just thinking of all that could crush her son before he got a good start in the world overwhelmed Ruth. She thought of both boys and how the world saw each of them in black and white, how they'd be forever defined by that distinction.

Ruth pulled a blue turtleneck sweater of Corey's from the laundry basket and held it to her face, covering her mouth and nose with the fabric, and breathed in the scent of the boy she and this other woman shared.

"I'll take that." Verna slid the sweater out of Ruth's hands and returned it to the basket.

Whether it signaled protection or possession, Ruth didn't protest.

Then Verna stooped to pick up dirty white socks. Ruth watched this woman, her child's mother, do something so basic, something she'd likely done thousands of times before without thinking anything of it. The seed Ruth had planted more than a decade ago was now the budding flower Verna would go on tending to keep it blossoming.

Thirty-Eight

RUTH

That afternoon, Ruth's car idled outside the little green house on Kirkland. Through the window, she could see that a tabletop tree with a tilted Santa were the only remnants of holiday cheer at Lena's house. Sometimes it took everything in a person to stand upright in a bent world. Tired of waiting and prolonging what was to come, Ruth got out of her car and walked to Lena's front door. She had no idea how long she stood out there, but the door opened and Lena invited her to come in.

"Happy New Year. Well, almost. He's in there." Lena walked down the dark hallway to her bedroom, leaving Ruth in the front of the house.

Ruth's eyes adjusted to the dim lighting and she saw Midnight sitting on the couch, his thumbs moving vigorously across the screen of his phone. The last time she'd been in this house, she'd been terrified, hoping and praying he'd make it back here safely. It had only been a few days, but it seemed much longer.

"Hi," she said. When he didn't answer or look up, she walked over to the tree by the window, found the extension cord, and plugged it into the wall. The string of colorful lights lit up that corner of the room.

Midnight startled, his lips parted. Still in his baggy pajamas, he appeared smaller than he had just days ago. A mere boy, with the palest skin under the shadowed canopy of the overcast winter afternoon.

"What you doing?" she said, perching next to him on the sofa.

He shrugged. "Playing a game."

"Something you got for Christmas?"

"*Assassin's Creed.*"

A million thoughts rattled in her head, but none of them formed coherently enough for articulation. She began regretting that she'd even come.

Midnight might lose a friendship and would likely suffer from hurt and disillusionment for a long time. But she knew he'd be okay. Just as markets corrected themselves over the years through the inevitable downturns and upswings of the economy, white boys who fell on hard times could often count on being made whole again. Not so much for the Black ones. She wanted the possibilities of the world to open up to him and Corey equally, but she knew that some wishes—even ones made at the start of a new year—would likely go unfulfilled.

She also sensed that the closeness they'd shared in the short time they'd known each other had somehow receded after what happened at the river, and she was just now assessing the storm damage: His sallow skin, and the unruly snatch of hair over his brow that barely obscured his shadowy eyes. His back bent as if an invisible weight pulled downward on him.

Ruth covered his phone with her hand, and he flinched.

"Look at me," she said.

Slowly, he lifted his eyes.

"What you did the other morning was extremely dangerous. You could've gotten yourself and Corey killed. It's not a game."

"I know that," he said, his voice tinged with frustration.

"You've been through a lot for a boy your age. I want you to know I don't blame you for being upset, for wanting to make all your hurt feelings go away." She thought about all the mistakes she had made as a teenager and how she would've done anything to erase the pain that had built up in her over the years. Pain she couldn't give a name to at the time, even as it consumed her.

Midnight twisted his mouth and said nothing, but it didn't matter as long as he heard what she had to say. She went on. "The other day at the river, you said I don't care about you. I do care. I was just starting to get to know you and like you."

He remained quiet.

When she picked up her purse, looped it around her arm, and began to get up from the sofa, Midnight spoke. "I'm sorry," he said, looking at her expectantly, as if awaiting her forgiveness.

She thought of Joanna, who had left her motherless despite her best intentions. And of Mama, who did what she did for what she considered all the right reasons but had still been wrong. She considered Midnight, his innocence corroded already by a world that had dealt him a bad hand. But he'd been reckless and put her son's life in danger.

Yet he was just a child, and maybe he deserved her forgiveness. Being Black, she came from a long line of people who were expected to forgive reflexively. But she couldn't do it. She hadn't sat long enough with all that had happened to set him free. Not yet at least. So, she gave him what she could. Her understanding.

"I know," she answered him. "I know you're sorry."

His shoulders drooped even more, and he reminded her of a ship bobbing in the ocean before sinking. She got up and walked to the front door, but then paused. Turning back to face him, she said, "At least nine days, maybe weeks."

When he gave her a puzzled look, she smiled. "I'm just answering your question. That's how long a cockroach can live with its head cut off."

The sliver of light she saw now didn't come from the little Christmas tree in the window, but from his eyes.

Thirty-Nine

RUTH

On New Year's Eve, Mama had always admonished her children to stay home and off the streets. To avoid drunk drivers and itchy trigger fingers and wayward firecrackers. She even skipped Watch Night services at Friendship. Usually, Ruth spent this night celebrating with Xavier and their friends at a downtown Chicago hotel.

There were some battles in life you had to fight alone, but your burden grew lighter—or at least it seemed that way—when you huddled close to somebody in the bunker. Xavier had always been by her side helping her soldier on. Being apart from him these past few weeks felt like having limbs idled and cut off from the heart pumping blood to them. She ached to see him and make things right. She ached to kiss him at the stroke of midnight, but that wasn't to be.

But this year, for the first time ever, Ruth sat alone with Mama watching Dick Clark count down until the ball dropped in Times Square and couples kissed openmouthed on national TV. They didn't say anything to each other, because any words they used would be sharp, jagged enough to cut and draw blood. When they'd had enough of viewing a million strangers usher in the new year, they retired to their respective bedrooms.

Sitting on her bed in silence, Ruth decided she couldn't avoid the inevitable any longer and knocked on her grandmother's bedroom door.

"It's open." Mama was still awake, in her blue terry cloth robe, tying her hair with a black satin scarf.

A wide-tooth comb lay on the dresser. Ruth picked it up and, with a trembling hand, held it out to her.

"Get down on the floor." Mama perched on the edge of the bed with Ruth sitting cross-legged at her feet. The comb sounded like the scrape of a rake as Mama pulled it through Ruth's tightly coiled hair. This had been their ritual every night when she was a little girl, and she eased into the feel of Mama braiding her hair again.

"Ouch." Mama's thick thighs tightened around the sides of her granddaughter's head.

"You're still tender-headed, I see." She tugged the comb more gently in Ruth's kitchen, the kinky hair at the nape of her neck.

They hadn't finished their conversation from Sunday about Mama's role working in cahoots with Pastor Bumpus and DeAngelo to fix things. Nor had they spoken about what had happened at the river. But all Ruth could think about now was how she had found her son after all these years and then almost lost him. Instinctively, Mama knew.

"You haven't said a lot since the other morning." Mama leaned down so she could look Ruth in the eye. "You finally met your boy. You all right?"

"I'm fine, or at least I will be. It's Corey I worry about. Those cops could've killed him. I keep thinking about Amadou Diallo all those years ago, and every Black boy who has to be tense all the time not knowing what might happen. Mothers and fathers are scared every time their sons walk out the door."

The movement of the comb through Ruth's hair stopped. Mama said, "Brings back those memories of Alfonso getting lynched. Just when you think things have changed, you get more of the same. I worried myself sick about your brother when he was growing up. Still do. That's why I doted on him so much. Thought I could love on him enough to keep him safe."

"I'm just glad Corey has the Cunninghams to lean on."

"Did I hear you right?"

Admitting that suddenly felt like giving in, acknowledging that Mama's machinations had yielded something good. But she'd meant what she said. "Yeah, I know he's where he's supposed to be."

"It's all about doing what's right by your child. Mothers sacrifice. We put our babies first. Before ourselves. I didn't want it all to come out like this, but it did, and there's nothing anyone can do about it now."

Mama seemed more than resigned now. Maybe unburdened after holding her secrets inside so long. Ruth hadn't thought to consider the toll it had taken on her grandmother trying to orchestrate everything behind the curtain.

"And someday Corey will get over finding everything out the way he did," Mama added.

"How did you know you were doing the right thing when I got pregnant?"

Mama paused before parting another section of hair, greasing Ruth's scalp. "There's no right way to be a mother. You do what you know how to do at the time and pray it all comes out okay in the end. I think of it like baking a cake. You pour all your best ingredients in the bowl. Flour, sugar, eggs, and real butter—no yogurt or applesauce substitutes, either. You mix it real good and then put it in the oven and you wait for it to rise. Take it out too early, it won't be done, or it may fall." She bent close to Ruth's ear and said, "You were my precious cake. Your papa and I poured everything we had into you. You still had a lot of rising to do in this world. I didn't want you to fall."

Ruth rested her cheek against Mama's thigh while she braided. It struck Ruth that every mother's choice had repercussions for generations, and it fanned out into a web that could ensnare you or catch you when you slipped. It all depended on how you looked at it.

"It's been good seeing Natasha. Watching her with Camila, I started wondering what my life would be like now if I'd married a guy like Luis from high school and raised a family here in Ganton instead of moving away from home."

Mama grunted. "You'd be going through a world of hurt and doing your best to convince folks you were happy."

"What do you mean?"

"Natasha's sharing her husband the way she shared her mother with that revolving door of men all those years. He's cheating on her, for sure."

Back in the day, Mama had disapproved of her friendship with Natasha, thinking her friend would hold her back somehow. But it was time to let that go. "Every family has its problems," Ruth said.

"Child, if you don't get your head out those fairy tales. Even truck drivers come home sometimes, but not Luis. You know how folks talk. They say he's got another whole family out there. Mexican, like him."

"He's Puerto Rican, Mama."

"Whatever. You get my point."

She could've chastised Mama, but what good would it do? They were finding their way back to each other, but she accepted some things would never change.

Mama scratched her granddaughter's scalp with the comb, freeing flakes of dandruff that dotted Ruth's eyelashes like snowflakes. Natasha had never let on that there were problems in her marriage. Ruth wondered if every woman harbored a secret tucked away in her heart, a cross she carried all alone.

She began thinking of Joanna now and how little she knew of the woman who had given her life. And she never would know her, because she hadn't bothered to stick around.

Twisting her head to look up at Mama, she said, "At least you loved Corey enough to try to do what you thought was right. My mother didn't give a damn about me and Eli. I know you don't like for me to say it, but I inherited the abandonment gene from her. I tried not to, but I ended up just like her."

Mama stopped combing, her hand suspended in the air. "I

should've given you the whole story. You're grown enough to handle the truth."

"What story? My mother was a druggie and she loved that high more than her own kids. What else is there to say?"

Mama pressed her hands into Ruth's shoulders. "No. No, that's not the way it was at all. She was on that stuff, yes, and it did have hold of her. But when she decided she wanted to get out of Ganton, she said she was going to take you and Eli with her. Her mind was made up."

"But she didn't, did she? She left us behind."

"Because Hezekiah and I begged her not to take you. We knew she loved you kids, but how could she be a real mother to you when she had all that poison inside her? It made no sense. It took a lot, but we convinced her to let us raise you two."

Ruth pulled away, moving out of the grip of her grandmother's heavy thighs. No, not again. Not one more way Mama had manipulated her life, pulling strings without her knowing it. Her body seized with anguish. How could this be true?

"Are you saying she really wanted us?"

"Yes, I am. You and your brother were always wanted. Your mother wanted you. Papa and I wanted you. You hear me? You understand?"

Tears filled Ruth's eyes. "I understand, all right. You played God with my life." When she spoke, her words emerged thin from exhaustion, all her anger depleted. All these years, she thought her mother had abandoned her without looking back.

"I wasn't playing God. I was loving you and your brother the best I could. I love Joanna something fierce. She was the only child Hezekiah and I had. It tore me up inside to see her walk out that door forever. And then to separate her from you and Eli? That's a special kind of pain. We put her in rehab so many times, but she'd get out and go right back to that stuff. Your grandfather and I knew we were losing Joanna to that dope. We couldn't lose you and your brother, too."

For so long, Ruth had wanted answers, the truth. And now, it descended upon her in an avalanche. As a grown woman, she now recognized her own mistakes. Why had it taken eleven years and Xavier's push to start a family for Ruth to come looking for her child? As she passed the blame around, she had to take her share, too. She saw that now.

And what about Joanna, coerced into leaving her babies behind? Did memories of Ruth and Eli haunt her the way the first day of Corey's life had haunted Ruth? Gazing out the window, she wondered if her mother was looking upon these same stars right now. The two of them knew better than anyone the price you paid for walking away from your child because someone else decided for you what was best.

This new understanding brought a measure of peace, but worry still needled her. If it ever became known that Corey's adoption was illegal, everything could be ripped out from under her son. If anyone questioned Ruth about the adoption, she would lie gladly this time. She was a mother, and what Mama had said was right—mothers protected their children. This much, she knew. And someday, she'd write a letter to Corey telling him she'd loved him from the moment she found out he was growing inside her. She'd apologize again. Over and over, as many times as she needed to until he believed her.

Mama's hands and the comb still rested on top of Ruth's head, but they hadn't moved. Ruth turned around and looked up at her grandmother, trying to read her thoughts. She followed her eyes out the window to the porch, which was aglow with light. Ruth said, "I see you finally got the porch light fixed."

"Dino came over and took care of it."

Ruth teased her grandmother. "Oh? Seems like he's spending a lot of time over here. You know, you could've invited him for New Year's Eve."

"Hush your mouth, girl." She felt a light tap of the comb on the back of her neck, but she still heard the smile in Mama's voice. "Now that there is exactly why I didn't invite him."

Then Mama got to humming something throaty and soulful, maybe gospel or jazz.

"Sing it, Mama."

"When I was a little girl, that's all I wanted to do was sing."

"You used to sing around the house all the time." She had stopped singing after Papa died and their house became eerily quiet.

"No, I wanted to really sing, onstage, you know. In front of lots of people. I'd heard about Leontyne Price learning to sing opera at the Juilliard School of Music in New York. They always make exceptions for one of us. But Black girls from Ganton, Indiana, didn't go to Juilliard in the fifties and sixties. So, I stayed here, finished school, and made do working at the hotel."

Ruth inhaled the Jergens lotion that Mama always slathered on her legs after her nightly bath. Greasing her fingers with oil, Mama slid them down the lines of Ruth's scalp and followed that up with a spray sheen. Ruth laughed to herself thinking of the *Coming to America* Soul Glo stains she'd leave on the pillowcases that night.

"What are you smiling about, child?"

"Nothing, Mama. I'm just imagining you living your dream, singing professionally, with all those people spellbound under the power of your voice. You never told me that story about your singing dream."

"I'm telling you now. And you know I've never been one for wasted words. Save your breath for when you die."

As surely as Ruth knew another year had begun, she understood that Yale had been her Juilliard.

Forty

RUTH

New Year's Day had been Papa's favorite holiday, and he'd even let her and Eli sip from his spiked eggnog over the objections of their grandmother. It had become tradition for Mama to cook a feast, and this late morning, Ruth smelled black-eyed peas, corn bread, and collard greens.

From her bedroom window, she watched Eli toss a football on the street below with his sons in the same spot where you could probably still see the faded hopscotch lines from their youth. When the ball rolled onto the neighbors' square patch of dirt, Keisha ran to fetch it.

By the time Ruth dressed and made it to the kitchen, she saw her sister-in-law mixing ingredients for a red velvet cake. By Mama's side, sprinkling onions and garlic into the black-eyed peas, stood Dino.

"Happy N-N-New Year, Ruth," he said, and wiped his hands on a red apron wrapped around his waist that read *Real Men Cook*.

"Same to you, Dino." She pecked him on the cheek, showing Mama she approved of whatever and whoever made her happy. Still, she wondered about the timing of his arrival that morning and whether or not he had slipped in before the sun came up.

Under her grandmother's careful supervision, Ruth rubbed brown sugar and vinegar on the pork roast. "Pick up that meat. It won't bite.

And don't be stingy with the rub. Make sure you get some on the backside."

"Yes, ma'am."

The front door opened and Ruth turned to greet her brother, but there, standing in the foyer, she saw Xavier, his face unreadable, looking like a mismatched piece of furniture in her old house. He started toward her like a horse just out the gate in a race, but pulled back, hesitant, suddenly shy and uncertain.

Her feet locked in place on the linoleum, and she froze there like a block of stone, her hands dripping with apple cider vinegar. All the lies and hurt feelings stood between them. Now, here he was in the house where she'd given birth.

People talked about straddling two worlds, but Ruth had never achieved that perfect balance. How could you find firm footing in one, enough to be rooted, without becoming a passing stranger in the other?

He took a halting step closer to her.

"Happy New Year."

"Xavier." Saying his name set her feet free. She ran into his arms and inhaled the woodsy scent of his soap. She felt the familiar beat of his heart. Hard and steady.

His hug felt different, though, not like one between a husband and wife, but more patronizing, the way rich society ladies hugged when they didn't want to get too close to the proletariat class.

"Oh, sorry. My hands," she said, realizing she'd smeared his coat. "Happy New Year." Pulling away to look at him, she noticed the razor bumps along his throat. She hadn't been there to remind him not to shave against the grain. Evidence that he might still need her. "I can't believe you're really here."

"Don't be mad at her, but Tess filled me in on things." He winked at her grandmother. "Then Mama Tuttle invited me over for her black-eyed peas. How could I say no to that?"

Mama popped him playfully with a dish towel and tried to hide her smile. Already, he had conferred a nickname on her grandmother, and she didn't seem to mind at all.

Ruth stood there, still in slight shock, gazing at her husband and trying to catch up on what was happening. Eli walked in with the kids trailing behind him and slapped Xavier's back. "Hey, man, let's watch the game," he said, and Xavier shrugged at her before disappearing into the living room.

Where did things really stand between them now? She couldn't be sure. In a way, she understood Mama's lies but hadn't fully forgiven them. Had Xavier forgiven hers?

HOURS LATER, AFTER THEY'D FEASTED ON PORK ROAST, BLACK-EYED peas, and corn bread, she waited for the right moment to pull him aside to talk. But now she found Xavier hunched over Mama's old record player.

"This is a classic right here, Mama Tuttle."

Mama rocked back and forth on the recliner until she got enough momentum to stand and move to the buffet table, where he had opened a drawer to reveal stacks of album covers. She nodded permission for Xavier to peruse them.

"Ohh. Temptations, Etta James, Al Green, James Brown. You're taking me way back now." He licked his lips and rubbed his hands together. It warmed her to watch him be so easy with her grandmother.

Mama put one hand on her hip. "I think some of these take you back way before you were even born, child."

"Oh, my folks raised me on the Supremes and Marvin Gaye, all of this. That's all they played in our house. May I?"

Before Mama had time to answer him, Xavier blew dust off an LP and placed it on the turntable, sliding the needle on the record. Within seconds, the song "My Girl" filled their living room for the first time since Papa died.

"May I?" Xavier asked again. This time, he extended his hand. Ruth watched from her position next to Eli and Cassie on the sofa, the kids on the floor, and Dino on a folding chair pulled from the closet.

Only their fingertips touched at first, and then Mama let her grandson-in-law take her hand and wrap his arm around her back. She stood stiffly in place at first until he crooned in her ear. As if her feet were brand-new and she'd never walked before, she moved into the curve of his arm and swayed woodenly with him to the melody.

Eli called out to her. "You can do better than that, Mama. Show that big-city boy what you working with. Show him how we do it in Ganton."

Mama shot Eli a look of feigned reproach and then turned her attention back to Xavier. She must have seen what had attracted her granddaughter to the man—his effusive charm, the way he made you feel like the most special person in the world.

A fullness she couldn't quite describe rose within Ruth, and she regretted not bringing Xavier around her family all these years. But now, when she tried to catch her husband's eye, he avoided looking at her.

Xavier took both of Mama's hands in his and gently twirled her, even dipping her twice, and she let him. Only then, when watching their fancy footwork, did Ruth notice her husband's shoes. The Magnanni leather shoes she'd bought him for Christmas. She'd left them wrapped in a box under the tree. He'd opened her gift and worn the shoes here. That had to mean something. Everyone clapped and catcalled at the end of their dance, encouraging an encore.

"You're all right now, Mama Tuttle. I like your style," Xavier said when she sang along with him. "And you can sing, too. I'm impressed."

"Oh, I do a little something," she said, taking a stage bow as if she were standing before thousands at Carnegie Hall.

After the others got up to dance, Ruth seized her chance to grab her husband's hand and lead him away from her family to her childhood bedroom. She cringed imagining how it must have looked through his eyes. Just being alone with him in this room where she'd brought a life into the world unnerved her.

"Look."

"Hey."

They spoke at the same time, stumbling over each other's words. Nervous laughter buzzed between them.

"You go first," Xavier said.

"I don't know where to begin or how to begin. We've been away from each other for such a long time and so much has happened that I haven't been able to process it all. I just know . . . I've missed you. *Really* missed you." She paused and studied his face, hoping for a glimpse behind the mask. "You're so quiet and it's scaring me."

Backing away from her, Xavier knelt over his luggage and pulled out a wooden box. Confused, she asked, "What are you doing?"

Opening the box, he pulled out a piece of yellow folded paper. Taking her hand, he placed it in her palm. It was one of the colorful notes from their gratitude box, she recognized. The last time she'd read what he'd written, their marriage had begun to splinter. Fear squeezed her heart and made her hands tremble. Unfolding the paper slowly, she sucked in a breath and read his neat cursive. *Us, Always Us*.

"I've missed you, too," he said.

She knew they still had unfinished business and a lot to work through to make things right again. But maybe it wasn't about going back to some earlier point in time in their marriage. Maybe you just continued wherever you were, wiser from all you knew, stronger from all the burdens you'd carried.

"All right, you lovebirds, get on out here," Eli called to them. They held each other's gaze for a moment longer and then rejoined the rest of the family.

Eli rose to get Mama's good glasses from the cabinet and fill them with eggnog, adding a shot of bourbon, and for once their grandmother didn't protest. They toasted everything they could think of. Old friends becoming lovers. The new president in all his swagger. And Papa, who was surely looking down and smiling on them all.

To Hezekiah. To Hezekiah.

Dino lumbered over to the record stack and found the Temptations Christmas album and set the needle to "Silent Night."

"This was Hezekiah's favorite, and I think we need something a little f-f-festive," he said, and pulled Mama into his arms.

They all moved with the music, letting the melody wash over them, the spiritual meeting the secular in some excelsis that could only be described as soulful.

Ruth had grown into both parts of herself in this town that did more than kill dreams. It birthed them, too. She could never escape this place, and she didn't want to, because these people were in her and she in them.

Perfect mothers didn't exist, only perfectly flawed ones did. She couldn't predict how far Corey would go in this world, just as Mama and Joanna couldn't have known what would become of Ruth and Eli. Yet they still believed beyond what they could see. This day here in Ganton was a love note to Hezekiah and Harriet, W.E.B., and Booker T. And at the start of this new year, Ruth imagined the ancestors dancing somewhere right along with them.

Acknowledgments

In a St. Petersburg, Florida, parking lot after a writing workshop, author James Anderson said this to me: "Whatever you do, don't let Ruth and Midnight languish on the side of the road. Only you can breathe life into them." About a decade earlier, journalist Byron Pitts sent me a note that I kept taped to my bedroom mirror for years. Quoting Maya Angelou, he wrote, "You are the hope and dream of the slave." Those wise words carried me through the still waters and the turbulent tides of this journey to publication.

First, thank you to my brilliant agent, Danielle Bukowski of Sterling Lord Literistic, for plucking me out of the Twitter slush pile, believing in this book, and being my escort to the publishing ball every step of the way.

To my incomparable editor, Liz Stein of William Morrow, whose razor-sharp editorial eye strengthened this book, you helped me make the story on the page match the vision in my head, and for that, I can't thank you enough.

While this novel is a work of fiction, I consulted subject matter experts for accuracy and authenticity. Thank you to Tammy M. Minger of Minger Law Office for background on Indiana adoption law; Evan Smith, a research and development and process engineer, for explaining the work of chemical engineers in the consumer-packaged-goods industry; and Sergeant Adam Henkels of the Chicago Police Department for details on gang recruitment tactics. Any factual errors are mine and mine alone.

This novel would not exist without these phenomenal beta readers who offered the most valuable, insightful critique: Erin Bartels, Julie Carrick Dalton, Alison Hammer, Alison Murphy, and Milo Todd.

The first person I call with book news—the good, the bad, and the petty—is Julie Carrick Dalton, my literary soulmate and the most generous writer I know. Every milestone on our journeys to becoming debut authors has been in lockstep. We're opposites in so many ways, yet I can't imagine a better sidekick on this crazy ride!

Alison Hammer is always up for meeting me at local book events and sharing wisdom from her own debut journey. I'm so appreciative.

Michele Montgomery, thank you for the long-distance account-ability writing dates in the home stretch and for all the candles you lit for my book's success.

I'm indebted to the writing organizations that helped me hone my craft and gave me a tribe: Eckerd College Writers in Paradise, Kimbilio Fiction, Tin House, Hurston/Wright Foundation, Grub-Street, Mystery Writers of America Midwest, Women's Fiction Writers Association, FLOW (For Love of Writing), StoryStudio Chicago, and Writer Unboxed.

Every accomplished author I studied under in workshops influenced the shape of this book and the ones to come: Ann Hood, Laura Lippman, Lori Roy, David Haynes, Tayari Jones, Nicole Dennis-Benn, and Donald Maass.

A special note of gratitude to author Caroline Leavitt, who was the first to review an early draft of the novel. Thank you for being my cheerleader and literary fairy godmother.

I'm also grateful to bookseller Pamela Klinger-Horn of Excelsior Bay Books and Ron Block of Cuyahoga County Public Library for being early and vocal champions of this novel.

The writing community teaches and lifts me every day. I wish I had enough space to tell the stories of how each of you has supported me, but know that I'm smiling and remembering as I type your names: Denny S. Bryce, Heather Webb, Therese Walsh, Rita Woods, Irene Reed, Catherine Adel West, Mary Hawley, Julie Clark,

Suzanne Park, Kristin Rockaway, Kathleen Barber, Lori Rader-Day, Heather Ash, Susanna Calkins, Mia Manansala, Ava Black, Cynthia Pelayo, Bo Thunboe, Lainey Cameron, Lisa Montanaro, Mary Chase, Amy Melnicsak, Kasia Manolas, Robb Cadigan, Cerrissa Kim, Beth Havey, Jane Rosenthal, Leah DeCesare, Kathryn Craft, Louise Miller, Amy Sue Nathan, Eve Bridburg, and Sonya Larson.

Publishing a book and building an author career require the expertise of a team. Thankfully, I have a dynamic one by my side, including Alice Lawson, my TV/film agent at Gersh. Also, the entire William Morrow/HarperCollins family: Tavia Kowalchuk in marketing and Bianca Flores in publicity; Greg Villepique, copy editor, and Jeanie Lee, production editor; Ploy Siripant, cover designer, and Nancy Singer, interior pages designer; and Vedika Khanna, the assistant editor who handled details, large and small.

So many teachers over the years have nurtured my love for books and writing. One in particular is Donald Nekrosius, my high school English teacher at St. Ignatius College Prep in Chicago. He told me I had something important to say and that the world needed my voice. He planted the seed, and eventually, I believed it, too.

Thank you to my college crew, who celebrated me throughout this writing journey: Yolanda Harris, Amber Maiden, Robin Fleming, Camille Meggs, Sabine Champagne, and Tracy Dumas.

De Anna Ward and Sharon Tubbs, thank you for the vision setting during our February birthday month each year. Dreams do come true.

Fhelt Brown and Aaliyah Thompson, you are chosen family and I appreciate your steadfast love and support.

To the ladies of P4, who are like sisters to me: Jada Hill, Cinterro Jones, and Elsa W. Smith. Love you to pieces. The talk-show circuit awaits our tell-all exposé, which is sure to be the real page-turner.

I stand on the shoulders of those who came before me, and I offer gratitude to my loved ones, especially the Johnson, Rudy, Compton, Smith, and Hines families.

I owe any success I've achieved to my parents, who have loved me completely, unconditionally, and endlessly. To my mother, Doris E. Johnson, you are the one who knows and loves me best, the wind beneath my wings. None of this would have been possible without your sacrifice and prayers. To my late father, Herman H. Johnson, you instilled in me an appreciation for education and a fierce sense of family pride. Weeks before your death, you taught me how to live without you, saying, "Carry on and do great things." I hope I've made you proud.

And finally, thank you to my readers for choosing *The Kindest Lie*. I wrote this novel to spark meaningful conversation and address my own questions about race and class in America. But mostly, I wanted you to enjoy the story. These characters grew from my heart. I hope they'll remain in yours for a long time to come.

About the author

About the book

Insights,
Interviews
& More . . .

Meet Nancy Johnson

Nina Subin

NANCY JOHNSON grew up on Chicago's South Side and worked for more than a decade as an Emmy-nominated, award-winning television journalist at CBS and ABC affiliates in markets nationwide. A graduate of Northwestern University and the University of North Carolina at Chapel Hill, she tells stories at the intersection of race and class. She manages brand communications for a large nonprofit and lives in downtown Chicago. *The Kindest Lie* is her first novel. ∾

Behind the Book

The first time I was called the n-word happened early in my career as a television news reporter, when a photojournalist colleague hurled the epithet in anger. The second time was when I had my first home built and someone spray-painted that ugly word on the drywall.

Just four years later, the election of Barack Obama was a balm soothing the wound, not only for me, but also for all of us who'd experienced the legacy of almost four hundred years of racial terror in America. My father survived the Great Depression, the Second World War, and Jim Crow; and then, shortly before he died of lung cancer, he cast the last vote of his life for Obama and got to see a Black man like himself ascend to the highest office in the land.

In *The Kindest Lie,* I wrote about a nation drunk with hope as it broke a seemingly impenetrable barrier. Even as the financial markets crashed and factories shuttered and people lost their jobs, a sense of promise persisted. Yet despite the opportunities presented when Obama won the 2008 election, I watched the vitriol between Black and white America bubble up and boil over. There was nothing post-racial about it. So many people who were just trying to make it and fulfill their dreams had a scarcity mindset; they believed life was an *us versus them* zero-sum game.

I centered the novel around Ruth ▸

Tuttle, a successful Black engineer on the rise in Chicago—a woman who's pulled back into the struggling community she managed to escape. Like me, Ruth is a Black professional who often straddles worlds without finding firm footing in either. When she meets Midnight, a young white boy who is adrift and trying to find his way, she sees herself in him while also recognizing the white privilege that often protects him. I created these complicated characters to show the parallels between two very different people who are both grasping for the American dream. This story was born out of my own burning question: Could the universal need for love and family transcend the chasm of race and class in America?

When I created the Black characters in my novel, I knew some readers would come to the page with preconceived, faulty perceptions of who we are. The complexity of the characters in the Tuttle family shows the range of our humanity and that we don't fit into a prescribed box. Mama is a ferociously protective grandmother who sacrifices and loves hard and sometimes lies to give her grandchildren the best shot at succeeding in this world. Yet we learn that at seventy-eight years old, she's a woman harboring trauma and unfulfilled dreams of her own. Eli, Ruth's brother—the character I most enjoyed crafting—is a proud Black husband and father who's lost his job at the local auto plant. He's bitter and he drinks too much, but even when his emotions are raw, he remains resilient, and we watch him protect those he loves over and over again.

The hopes and dreams of the white characters in *The Kindest Lie* are just as powerful and palpable as the Tuttles'. Midnight's desperate need to be loved twisted my heart in every scene I wrote. As a kid who was bullied for being too tall, too smart, and too nerdy, I've always connected with what it feels like to be on the outside of things. Those personal experiences of isolation and longing fueled the character of this young boy. Like Eli, Midnight's father, Butch, also lost his job at the plant. His behavior shows how economic anxiety can lead to toxic masculinity, regardless of racial background. There's no question that Butch is a hateful bigot, yet he is also capable of fierce love. As incongruous as it seems, both can be true at the same time.

I'm convinced that we're all reaching for our own version of the American dream. The lies we tell, the secrets we keep, and the mistakes we make are all part of that journey. I don't have any easy solutions; however, I am convinced that children are watching us and repeating our mistakes. In *The Kindest Lie*, we see the disastrous fallout of what happens when racism goes unchecked and the children follow our lead. We need to have an honest dialogue. I hope that my novel can be a starting point for the conversation.

Q&A with Nancy Johnson

Q: The Kindest Lie is a searing exploration of race, class, police brutality, the American dream, and so much more. The novel is set in the recent past, but these topics remain highly relevant to this day. How do you see The Kindest Lie *fitting into the current cultural and political conversation?*

A: Stories are timeless because universal truths are. The ways we hurt and hope transcend time and overlap generations. Anti-Black racism has a four-hundred-year-plus history in America, and its potency has never waned. In the book, what Ruth, Xavier, and Corey feared in every encounter with white police officers was realized in 2020 in the deaths of George Floyd, Breonna Taylor, and Rayshard Brooks.

I believe our nation is still just as bitterly divided and as roiling with racial strife as it was in November 2008, when my novel opens on the night America elected its first Black president. Back then, people were struggling to survive an economic downturn that left many jobless and financially strapped. Now, more than a decade later, a global pandemic, an historic presidential election, and a racial reckoning have tested our nation in profound ways.

Q: When Ruth, an Ivy League–educated Black engineer, meets Midnight, a young white boy adrift and armored with white privilege, they find themselves on a dangerous path that could upend both their lives. What commonalities do these two characters share? In what ways do they shape our understanding of Black and white communities in middle America? How do the challenges of their friendship reflect the deep divide between these two communities?

A: Both Ruth and Midnight grew up in working-class neighborhoods in Ganton, Indiana. They're science geeks with big dreams. As a girl, Ruth wanted to pursue an Ivy League education and become an engineer. Midnight dreams of becoming a microbiologist. Dreams can be elusive and easily slip away, even once they're in our grasp. That's why Mama told a series of lies and kept secrets to ensure Ruth's future would remain intact. Similarly, Midnight's father admonishes him to forget baseball and become a doctor so he can cure cancer someday. However, the most durable bond Ruth and Midnight share is their desperate need for love and family connection. Still, the world reminds them over and over that expectations and outcomes don't operate so equitably. Black and white America remain divided, and it's that chasm that threatens the budding friendship between Ruth and Midnight.

Q: The novel focuses on Ruth then segues into Midnight's story with great skill and ease. What was it like to write from the perspective of a young white boy, and how did you find the balance to juggle these two narrative voices?

A: I'll let you in on a little secret. In an early iteration of this story, Midnight was a Black boy. However, when I decided to tackle the racial divide, I knew that Midnight needed to be white. I've never been white before, but as a Black person in America who has had to navigate white spaces in school and on the job, I'm fairly fluent in whiteness. I relied on friends with sons to fill me in on favorite video games and mischief. Where I really drew inspiration for Midnight's character, though, was my own experience as an outsider who was bullied as a kid. I understood his loneliness and longing for acceptance because I'd experienced that myself.

I was able to easily move in and out of both Ruth's and Midnight's perspectives because they're so different in terms of age, race, and gender. I had fun discovering the many parallels in their lives and watching their journeys intersect in the most explosive and emotionally charged ways.

Q: How did your background as a Black female professional, as well as your own coming-of-age experiences, influence the creation of Ruth's character?

A: I grew up in a solidly middle-class family, where both of my parents were college graduates. That experience differs from Ruth's; she came of age in a poor working-class family. Yet there are ▶

commonalities, in that we both wear the mask of the Black professional and code-switch as we navigate predominantly white spaces at work and then go home to our Black communities. There's a scene early in the novel where Ruth is in the workplace trying to maintain her professionalism while recognizing she's being marginalized. I've had that experience a few times in my career, and those challenges helped me craft a believable scenario for Ruth. Also, I've had to be discerning when interacting with those from my own community, determining which Black colleagues are allies and which are detractors. Ruth finds solidarity with the Black office receptionist instead of with her fellow scientist, who shares her skin color but not her Black consciousness.

Q: The Kindest Lie *opens with the rise of Barack Obama, a time of hope. Was it always important for you to start the novel with that moment, or did an earlier draft have a different beginning?*

A: It's often a challenge to know the right way to open a novel. I'd always been taught to begin at the moment when everything changes. In an early draft, I opened with Ruth giving birth at seventeen to her baby boy. But then I realized that the change moment was bigger than Ruth and her individual circumstance. Barack Obama's ascendance to the presidency birthed hope and promise in many across the nation, but especially in Black people. Election Night 2008 marked a celebration for those who lived to see it, and in honor of those who had made it possible. Yet as powerful as that hope was, it had its limits in a country that had never healed its racial wounds. Starting with the celebration made the painful reality of what followed even more poignant.

Q: *What inspired you to explore the sacrifices and expectations that are inevitably linked with motherhood? How do you expect readers will perceive your portrait of being a Black mother in contemporary America?*

A: Society lauds motherhood as this calling that requires perfection and provides little room for deviation from accepted norms. We rarely see narratives about mothers who walk away from their children. Mothers who lie and break the law to protect those they love. Mothers who question their fitness to be mothers. I find those messy mothers to be the most interesting. I'm curious to know who they are, how they define themselves, and why they make the choices they do. In my novel, readers get to see a range of Black mothers in Ruth, Mama, and Verna. They love fiercely, sacrifice, and make mistakes. They're flawed and they're human. All of them are struggling to mother and protect Black children, trying to keep those children and their dreams alive.

Q: The Kindest Lie *is your debut novel. How did you become a writer, and what was the first seed of inspiration for* **The Kindest Lie?**

A: I can't remember a time when I wasn't writing. From penning school essays on how I spent my summer vacation to serving as managing editor of a citywide youth newspaper in Chicago, I made writing central in my life growing up. Although I've always loved books, I didn't pursue fiction writing until after my news career. I began to reflect then on my purpose and my passion. Writing is my gift, and I knew I had to use it to tell untold stories and amplify the voices of Black people in America. The bitter divide between Black and white America in the 2008 presidential election saddened me because I couldn't understand how half of America saw things so differently than I did. That's something I wanted to explore, and it turned into *The Kindest Lie*. I believe fiction helps us transcend those barriers and have honest, difficult conversations. The world begins to make sense when we understand it through the lens of our characters.

Q: Which character came to you most naturally, and which was most difficult to write?

A: Eli represents so many Black men in America who are proud and hardworking, trying to make it in a world that wasn't designed for their ascent. I connect with that truth in a fundamental way, and that's why his story flowed effortlessly. It was a joy to write his character. ▶

Q&A with Nancy Johnson (*continued*)

One of the most difficult characters to craft was Mama. She's a feisty, strong-willed old woman, but I worried about drifting into caricature. Initially, I showed her anger and frustration with her granddaughter but revealed little motivation for those emotions. However, once I added layers to Mama's character—giving her a love interest and dreams of her own—she came alive on the page, and I believe readers will understand, even if they don't agree with, the choices she makes. ❧

Reading Group Guide

1. The novel begins in 2008, with the election of Barack Obama. Why do you think the author chooses to open the story with this pivotal moment in history, and how does that moment set the tone for what unfolds in the rest of the book? How would this story be different if it took place in the present day?

2. Ruth's long-held secret from her past sends her back to her impoverished hometown and threatens to upend the upscale life she's created with her husband, Xavier. What does this reveal about being Black in America? What is the cost of that double identity? Does one ultimately have to choose between the two?

3. When Ruth encounters Black panhandlers in downtown Chicago, she refrains from giving them money; however, she donates to a white family she's never met that lost a child in a Ganton house fire. Later in the novel, she locks her car doors when she sees two young Black men jostling in the street. Ultimately, she befriends Midnight, who is white. Do you think Ruth suffers from internal racial bias or selective classism?

4. Ruth wrestles with the moments after she gives birth, when Mama leaves the bedroom with her baby, telling her not to think about her son and to instead pursue her Ivy League education. Is Ruth to blame for walking away from her child? Do you think she had a responsibility to pursue the truth about her son's identity and whereabouts over the years? Did she have a choice, or was she robbed of it?

5. The threat of police violence is a constant throughout the novel. How does that impact Black and white characters differently? ▶

6. Butch is portrayed as a racist who makes hateful remarks and projects a bitter worldview. Despite this negativity, does he have any redeeming qualities? How does Midnight's attachment to his father inform his own understanding of race?

7. Midnight got his nickname from his Black and brown friends from school because he was a little white boy trying to "act Black." Is Midnight guilty of cultural appropriation? Do you think his behavior could be interpreted as offensive?

8. When the boys have the run-in with Dale at the convenience store, Corey and Midnight process that encounter very differently. How do their racial identities shape their reactions?

9. Mama reveals many explosive secrets throughout the novel. Are the choices she makes to protect Ruth and Eli understandable and forgivable?

10. *The Kindest Lie* examines the sacrifices and complexities of motherhood. What do Ruth, Mama, Lena, Verna, and Natasha reveal about what it means to be a mother in contemporary America?

11. Eli and Butch are both victims of the economic downturn. How does toxic masculinity infect Black and white men under this type of pressure?

12. Midnight is trapped in the web of poverty that Ruth managed to escape. Yet he's white, and she believes he will always benefit from the privilege of his race in spite of his unstable home life. Do you think that's true? Will his whiteness supersede his economic disadvantage? Corey is raised in a middle-class two-parent household, but he's still Black. What do you think

his future will look like? How do these dynamics impact the trajectory of these characters' lives, and how do their perceptions of each other evolve over the course of the novel? ◠